MIDNIGHT CONQUEST

Book 1 of the

Bonded By Blood

Vampire Chronicles

ARIAL BURNZ

MIDNIGHT CONQUEST
Book 1 of the Bonded By Blood Vampire Chronicles

June 2011
March 2013 – Second Edition (minor corrections)

Published by
Mystical Press
Rancho Cucamonga, CA 91701
www.MysticalPress.com

ISBN 10: 1463539061
ISBN 13: 978-1463539061

Printed in the United States of America

This book is a work of fiction and any resemblance to persons—living,
dead, undead or magical—or places, events or locales is purely
coincidental. The characters are productions of the authors' imagination
and used fictitiously.

MIDNIGHT CONQUEST

Book 1 of the

Bonded By Blood

Vampire Chronicles

ARIAL BURNZ

MYSTICAL PRESS—RANCHO CUCAMONGA, CA

Writing as Arial Burnz

Bonded By Blood Vampire Chronicles:
Midnight Conquest—Book 1
Midnight Captive—Book 2

Writing as Christine Davies (children's books)

Where Art Thou Unicorn?

Buy Arial's books at
Amazon, Barnes & Noble and iTunes

DEDICATION

A Thank You to Sting
For "Moon Over Bourbon Street"
He fed me the intro
To Anne Rice's treat
She's planted the seed
To all that I have written
If it wasn't for her
I'd have never been bitten

Broderick MacDougal—Gypsy. Rogue. Vampire.

With a groan, he dashed around the table, and before she could gather her wits, he pulled her to her feet, wrapping her in his embrace and crushing her arms between them. Davina's hands upon his chest spread warmth over his body. The wild thumping of his heart beneath her palms matched her own heart's cadence, pounding in his ears. Davina stared up at him with parted lips, full and tempting, begging to be tasted, and his mouth descended upon hers. With a dexterity that surprised him, she dodged him.

"Stop!"

Amusement played havoc with his features and he eased the tension of his embrace just enough to allow Davina some breathing room. His voice purred, "Stop? You are ripe and ready, lass. What say we indulge in each other in a more private atmosphere?"

Davina stepped out of his embrace and cracked her hand against his cheek.

"What in—" Broderick's brow scrunched in confusion, and then smoothed as he tipped his head back and hearty laughter poured out of his mouth, his fists planted on his hips. *Oh, I like her!*

ACKNOWLEDGMENTS

It goes without saying that I could never achieve my dreams as a writer without the unfailing love and support of my husband, DeWayne. He gives me the freedom to spread my wings and fly. He also puts up with my endless brainstorming sessions and overloading his brain with all the information about my characters. What a trooper! He deserves a medal!!

Nor can I forget to mention my mother, for without her, I would not be here. She is my number one fan, boosting my ego because she thinks my writing is perfect from the first draft. Gotta love moms! Furthermore, my very talented mother painted the scenery on the bottom-half of my first cover. Thank you for such an excellent vision of the world I built for my characters. You really brought it to life!

Additionally, my heartfelt thanks and appreciation goes out to all my beta readers. Your input, comments, honesty and encouragement through the various stages of this novel are invaluable. Hugs to (listed alphabetically) **Elizabyth Burtis**, **Michelle Ferguson**, **Mildred L. Losee**, **Dallas Maupin**, and **Lori "Beanie" Tunno**.

A special thank you goes to my editor, **AJ Nuest**. I dragged you into this and you embraced my project with open arms, being a great contributor in helping me close this 20-year endeavor with a bang. Not only has your keen eye helped me fine-tune my prose, but you loved, defended and coddled "my baby" as if it were your own. You also fell in love with Broderick as much as I did...and that says a lot! Your friendship and partnership are cherished treasures. I can't wait to work with you on Book 2! (And for those of you interested, her last name is pronounced NOOST.)

Two more people must be singled out. A big hug and an I'm-not-worthy-groveling-before-you to **HP Mallory**. Your friendship, encouragement and guidance have been priceless. You're an inspiration! And a heartfelt thank you to **Steve Anderson** who graciously provided advice and translation for the Hebrew I'm using in my vampire lore and prophecy. I could not have done any of it without your assistance. Your knowledge of the language knocked my socks off and I am humbled in your virtual presence.

If I thank any more people, my readers are going to abandon me, as there are too many people to mention here without taking up an additional ten pages. Most of you know who you are, and many of you know I started this particular project over twenty years ago. Thank you all for never giving up on me and being my cheering section.

For those who tried to interfere with my dream and douse my fire, I'm happy to say I proved you wrong…and you can kiss my unicorn.

Reader Advisory: This story contains explicit love scenes, described using graphic and direct language. This story also contains explicit, nail-biting scenes of violence and domestic abuse. (Don't worry…the bad guys get it in the end!)

AUTHOR NOTES

Make no mistake, this novel is not classified as *historical fiction*, but instead a *paranormal romance novel* with an historical backdrop. As such, I wrote most of my story in a fair amount of contemporary language. I strived to ensure the dialogue of my characters had a "flavor" of the Renaissance period, with a few Scottish words thrown in here and there. I make no claims the language is historically accurate. Imagine a modern person reciting an old tale. That is the spirit in which this story is conveyed. (Besides, there are only so many modern words to describe the male and female genitalia, let alone limiting myself to the meager supply of 16*th* century vocabulary.)

I have been warned, by many of my writer friends who craft historical novels, that if their readers find any historical inaccuracies, they receive plenty of e-mail detailing their mistakes. My own grandmother is a History Nazi—a history book to her left and a romance novel to her right, checking all the facts—so I know how much people enjoy this endeavor. Forasmuch, I have done my best to be as historically accurate as I could be. Though I've collected information from various sources, the most recent resource I used was Alison Sim's wonderful book *The Tudor Housewife* (ISBN 0-7735-

2233-6). It's a well-encapsulated reference for how life was during the time of my novel and has a generous amount of information that debunks a lot of misconceptions about this time period (e.g., the average age of first marriage was mid-twenties, not the teens!)

I am not an historian. If there are any mistakes in the history presented in this book, they are my mistakes and I offer my heartfelt apologies in advance and sincerely hope these inaccuracies do not interfere with your ability to enjoy the story. All in all, this *is* a paranormal/fantasy romance novel. I do, however, welcome your comments so that I may learn from these mistakes. Please be kind. :D

I encourage you to visit my web site (www.ArialBurnz.com) for more information on the Bonded By Blood Vampire Chronicles.

Without further ado, and at long last, I give you...MIDNIGHT CONQUEST.

That's my two pence...
Arial
June 2011

CHAPTER ONE

Scottish Fortress of the Vamsyrian Council—1486

"Death? Shall I—" Another wave of agony pressed upon his chest. Broderick MacDougal braced as razor-like pain raked through the inside of his body and coursed through his veins. He dropped to his knees. Putting his hands in front of him, he kept his face from hitting the sandstone as the breath was knocked from his lungs. Panting, he laid his cheek against the floor. The cold stone soothed the fever of his skin. The sound of his ragged breaths echoed off the vastness of the Vamsyrian Fortress. As the agony subsided, he struggled to right himself and stared at the youthful faces of the Elders.

The Elders of the Vamsyrian Council sat on their black iron thrones behind the expanse of their black marble table, looking like anything but elders. They glared down at Broderick, who knelt on the floor before them. All three men of various unknown nationalities and features, garbed in formal brocade robes of deep red, seemed no older than five-and-twenty years. Yet they measured their ages in centuries, Cordelia had told him.

Able to stand once more, Broderick cleared his throat. "Death?" he repeated. "Shall I not be permitted to live should I choose neither of the other options?"

Elder Rasheed, who had given Broderick his three choices, raised a coal-black eyebrow. "If you choose to go with the Army of Light, we are not permitted to kill you; but yea, if one does not choose them or us, it is customary to kill those who have rescinded from making this choice. That is a rare occurrence, but has happened. Killing you would be more out of mercy than preserving the secrecy of our race."

Through the fire licking through his body, Broderick managed to raise his own eyebrow. "Mercy? Why is that?"

Elder Rasheed glanced sideways at his peers. "Surely you have been told your fate as a Blood Slave. Is it not why you are here?"

Broderick didn't like the sound of that and shook his head, a tear of perspiration dripping from his eyebrow onto his cheek. "What is a Blood Slave?"

Frowning, Elder Rasheed turned a critical gaze to Cordelia. Broderick turned his head to the right, clenching his jaw from the effort, and stared at the woman who had brought him here. Cordelia Harley stood regally, yet avoided everyone's eyes, red mottling her cheeks as she studied the tapestries on the stone walls.

"In short," Rasheed continued, "becoming a Blood Slave is a death sentence. The exchange of blood you experienced is what creates your condition."

Over the last several months, Cordelia had fed from Broderick, her small fangs piercing his throat as she drank a small amount of his blood. Then she cut her wrist and fed her blood to him which had his blood mixed with hers. This swapping of blood was necessary...so she had said. "Cordelia told me this was part of the transformation."

Rasheed dropped his jaw, and turned a murderous glare on Cordelia. "*You* created this Blood Slave?" Cordelia still refused to make eye contact with anyone. "Look at me, woman!"

The pale, yet devious, beauty glimpsed at the Elder from under her raven eyebrows, then dropped her gaze to the floor and nodded. Broderick grumbled.

"You led us to believe by calling for this transformation, you were saving him from this condition, not that you had created it!" Rasheed rose from his chair like heat from a fire pit, slow and radiating with anger. "You dare move from that spot before this is over, I will personally skin you alive and leave you on display in this Grand Hall until *I* feel you have suffered enough."

Cordelia's breath quickened as she stared in wide-eyed horror at the Elders. She offered a small nod as consent.

Rasheed sank into his seat, still training his eyes on her. "Nay, Broderick MacDougal. This small exchange of blood binds you emotionally and physically to the immortal and, in essence, turns you into a slave of her will. That is why it is termed 'Blood Slave.' It is also why your body experiences such pain. The immortal blood fights within your body, trying to make the transformation. Since there is not enough of the immortal blood inside you, your body will die fighting this battle."

Broderick gritted his teeth, struggling both with his rage toward Cordelia and the ache of his condition. This explained why he had followed her so blindly—he had no control over his emotions. Again, he permitted himself to be betrayed by a woman.

Of the two women he trusted, which was more responsible for his current position? His lifelong pursuit of killing his clan enemy motivated him to eagerly accept anything Cordelia promised. However, Evangeline's betrayal caused the massacre of his brothers and their families, further fueling his vengeance and giving him no other choice but immortality to achieve his goals. And yet the broken heart within his chest would demand nothing less. Broderick turned his eyes to his left to gaze at the bane of his existence...his clan enemy, Angus Campbell.

Since Broderick's childhood, his father Hamish MacDougal warred endlessly with Fraser Campbell in a private battle, whose roots remained—even to this very moment—a mystery. Caught up in one bloody fight after another, watching those he loved perish under the sword, Broderick built his own reasons for revenge against this branch of the Campbells.

His enemy stood beside him now, veins pulsing at his temples, fury burning in his emerald-green eyes as he glared at Broderick and Cordelia in turn.

"Your choice will determine your fate," Elder Rasheed said.

"Who is this Army of Light?" Broderick asked, resisting the urge crack Angus across the jaw, but turned his attention to the Council.

Elder Ammon explained in an accent even stranger than Rasheed's. "They call themselves God's *special* children," he said with disdain, staring down his aquiline nose. "They are a perversion of what we are. They claim to offer eternal life; and yet with our immortality, we remain undying while their mortal lives expire."

"If they're mortal," Broderick asked with a quivering voice, "what would going with them afford me? I thought I was doomed to die."

Elder Mikhail smirked. "We have been told their god can perform miracles and heal. Since we have never seen those who have joined with them—and be assured, those have been very few indeed—there is no way we can confirm or deny these claims. If you go with them, they may be able to heal you…they may not. We make no guarantees as to what they offer or what they claim to do." Mikhail waved his thin fingers dismissively.

"But face them you must," Elder Ammon said, pointing at a door to Broderick's right. "They will offer you their side of this choice you make. All those choosing to become a member of the Vamsyrian race must do so willingly and make an educated decision. You will hear what they have to say before you decide."

Two men, whom Broderick just noticed stood behind the Elders, came forward and assisted Broderick to his feet. Leaning on them, he shuffled laboriously toward the door where a new possible destiny awaited him. He glowered at Cordelia. She still refused to make eye contact with him as he passed, her mind shuttered from his attempts to peer into her private, demented world. She had taken him for a fool. She had never intended to give him immortality, but only used him to get back at Angus, denying him the revenge of killing Broderick himself. Angus's obvious anger at both Broderick and Cordelia confirmed she'd succeeded. But Broderick could only guess why she brought him before the Council. Why not just taunt him in front of Angus? Why bring him here? Furthermore, Angus's presence at this gathering made no sense. Was he here to protest the transformation? Why didn't the Council just let Angus kill him? He certainly couldn't defend himself, and yet Angus operated as if his hands were tied.

Then an idea struck him. If he went into this room and chose to become a member of the Army of Light, Angus would most certainly not have his revenge. Broderick would be under their protection. If, by some chance the Army of Light could cure him, he could possibly live to fight another day and still have their protection even though he was mortal. And if they couldn't cure him, at the least, if he died, he would die knowing Angus wouldn't have his retribution…a last act of defiance, albeit a weak one. None of this sat well with him, but what choice did he have?

One Vamsyrian heaved open the heavy, oaken door. The two immortals helped Broderick into a single wooden chair in the room, facing another door on the opposite wall. They nodded and retreated to the shadowed corners behind Broderick. The silence of the chamber fell around them like a fog.

A standing brazier burned on Broderick's right, crackling and hissing, casting the stone walls with flickering orange light, but not providing much illumination. Broderick winced as another breathtaking wave of fire coursed through his body. He gripped the arm rests, bracing against the agony, waiting for the pain to subside. *This needs to end or I would go mad with the torture of this condition!*

A bolt thrown back on the other side of the door jarred his body. More ripples of pain wound down his legs and curled his toes. A hooded figure stepped into the chamber. The door swung closed behind this person, and the bolt clanked once more, locking them in together. His body recovered as the stinging subsided, and Broderick breathed easy once more.

The figure faced him. "I know your condition may seem hopeless, but God can cure you of this blood affliction."

Broderick stiffened and leaned forward to try and see her face under the cloak, but the brazier lent little aid to his eyes. "'Tis impossible," he grunted through his teeth. "The voice I hear must be from the grave."

The woman before him pushed back her hood to reveal the long, golden hair he knew so well.

Evangeline, his whore of a wife, shook her head and gawked at him with eyes like saucers. Broderick's lip curled into a snarl and he swallowed the bile rising in his throat.

Evangeline whimpered and fell to her knees. "Dear Father in heaven, how could you have selected me as the one to face my husband? Surely he will choose the path of darkness if I am the one to show him the light. Why could you not have sent someone else?"

Rage muddling his senses, Broderick rose and stepped toward her. The grief rising in his heart threatened to drown him like a torrent of waves and he fought the tears stinging his eyes. He would watch the light expire from her as he had seen Maxwell and Donnel's lives snuffed out.

Evangeline gasped and held her palms up, rambling a rapid string of words, "*Veh atah adonai mahgen bah-adee, k'vodee u-merim roshee.*"

Broderick slammed into an unseen wall and fell to the ground. Writhing in agony, the rage was knocked from his senses. Through a dim cloud of awareness, he teetered as the two Vamsyrian guards helped him back into the chair before retreating to the corners. Evangeline lowered her hands and remained kneeling on the stone floor across the space. Once he regained his wits, he cleared his throat. "What is this magic, witch?"

She frowned. "I am no witch, Broderick. I am a member of the *Tzava Ha'or*—the Army of Light. God has given us certain measures of protection against…" She pursed her lips and dropped her gaze. A shuddering breath shook her shoulders and she raised her chin, facing him with tear-filled eyes. "Against the blood of the cursed."

Broderick grasped the arms of the chair to stand, but reminded of his last encounter with this protection of God, he reconsidered. "How is it that you're alive and among those who are supposed to be *special* children of God?" Hatred seasoned every syllable he managed to grit through his teeth. She implored him with her eyes, which only made rage and grief tremble through his body all the more. "Why do you still live?"

"I ran," she whispered through her tears and stared into the past. "I ran from the battle into the forest for hours. When I dropped from exhaustion, I was set upon by thieves who…" She closed her eyes and swallowed. "Forced themselves upon me…leaving me for dead."

"And yet you kneel before me." Broderick fought back his sympathy. "Proceed."

"I don't know how long I lay there, but awoke and stumbled onto the road where a group of monks nearly trampled me with their horse and wain. They secreted me to a convent where the sisters nursed me back to health; where I became a member of the Army of Light." Evangeline peered up at Broderick with a flicker of hope in her glassy eyes. "They taught me that God is a forgiving and loving God, Broderick. Please don't turn your back on Him by choosing this path of darkness. He *can* heal you and forgives anything. He even forgave me."

"*I* have not!" Ire shook his limbs and gave him the strength to stand against the agony ripping through his body. The trembling in his voice broke his words, making speech difficult. "Do you think all the lives you took with your betrayal can be so easily tossed aside? You are the reason I stand here seeking retribution against my enemy whose bed you shared. You remain in the protective arms of God while my body dies as a Blood Slave."

"God can cure you, Broderick! He has released those like you who were Blood Slaves. Join the Army of Light and He can cure you."

The two Vamsyrian guards flanked Broderick as he stepped toward her. He fought against their arms, against the anguish in his soul, against the injustice that continually plagued his life. "You are mad to think I would take anything from you or a God who harbors betrayers. You should be dead, and yet you sit before me offering me salvation. Did you think I would forgive you because you have such an offer?"

Evangeline bowed and shook her head. "Nay," she whispered. "I am just as surprised that you're alive. As such, I am still your wife, and you maintain the right to do with me as you will." Evangeline raised her palms again, mumbling another string of strange phrases, "*Pitkhu li sha-ahray tsedek, avoh bahm ve odeh yah. Zeh ha-sha-ar adonai. Tsadikim yavou bo.*"

Broderick breathed easier at the noticeable difference in the atmosphere, the lessening pressure on his body. The Vamsyrians at his side also looked around with wonderment in their eyes. The unseen wall she erected must have dropped. Broderick tried to lunge forward, but the Vamsyrians held him back. Unable to fight against them, he surrendered. "I choose the path to immortality, rendering myself dead to you. Since God has forgiven your transgressions, I'm sure the church will annul our pathetic excuse of a marriage. God is your husband now and may you both suffer for it!"

Evangeline fell to the floor in a weeping heap as they escorted Broderick from the room.

Positioning him before the Council once more, the two Vamsyrians released Broderick, and he gathered every bit of strength he could muster to remain standing. "I choose to become a Vamsyrian," he announced with a raspy voice. Broderick glared at Angus, who shockingly displayed a smirk of satisfaction on his lips.

The Elders nodded and turned their eyes to Cordelia. She stepped forward and glanced toward Angus. Raising an ebony eyebrow, she crossed her arms over her ample breasts and turned to the Council. "I revoke my claim on Broderick MacDougal."

Elder Rasheed's eyes grew wide, along with his peers. "Are you stating that you do not wish to transform Broderick MacDougal, which is the reason we have been summoned?"

Cordelia stepped back and swallowed. "Aye," she responded in a trembling voice.

Elder Rasheed stood and Cordelia had the sense enough to cower. "You try my patience, woman! I may skin you yet!"

"Elder Rasheed, if I may." Angus stepped forward, uncrossing his arms.

Rasheed sighed in resignation. "Aye, Angus Campbell," he said with a dismissive wave. "As you originally requested when you came before this Council, this poor creature is yours to do with as you will. Put him out of his misery." Sitting down, Rasheed put his head in his hands.

"Nay, Elder Rasheed." Angus regarded Broderick. "I am proposing to make the transformation myself."

Broderick's wide eyes were not the only ones to rivet their attention on Angus Campbell. "Why would you do such a thing? You have the opportunity to finally rid me from your existence. Take it and do as Elder Rasheed said…put me out of my misery." Broderick shuddered from a wave of pain.

"Although I do enjoy seeing you suffer," Angus sneered, "there is no satisfaction in killing you in such a weakened state. My spirit will never be at rest." Angus stepped closer to Broderick, smirking at his bent and desecrated body. "You must be willing to do the transformation, Rick, or I cannot perform the deed. What be your choice?"

Broderick glanced at everyone, Cordelia's gaze intent upon him. Each person seemed to be holding their breath, waiting for him to say the word.

"Live to fight another day," Angus taunted. "Be a worthy opponent."

Broderick glared into the mocking eyes of his enemy. A long stretch of silence wound between them, thick with opposition. The souls of his brothers, their wives and their wee bairn called for vengeance from the nether regions of his soul. "Do the deed, then," Broderick snarled. "But you shall regret your decision."

Angus chuckled and waited for Rasheed's approval, who stood staring at the absurdity of this scene. With barely a nod from the Elder, Angus pounced on Broderick, pulled his head back with a fierce yank on his hair and sank his fangs into

Broderick's tender neck. He bellowed and clawed as Angus gashed his throat. However, the pain coursing through his body and burning at his neck soon vanished for the euphoria of feeding, just as he had felt with Cordelia, and Broderick slumped in Angus's arms. The contact with Angus stretched into a deep fog. Cordelia usually probed his mind when she drank from him, but he experienced none of that with Angus. Broderick slipped deeper toward death, his life draining away. Angus may drain him of life and kill him after all.

At long last, Angus broke contact and lowered Broderick to the floor. Rasheed stood by and handed Angus a black-handled dagger. Slicing his wrist open, Angus fed the open wound to Broderick. But Broderick couldn't get his mouth to open and accept the Vamsyrian blood pouring down his chin. Best he should just refuse and die anyway.

"You made this choice, Rick!" Angus barked and re-cut his rapidly-healing wrist. "Open your mouth!"

Before Broderick could revel in the triumph of defeating Angus at the last, the smell of the blood assailed his senses and he opened his mouth to receive immortality. He drank deep and gasped when Angus pulled his wrist away to cut it anew.

"Aye, Rick," Angus coaxed as Broderick latched his mouth around the cut, swallowing in gulps the life-giving liquid.

Strength returned to his body, a soothing sensation moving through his veins as the blood worked its way into his limbs. His throat tingled. Angus yanked his hand away. Though Broderick still couldn't get his body to respond to his wishes, he lay marveling at his new-found acute senses. The breathing of the Vamsyrian guards across the room fluttered against his ears; the delicate aroma of Cordelia's verbena touched his nose as when he fed from her; the veins in the black marble table seemed to glow, the hairline fractures visible with his new sight.

Angus turned to Rasheed, wiping his mouth with a kerchief. "Why could I not read his mind? Why could I not glean all his memories?"

Cordelia grinned and clenched her fists at her sides, joy lighting her eyes. "Because my blood ruled his body. You cannot glean such memories from another Vamsyrian, Angus. You wanted to gain such an advantage over Broderick to know everything about him, but you couldn't because he was my Blood Slave." She seemed giddy over a revelation. Broderick jerked and convulsed on the floor, as the two hulking Vamsyrians cut short Cordelia's moment of glee. Flanking her, they grabbed her arms and escorted her from the room.

"My lord," she protested and yanked against their hands shackling her wrists. "My lord, please!"

Cordelia's objections faded behind the closed door, leaving the room in a heavy hush and Broderick to ponder Cordelia's involvement in this charade. She knew Angus would make the transformation, though she may not have known about the results. Why had that information caused such elation?

Rasheed contemplated Broderick lying on the stone floor with narrowed eyes. After a long moment, the Elders filed out of the room through the same door in which Cordelia disappeared, none of them uttering a word. Angus stood over Broderick's body, shaking with a fever from the Vamsyrian blood purging the last of his humanity. The scent of his enemy—a distinct, musky spice— wafted around Broderick and he committed the aroma to his memory. "Brothers for all eternity now, forever bonded by blood." Kneeling beside Broderick, Angus whispered, "I will give you this time, Rick, to learn what you have become. Use the time wisely. Once 'tis over, I *will* hunt you." Rising, Angus nodded and whirled toward the exit.

"Not if I find you first." Broderick grinned as he lay shuddering and scowled at Angus, who marched from the Grand Hall.

Stewart Glen, Scotland—Late Autumn, 1505
Nineteen Years Later

Davina Stewart's eyes danced with delight around the colorful tents and caravans of the Gypsy camp. So many exotic scents drifted through her senses, her mouth watered one moment and she heaved a pleasurable sigh the next. Among the flickering torches and fires, acrobats tumbled, jugglers tossed flaming batons high into the air, and merchants waved their wares from around the world at the passersby. Davina's father Parlan and her brother Kehr excused themselves and ambled over toward the horseflesh the Gypsies had for sale.

"Davina." Her mother Lilias pressed a hand to Davina's arm, then gestured toward a tent in the distance. "Myrna and I will be at that tent. I mean to get your father a gift before he and your brother return. Stay close to Rosselyn and do not wander off."

"Aye, M'ma." Watching her mother and Myrna join arms and stroll off, Davina clenched her jaw to contain her excitement.

Rosselyn stood with her mouth agape.

Davina cleared her throat. "If you wish to stand here and stare after our mothers, then you will do so by yourself. I, for one, am not going to miss out on this rare opportunity to explore my freedom." Davina turned and scampered in the opposite direction to put some distance between her and her mother.

Rosselyn scurried to catch up, and linked arms with Davina. "As your handmaid and entrusted guardian, need I remind you she said not to wander off?"

"Can you believe she left us to explore?" Giddiness bubbled up inside Davina and giggles spurted through her hands as she covered her mouth.

"Do you not get enough exploring while you visit with your brother at court?" Rosselyn tucked a stray, chestnut curl under her coif.

"Bah!" Davina scoffed, imitating her brother's favored exclamation. "Court is a horrible place to be, I have learned. The women backbite each other, supposedly friends, and all they ever talk about is the tossing of skirts and secret meetings with bonnie lads in the garden." Heat rose to Davina's face at her bold proclamation.

Rosselyn giggled. "Davina Stewart, you're blushing! And as you should! Your mother would take a strap to you if she heard you say such things."

"At court, M'ma keeps me close at hand, so nay, I don't explore much there, either. I shall revel in my freedom this night!" Davina laughed. The glee vanished over the realization of how she must sound. "Oh, don't misunderstand me. I adore M'ma, but…"

"Aye, she hardly ever allows you out of her reach, let alone her sight." Rosselyn was two years older than Davina's thirteen and had grown up in their household. Naturally, she fell into the role of Davina's handmaid since her mother, Myrna, was Lilias's handmaid. Though Rosselyn served her station well, Davina loved the older girl more like a sister.

Borrowing her mother's idea, Davina dragged Rosselyn along to peruse the wares of the tents, searching to buy gifts for her family. A particularly fine boot dagger caught her eye. The Gypsy pulled the small blade from the sheath. "A splendid blade for a lady such as yourself," he pressured.

"Oh, 'tis not for me, but for my brother," Davina countered.

"Ah, a fine weapon to tuck into his boot! See the silver inlaid designs down the blade?"

"'Tis truly silver?" Davina lifted the boot dagger and studied the decorative, Celtic designs swirling down the narrow blade.

"Aye! A work of art." When he told her the price, she squirmed. "Real silver, I promise."

She handed the blade back, but the silversmith wouldn't take it. He glanced around, and then conspiratorially whispered a lower price. Not much lower, but enough. Davina surrendered her coin.

Rosselyn tugged on Davina's sleeve. "Look, Davina," she said pointing to an aging woman. The Gypsy had a long silver braid and a scarlet scarf covering her head.

The woman beckoned to them. She sat beside a canvas tent painted with an impressive scene of a fair-haired woman sitting behind a table displaying a spread of tablets. Stars, moons and other strange symbols Davina didn't recognize floated around the woman's cascading blonde hair. "What are her services, do you suppose?" Davina whispered in awe.

Rosselyn glanced across the circle of tents and wagons toward their mothers. Lilias and Myrna stood before an array of ribbons draped over the arms of a man. Grabbing Davina's hand, a wide grin spread on Rosselyn's thin lips and a sparkle of mischief touched her hazel eyes. "Come!"

Davina struggled to keep up as Rosselyn tugged at her hand, and they ran until they stood breathless before the Gypsy woman.

"Eager to have your fortune told, I see," the Gypsy chimed in her lovely French accent, and waved a wrinkled hand toward the tent flap. "Only one at a time, *s'il vous plaît.*"

"You go first, Roz," Davina encouraged.

Rosselyn stepped toward the tent opening, and then stopped. Turning back she glanced between Davina and the Gypsy. "She is not to go anywhere." Diverting her eyes back to Davina, she pointed a scolding finger. "You stay right here, you understand? Your mother will have my head on a pike if you wander off without me."

The woman grasped Davina's hand and rubbed it affectionately with her warm touch. "Fear not, *mademoiselle*, I will guard her with my life as we share some tea." Ushering Davina to a small stool beside the fire, Rosselyn seemed content with this arrangement and rushed into the tent, anxious for her session.

"You enjoy tea, *oui*?" The woman glanced at Davina's palm. "I am Amice."

"My name is Davina," she answered in French. As was customary in the Scottish courts, Davina had studied French, even though her family's court connections were somewhat distant. "And yea, I would be most grateful for a cup of tea." A broad grin spread across Amice's mouth as Davina spoke the old woman's native tongue, and Davina watched as the Gypsy studied her hand, squinting at the lines. "What is it you see?"

Amice shrugged, rubbed the center of Davina's palm and grinned up at her. Youthful eyes gazed back at Davina amongst the wrinkles of time settling on her face. "My eyes are old and I see nothing. You will have your palm read, yea?"

"My palm read?" Davina scrunched her eyebrows together. "You can read a palm like one reads a book?

Amice waved her hand dismissively. "In a manner of speaking." She gently urged Davina to sit and, before taking her own stool, handed Davina two clay cups. Davina placed her brother's gift upon her lap to free her hands. Amice reached behind and grabbed a small basket. Sprinkling some tea leaves into the cups, she put the basket aside. From the cut stump between them, which served as a makeshift table, Amice snatched a hefty cloth to grab a kettle resting on the fire. She smiled and poured hot water into the two tea cups, filling one cup only half way, which she took for herself, leaving Davina the full one.

The chill of the night air tingled on Davina's cheeks and she held the warming cup between her palms, blowing on the amber liquid.

A creaking sounded behind and she turned to see a young girl with tangled, golden hair peeking through the door of the Gypsy wagon. The girl appeared but a few years younger than Davina's thirteen. Davina smiled and timidly waved. The girl frowned, stuck out her tongue, and ducked back inside. Her mouth dropping open at the rude child,

Davina turned back and scowled over her tea. More than half of her cup was finished when she noted Amice had not yet taken a sip, but instead had set her cup on the stump. Before Davina could inquire, Rosselyn emerged from the tent, rubbing her palm and smiling. "Fascinating, milady!"

"My goodness! That was done in haste." Davina cast a look of regret at Amice.

Amice beckoned Rosselyn with a wave. "Come, I have made you a cup of tea." Leaning forward, she reached for the kettle and filled the cup on the stump. With the leaves already steeped, the fresh water made a cup of piping hot tea.

How smart! Davina thought.

As Rosselyn and Amice exchanged introductions, Davina finished the last of her tea— careful not to swallow the loose tea leaves— handed the cup to Amice, and stepped into the tent. The spicy aroma of incense drifted through the air and she sighed from the exotic scent. Dim lighting created a soothing atmosphere; the outside firelight cast shadows upon the cloth walls, infusing a dreamlike ambience. A table stood at the far end, a small stool set before it. Oil lamps on iron stands illuminated a basket on one corner of the tabletop, and behind the table sat not another old woman or bejeweled Gypsy girl as Davina expected, but the largest man she had ever cast her eyes upon. And very handsome! Her inexperienced heart thumped inside her reedy figure when his penetrating gaze met hers.

This giant dwarfed everything in the room. His chest and arms bulged under the thin material of his brown linen shirt. A small opening in his collar revealed a mass of curled auburn hair, as fiery as the hair upon his head—striking in the lamplight. A flush heated Davina's face over the mixture of unfamiliar emotions running through her at the mere sight of him, and she reached for the tent flap, thinking to run from this bewitching man.

"Please, lass," he said, his voice deep and smooth, like cream. He leaned forward, resting one elbow on the table and reached toward her with his other hand, the table creaking in protest. "Let me read your palm."

Drawn to that creamy voice and those hooded eyes, Davina released the flap and sat before him. "My name is Davina," she offered, trying to delay.

"An honor to meet you, mistress. I am Broderick." He smiled and Davina's insides melted like snow in spring.

"Broderick," she whispered, tasting his name. Clearing her throat, she gathered strength, put Kehr's gift on the table and gave him her hand.

"You have nothing to fear, lass," he assured her, and when he touched her hand, her anxiety vanished.

Broderick closed his eyes, letting his head fall back slightly, his hawk-like nose shadowing a chiseled cheek. Davina inclined toward him, drawn to his handsome features and the strength emanating from his body. She couldn't help comparing him to her brother Kehr. Not one man she'd ever seen lived up to the vision of her brother—handsome, witty, charming, humorous, large in stature and character. Yet this Gypsy giant was something to behold. He smiled subtly, and an attractive dimple appeared just to the left of his mouth, enticing her to smile.

"You have a happy life, lass. A family filled with love and warmth. You have a special place in your heart for…Kehr."

Davina gasped. How did he know her brother's name? Then she pursed her lips. "Rosselyn told you of my brother."

He opened his eyes and grinned. "Well, I saw the lad in her life, too. But what I said of your brother is what I learned from you. You don't believe in fortune telling?"

Davina harrumphed. "You have said nothing to convince me you're a marvel, sir."

A chuckle rumbled deep in his chest, and her heart thudded against her ribs. His eyelids dipped close in concentration. "Honey. You have a particular passion for honey. And your brother shares this passion with you." He opened his eyes and shook his head. "*Tsk, tsk, tsk.* Come, lass. You and Kehr needs be more cautious on your night raids. You two will give yourselves away if you eat

26

so much at once. I suggest you taper your stealing, to avoid trouble." He winked.

Davina's face burned with embarrassment, but that soon gave way to wonderment. How could he know she and Kehr snuck through the castle halls at night to rob the honey supply?

Broderick leaned forward and whispered, "Fear not, lass. Your secret is safe with me."

Davina bowed her head, hiding her smile, and then sat mesmerized as the giant turned her hand into the lamplight and studied the lines on her palm. She scooted forward when a furrow formed on his brow. "What do you see, sir?"

Their faces were very close as his deep voice cautioned her. "I cannot lie to you, lass. Doing so would be a disaster."

"A disaster?"

"Aye." His emerald eyes bore into hers. "Times ahead will not be pleasant. But you must not lose faith. You have much strength. Draw on that strength and hold tight to what is most dear, for that is what will bring you through these troubled times that are yet to come."

"What will happen, sir?" she pressed.

"'Tis unknown to me. I know not the specifics. The lines on the palm do not reveal such details, only to say that strife is in your future. Just remember what I told you. Hold tight to your vision of strength." He brought his lips to her hand

and kissed her knuckles before releasing. Dazed and openmouthed, she stared at him, rooted to the chair. The corner of his mouth turned up, bringing forth his dimple, and she returned the smile, listening to her heart bang inside her chest.

Broderick cleared his throat and nodded toward the basket. She smiled wider, still staring at him, and he nodded toward the basket once more. She returned the nod, glanced at the basket and gasped in realization. He wanted her to pay him! Too embarrassed at her ridiculous, gawking behavior, she fumbled to pull some *billon* pennies from the purse at her waist and placed them in the basket, scurrying from the tent without looking back.

Davina stood near the entrance, catching her breath and willing her face to stop burning. Swallowing hard, she turned to the Gypsy woman. "Thank you for sitting with Rosselyn, Amice." Pressing more coins into the woman's hand, Davina offered an uneasy smile as Rosselyn surrendered her empty teacup to Amice. Snatching Rosselyn's hand, Davina dragged her handmaid away, trying to leave her embarrassment behind.

"Mistress, what troubles you?" Rosselyn stopped Davina, grabbing her by the shoulders and confronting her.

The words poured from Davina's mouth in a rush while she fluttered her hands like a wounded bird. "Oh, I acted like a fop! I sat gazing at him like a doe. He was so handsome, Rosselyn! My heart will not cease ramming in my breast! What plagues me?" Davina fanned her face in a failed attempt to cool the burning in her cheeks.

Rosselyn laughed and hugged Davina. "My dear Davina, I do believe that Gypsy has stolen your heart!"

Davina clapped her hands over her mouth. "By the saints! I left my brother's gift on the table!"

Sobering up marginally, Rosselyn turned back to the fortune teller's tent. "Come, then, let us return and fetch it."

Davina tugged on Rosselyn's hand with all her might, yanking her friend back. "Nay! I cannot face him again! I shall surely perish from…from…"

Rosselyn rubbed Davina's shoulders as if to warm her. "Do not fret so! I will fetch it for you. Come with me and stay behind the wagon so he won't see you."

They crept alongside and peered around the fortune teller's wagon. Amice seemed to study the teacups, tilting them to and fro. Broderick emerged from the tent and Davina clutched Rosselyn, pulling her back out of sight.

"And just what are you up to, Amice?" The sound of his deep voice made Davina's knees buckle and she dared to peek around the wagon with Rosselyn.

"A little tea leaf reading," she said in French, keeping her eyes trained on the tea leaves.

Rosselyn turned to Davina and shrugged, as Rosselyn did not speak French. Davina indicated she would tell her later and switched places with Rosselyn to better hear their conversation.

"From the two young girls?" he asked.

"Aye." Amice smiled. "You have her heart forever, my son."

The giant cocked his eyebrow curiously. "Which one?"

"The sweet Davina," Amice said, waving one of the cups in the air as she eyed the other. Davina nearly fainted from the rapid pounding of her heart.

"Nonsense, the girl will not remember me when she finds herself a husband." He chuckled. "Her open admiration for me was very flattering, though. She's pretty now, but she will be the one stealing hearts when she grows to womanhood."

He thinks me pretty! He thinks me pretty! Davina spent all her energy not jumping up and down like a flea. She bit her curled index finger to silence a heady giggle.

"*Your* heart is the one she will steal, my son." Amice handed him the cup, and Davina opened her mouth in awe.

He peered into the cup, frowned and gave it back to Amice. Shrugging, he grinned and handed her Kehr's wrapped gift. "Well, since she'll return to be my true love, give her this." Amice at last diverted her attention from her cup-gazing to eye the package. "She left in such haste, she forgot to take her fardel with her." Shaking his head, he turned and went back into the tent. Amice sat smiling, reading the tea leaves.

Davina gripped the side of the wagon, her mouth still hanging open. Seeing Broderick gone, Rosselyn stepped forward, quickly made her excuses and retrieved the wrapped boot knife. Ushering Davina away from the wagon, she spoke when they were out of earshot. "What did they say? You seemed ready to faint!"

Davina stumbled forward as if in a trance, her mouth open and her body numb. The faintest smile appeared on her lips.

CHAPTER TWO

Stewart Glen, Scotland—Summer, 1513
Eight Years Later

"I beg you to forgive my son, Parlan."

Davina Stewart-Russell halted at the sound of her father-in-law's voice and stopped short of the doorway she was just about to walk through to the parlor of her childhood home. The quick glance into the room, before she stepped back to hide, afforded her the moment she needed to see the scene. Her father, Parlan, stood before the stone hearth built from the jagged rocks of the local area, his arms crossed and his back to the room. Munro, her father-in-law, stood to the right side of the hearth, his hands clasped and resting on the hilt of his sword, addressing her father. Her husband, Ian, stood further back and between the two men, his head down and shoulders hunched in a very uncharacteristic position of submission. All of them had their backs to Davina, so didn't see her approach or her hasty retreat. Peering around the doorway and staying hidden behind the partially opened door, she peeked through the crack at the hinges.

Munro continued his petition for his son, talking as if Ian wasn't in the room. "As you and I have both discussed at length, this position of responsibility isn't sitting well with Ian. I appreciate your patience and your willingness to work with me on settling his role as husband and father."

"I will not make efforts toward introducing him to any royal contacts until Ian has shown some signs of maturing." Parlan turned toward Munro and crossed his arms over his chest in that position Davina knew so well that bespoke his solidity in the matter. "And you would do well to close your coffers to him. As you know, he has already gone through Davina's dowry."

"Aye, Parlan. I—"

"Da, please!" Ian protested.

"Hold that tongue, lad, or I will cut it out!" Munro glared at Ian until his head bowed.

Davina's drumming heart made her breathless with fear of being discovered and over the rare display of her husband so subservient. Davina almost swooned at the mixture of excitement and trepidation surging through her. How many times had her husband made her feel the same way? How many times had he silenced her with a heavy hand? To see Ian subject to another authority made her want to cheer. Yet, her limbs trembled at the notion of Ian catching her witnessing this moment and relishing her private victory in his discipline. She struggled to remain a silent audience.

Parlan's forehead creased, pensive, as he studied Ian and Munro. When Munro appeared satisfied his son would remain silent, he turned his attention back to Parlan. "I fear you're correct, Parlan. I had hoped that he would curb his spending, and I wish I could say where the money is going…" He glared at his son. "But I agree with your next suggested course of action."

"Da, I have tried!" Ian disputed. "Have I not proven to be a better husband?"

Munro stepped forward and backhanded his son, causing Ian's head to thrash to the side, splattering blood to the stone floor. A measure of guilt pulsed at Davina's conscience from enjoying her husband's situation. At the same time, she pondered at what he could possibly mean by "a better husband." If anything, Ian had become more brutal over the last four months or so. Did he think that disciplining his wife more harshly was the quality of a sound groom? Munro raised his fist and Ian shielded himself for another blow.

"Enough!" Parlan barked. "I can see now where your son learned his order of discipline."

Munro drew up tall, pushing his chest out in defiance. "Harsh discipline is the only thing he'll listen to, Parlan. Trust me on this."

"That may be so, as I don't know your son well enough, but I know Davina, and that manner of punishment isn't necessary with her. Though she can be rather dramatic, she's a reasonable woman and can be spoken to. I realize a man has the right to do with his wife as he wishes, and some women do need to be disciplined with an element of force, but not my daughter."

Davina fought to see through the tears flooding her eyes over her father's defense. She was not aware her father knew. The pride and relief swelling in her breast would surely burst her ribcage!

"We arranged this marriage contract for mutual benefits," Parlan continued. "As I'm second cousin to King James, this gives you valuable connections. The Russells have wealth for investments and business opportunities for me and my son, Kehr." He stepped toward Munro with menace in his eyes, his voice barely a whisper, and Davina strained to hear him. "But I didn't bargain the brutality of my daughter in the exchange."

Munro glared at his son. "Again, Parlan, I must beg you to forgive my son." He turned toward her father more contrite. "And I implore you to forgive me for whatever I may have done to contribute to my son's overzealous duties as a husband."

A chill ran through Davina. Though Munro may have sounded sincere—and the expression of acceptance on her father's face indicated he believed her father-in-law—that same tone of feigned humility came from Ian often. Such humility always proved to be an elaborate masquerade, however. Even his words indicated he didn't think he was at fault: "Whatever I *may* have done..." In the fourteen months Davina and Ian had been married, she had come to notice these veiled signs meant to draw sympathy and surrender but instead indicated the truth behind the façade.

Munro turned his piercing eyes toward Ian as he spoke. "To show you my efforts to make this right, Parlan, I will indeed do as you suggest and close my coffers to my son." A subtle flavor of smug satisfaction touched Munro's features as he held this position of power over his son. Davina easily recognized Ian's body trembling with hidden rage, his fists clenched behind his back. A foreboding terror flowed over her, like the freezing water of a winter current taking her down into its murky darkness. She would surely be the object of his frustration once they were alone and back at their own, cold manor.

Hold on to that image of strength, Davina chanted in her head, as she had done countless times before, the voice and the face of Broderick being that strength. Whenever sorrow or despair threatened to consume her and drive her mad, she focused on his flaming red hair, his broad chest and strong arms encircling her in a cocoon of safety, his full lips pressing a comforting kiss to her brow. Broderick would never treat her in the way Ian did and she found refuge in the fantasy of being the Gypsy's wife. In that world, that realm of fantasy, Ian could not touch her, break her spirit, nor destroy her pride.

Pivoting on his heel, Munro faced Parlan once more and gave a curt nod, drawing Davina's attention. "A very wise counsel, indeed, and I'm ashamed I didn't think of it sooner myself."

"There is more to responsibility than the managing of finances, Ian." Parlan stood before his son-in-law, glowering down at the top of his bowed head. "Davina is a kind heart, a loving soul—"

"All the more reason why I'm overjoyed at the union," Munro interrupted, standing beside Ian. "She's the sweet hand who will gentle the beast inside my son. I'm sure you have seen the wisdom in this and why you agreed to the union. Davina will succeed in wooing my son into a loving husband and father."

Parlan's face grew dark and he stepped within a breath of the two men. Studying them, his eyes settled on Ian, who met his gaze. "'Tis difficult to become a father, Ian, when you beat the vessel that contains your child."

Davina used the sleeve of her dress to muffle her tears of release. Loneliness had been her only companion under the brutal hands of her husband, and the unborn child she lost was more grief than she could bear. She had no idea her father knew what she had endured. Ian threatened her repeatedly, saying he only did the duty of a husband disciplining an unruly wife, and if she said anything to anyone of the constant deserved correction, she would regret it. After fighting against him proved to bring more of his dominance, she began to believe she was at fault, and indeed brought his wrath upon her. After all, many of her cousins spoke of the discipline all women must endure at the hands of their husbands, even the cruel methods their husbands chose to bed them. Why should her situation be any different?

Ian's inconsistent moods made her guarded at all times. One moment he displayed loving attention and whispered promises; the next he blamed her for whatever fouled his mood. Her mind spun with the torrent of various accusations and reasons for his shifting disposition. At times, Davina could hardly tell up from down and all rationalizations fell short to the chaos of her circumstances. Seeing her father come to her defense and knowing he did have eyes to see the truth, she gripped the wall to steady her legs buckling from sheer relief. She wasn't crazy! She wasn't at fault!

"Hold your coffers, then, Munro. Until Ian can prove to be gentler to Davina, she'll come back home here and the courtship will begin anew."

Ian snapped his head toward his father, and Munro dropped his mouth open. "Now, Parlan, I believe that's going a bit too far. There is no need to upset Davina with having to move her back here and endure the instability of a shifting home life."

"A safe and loving home life is better than the holdings she has endured under your roof. I will make arrangements to have her things brought back at once." Parlan narrowed his eyes on Ian. "You want those covetous connections to the crown, lad, you had better prove yourself to be a doting husband, worthy of the fruit of my grandchildren."

Davina fought to calm the thundering of her heart, thrumming out of control. She would be home!

"Parlan." Munro put a comforting hand upon her father's shoulder. "I can assure you Davina will be safe under my roof. Now that I'm aware of the situation—"

"The mistreatment was happening under your nose and you could not see it!" Parlan roared.

Munro bowed his head, backing away, and nodded. "You are correct, Parlan. I cannot express the grief of my ignorance over the pain I have caused your precious daughter. I have come to see Davina as the daughter I have always wanted and regret that my wife did not live to know her." Munro turned away to submit to forlorn pacing, his hands behind his back, a vision of repentance. "Methinks if Ian had the loving influence of my wife, he might have learned to be a kinder husband. I fear my attention to matters of estate and wealth gave me little time with him, so I failed in my duty to teach him such things." Turning sorrowful eyes to Parlan, Munro pleaded his case. "I understand your decision, and if you wish to maintain your position, I won't fight you. Nevertheless, I implore you to give me the chance to set this right. My eyes are opened and I will be Davina's protector. I will maintain control over Ian."

Davina waited, her breath caught in her chest, as she dared to hope in the safety her father offered. The moments stretched on endlessly as she watched Parlan consider Munro's words. With a deep sigh, he nodded. "I will concede."

Davina dropped her mouth open and her heart plummeted into the depths of her being.

"On one condition: You will all stay here as our guests for a fortnight or more. I wish to spend time with my daughter and give her a chance of reprieve and a period of observation over your son." Parlan pointed a finger at Munro's face and snarled his lips. "But if I see the tiniest sign of sorrow in my daughter's eyes, any hint of a mark on her body, if I don't see her demeanor change to that of a blissfully happy woman in a short time, I'm dissolving this marriage, and I care not what scandal it causes or what it costs me."

Munro tightened his jaw and his eyes grew cold. "Aye, I'm sure scandal is something you're well-equipped to handle, considering your background."

Parlan's face flushed crimson. "Regardless of my background," he gritted, "I'm still the one who has the connections to the crown, and not just through my illegitimate birth. Being nursery mates and close cousin to the one currently on the throne has its privileges."

The two men stared at each other in a silent contest, but a broad smile eventually broke across Munro's face. "Not to worry, my friend! You won't be disappointed. Ian will be a model son-in-law, and we will have many grandchildren to be proud of!" Munro's hearty slaps on Parlan's back did nothing to wipe away the determined line of Parlan's mouth, but he still nodded his assent.

Davina gulped down the new tears of dismay that threatened to give her away. Easing back from the doorway, she padded silently down the hall, away from this meeting of men, this gathering of male dominance deciding a doom-filled destiny for her life. As she staggered through the kitchen, out into the empty courtyard and behind the stables, her heart sank even further at the idea of Munro's protection in which she had no faith. She had never said a word to her father, and Parlan knew Ian was maltreating her in the few visits her parents had paid her, or their brief visits back to her home. How could Munro stand there feigning ignorance of what happened under his own roof? She sank down onto a small pile of straw behind some rain barrels, pulled her knees to her chest and buried her face in her arms, letting her tears flow.

Not once during this horror and farce of a marriage had she confided in her brother Kehr. Even now, she couldn't go to him, as he was away in Edinburgh, at least three day's journey from their home in Stewart Glen. Why she never shared any of her woes about Ian with her brother, she couldn't reason at this moment. She shared everything with him, including her fantasies of being the wife of the Gypsy fortune teller. Not the intimate details, of course, but the ideas of him coming back and declaring his true love. She had been grateful her brother was accepting of her dreams, though he did tease her from time to time. Kehr was always supportive, but he did caution her not to get too wrapped up in her dream world. It was, after all, a fantasy.

Drawing in a deep breath, she calmed her thumping heart and shaking hands, seeking her fantasies to ease her worry. What an impression he had made on her, the giant Gypsy fortune teller. She had enjoyed many trips to the Gypsy camp during their last stay, conversing with Amice while they sipped tea by the fire. Hardly glancing at Davina, Broderick came and went, telling fortunes and going about his business. Too shy to address him directly, Davina drank in every opportunity she saw him, her infatuation growing. And when he did address her, she couldn't form more than two words without a flurry of giggles. But she memorized every feature of Broderick's face—the curve of his hawk-like nose, the handsome angle of his cheekbones, the set line of his square jaw. At the tender age of thirteen, innocence and inexperience flavored her daydreams with strolls through moonlit forests and stolen kisses. As she grew older, those fantasies matured and burned with passion-filled embraces. Amice said they would return. In the eight years since she met him, every group of Gypsies traveling through their little village of Stewart Glen set her heart aflame, only to be doused by the disappointment of his not being amongst them. When her father made the marriage contract with Munro, giving her hand to Ian, she forced herself to abandon her dreams and come to the realistic conclusion she had to put her whimsies aside, as her brother encouraged.

The dark reality of this union with Ian, though, resurrected those fantasies and she clung to them with her life.

Kittens mewed somewhere in the stables, their helpless little cries drawing her attention and turning the corners of her mouth up in sympathy. She sighed. At least her heart stopped pounding, and her hands were steady once more.

Leaning her head against the wooden structure of the stables, she stared at the stones of the perimeter wall across the way...stones that her father placed by his own hands. She smiled as she recalled his attempt at engineering the secret opening located in the north side of the perimeter wall, at the back of their grounds just to her left. He complained how imperfect the mechanisms were. Kehr and Davina delighted in using the secret passage for fun through the years, though with stern warning from their father not to give away its whereabouts. Though their home was not designed to be a formidable fortress against an army, the walls did keep them safe by directing all traffic through the front gates. Parlan was ever mindful of his family, as a responsible father should be.

She started at a clatter on the other side of the wall and held her hand to her breast, forcing her breathing to slow. Not moving a muscle or daring to breathe, she waited for any other sounds to reveal what happened. The blood drained from her face as Ian's grumbling reached her ears. Deep, nervous protests rumbled from the horses in the stables as Ian kicked what sounded like buckets or stools. "Bitch! This is all her fault!" The jangling of buckles and tack sounded amongst the commotion. "Hold still, you stupid animal!"

Davina inched into a crouching position from her seat on the ground, and peered through the cracks in the shutters of the opening above her. Ian struggled to saddle his horse. She winced at each tug and shove the horse endured from his master, until their stableman Fife cleared his throat when he stepped up to the stall. "Can I be of assistance, Master Ian?"

Ian recoiled at Fife's voice and then took a calming breath, backing away from the horse. "Aye, Fife, I would appreciate that."

Davina's heart twisted at the sight of Ian's handsome smile and charming air. He had been that way with her during their courtship, but now showed that side of his personality to everyone but her. Little did people suspect the ruthless man beneath the attractive exterior.

"Something upsets you, Master Ian?" Fife rubbed his large, round nose, squinting his age-lined eyes as he patted the horse's neck and walked around the other side to secure the leather straps.

"Oh, just a little disagreement with my father. Nothing serious." Ian grinned and shook his head. "Do we ever stop having disagreements with our parents, I wonder?"

Fife chuckled and shook his head, dropping his guard. "'Tis an endless battle we must endure a lifetime, lad. A lifetime." They both shared a laugh in this wisdom. Fife handed the reins over to Ian. "Be easy on her, Master Ian. Have a good run to ease your tension and be back in time for supper."

Ian shook his head good-naturedly and mounted his trim form into the saddle. "I feel I have more than one father around here with the way you and Parlan dote over me."

"Just lookin' out for you, Master Ian." Fife waved as he watched Ian turn his horse and head for the front gate. "Nice lad," he whispered as he straightened up the stables.

Davina bit her lower lip in frustration. Was she the only one who understood Ian's cruelty? Clenching her fists, she marched from behind the stables and headed back to the castle, Fife giving her a puzzled glance as she closed the door behind her. Nay, she wasn't the only one. Her father had eyes to see, and she would be sure he knew the extent of Ian's brutality.

She headed straight back to the parlor, but found the room empty, the fire still burning in the hearth. Turning on her heels, she almost bumped into her mother.

"Oh! Davina, you gave me a start!" Lilias put a hand to her breast and caught her breath. "Your father sent me to fetch you."

"I was just looking for him, myself."

Taking her daughter's hand, Lilias led Davina through the ground floor of their home to the first floor, housing the private bedchambers. Every stone they passed on their way to her parents' chamber reminded Davina of the pride in her father's efforts, and the confidence in his wisdom to listen to her pleas.

When her mother opened the door to their chamber, Lilias ushered Davina through, closed the heavy door behind them, and sat on the lounging couch by the fire taking a quiet, yet supportive place at her husband's side. Parlan stood at the hearth, his back to the door, much the way he had in the parlor. "I'm not sure how much you heard outside the parlor, Davina, but I am sorry the conversation caused you such distress." He turned to face her, his eyebrows scrunched in sorrow. "Fear not, I was the only one who witnessed your tearful retreat." His last words were a comforting whisper.

Davina drew her quivering lip between her teeth to steady it and stand strong before her father. "'Tis nothing you caused, Da. I'm grateful to know you're aware of my situation." Her voice trembled, but she cleared her throat and kept her tears at bay. "I was on my way into the parlor to fetch my embroidery when my father-in-law begged for your forgiveness for my husband."

Parlan's eyebrows rose, apparently surprised she heard so much. He nodded. "Then you know Ian's punishment for his inability to manage his responsibilities."

She nodded.

After a long pause, he said, "I realize the condition of this arrangement sounds like I'm sending you back into the lion's den." Parlan studied the soft brown leather of his boots before returning his gaze to her. "Ian is especially not happy about the tightening of his purse, which I trust Munro to enforce. That's why I'm insisting they stay here under my roof, so I can give you a measure of safety and assurance you will be protected."

Davina let the flood of her sorrow loose. "Da, please don't let me endure another moment of this union! Can we not do as you said and dissolve this marriage?"

Parlan tightened his jaw and turned his sorrowful eyes toward his wife. Lilias grabbed his hand, seeming to give him support. "Davina, the Russells provide immense business opportunities, both for me and your brother, and I cannot rely on my cousin the King forever. We must make efforts to increase our holdings on our own." Focusing back on Davina, he stepped toward her and took both of her hands into his. "I'm sorry you endured more than any woman's share of heavy-handedness from your husband. Now that I can deny his treatment of you no more, I hope you can forgive me for not speaking for you sooner. I will take measures to ensure you're protected, and with your help, methinks we can make this work."

Davina exerted great effort to speak over the lump forming in her throat. "Be the gentle hand to tame the beast," she whispered, repeating the words of her father-in-law.

Parlan nodded. "Munro has obviously done a poor job of showing Ian how to be a man. Your stay, their stay here will be indefinite. Ian and Munro will each be staying in the guest rooms above, and you will, again, have your room to yourself on this level. I have pressed the matter further with Munro, and we will both be supervising Ian's behavior over the next several weeks. Munro has humbly accepted my guidance as a father, and Lilias as a mother, to put Ian on the right path. Only when we see improvement will you be allowed to venture back to their home. Only when I feel confident you will be cherished and taken care of as the precious woman you are, will you be allowed to go with them."

Though relieved the beatings and cruel sexual engagements would stop, Davina's world still crumbled about her. "Da, you don't know the true Ian. He's a master of donning a mask of charm over the monster he is. He'll—"

"Davina, there is no way I will let him harm you. I agree that he takes his responsibilities too far in exercising his dominion as a husband, but he isn't a danger to your life. If I thought he was, I would dissolve this marriage now. We will protect you." Davina hated knowing her family believed she had a flare for the dramatic. He kissed her forehead and pulled her into a tight embrace. "I won't let him harm you. You must do this for your family. One day, when Ian has learned his role and duties as a husband, you may grow to forgive and love him. If not, you may at least find solace in the children you will have one day."

She let her tears flow, wetting her father's tunic and holding him tight for strength as she submitted to his wishes. She would be the sacrificial lamb for the stability of her family's future.

50

Steel clashing against steel rang about the air, bouncing off the walls and high ceiling of the Great Hall, which mingled with the grunts, panting, and groans of Kehr and Ian as they dueled. Kehr parried Ian's thrust, turned around, and swatted Ian's open side, initiating a grunt from him. With a grin on his face, Ian shoved Kehr forward, and Kehr returned the grin with his own thrust; however, Ian effectively blocked with his shield.

"Good!" Kehr encouraged.

"Thank you!" Ian said with another slash of his sword, which Kehr dodged.

Davina smiled at her brother, warmed by his presence. He had finally come home after a long stay in Edinburgh visiting at court. He only just arrived, late the previous evening, and though she anticipated his arrival and the opportunity to spend time with him, the news about King James's visiting apparition sent her spirits sinking.

All of Scotland was abuzz with the King's experience, and Kehr had relayed the story with a grand reenactment in the parlor. With a fire blazing in the hearth, casting ominous shadows across the room, her family sat in a circle, fixed on Kehr's dramatic performance.

"'Bow before the King of Scotland!' the king's advisor bellowed as he chased after the man who burst into the king's private prayer chambers." Kehr imitated Marshall John Inglis, running after the intruder. "But the king raised his hand and stayed his advisors, for the man stopped before he reached his majesty."

Ripples of laughter circulated the room, and Davina put her hand upon her mouth to stifle her own chuckles. "And you say *I* have a penchant for drama!" she teased.

Kehr laughed at the interruption, but proceeded. "'Enough,' said the king. 'Let him speak.' After they stared at each other for a long stretch of silence, the man reached forward," Kehr mimed the actions of the intruder, bending forward with his fist before him. "And yanked his majesty by his tunic, saying, 'Sir King, my mother has sent me to you, desiring you not to go where you are purposed.'" Kehr's brow furrowed with the grave message the man delivered to the king. "'If you do, you shall not fare well in your journey, nor none that is with you.'" Kehr stalked along the edge of those seated around the room, looking each of them in the eye. Davina shook her head at the pause he used for effect. Kehr centered before his audience. "And just like that..." Kehr snapped his fingers. "The man vanished like a blink in the sun!" The family gasped and murmured to each other. Kehr shrugged his shoulders. "And so the king has decided not to declare war on England."

Davina steadied as the breath left her chest in rush...while everyone else broke into applause, cheering and celebrating the grand occasion. Grabbing his mead, Kehr nodded to Davina and raised his mug. She returned the nod with a forced smile. Her brother sat down amongst the applause, while the family congratulated him on his performance and the wonderful news.

Davina had made every effort to appear happy, just as she did now, struggling to maintain her smile as a mask, clinging to the knowledge that Kehr and her father were not going to war after all. Thankfully, talk of war always kept her away from court, where she loathed spending time. Besides, she wanted Ian in the battlefield…not her brother and father.

"Hold tight, Ian," Kehr warned and unleashed an onslaught of swings, clashes, and advances that had Ian backing up across the length of the room. Not watching his footsteps, Ian tripped and fell backwards, but with rapid steps, regained his footing and turned around to avoid Kehr's assault.

"Getting caught up in the excitement, niece?" Her mother's brother Tammus stood beside Davina.

Davina realized she gripped the back of a chair while watching her brother and husband engaging in their mock battle for part of Ian's training. Easing her hands off the hard wood, she only just noticed the ache in her fingers. She regarded her uncle, whose face glowed with a warm, orange hue in the light of the torches set about the hall. "Aye, Uncle. I fret for them both," she lied.

Tammus put a warm arm about her shoulders and hugged her to his side. "Oh, worry not, lass. Mock battle is most certainly different from the real engagement, which, thankfully, we don't have to endure after all."

"Aye, Uncle." She grinned and turned her attention back to the dueling pair.

When Kehr winked at her, his back turned to Ian, her husband slapped Kehr in the bottom with the flat of his sword, causing her brother to yelp. Ian raised his eyebrows in mock surprise, and Kehr set off chasing Ian, who ran away screaming like a little girl, encircling the wide expanse of the room. Everyone erupted into laughter at the comical scene, save Davina. Ian's display made her sick. Over the last six weeks since Ian's punishment of tightening his purse strings, Ian had been putting on a stellar performance of winning her family over at every opportunity. Though they didn't allow the two of them to be alone together, to her great relief, those rare moments when he could steal a glance in her direction or corner her in the castle, he let her know privately that this would all come back to haunt her once he achieved his goal of gaining back his control and his money.

"'Tis a delightful game of cat and mouse, is it not?" he had asked her on one of those cornering engagements.

"You won't be able to fool my family," Davina said confidently.

He closed in on her, backing her into the corner of the stairs and bracing his arms on the walls. "They think to control me," he hissed, "a puppet on their strings, dishing out meager helpings from their purse? Let us see how they like being controlled. They are a trusting lot, just as you are." He cursed her with an evil smile and strutted away. She started carrying a dagger in her boot after that encounter. Watching her family now, playing right out of Ian's hands, his statement seemed true enough. Ian enjoyed this masquerade, enjoyed manipulating people to think and do what he wanted, a game he relished in perfecting. How far would he go?

Kehr succeeded in tripping Ian, who went sprawling across the stone floor. Everyone rushed to his aid, Kehr at the head of the crowd, apologizing. Ian sat stunned for the moment and Davina allowed herself a secret smile. Gaining his composure, Ian wiped the blood from his bottom lip and looked at her. Raising an eyebrow, he smiled briefly—just long enough for her to notice—before his face turned somber. Ian dropped his gaze as though heartsick. Glancing at

Davina, he rose from the floor and dusted his breeches. The slight gesture caused her brother and father to turn toward Davina. Before she knew Ian's ploy, Davina had been caught gloating at her husband's accident, exactly as Ian wanted.

Heat climbed into her cheeks. Parlan glared at her, causing the rest of the group to turn toward her. Excusing herself from the scene, Davina left the Great Hall into the corridor past the parlor, through the kitchen and outside toward the stables, choking down her sobs. Dusk settled around the castle, casting everything in hues of gray. Halos of amber light ringed the torches set about the grounds, lighting at least a guiding path. She stomped into the stables and kicked an empty bucket on the ground. The commotion awakened the kittens and they stirred.

"How can they believe his performance?" she hissed and folded her arms under her breasts, clenching her fists and pacing. After the first incident, Davina had gone to her father explaining Ian's plan, and he believed her. But when Ian was brought before Munro, Parlan and Davina for accountability, Ian claimed Davina misunderstood him and apologized for being a fool with his words, not saying things correctly. At first, even she believed she was hearing him wrong, until he cornered her another time. There was no mistaking anything. After a time, her father grew to believe

Davina was trying to discredit Ian while he was trying so hard to change. These failures didn't discourage her from continuing to try, though.

Three kittens emerged from under the crate at the back of Fife's work area. Davina stopped and stared, waiting. Where were the other kittens? She crouched down upon her heels, peering into the dimness. One more kitten crawled out, mewing. They grew so much in the last six weeks…but only in size. Their shrinking numbers is what concerned Davina. When she had first seen the kittens, she counted eight. A week later—the week after Ian's punishment and supervision began—there were seven. She sloughed off the difference of numbers as a miscount. When the second kitten went missing the following week, she surmised the poor thing might have been snatched by an owl or other predator. *Other predator, indeed.* Fife told her about the third kitten gone missing two weeks later, saying Ian brought it to him near heartbroken. Its head had been crushed…by a horse, Fife guessed. Davina tried to tell Fife of her suspicions, but with fatherly counsel he told her she was being too hard on Master Ian and needed to learn to forgive him for his past transgressions, and how Ian confided in Fife about ways to try and be a better husband.

Too many kittens had gone missing for her not to be suspicious in spite of what Fife said. She crouched, waiting for the fifth kitten to emerge from the crate. Still nothing. Taking a lantern off the wall, she brought the light into the growing darkness of the falling night, into Fife's work area. The crate lay empty. Four kittens roamed about her. Four out of the eight. Where was the fifth?

She replaced the lantern and paced two circuits around the area in front of the stalls before she entered the gate to her own horse Heather. Grabbing her saddle, she heaved it atop Heather's back.

"Going somewhere?" Ian's voice caused her to jump, and icicles danced up her spine.

She clamped her lips shut and instead focused on pulling the leather straps tight, straining to hear his actions over the incessant pounding of her heart. Shuffling to the other side of her horse, her foot fell upon something soft, and she jumped back with a yelp, thinking she'd stepped on a rat. Nothing moved. With the toe of her boot, she touched the straw where she had stepped. Still no stirring, so she knelt down, extended a trembling hand, and lifted the straw away. The fifth kitten.

"Awww," Ian said, sounding forlorn, but when she saw him peeking over the stall, he had a smile on lips. "Not another one?" She marveled in terror at how he could make his voice sound loving or concerned when he held such a menacing grin on his face. The hair on the back of her neck bristled.

"Why?" she whimpered. "Why are you doing this?"

He glanced over his shoulder and smiled. "Gullible to the last," he whispered and winked.

She grabbed a rag off the nail at the back of the stall and scooped up the cold body. She sobbed as she showed him the kitten. "Do you have so much anger inside you that you must take it out on innocent animals since you cannot take it out on me?"

"Davina, what are you saying?" Ian stepped back toward the opening of the stables. "Are you saying that I—?" Ian shook his head, standing just outside the stable entrance; his eyes filled with sorrow and reflected the flickering light of the torch, adding to his demonic aura. "I know I have done you wrong, but have I not done everything I can to prove to you I have changed? What more—?"

"There, there, Master Ian," Fife said, coming into the stables. "What has you so upset, lad?"

"Is that what you think of me, Davina?" Ian said, grief-stricken.

"Fife! Look! Another kitten!" She sobbed uncontrollably, dreading how this would turn out. "'Tis as I told you! He saw me find the kitten and held no remorse!"

Fife stared at her open-mouthed, and then glanced at Ian with regret. Davina ran past them, around to the back of the stables, and put the kitten down on a small pile of straw. Crying, she washed the blood from her hands and splashed cool water from the rain barrel on her face to try and clear her head. Resting her hands on the edge of the barrel, she panted, trying to think of how she would handle this. *This cannot be happening! Why is this happening?*

At the edge of the rain barrel, a crusted, brown mark resembled a partial hand print. A bloody handprint.

Ian grabbed her by the shoulders and turned her about so quickly, her head spun. Holding her against the back wall of the stable, he said loud enough for Fife to hear, in a voice dripping with affection so sincere, she almost believed his words...if not for the ominous mask on his face, "You are just as delicate as those kittens. I would hate to see something like that happen to you. It would crush me." He squeezed her shoulders harder on the word "crush" for emphasis.

Through the shutters to her left, above the rain barrel, retreating footsteps faded and Ian waited for Fife to be out of earshot.

"Gullible to the last, Davina," he taunted. "I will have them accepting me into your family, and *you* will be the one under restrictions. They may even think you mad after I finish my work."

Her world closing in around her, she shoved him away and scrambled toward the castle. Bursting through the kitchen entrance, she bolted down the hall to the parlor and stopped short at the door. Her family was seated around the room, their eyes wide and questioning. Fife stood to her left beside her father, crushing his hat in his nervous hands, guilt on his face.

"Fife, what have you told them?" Davina laid her cold fingertips against her wet, flushed cheeks.

Her father crossed his arms. "What is this about Ian killing kittens?"

She rushed to grab her father's forearm. "Da, he's taking his anger out on these poor defenseless animals instead of me." She couldn't control her sobbing as she pleaded.

"Now, Mistress Davina," Fife admonished gently. "Master Ian said he could no more hurt those kittens than he could you. You just misunderstood what he said."

"Thank you for defending me, Fife, but methinks 'tis hopeless to try anymore." Ian stood at the door, sorrow pulling down the corners of his mouth. "Methinks she's right, Parlan. We should dissolve this union. She'll never forgive me, no matter how much I try to change."

"Why are you doing this!" she screeched in Ian's face.

"Now you want me? What is your game, Davina?" Ian threw his hands up in frustration and shuffled to the center of the room to plead his case, leaving Davina back at the doorway.

"Nay, that's not what I mean to say and you know this! Why are you trying to make my family see me as mad?"

Ian dropped his jaw as if he'd been slapped. Closing his mouth and then his eyes, he nodded. "Parlan, I have tried." He regarded her father with such sorrow, her mother sobbed. "I love your daughter, and I hoped we could make this work, but 'tis plain to see she won't forgive me." Turning to his father Munro, he said, "I will be in my chamber packing my trunk. 'Tis best we leave on the morrow." Facing Davina, he stepped forward with his back to the room and gave her that private, evil smile his voice never betrayed. "Farewell, Davina," he whispered, and departed. Munro followed, scowling at her on his way out.

Davina stood stunned at the accusatory glares from her family. Parlan sighed and marched to the hearth, turning his back to her. Lilias sobbed into the kerchief she pulled from her sleeve. Kehr stepped forward, his eyebrows turned down. "Davina, 'tis time to put away your Gypsy dream lover. Not one man, never mind you Ian, will ever be able to live up to this fantasy. 'Tis time you grew up."

Parlan turned around with fluid expressions that alternated between confusion and anger. Davina almost choked on the lump forming in her throat. Even her beloved Kehr betrayed her, thought her mad! Running from the room, she went back out to the stables. Pulling Heather from her stall, Davina mounted her horse and bolted through the grounds and out the front gate, away from the madness. Her cheeks, wet with tears, grew cold as the wind whipped past and tangled her hair. At a clearing where she frequently found solitude, she pulled on Heather's reins and jumped from her horse, falling to the ground covered with the leaves of last fall, damp from the evening dew.

Kneeling in the middle of the moonlit forest, Davina sobbed into the leaves. How right her Gypsy dream lover had been! The doom Broderick predicted for her life as a young girl entrenched her. But why was this happening? She only wanted to continue the happy life she had prior to meeting Ian. Why did God wed her to this madman who thrilled at manipulation and control? She only wanted a family and someone to love. Pushing up, she settled her trembling hands upon her belly. Losing her first child grieved her deeply, but in the end, she reasoned, wasn't not having the child for the best? Davina couldn't bear to see her own flesh and blood forced to submit to the same fate as she, to this frenzy she endured. Curling her knees to her chest, she pulled her legs close, hugging the baby nestled inside her now. She missed two monthly courses—one before Ian's *punishment* and this last month—thus had become with child before she and Ian had separate chambers. What would happen then to this baby if they perceived her a lunatic? Rocking back and forth, her forehead against her knees, she let the river of tears flow.

The crook of her arm touched the dagger in her boot. She held her breath, frozen by an idea that touched her mind. Hiking up the hem of her gown, she pulled the weapon from her boot and sat on her heels. Her heart warred over this decision. *I am mad. But what other choice do I have?* She squeezed her hands around the hilt of her dagger, the tip of the blade poised over her heart. White-knuckled and trembling, her hands throbbed painfully. Whether she gripped the knife out of fear or for strength was unclear. A soft breeze touched her tear-stained cheeks, cooling her flesh in the evening air. She didn't want to do this—to take her own life and the life of her unborn child—but how could she face the madness awaiting them both? How could she face the betrayal of her family? Or was this just a coward's excuse?

She gritted out a cry of frustration and drove the blade into the soft, damp earth, collapsing to the ground. Her body wracked with sobs, and the smell of dirt mixed with the stale, decaying leaves, like a grave. "So close," she whimpered. "So close to being a widow. So close to freedom." Over one decision made by the King, all her hopes shattered like icicles against stone. Even this member of her family—her royal cousin—betrayed her; the apparition of James seemed to be sent just for her, just to torment her existence. Davina sobbed deeper as hopelessness engulfed her.

Heather stamped her hooves and tossed her head. Davina darted her gaze around the darkened forest in search of the source of the animal's agitation. Her stomach lurched in fear.

Oh, God! Have they come for me? She paled. Ian might have come after her…alone.

Cold silence answered her, save for the slight rustle of the trees in the wind. She searched the terrain but saw nothing. After a moment more of silence, she heaved a tentative sigh and relief bathed her. No one came with horses to seize and take her back. Davina rose to her feet, wiping her nose, and crept toward her mount, still darting her eyes around. "There, there," she soothed, her hand outstretched.

Before she could lay her fingers on Heather's flank, an unseen force knocked the wind from her lungs, and she thumped her head on the ground. Davina's face pushed into the leaves, head throbbing, and someone crushed her body. Unable to breathe or think, she struggled to force air back into her lungs as panic set in.

"Relax, lass," a deep voice whispered against her ear. "Your breath will return in a moment."

In a whirl, her attacker yanked her to her feet and turned her to face him, his hands biting into the fresh bruises on her arms made by Ian when he held her against the stables. Vision-blurred and her mind still reeling from the encounter, she managed to steady herself and soon the summer night air filled her lungs once more. She breathed in hungry gulps.

"There you go, lassie."

Fear jolted her body and she fought with the man holding her captive against him. A molten silver glow in the pupils of his eyes drew her into their depths, and she calmed. A wave of curiosity and confusion flooded through her when her eyes settled upon his familiar face—that hawk-like nose, those emerald-green eyes, that fiery-red hair. Had her Broderick come back to rescue her at last? She pushed against his chest to gain some distance from his face for a better view of him.

Nay. This face appeared younger, his jaw not as wide, his cheekbones not as chiseled. *I have lost my mind!* She should be frightened senseless in the arms of her attacker, and yet she wondered if he was the man she longed for since her youth.

The danger in his eyes transformed to confusion as this dark stranger searched her face. Clutching her hair, he pulled her head back. A cry escaped her lips as he pulled the hair against the lump on her head. She was forced to gawk at the black sky and pregnant moon above. She held her breath as his mouth latched onto her throat, and sharp teeth pierced her tender skin. A brief pain…then an unexpected, warm flow of pleasure streamed through her veins, and she collapsed against him with a moan, falling into euphoria.

This man—this creature—probed her mind, a seductive invasion of her thoughts, learning everything about her as he drank. Within moments, she relived the pleasures of her childhood, the frustrations of her youthful womanhood, and the fantasies of her Gypsy dream lover. These distant memories of Broderick came rushing forward and surrounded her…the exotic aroma of the incense, the heady presence of his heat, the fluttering of her belly at the sight of him.

Davina relived the night she met Broderick.

"What do you see, sir?"

Their faces were very close as his deep voice cautioned her. "I cannot lie to you, lass. Doing so would be a disaster."

"A disaster?"

"Aye." His emerald eyes bore into hers. "Times ahead will not be pleasant. But you must not lose faith. You have much strength. Draw on that strength and hold tight to what is most dear, for that is what will bring you through these troubled times that are yet to come."

"What will happen, sir?" she pressed.

"'Tis unknown to me. I know not the specifics. The lines on the palm do not reveal such details, only to say that strife is in your future. Just remember what I told you. Hold tight to your vision of strength." The rest of her memories leading up to this moment in time, quickened by and brought her back to the despair she experienced today.

Aye then. Let this stranger drink the life flowing through my body. Let him do what I cannot bring myself to do. I will have peace at last and die in the arms of the man who I imagine, for the moment, is the one I love. In the seconds from the time he'd latched onto her throat until this moment, serenity engulfed her.

The stranger broke from her and dropped her to the ground. Davina's neck throbbed. Her head churned from the rapid memories swirling through her mind, displaying her life like a poorly performed play.

Scrutinizing his hazy image beginning to clear, she discerned him tip his head back and laugh maniacally. "After two decades of searching, I finally have what I have been looking for!" He knelt down before her and cradled her face in his palms. "God doesn't look well upon my kind, so I can only credit the Dark Lord himself for bringing me such a prize!" He breathed deep, his smile growing. "As sweet as your blood is, my dear lady," the man licked her blood from his lips, "I will leave you to your tragic life." The molten silver glow faded from his eyes.

The questions swirling through her mind vanished in the familiar despair moving through her and gripping her heart. What twisted games were the Fates playing with her? Why relive all those moments, with Death so close in her arms, only to have her chance at freedom yanked away from her. She reached for him, but weakness lorded over her body. "Nay," she tried to say over the lump in her throat, choking back the tears stinging her eyes. "You cannot leave me to this. Please…finish the task."

He curled a finger under her chin. "All will be well." He laid his palm to her forehead and Davina's mind became a fog. All went black.

Stars sprinkled the sky above with the moon overhead. Davina sat up, her head pinning, and touched the lump throbbing on the back of her skull.

"Thank God!" a deep male voice exclaimed. A hazy figure knelt beside her, and she struggled to clear her vision to try and identify him. "What were you thinking!"

She scrunched her eyebrows in confusion, her mind a muddled mess. "Wha—?"

"I apologize. I may have been a little overzealous in trying to save you from yourself." When she tried to stand up, his warm hands on her shoulders pushed her back down. "Methinks you need to stay seated for a moment longer. Do you know where you are?"

Davina scanned the area, the world coming into view. She sat in the middle of the forest clearing she frequented for solitude. Heather stood a distance away, nibbling at some leaves on a bush. Why was she here? Glancing at her trembling hands, she hoped to find the answers. Her eyes wandered, and in the stranger's hand, she recognized her dagger. She beheld the stranger, his emerald eyes filled with concern in the silver light of the moon. How familiar he seemed. Her breath caught in her throat. How very much like her Gypsy dream lover, yet not like him.

"You remember," he said, nodding. "You are very fortunate I came along, mistress. What would possess you to take your own life, only God will know, but for the sake of your soul, I hope you do *not* try to repeat that ghastly task."

"Sir, if you please." She laid an imploring hand upon his arm. "What happened?"

"Oh, I thought you remembered." He cleared his throat. "You were going to take your life, so I stopped you. In the process, you hit your head. I hope you can forgive me." He rolled his eyes and mumbled, "I may have almost finished the deed for you myself, with my clumsiness."

"Not to wish you ill tidings, sir, but I wish you *had* finished the deed."

"Nonsense!" He inhaled a breath and seemed to gain control over his outburst. "Why do you suppose I'm out here, young miss?"

"I'm not sure I understand what you imply, sir."

"I will come right out and say it, in spite of how mad my words will sound." He took both her hands in his and stared pointedly into her eyes. "'Tis not by chance that I wandered these woods this night. I say this after having saved your life, but I doubted my sanity at first. I was passing through your humble little town below and these woods called to me. A message came into my mind as I searched, not knowing what I searched for. The message said, 'You must tell her that he will return, that he will rescue her. You must tell her not to give up hope and hold tight to that vision of strength.'"

Davina gasped.

"Do you know what that means?"

She nodded.

"Good, because I certainly do not." The corner of his handsome mouth turned up when she offered no explanation. "Well, it matters not. I'm glad I'm not cracked after all."

"So am I, sir," she replied in awe. A new hope blossomed in Davina's chest. "I thank the Lord you were listening to Him this night. Thank you for stopping me." She resisted the urge to hug this dark stranger, who became her savior and messenger in the form of the man she loved, and instead kissed his knuckles in gratitude.

"Well, that's more reward than I have already received and could have hoped for." He helped her to her feet, not letting her hand go until she proved she was sound on her feet and assured him she was able to ride. After she mounted Heather, he held the dagger up to her, offering her the handle-end. When she reached for it, he pulled it back. "I hand this over with much hesitance, dear lady. Will you promise me you will never have this blade pointed at your heart again?"

"Aye, sir, I promise." He gave her the knife and she tucked it into her boot. "The message you delivered has given me a reason to live."

"That's a great relief." He patted her knee. "You can ride back on your own, I trust?"

She nodded and her face flushed with shame. "Aye, I'm sure my family didn't know my intent when I left in such a state. Having to explain how you saved me from myself would put us both in an awkward position."

"That it would. As much as I would like to accompany you back, I have other pressing matters. I have been biding for someone for a very long time, and I believe I will bide no more. You have given me a sign of my own, my dear lady. I'm sure we will see each other another time, though." He walked a few steps backwards and waved before he turned to leave. "Good night, fair lady!"

"Oh, sir! What is the name of my savior so I may include you in my prayers?"

"Angus!" he called back without missing a step.

CHAPTER THREE

Stewart Glen, Scotland—Late Autumn, 1514
15 Months Later

"Leave me alone! Don't touch me!" Davina struggled against the hands restraining her.

"Davina. *Davina.*"

The softness of the voice stopped her, and she scooted away, uncertain of her surroundings.

"'Tis I, Davina, your mother!" Lilias lit a tallow candle and climbed onto the bed beside her daughter. Wrapping comforting arms around Davina and rocking to and fro, she hushed her. "All is well. He's dead. Remember? He's long in the grave, sweet."

"Aye, M'ma." She sighed and let her mother wipe her sweaty brow. "Cailin?"

"Cailin is well," her mother assured her. "Myrna is attending her. Rest easy, Davina." Lilias sighed and continued to rock her daughter. "Many weeks have passed since a nightmare has troubled you."

Davina nodded. Her husband Ian had been dead over a year, and the nightmares still plagued her; though, they appeared to be dying off as of late, which gave her some hope.

So much had happened since that night she tried to take her own life. The time went by so quickly it seemed to have vanished; and yet as she waited with patience for Broderick's return, as the dark stranger Angus promised, the time seemed to stretch on into eternity. Though Ian gained a foothold with her family, a long and heartfelt conversation with them eased the tension, and they gave Davina the benefit of observing Ian more closely. The bruises she received from his rough handling behind the stables aided her cause. And even though she braved showing them the scars on her body from past beatings, dissolving the union was no longer an option. Davina told them about her pregnancy, and though her condition gave them more reason to keep Ian away from her during this observation, it solidified their marriage.

Thankfully, this evidence betrayed Ian's true nature, but prior to pursuing any other disciplinary measures, King James changed his mind and declared war on England. Before the men were called to arms, Ian tried to escape, taking as much as he could from his father's estate to support himself, but Munro and Parlan intercepted him. They kept him under lock and key until their time to go, with the threat of treason hanging over his head if he tried to escape once more. On the eve of their departure, Ian vowed he would return, and Davina would wish she had never been born. Kehr vowed to Davina, in his own private farewell, that Ian would *not* return.

On September 9, 1513, the Battle of Flodden Field ravaged Scotland's countrymen—even taking their brave King—and left a mass of women heartbroken in its wake, including Davina and her mother. The war dragged not only her husband into the battlefield, but her brother Kehr and her father Parlan as well, proving to be a bittersweet victory. True to Kehr's word, Ian didn't return. His death freed her, but at the cost of losing her beloved brother and father. Uncle Tammus— having been one of the few who survived—trudged home, bringing the bodies of Parlan and Kehr with him. Among so many others in the massacre, Ian's body couldn't be found, so great was the loss. They buried Kehr and Parlan on their land, and seeing them lowered into the cold earth put finality to their lives. However, with Ian's death, the babe inside her—three months along—would have the chance to live a peaceful life.

Munro also fell in battle, leaving Davina the inheritance of his estate and funds. She couldn't bear returning to the place where Ian terrorized her, so she returned home. That chapter now closed upon her life, new responsibilities awaited her, assisting her mother in the care of Stewart Glen. In addition, Tammus took upon the role of guardian for them, spending half his time at Stewart Glen and the other half at his own holdings. With his son also fallen in battle, and his wife dead at childbirth, Tammus welcomed the family responsibilities.

So if her torment was over, if Ian was dead and long in the grave, as her mother said…why did he still haunt her dreams? Why could she not escape this dread of his return? Maybe the nightmares came from never finding his body, and Ian's hanging threat. Maybe she just needed to forgive him at last and release her hatred.

Myrna entered the room, cradling a crying babe. "She calls for you, Mistress Davina."

Davina could feel the milk in her breasts rush forth and seep through her gown at the sound of her child's baying, and she winced in discomfort. She reached out and took her eight-month-old daughter from her mother's handmaid. "Aye, precious," she cooed, and soothed the infant with kisses and strokes to her tiny face. "Thank you, Myrna." Davina noted how much weight Myrna lost over this last year, the death of Parlan and Kehr seeming to take its toll on her as well. Davina turned to her mother. "I will be fine, M'ma. Cailin can stay with me for the rest of the night."

Lilias gave mother and child a kiss to their brows and left them alone in the candlelight, Myrna following close behind. The glow of the flame flickered and danced in the silence, casting soft illumination upon her baby's face. Davina's lips touched Cailin's cheeks, and she wiped the tears away. Her infant in her arms made the nightmares so easy to forget. Positioning her child at her side, she opened her damp gown, and the eager mouth closed around her nipple. Cailin stopped crying and breathed soft, warm puffs against Davina's skin.

Davina studied her nursing child—her tiny nose, soft lashes upon her pudgy cheeks, cinnamon hair, thick and curling, around her angelic face. Burying her face in her daughter's silky curls, Davina shed silent tears into Cailin's downy locks. "What a blessing from the curse," she whispered. She vowed, as she had a hundred times since Ian's death, she would never let a man brutalize her again.

The morning sunlight kissed Davina's face and she stretched in its warmth. She watched her handmaid, who opened the curtains, humming a simple tune while fetching Davina's clothes from the wardrobe.

"Good morrow, Davina."

Davina smiled. "Good morrow, Rosselyn." Rising from her bed, she held Cailin in her arms and carried her half-sleeping daughter through the double doors to the landing outside. She drew a deep, cool breath of air and sighed. With the winter months coming upon them, the morning sky was still shadowed, and not yet brightened by the late-rising sun. She placed her hand atop the cold, gritting stone wall. Pride swelled in her breast over her father's ingenuity. He had used the remnants of a walkway atop the curtain wall of the older structure, creating a terrace. This was Davina's favorite feature of her bedchamber, providing a view over the courtyard, the dense forest off to the left, and the village far in the distance. For no apparent reason, a tickle of excitement fluttered in her stomach, not unlike the anticipation of a long-awaited gift. *Curious.*

Davina grinned and stepped back inside to sit down in an embroidered chair, where she cradled her baby. Davina opened her robe and gown and offered one of her swollen breasts. With greedy enthusiasm, Cailin suckled as she clutched a handful of Davina's hair and closed her eyes. A live-in wet nurse was expensive, and though she had a sizable inheritance from her late husband's family, Davina erred on the side of caution in maintaining those funds. She and her family held no titles, their connections to the crown through her father's illegitimate birth too distant for such luxuries. But they fared well enough to own land and have a mutual relationship with the growing community of Stewart Glen. This arrangement suited Davina well. Her age and position allowed her to maintain a low profile, so finding suitors was not a concern. All that aside, neither would she send her daughter away to be nursed, as she enjoyed the bonding breast feeding Cailin afforded.

After a while, Cailin stopped suckling and Davina turned her around to offer her other breast. Lilias strolled into the room and kissed Davina on the crown of her head. "I would like you to help Caitrina and her girls with the laundry today, Davina. Rosselyn, Myrna, and I will have Anna help us with the sweeping and changing of the wormwood."

"Of course, M'ma," Davina said, rising and handing Cailin to Myrna, who took the baby to the nursery. "Are we still for the markets this day?"

"As to be expected!" Lilias said with mock astonishment. "I must continue my eternal quest for ribbon!" They snickered and Lilias left to be about her chores.

Rosselyn smiled. "I shall make haste with our food." She broke her fast with Davina when she returned with a tray, then helped Davina finish dressing. To prepare for the morning of laundry chores, she gathered Davina's long coppery tresses cascading down her back into a tight braid and tied it up under her coif.

How should I breach the subject? Davina pondered as Rosselyn worked at securing the last of her hair. As of late, Davina ached to talk about her brother and father. *What would be a subtle way of easing into the topic without springing it upon her from nowhere?* She glanced at their trenchers and eyed the honey.

"Where is your mind, Davina?"

Relief washed over her that Rosselyn created the perfect opportunity. "I was thinking upon my brother, Roz. The honey with our meal made me recall how many years Kehr and I went on our little midnight raids."

Rosselyn made no comment while she helped Davina dress in her chemise. Rosselyn laced the brown wool kirtle, avoiding eye contact, tears building in her eyes as distress marred her brow.

Davina's cheeks flushed warm over Rosselyn's silence, but she pressed onward. "Up until the day I married, Kehr and I snuck through the dark halls to the pantry, giggling like babes in the nursery."

Rosselyn never took her eyes off her duties, worrying her lip between her teeth.

Davina turned to Rosselyn and stayed her thin hands. "Please share this with me, Rosselyn. Since the death of my father and brother, no one will speak to me about them. I fear I will lose their memory."

Rosselyn's bottom lip trembled. Tears spilled down her cheeks and past the attractive mole on her jaw line. "Davina, I…" She stared at Davina for a long moment.

When Davina thought her friend would say something more, Rosselyn stepped away and disappeared into the wardrobe. As much as Davina wanted to go and comfort her, feeling responsible for her current mood, Rosselyn's retreat meant she needed time, so Davina granted her a few moments alone.

Davina turned when Rosselyn emerged from the wardrobe with pink-rimmed eyes. "Thank you for helping me dress, Roz."

Rosselyn nodded and excused herself, leaving Davina with an uncomfortable silence and an empty heart at another failed attempt to reminisce with someone. Davina pulled a fresh kerchief from her dresser drawer and sat on the lounging couch before the hearth, burying her face in the soft linen. Wiping her face and tucking her kerchief into her sleeve, she straightened her shoulders and focused on the day ahead. The chores would be a welcome distraction.

With most of the larger chores finished for the day, Davina and Lilias freshened up and dressed more appropriately for their trip to the village. Davina wore a gown of pleated gold and maroon, embroidered with moss-green designs across her breast. Gold embroidery trimmed the square neckline of the kirtle, laced tight for support. The soft moss-green linen of her chemise peeked through the slits of the maroon sleeves.

"Oh, none of this will do!" Lilias complained to Davina in front of the vendor. "All my ribbons are old. 'Tis nothing bonnie here for a replacement!"

The merchant frowned at her as they strolled away. Davina cast an apologetic glance back at the man. "Oh, you do carry on, M'ma. I only just bought some ribbon for you a few months ago."

"Aye! 'Tis old!"

A chuckle fluttered from between Davina's lips and she ushered her mother through the market, making their way past the hawkers and sing-song calls of the merchants, trying to entice them to buy their wares. The gathering crowd by the entrance to the square gave Davina pause and caused her eyebrows to rise with curiosity. "M'ma, look," she said, pointing.

They craned their necks, trying to see over the crowd. Laughter rippled through the congestion, and the gathered people parted to let the procession through.

"Gypsies!" a young woman squealed as she squeezed through the crowd to join the people standing to Lilias's side. "The Gypsies are in town!"

Davina's heart hammered against her ribs, and her hand flew to her chest. At least two years had passed since any Gypsies came through Stewart Glen, and not since nine years ago had she seen the group her giant Gypsy belonged to. Davina mumbled a hopeful prayer.

Lilias patted Davina's arm with authority. "They'll surely have a bonnie selection of ribbons from all over the world."

"Aye, M'ma," she said, surprised at her own breathlessness.

Davina and Lilias pushed their way through the forest of bodies to see the parade go by. With festive music tinkling over the crowd, acrobats tumbled in the street, and jugglers tossed flashing blades and torches into the air. Caravans rumbled by in a rainbow, all of them painted in bright blues, greens, yellows and reds, trimmed in brass or copper. Some had carved, wooden designs of excellent craftsmanship; all teetered, loaded with wares, pots and utensils, beads and scarves, happy faces and waving hands. A caravan painted with stars and mystic symbols lumbered by, driven by a pretty young woman with mounds of golden hair about her shoulders. Beside her sat a dark, wrinkled woman, who ogled Davina, her lips parted and eyes wide with recognition.

"He has returned," Davina whispered.

She watched the great wagon roll by. The old woman strained to look at Davina over her shoulder, pushing aside the dangling scarves and beads.

Excitement surged through Davina. *He has come back! He's truly here!* She watched the caravans wobble through the square and disappear down the center street. Her eyes jumped from one face to the next in the procession as the people passed by, but she didn't see him anywhere.

Lilias nodded, watching the trailing acrobats throw each other into the air. "We should come back tonight and watch them perform, Davina. This promises to be a very entertaining evening. "

"Aye, M'ma," Davina said at last with a growing smile. "That it does!"

A cry sliced through the blackness and Broderick MacDougal ran toward it, urgency knotting his gut. She ran out of the forest toward him, her carrot-red hair flowing behind her like a banner, her eyes wide and filled with terror.

"Broderick!" the young girl yelped. She glanced back over her shoulder, as if running from some hideous monster. Her thin, frail body ran into his arms and he encased her in his

comforting embrace, soothing the freckle-faced child. "There, there, lassie. 'Tis safe you are."

Broderick pulled back to wipe her tears, but no longer held the youth in his arms. A mature woman, who resembled the maid, clung to him now, cascading mounds of rich auburn hair framing her exotic face. Her sapphire eyes, glassed with tears, gazed at him with hope, her bow-like mouth trembling and tempting. Her full breasts pressed against his chest, and Broderick moaned in response.

A guttural growl in the distance returned his attention to the one who pursued her. Turning away from the darkened trees and carrying her in his arms, he headed for a white fog bank in the glen where she would be safe. She nestled her head against his chest, clinging to him, her warmth seeping into his flesh.

Once they reached the safety of the fog, she pressed her palm to his cheek. "I knew you would return." The huskiness of her voice teased the desire stirring his loins.

Broderick let her figure slide down the front of him, and against his arousal, as he set her to stand. He groaned as his hands caressed her curves, realizing the only barrier between his touch and her skin was her whisper-thin night dress.

"Broderick, I knew you would return," she breathed and touched his lips with her fingertips.

Broderick bent forward and seized her mouth in a hungry kiss, and she opened to him, inviting him to delve into her sweetness. The physical contact alone was enough to excite his cravings —the heat of her skin, the scent of roses and her blood, the taste of her mouth, the sound of her sighing his name—and yet a deeper connection caused his body to respond with a surging need that settled in his groin. His hands sought the hem of her night dress, pulling the material up to her hips where Broderick smoothed his palms over the soft mounds of her bottom. Lifting her into his arms once more, he persuaded her to wrap her long legs around his waist, and his fingers explored the wet folds of her quim. She gasped and threw her head back, clutching at his shoulders.

"Aye, lass," Broderick encouraged. He toyed with her sensitive bud and she bucked her hips against his hand, grunting her pleasure as she writhed in his grasp.

Wrapping her arms about his neck, she fused her lips to his and whimpered her orgasm into his mouth. Shuddering, she broke from the kiss, panting and gasping. "I want you inside me, Broderick."

His rod surged with anticipation. Cradling her backside in one arm, he unfastened his breeches, letting his erection spring forth. Already wet and pulsing for him, she slid onto his shaft with an ease that weakened his knees, and he dropped to the cool grass, positioning her to straddle his lap as he knelt. Broderick cupped her bottom, bouncing her as he buried his cock deep, watching her full lips whisper his name. With a firm grip on her hips, he drove deeper and harder, grinding her against him, not able to get enough of this woman, rocking closer to climax.

Her hot breath against his ear, she pleaded, "Say my name, Broderick." She locked eyes with him. "Davina," she encouraged. "I want to hear your voice thick with passion as you say my name."

A grin spread his mouth wide and he eagerly obliged. Bending forward, he laid her under him, tilting her hips to give him better access, and grunted into her hair.

"Davina!" Broderick MacDougal sprang up in the darkness of his cave, rousing from his sleep and rubbing his erection. In the blackness, his eyes searched his surroundings. As the haze of his daytime sleep cleared from his mind, he relaxed and laid back down.

A sheen of moisture covered his body, and he lay panting. Dreams. They seemed to be meant for mortals, and yet after so many years, he had one. Touching his turgid shaft, it dawned on him that he hadn't had a stiff member upon wakening since before his transformation almost—

He stopped and calculated. *Has it actually been almost thirty years since I crossed over?* The time escaped him with such haste. His brow furrowed. He wished some of the memories would disappear with the same effectiveness. Still, no matter how many years went by, the ache of the past would not diminish.

Shaking his head to clear the memories threatening to rise, he drew in a deep breath to will them away and reflected on the dream, instead. A long, tortured moan escaped his lips. Where had the detailed vision come from? He lay smiling, wishing such images filled his mind every time he slept, though he admonished his himself for not finishing the deed and being so unfulfilled. How strange that he dreamt of the young, freckle-faced girl whose palm he'd read the last time they'd been to this little town—and recalling this caused his member to sag.

Broderick laughed at his body's response.

He saw her enough during the many visits she made to Amice. Her secret trips to the pantry with her brother to steal honey tickled his mind; and the way her heart thumped away in her breast every time she saw him. Pretty and innocent, she had been destined to break some hearts. A soft chuckle quivered out of him as he recalled Amice's divination: *You have her heart forever, my son.*

After so many years, how many hearts had she broken? How many, indeed, if she turned into the vision of beauty in his dream. He growled a predatory sound and his shaft resurrected with need. Was she still here after all this time? *Most likely grown up and surrounded by a brood of wee bairn.* If she were his wife, and if the dream was any indication of what she'd be like in his bed, the woman would be eternally pregnant.

What a strange dream to have after all these years. Had returning triggered some kind of craving to protect the lass after the fortune he read for her? Did she experience the tumultuous future he divined? These cravings to protect her must have been quite strong to elicit a dream after so many decades. *Interesting.*

Broderick rose to dress. His silver sword sat propped against the stone wall, along with his clothes, boots and sporran—the leather pouch he wore upon his belt. He had his sword especially fashioned in preparation to confront Angus Campbell, having the blade crafted in silver—the only weapon he knew that had an effect against a Vamsyrian. Though he didn't have much cause to use his sword over the last few decades, Broderick practiced with the blade, using his immortal strength and speed to wield the weapon in ways he never learned as a mortal. Holding the sword in his grip, enjoying the weight of the weapon, gave him comfort in a mortal sense. He rarely carried it with him to the camp, though, and left it propped against the cave wall. If Angus was close by, Broderick would know.

Dressed, he stepped out of the cave and inspected the surrounding forest. Going ahead of the caravan of Gypsies, knowing where they headed, he found the cave he used the last time they visited Stewart Glen. Caves were ideal, but not plentiful in the smoother terrain of the eastern end of Scotland. Fortunately, this town sat nestled into the rising mounds of rocky terrain covered in a dense forest, perfect for hiding in the hours of daylight. Broderick preferred something like a cave, or abandoned dwelling, which took little preparation. On the other hand, if they weren't available and the area didn't seem safe, digging sometimes became necessary—a task Broderick loathed because it reminded him so much of a grave. He knew he slept the trance of the undead during the light of day, but delving into the earth at such a time was not the reminder he needed—too nightmarish for his tastes.

The low stirrings of the Hunger needled his gut. Immortality had benefits, but was not without its banes. Though he could still eat, normal food did nothing for him. Vamsyrians must feed on human blood. Not because the lack of blood would be fatal—this Broderick found out five years after he crossed over, taking his own personal journey to discover his limitations, despite the advice of his mentor, Rasheed. That personal journey gave Broderick advantages over his mentor and the other Elders, and he chose to keep his private lessons secret to maintain that advantage. The Vamsyrians proved to be a suspicious breed. *A contagious state of mind*, Broderick reluctantly admitted. Once more, the past tried to resurface and he pushed the rising dread away. Enough of this review of his history. The time had come to satisfy the Hunger.

The hairs on the back of his neck tingled and Broderick darted his eyes about the forest. This sensation proved to be something else he'd not experienced in some years—the presence of another Vamsyrian. Ducking back inside the cave, Broderick donned his sword, and opened his senses to the experience, closing his eyes and taking in the area around him. The cool night air touched his cheeks and a faintly familiar chill rippled through his limbs. *Angus?*

Broderick pinpointed the direction of the presence and dashed through the forest, trees and brush flashing by in a blur. Though sensing the presence of his kind was not a skill he alone possessed—as any Vamsyrian could feel the spirit of another—he did take many years to increase that range beyond anyone he'd known. This was one of the advantages he kept from his mentor. As he pursued, he turned this way and that along with the presence, certain whoever it was came within range of what Broderick called the standard boundary. Surprising Broderick to a gradual stop, he lost the sense of the presence. He closed his eyes and extended his perception. Still nothing. Broderick clenched his jaw in defeat.

A quick search of the immediate area revealed a lair—a deep hole dug into the ground, the entrance hidden behind a large boulder in which only one of their kind had the strength to move. Broderick could hardly stand up inside the shelter and the width was just enough to accommodate a sleeping area for someone his size. Broderick eyed the wool and linen bedding in the dimness, his immortal vision giving him the ability to make out the sparse personal belongings. Whoever's lair this belonged to didn't leave enough behind to give Broderick many clues...save one. The spicy scent he caught rising from the bedding seemed vaguely familiar.

Broderick shook his head and left the lair. He couldn't be certain this belonged to Angus. Too many years passed for him to be sure the essence he sensed or smelled was indeed his enemy. This hole could very well house another, whom he may have met in his many journeys. *He* wouldn't be pleased to find his hiding place demolished, so until he was sure, he left this one alone. He took note of its location, though, and turned to head back toward the village of Stewart Glen. He still must feed.

The Gypsies set up their camp at the edge of the woods, at the rim of the small town of Stewart Glen. They erected tents, unloaded caravans, and displayed wares for the coming fortnight of bartering, begging, performing, and even some thieving. They would stay longer if there was a steady flow of visitors willing to spend their money. Or if they could find work on farms, but the harvest was over, so work would be scarce. Even the weather might keep them around, but long stays in general were to be avoided. They never wanted to wear out their welcome. Not many places embraced the Gypsies in these troubling times of plague and poverty.

The darkened sky let the fires and torches illuminate the encampment in a dancing yellow light. Broderick scanned the many tents and caravans as he approached the settlement, to ferret out Amice and Veronique's camp. There sat the mystical wagon. The tent sagged and Broderick groaned. He had shown Veronique several times how to help Amice erect the tent. She needed to start taking on more responsibilities. Was she being lazy or did she truly lack the aptitude to stake the tent properly? How many more times did he need to show her how to complete the task? He shook his head. At least their camp was nested in a good vantage point at the edge of the settlement—close to the town where the villagers would file into the encampment. An inviting fire burned with a warm glow and Broderick sauntered up to the tent where he could see Amice's shadow as she prepared for the evening of fortune telling.

"*C'était la fille*," Amice said under her breath, his immortal ears picking up her voice even at this distance. "I know that was her."

Broderick stood at the opening of the tent. Her hunched figure bustled around, arranging the table and stools and lighting the oil lamps. Amice's protective nature mothered him, and he frowned. She learned something of his past, though he never spoke of his history in length. She picked up bits and pieces of his life through the years, images she divined from him before she taught him to control his thoughts. Broderick's tongue slipped during their conversations, revealing more details of his tragedies. As a result, she believed she knew what Broderick needed.

Broderick entered the tent and gave her a hug. "*Bon soir*, Amice."

"Good evening, my son," she responded in French, returning the hug, and continued setting up the table for the night. She lit the incense and blew at the coals until they glowed red. Now close enough, Broderick could hear her thinking. *I must not mention her. He will not listen. I'm better off not mentioning her at all.*

Broderick came up behind Amice and whispered in her ear, "Planning to marry me off, eh?"

She spun around and glared. He jumped back to avoid her scolding finger. "You stay out of my thoughts, Broderick MacDougal! I do not invade your mind! I expect the same courtesy!"

"I heard your words upon my approach," he protested. Her thoughts were her own, and Broderick knew she abhorred the invasion of privacy, but he couldn't help teasing her. These mind games were harmless enough. "So fiery for an old lass! And just who do you have in mind?"

"I never should have taught you how to perfect your mental powers!"

"I make too much money for you to mean what you say." He laughed.

"You just keep invading me and we will see how fiery I can get! I will cast a spell on you, and you…you will fall in love with a chicken!" She nodded emphatically.

Broderick held his laughter back at the ridiculous threat for about as long as he could manage, his lips clamped tight, but eventually spit out a flurry of chuckles. "I did not choose to hide amongst the Gypsies to be eternally wed to a chicken! And what in Hades made you think of that punishment?" He shook his head, still laughing.

Amice laughed at her own silly curse, her hunched figure giggling like a little girl. Shaking her head, she breathed deep and gained control of her laughter. "It was the first thing that came to my mind." Patting his face, she said, "Please tighten our tent before you are on your way. I know you must feed."

"Aye."

Rain pelted his face, his head back and his eyes staring up at the grey clouds. Too weak to move, too weak to even raise his head, his breaths puffed out of him, shallow and quivering. With his head spinning, he couldn't orient himself to his surroundings. Blinking his eyes, he tried to clear his senses. He bled. The cut through his thigh drained his life onto the battlefield. Movement out of the corner of his eye caused his weak heart to patter. Flickering whiskers and a twitching nose seemed larger than life so close to his face. The rat's wet fur matted in spikes, dripping with droplets at the ends, off its whiskers which tickled his cheeks. He could feel tiny feet crawling across his slashed belly, another around the side of his wounded leg. With all his strength, he let out a tortured cry from his trembling lips.

Sitting up in his bed, sweat dripping from his nose, he startled out of the nightmare, breathing deep to calm his pounding heart.

Calloused hands chafed over his bare chest and he started from the scratchy sensations, so much like the rats. "There, there, love," the hoarse voice grated. "'Tis just another nightmare."

He shuddered and turned onto his side, away from her. She made his flesh crawl, but she was a means to an end. His nose wrinkled from the musty, straw mattress in the bed box as he curled into a fetal position. *Not much longer,* he comforted himself. *Just another week or so and I will be free.*

The structures housing the shops and businesses of Stewart Glen hung with oppressive judgment over Broderick as he made his way through the narrow, cobblestone streets. He walked tall, refusing to surrender to their scrutiny. The little village of Stewart Glen had grown over the last nine years, especially good for him since that increased his chances of finding the malevolent souls to feed from. Thick moisture hung in the chilling air, making everything faded and worn. His footsteps made no sound upon the stones, and he watched for movement in the shadows. A muffled cry drifted out of the distant darkness. Scuffles and whimpers tugged at his sensibility. A harsh voice stabbed at his compassion. He stalked forward.

"You owe me! Now where is it?"

The unmistakable sound of a hand striking flesh—like a cut of meat slapping onto a marble slab—echoed in the dimness. When Broderick rounded the corner of the building into the alley, he stopped at the edge of the shadows. An ogre of a man stood over a waif crouched in a corner, the lad's arms over his head, trying to defend himself from his attacker.

"Whatever you think he has," Broderick said, interrupting the man, "I'm sure he would have given it to you by now."

The lad dared to peer around the beefy legs of the man in front of him. The boy's face swelled and pulsed red, his right eye swollen shut and his lips split and bleeding. The Hunger stirred, but Broderick kept the blood lust in check.

As many times as Broderick saw this kind of abuse, the results of such brutality still shocked him. Broderick stepped into the alley and stood towering before the man.

He listened to the man's musings. Gaining his senses from the shock of someone confronting him, the man assessed Broderick's massive frame and quailed. *I can take him*, the man considered. He puffed his chest out and poked his finger into Broderick's shoulder. "This be none of your business! Now you turn 'round and forget any of this or—"

Broderick grabbed the man's poking hand, crushing his bones like dry twigs and bringing him to his knees. He glared down upon him in disgust. Two moments ago, this man stood over a defenseless child, having no regard for him. Now the coward whimpered and begged for his life, getting a taste of his own brutality.

Broderick released his hand, grabbed him by the front of his grease-stained shirt, and raised him off the ground, bringing the man's face very close to his own. The sounds and smells of fear played like a symphony to Broderick's senses. Closing his eyes, he enjoyed the melody. The man's heart pounded a fear-filled cadence; his blood chorused through his body, heating his skin. Breathing deep the warmth caressing Broderick's face and nostrils, he welcomed the Hunger that rose inside him, and a familiar sting tickled over his gums as his incisors extended. His body trembled with the desire for blood. Broderick snarled at the man, all too willing to appease the Hunger within. Smiling in satisfaction, he exposed his fangs for the man to see.

The coward widened his eyes and pushed and kicked at Broderick, trying to escape, his bloodcurdling cries vibrating through the alley. But as soon as his cries began, Broderick threw the man against the wall, silencing him. Groaning from the impact, he squirmed in agony on the alley floor. Broderick set the man on his feet, his victim now more compliant, and grabbed his face, forcing him to gaze into his eyes. Turning his face to the side, Broderick sank his fangs into the man's throat.

Feeding from his victims allowed him full access to the memories of their lives. Once Broderick fed from someone, they held no secrets. He learned everything about them up to the time of the feeding…and at times like these, he wished he could block some of the experiences. What horrific images Broderick witnessed! Though this man had been victimized as a child, he grew to thrive on molesting and abusing children of all ages and both sexes. And worst of all, he lorded over a small chain of children from the larger town of Strathbogie, selling their bodies for profit to demented men and women of the court, noble ranks who thrilled in the pleasure of knowing the body of a child. This child in the alley tonight was one of the few of the new chain he'd started in Stewart Glen.

Broderick filled this man's mind with terrifying images of hell, demons, and eternal torture—the kind of torture and abuse this man gave to these children. Broderick wanted to drain this man of the blood left in his body. And yet, before Broderick could claim his life, he reined in the Hunger and forced himself to stop, dropping the man to the dirt. Broderick drained the man of more than he should, and he guessed the recovery would be longer than usual, but he stopped feeding in time. The point of no return had not yet been reached. If the man feared his possible future, as Broderick hoped he would, he would hide away for a while to nurse himself back to health. He would live. Broderick snorted. If luck were any influence, the man wouldn't be able to live with his sins and take his own life. Though Broderick thought the death of this man would be justice, he had no right to end his pitiful existence.

Turning to the lad, Broderick stepped toward him, but he crouched further into the corner. "I know this terrified you. Please believe me when I say I'm not going to hurt you."

The lad remained in his place.

Broderick tried for a second time, but no attempts to win the lad over prevailed. He couldn't leave the child with such horrific memories, though. Like a snake striking, Broderick snatched the lad from the shadows and held him in his arms. Before the boy could realize what happened and cry out, he pressed his palm against the lad's forehead and closed his eyes. With careful concentration, he lulled the child into a deep sleep.

"Remember nothing, laddy," Broderick whispered, wiping the experience from his mind.

Easing the child's limp form to the ground of the alleyway, Broderick assessed his wounds. Taking his dagger from his sporran, Broderick sliced his palm open and applied his immortal blood to the child's sores like a liniment. In moments, the wounds healed as if they'd never been there. Broderick's cut healed with the same speed, and he reopened the lesion more than once to continue to administer to the injuries. Once finished, Broderick put the lad back into the corner with a gentle hand, curling him up into a decent sleeping position, and then placed a few *billon* pennies in his pocket. The lad would awaken from the ordeal as if the experience were a terrible nightmare. He would only have the coins in his pocket to ponder.

Turning to the coward lying motionless in the alley, Broderick pierced his own thumb and smeared his immortal blood across the two puncture wounds at the man's neck. The wounds faded away like smoke dissipating on the wind. Broderick hefted the man over his shoulder and carried him to the edge of town. He didn't want him anywhere near the lad when he awoke. With little remorse, he dumped the man into the bushes along the road that led north to Strathbogie.

When Broderick returned to the Gypsy camp, Amice greeted him with a furrowed brow. "Is everything quite well, my son? You look troubled."

"Aye, Amice. All is well." Broderick forced a smile and kissed Amice on the crown of her head, disappearing into the tent. Amice recognized his moods, but she also discerned when to keep her distance. She would not follow him into the tent and pry for more information.

Broderick closed his eyes and cursed his emotions. The wrath he allowed to freely reign on his victim tonight was a release of his failure to pursue the person he sensed. *He still deserved what he got.* Opening his eyes, he paced the tent, uneasiness tingling in his limbs. A brooding man his size did nothing to gain the trust of customers to be generous with their purses, so he took a moment to quiet his mind and get ready for the night of fortune telling, being sure to keep his senses alert. Broderick sat behind the small trestle table with his eyes closed and his arms crossed. Taking a deep and comfortable breath, he imagined the tension leaving his body like sand through a sieve. *Aye, release it all.* Meditating upon his dream would be a nice distraction. A smirk formed on his lips.

"Davina!" Lilias called, pulling Davina's attention away from the astounding display of a man putting a fiery torch into his mouth. Lilias stood before a Gypsy, whose arms dripped with ribbons, and motioned for Davina to come to her.

With much reluctance, Davina pulled away from the show and shuffled to where Lilias spoke with the ribbon-clad Gypsy. "Oh, these look much better than what we saw earlier this afternoon," Davina agreed.

Lilias raved over the wealth of colors, the variety of materials and patterns, and picked out as many as she could stuff into her bag. She paid the merchant and they strolled to the other tents, admiring the trinkets and wares from every corner of the earth. All the while, Davina kept her eyes open for the old Gypsy woman and her mystic caravan. Where Rosselyn wandered off to, she didn't know.

Lilias and Davina watched a knife grinder's fine skills as he sharpened a blade to a gleaming point, and then held their purses close to their bodies when Lilias spied a young lad cutting a sack of coins free from a man's belt. Davina roamed her eyes over a table filled with brooches and pins of all designs and jewels. The merchant leaned forward with a pin, trying to tempt her into buying the piece of jewelry, but Davina refused with a polite shake of her head as she touched the brooch Kehr gave her, fastening her cloak on her shoulders. A sad melody poured out of the perfect "O" of a tiny Gypsy girl's mouth, her aging grandfather holding a dented tin cup in his knotted hand, beckoning to the many passersby. Davina dropped some *billon* pennies into the cup.

As Davina and Lilias continued through the maze of activity, a man kicked a melon-sized ball of clay out of the fire beside his caravan, which rolled into their path, startling them. He approached with apologies and picked up the hot ball with a cloth, bringing it back to his seat. Davina veered toward him as he broke the clay ball open with a rock. Taking his knife from the ground beside him, he cut into the ball, revealing a steamy, white center.

Davina stepped further toward him, peering at his ministrations. "What do you have there, sir?" she inquired.

"Baked hedgehog," he replied, offering a piece of meat at the end of his dagger. "Would you like to try some, milady?"

Lilias wrinkled her nose. "Oh nay, Davina!" She grabbed Davina's outstretched hand and gawked at the Gypsy as if he were mad. "Thank you, but nay!"

Davina laughed at her mother's reluctance. "Come, M'ma. Be bold!" Davina took the offered meat and blew on the flesh to ease the heat. She sniffed and her mouth watered. "Oh, this smells divine!" Placing the morsel in her mouth, she explored the new taste with slow and deliberate chewing, savoring the succulent flavor. "Almost like rabbit."

Her mother still shook her head and even clamped her lips tight to get her message across. She pulled Davina away as Davina thanked the man for the sample.

Lilias nudged her daughter and pointed, indicating the tent painted with a golden-haired woman touching an array of cards, the midnight background and mystical symbols around her. Standing beside the flapped entrance, the old woman beckoned them closer. Davina's heart pounded against her rib cage.

"You must have your palm read," the elderly woman said when they approached, her voice thick with a French accent.

"You seemed very interested in my daughter earlier this afternoon, *madame*," Lilias said.

Davina locked eyes with the Gypsy's. "M'ma, this is the Gypsy I came down to the village to visit those many years ago." Lilias expressed her delight, and Davina stepped forward, taking the woman's offered hands. "*Bon soir*, Amice."

"It is good to see you, child." Amice stepped back and inspected Davina. "Oh, *chérie*! You have grown into such a beautiful woman! It is a miracle I recognized you as we passed! How I have missed our little conversations by the fire. I was delighted each day you came back." Amice regarded Lilias. "It is plain to see you have passed on your beauty, *madame*."

"You are too kind, Amice." Lilias grinned with pride at her daughter. "You must have your fortune told, sweet."

"Then you, *madame*."

"Oh, nay. I'm sure my future holds nothing worth discussing." Lilias's features turned down, weighted with sadness, which she tried to mask with a smile, but Davina knew her mother mourned for her husband Parlan and her son Kehr. "Knowledge of the future would benefit my daughter more than it would me." She turned to

Davina. "I will bide for you here, sweet." Amice ushered Lilias to sit by the fire pit and handed her a clay cup filled with steaming tea. Two young men Davina recognized from the township stumbled out of the tent, laughing, and stopped short to prevent colliding with her. They bowed their apologies and left.

While her mother and Amice conversed privately, Davina pushed away her growing uneasiness before she entered the tent. She couldn't let her apprehensions destroy this exciting moment, upon her at long last. The spicy aroma of incense drifted through her senses, and her body tingled from the memories of the last time she stepped into this exotic world—memories she revisited time and time again over nine years.

She turned and faced him.

CHAPTER FOUR

After the lads and their antics left the tent, a woman stepped through the opening. A soft evening breeze blew by, bringing her scent into the space, and Broderick's loins tightened at the familiar aroma of rose oil and her blood. He closed his eyes and inhaled deep, the smells thrusting him back into the dream he experienced upon awakening. Settling a curious but lusting gaze upon her, he crossed his arms over his chest and waited for her to advance, listening to what thoughts he could glean across the space. Even as she stood in the shadows, Broderick saw her eyes roam over his form, examining him, hints of desire floating on her rambling thoughts. She advanced into the light of the hanging oil lamp, allowing Broderick a more colorful view of her figure. *It* is *her. Davina.* His cock twitched in response. She had stepped right out of his dream, her full lips and luscious curves promising everything he experienced in his mind.

He leaned forward with his elbows on the table, which creaked in protest to his weight. "Do you wish to have your fortune told, lass, or shall we continue to eat each other with our eyes?"

She continued to stare at him with a creased brow, silent and hesitating.

The corner of Broderick's mouth turned up in a roguish grin, and he rose to his feet. From here, the sound of her pattering heart fluttered against his ears like butterflies.

She managed to swallow and find her voice. "Do you not remember me?" she asked.

Broderick raised an eyebrow with interest. *Aye, we rutted in our dreams, fair lady. Care to have a go at it again?* His eyes traveled down her body before he answered. "A face such as yours would be hard to forget."

Though her cheeks mottled red and he caught whispers of embarrassment, she uprooted and sat before him. *"Does he not remember me, or is he pretending not to?"*

Broderick straddled his chair and leaned forward, coming very close to her. "Lend me your hand, lass," he whispered.

Davina obeyed, her fingers trembling and cool in his hand. She gasped and tried to pull away with a reflexive jerk, and he sensed the heat of his skin startled her.

He held tight, though, his gaze meeting her sapphire eyes. "Relax, lass."

Relax, lass. The phrase had a male essence and echoed out of her memories.

Broderick closed his eyes and his thumb rubbed slow circles in the center of her palm while he concentrated on divining her thoughts. He could almost see himself through her eyes as she leaned in closer to peer at his face in the dim lighting, studying his features.

Relax, lass. Your breath will return in a moment.

The masculine phrase whispered from the dark recesses of her mind, a clouded and shadowed memory that, try as she might, would take no shape. Broderick sensed her struggling to recall the memory. Then he saw through Davina's eyes as she sat in the center of a forest clearing, her vision blurred and a dull throbbing at the back of her head. A man crouched next to her, asking about her welfare, and when she focused her attention on his face, he came into view—Angus Campbell.

Heart thundering in his chest, Broderick opened his eyes and narrowed them at her, searching her face. *Broderick is far more handsome,* she thought, *but there is no denying he does resemble Angus.*

His breath caught in his throat and he clenched, drawing his eyebrows together. *How did she know Angus and—*

"What—?"

"Hush!" He searched her mind for more information.

"Sir, if you please." Davina tried to pull away from him, but his hands held her tight.

His muscles tensed as he tried to reach deeper into her memories. Flashes of Angus's evil grin mocked Broderick, as if to say, "Come and get me, Rick!" More of the visions of a kinder, more compassionate Angus reemerged, conflicting with the Angus he knew. Then blackness rolled in like a fog, blotting out everything. He focused on the woman in hand, her eyes saucers of fright as she quailed away from him.

Raising his eyebrows, he eased his tension, but didn't release her. "My apologies, milady. The visions I saw…" He brought forth as much compassion as he could muster, stroking her hand, and entertained the desire to feed from her to get what he wanted. He wondered if he should take the chance, and glanced at the tent flap, hearing the many voices outside, but reconsidered. He would have to calm her. "Fear not, milady. I didn't mean to cause you such distress. The visions I saw…you have been through a lot, aye?" He hoped the predictions he made of her future in their last encounter were true or his bluff would be called.

Nodding, Davina took a calming breath as her lashes dipped to her flushed cheeks, then her eyes met his. She shrank from him.

Calm her. He closed his eyes, allowing the tension to ease from his face, the crease on his brow smoothing away, and he caressed and massaged her hand methodically. Using his immortal influence, he willed a peace to flow over her, like warm water pouring over her head and trickling down her body, washing away the fear and apprehension. She sighed, accepting the calming spirit surrounding her, the time languishing by in luxury.

Now more tranquil, Davina surrendered to his ministrations.

Her mind was a little difficult to navigate, her emotions swirling around in many directions, and her ability to block those memories baffled him. The more she relaxed, though, the more the fog began to lift. Broderick saw through Davina's eyes and couldn't resist the wicked grin that surfaced at seeing her memories of dressing for the evening. She stood in front of her looking glass, pulling her shift up her slender form, the thin material caressing her full, jutting breasts. Those images swirled and reformed to show Davina's reflection fully dressed and applying her perfume.

"I see blossom oil in a glass vial." His smile broadened. "Intimate places are touched by this fragrance," he whispered as he saw her touch the valley between her breasts, the two sensitive skin patches behind her knees. Broderick opened his eyes and breathed in deep through his nose. "A fragrance I smell coming from you, lass."

Fire flew to her cheeks and warmth emanated from her.

He settled his eyes upon her square neckline, where she had dabbed her rose oil, to linger before they traveled up to her sapphire eyes. Without releasing her gaze, he dipped the thumb of his free hand into a bowl of oil heated by a candle.

She tried to pull away once more, but he refused to let her go. "For what is the oil used?" Her voice trembled in spite of her efforts to keep it steady.

"The oil makes the lines upon your hand easier to read," he explained, and he smoothed the warmth over her palm, each stroke of his thumb slow and deliberate.

The sound of Davina's heartbeat quickened. Broderick sensed a hunger blossom inside her, and her eyes roamed over his neck and shoulders. Those swirling emotions diluted the last remnants of fear and became a mixture of curiosity and desire. Davina struggled to maintain a slow even breath, fighting the urge to pant. She wondered what his body pressed to hers would be like; feeling his weight upon her and hearing him call her name, his voice thick with desire.

Even with his eyes open, his mind flooded with her erotic images, which joined with Broderick's own recollection of his dream. He could taste her when he examined her mouth; could feel her sliding down his shaft when his eyes traveled over her curvy figure. Seeing the erotic images she entertained in her mind, mimicking the dream, was his undoing.

With a groan, he dashed around the table, and before she could gather her wits, he pulled her to her feet, wrapping her in his embrace and crushing her arms between them. Davina's hands upon his chest spread warmth over his body. The wild thumping of his heart beneath her palms matched her own heart's cadence, pounding in his ears. Davina stared up at him with parted lips, full and tempting, begging to be tasted, and his mouth descended upon hers. With a dexterity that surprised him, she dodged him.

"Stop!"

Amusement played havoc with his features and he eased the tension of his embrace just enough to allow Davina some breathing room. His voice purred, "Stop? You are ripe and ready, lass. What say we indulge in each other in a more private atmosphere?"

Davina stepped out of his embrace and cracked her hand against his cheek.

"What in—" Broderick's brow scrunched in confusion, and then smoothed as he tipped his head back and hearty laughter poured out of his mouth, his fists planted on his hips. *Oh, I like her!*

She stammered back, speechless, and her mouth fumbled with what to say. Before she could begin her insults, Broderick snaked his arms around her again. Davina struggled, pushing her fists against his broad chest still rumbling with his laughter. After much effort she found her tongue. "Let me be, you— you—!"

"Brute?" he supplied, unable to keep from chuckling at her passionate display. "Or am I more appropriately a—"

"An animal! That's what you are!" She pushed against him with all her might. "Let me—!"

He hadn't meant for her to fall. He just released her as she wanted and before he could think to snatch her hand, the force of pushing against him landed her right on her bottom.

Davina sat on the ground, dumbfounded, staring up at him. His arms folded across his chest, Broderick smiled down at her for a moment before stretching out a helping hand. Davina refused to take the offered help and rose to her feet unaided, dusting the dirt from her skirts and hands in furious gestures. His continuing flutter of laughter deepened the furrow of her brow.

When she faced him, they stared at each other in silence—his face sparkling with amusement; hers twisted in agitation. The fires of her temper were so easy to stoke, he couldn't resist teasing her. He nodded toward the offering basket on the table.

She gawked for a moment then gasped. "How dare you ask for contributions when you have done nothing but manhandle me!" Picking up the basket, she threw it at him.

He ducked with ease and chuckled. "Methinks if you had gone with me to more private quarters, you would have been more charitable."

Fury trembled throughout Davina's body and he knew she caught his twofold meaning. With a huff, she stormed out of the tent.

Broderick remained thunderstruck from the encounter. Taking a deep breath, and securing his sporran over his erection, he stepped out of the tent and welcomed the cool air and the retreating figure of the enticing, but mysterious, Davina. She stomped into the crowd, and with great reluctance, Broderick tore his eyes away from where she vanished and faced Amice. He took a cautious step back from the piercing glare the old woman leveled at him.

"Davina will not be one of your conquests, Broderick!"

"She's not a maiden untouched, Amice." However, this woman's virtue was not the pressing topic on his mind. Broderick stared off into the crowd, which long closed up behind her, still reeling from her visions of his enemy.

A sharp punch to his shoulder brought him out of his musings. Amice clutched her fists and faced him. "Her lack of innocence does not give you the right to break her heart!"

"What do you mean 'break her heart'? She doesn't—"

"I mean she is not one of those tavern wenches you manhandle for a mere handful of coins! If you pursue her, like you have other women in the past, you will crush her!"

"You exaggerate, Amice. She's a strong-willed woman. No one can break her heart or the wall she has built around it. I saw her defenses. A rousing fiery affair would do her some good." Broderick stepped into the tent to gather the money from the floor. Closing the tent flap behind him, he handed the coins to Amice. "'Tis done I am for the evening. I will be in the tavern if you need me."

Broderick didn't drink for the sake of getting drunk, but he still enjoyed the taste of good ale. Though becoming a Vamsyrian magnified his senses, neither spirits, wine nor ale influenced him. Besides the drink, Broderick enjoyed the busyness of the taverns, the laughter, the brawls—the women. A tavern wench leaned forward and set the mug of ale before him, and a generous amount of cleavage swelled under the dazzling smile on her face. He grinned at her distraction and winked. He would keep her in mind if need be. She sashayed to another table with a delicious swing to her hips, but he frowned. Her seductive dance wasn't enough to keep Broderick's mind from what drove him to the tavern in the first place—the lovely Davina.

He rubbed his cheek, remembering the sting, and chuckled. Like it or not, this woman intoxicated him. The scent of roses and the sweet fragrance of her blood mingled and teased both the Hunger and his desires, a powerful—even fatal— combination which Broderick needed to secure.

He pushed aside his desire for the moment. The mystery of how she managed to manifest in the flesh was a pressing matter. Having a dream had its own questions. Vamsyrians didn't dream—or so Rasheed and thirty years of silence during his sleep told him. And they were unlike any mortal dreams he remembered. As was the characteristic of mortal dreams, these reflected daily experiences and were fleeting. It was one thing to have a rekindled memory—she did spend a lot of time with Amice on their last stay in Stewart Glen—but to see her grown into adulthood and the dream match the reality...that was something different. This dream bordered on prophetic and was closer to waking feelings and sensations. Broderick didn't like it.

Nor did he like her surprising connection to Angus Campbell. Broderick couldn't put a time and place on the incident, but his experience with memories told him the encounter was recent. Angus spared Davina and did not wipe the memory from her mind, though the fogginess of the initial images made Broderick wonder if Angus had done some alterations.

"Leaving mental bread crumbs, Angus?" he mused under his breath.

He would need to feed from her. Then he would have full access to everything about her and her possible involvement with Angus, if she held anything deeper than just that encounter...such as her part in what Broderick knew to be a trap. Just as Broderick would have the information of her life in feeding from her, Angus was sure to have the same information. Which meant Angus learned Broderick had been through these parts once before, and now Broderick was sure who the lair belonged to. The time had come for his revenge. Broderick was ready.

But he had to tread with caution. Broderick wanted the advantage over his enemy, not to get sucked into his trap.

He nodded and gulped from his tankard. Pursuing Davina would be a dangerous challenge indeed, and Broderick never stepped down from a challenge. Davina would be a delight to explore while Broderick let Angus think he'd fallen for the bait. And the sooner he explored her, the better.

Davina pulled her knees to her chest and rubbed her palm in the flickering light of the bedside candle. Sleep would be fleeting this night, so Davina waited for Rosselyn to bring the chamomile tea she promised. The softly glowing embers in the hearth provided no illumination in the room at this distance, but did their job at keeping the cold outside at bay. Staring at her palm in the candlelight, she reflected on the powerful man who held her hand with his fiery touch. She could still smell the spicy oil upon her skin, stirring the memories of his penetrating emerald eyes and roguish smile. Her face flushed at the possibility he'd read her mind when she pictured herself beneath his body, in a wanton display of pleasure. Considering the other intimate things this stranger told her, that embarrassing probability loomed over her and her cheeks grew hot.

A subtle stirring of the curtains at the outside landing of her chamber drew Davina's eyes for just a moment, distracting her thoughts. A small gust of wind through the cracks in the double doors, no doubt. Hugging her covers closer around her body against the invading draft, she turned her palm into the light once more, as he had, and traced the lines he traced with his finger. How could he read the marks on her hand? The creases and scrawls slashing over the surface of her skin made no sense at all, and they blurred as she continued to stare at them through her building tears. She covered her eyes and fought to keep control over her emotions. *He doesn't remember me!*

Broderick stood on the landing outside. He hoped she was asleep, giving him the opportunity to feed from her and delve into her dreams for information. No such luck—she was awake. Not impossible, but would require more manipulation. Davina's thoughts drifted into the air like mist, where he could only catch a word or two, or some distant feelings of regret and sadness. Broderick stole into her chamber, moving unseen into the shadows, to get closer.

He doesn't remember me! her mind said.

Aye, by being this close, he could hear her thoughts much better.

Perhaps he didn't have to feed. Taking advantage of this situation, she wouldn't be guarding the musings of her mind, thinking she was alone in her own chamber. He would catch her off guard and confirm his suspicions. If that didn't work, he would feed.

From the concealing shadow of the tall armoire just inside the doorway, Broderick observed Davina. She shook her head as she stared into her palm. Broderick closed his eyes to catch the images of her imagination. Without actually touching her, those only came in flashes, like lightning illuminating an object in the darkness. He saw a version of himself in her mind, first standing as she came into the fortune-telling tent, then surprise on his face, which transformed into recognition and relief. In these unfolding flashes of her fantasy, he held Davina in his arms, showering her face with kisses, professing how much he had missed her and how he would never let her go.

Bitter laughter whispered out of Davina's mouth. *Of course he doesn't remember me. Nine years have passed—nine long years of him traveling the lands, meeting countless people, reading an endless amount of fortunes. He must have read the palms of a thousand young, love-struck girls like me. What makes me any different? Fool! How I wish he never came back. At least I would still have my fantasies in one piece!*

Broderick felt a measure of frustration and embarrassment emanate from Davina as she relived their recent meeting in the tent. Davina's view of the lustful and teasing encounter did not sit well with Broderick. Through the flashes of her memories and emotions, he saw himself as an aggressive rogue, taking liberties with her, acting like a hungry animal, pouncing on her at the first opportunity, treating her like some common wench, and then laughing at her. He had been so wrapped up in his initial shock of seeing her manifest in the flesh, in his own physical response to her, and then, more dramatically, the visions of Angus in her memories. How Broderick appeared to her was the furthest thought from his mind at that time. And here he stood, sneaking into her private bedchamber, embodying the animal she perceived him to be. Pushing down his rising shame, he reminded himself why he stood in the shadows of her room—to get information. These matters were trivial in comparison to preventing Angus from gaining the upper hand. He would bide until she settled into a peaceful sleep and do has he originally intended.

Davina punched her pillow before settling down under the covers. "Bastard Gypsy!"

An uncontrollable chuckle fluttered from his mouth. She sat up in bed, clutching her bedspread to her throat. *Damn, now I have to come out.* He sighed. "My word," he said, surprised at the deep resonance of his voice echoing through her chamber. "I'm flattered I haunt you so, milady."

"Like an unwanted specter!" she hissed.

Broderick stepped out of the shadows and into the dim candlelight, bowed before her and stood, crossing his arms over his chest in a stance he hoped appeared casual. Her eyes roamed over his body, leaving a trail of heat in its wake, and Broderick's lips parted with an intake of breath. The mixture of desire and fear in her eyes stirred Broderick's loins, and he adjusted his sporran, grateful it covered his groin.

With that candlelight glowing in his eyes, Lucifer himself would envy the Gypsy's form, Davina marveled. *Only the Dark Lord would come forth in the most pleasing form to seduce and entice me into giving away my very soul.*

The corner of Broderick's mouth turned up in amusement at how she perceived him. Davina was both afraid and enticed by him, so he would have to do what he could to quell the fear and heighten the seduction. A delightful shiver ran through his body and he sauntered over to her bed. A combination of panic and titillation radiated from Davina, and she brought her legs under her, assuming the position to leap at any moment. He stopped at the head post of her bed and leaned against it, keeping his arms crossed. The wooden structure groaned from his weight, but did nothing else.

"Get out," she said, not at all convincing.

He raised an eyebrow and let his eyes roam down her form, his smile widening. He stood just out of reach, so close to her body, clad only in her thin night dress—like the one she wore in his dream—the scent of roses and her blood teasing his desire, the heat of her body caressing his skin over the distance. She hugged her blankets closer in defense and shrank back from his intense gaze. Broderick chuckled, an almost evil sound he regretted hearing.

"Get out of my bedchamber," she said, sounding a little more determined.

"I offer a sincere apology at my brutal behavior earlier. I hoped you and I could continue our conversation in the privacy of a more peaceful setting." He glanced around the room. "'Tis a lovely bedchamber." He sat on her bedside.

The desire pulsing from her body betrayed her wide-eyed astonishment. "Just who in hell do you think—"

"*Tsk, tsk,* milady," he scolded. "What foul language coming from such a tempting mouth." Broderick admired her lips, full and slightly parted with surprise, and the heat increased between his legs. "Let us forego the charade. 'Tis obvious you desire me." He sent a wave of peaceful influence toward her and saw her visibly relax by a small margin. As he learned in the tent, the change must be gradual for her not to resist the seduction.

Davina scooted away from him, trying to take her bedcovers with her, but unable to pull them from under his demanding weight. She huffed and frowned. "You are arrogant to think I want anything to do with you." Davina deeply inhaled through her nose. Her mouth dropped open. "'Tis drunk you are!"

Fear filled her eyes and the peace he'd sent her vanished. He concentrated on sending another wave, which she responded to, much to his relief.

Another flutter of laughter rumbled from his chest. "Hardly drunk, but I have been drinking." He trailed his fingertip down the length of her arm, giving himself the opportunity to touch her, thereby increasing his immortal influence. She shivered and more of the fear melted away. "You forget, the mystic gifts I possess tell me otherwise. I can sense your desire, milady."

As he closed in, Davina threw a pillow at his face and pushed away. Yet within an instant, Broderick had her back on the bed, pressed beneath his thigh and arm. She struggled to break free, but gained no purchase against him. As he positioned his body over her, he nuzzled her hair away from her ear with his nose and breathed in her scent and warmth, sending more waves of peace and adding to his influence, currents of desire.

A retaliating flood of fear pulsed from her, and a menacing face of some unknown man flashed, before her mind closed like a trap. "Oh, dear God," she whispered. "Please, harm me not."

Broderick eased down beside her, his leg and arm still holding her to the bed, and stared at her face, her eyes closed tight. She imitated a child trying to wish away a nightmare, reminding him of the freckle-faced lass of his dream. The peaceful seduction he tried to wrap around her faltered under the fear she experienced. His eyebrows knit together and he touched her face. His palm resting against the warmth of her cheek, he brushed his thumb over her full, trembling bottom lip. She shrank from his touch and Broderick felt a stab of regret in his heart. He pulled his leg and arm from her. "Who has taught you to fear such contact?"

Davina pushed out of his embrace and fetched her robe from the settee. Donning the garment for protection, she faced him across the room, her pose regal and defensive. "Are you so audacious and absurd to think I would leap at the opportunity to bed you, after you stole into my private chambers uninvited?" Her voice trembled, and Broderick could feel her efforts at maintaining a strong façade. "You, sir, are not welcome here. Remove yourself at once." She gave him a final nod to secure her position on the matter.

Broderick rose from the bed, not at all pleased with this outcome. His muscles tensed as he stalked toward her across the room, ready to do what he hoped he didn't have to. Davina gawked at the ethereal presence he emulated. She stood mesmerized by his actions until he stopped in front of her, his body so close he could feel her warmth. When she stepped back to avoid him, his hands grasped her shoulders, keeping her in place. His gaze locked with hers, he tried one last time to delve into her mind for what he wanted. Nothing. Blackness. A void.

He would have to feed from her.

Closing his eyes, he sent waves of influence, charming her senses. He caressed his lips against her cheek and drew her into his breath. The scent of this woman—a mixture of her blood, her womanly essence and the rose oil she wore—made him drunk with desire. He kissed his mouth over her skin to touch the tip of his tongue against the sweet shell of her ear. The pulsing of her heart, strong and rapid, matched the panting of her breath and pounded against his senses. She moaned and pressed her palms to his chest. The notion of tasting the nectar running through her veins ignited the Hunger and the familiar pain shot across his gums as his fangs extended and his mouth watered.

CHAPTER FIVE

Davina started at the sound of the door closing to her chamber. She sat up in bed.

"Forgive me for taking so long, Davina," Rosselyn said as she headed toward her bedside with a tray of chamomile tea. "Oh, 'tis fast asleep you were and I woke you. Well, methinks falling asleep won't be so difficult, after all."

Davina stared in disbelief at the bedchamber, void of the giant Gypsy, her position in her bed, the covers strangely cool about her body. Why were her covers so cool if she had been lying in bed? Rosselyn set the tray down upon the bedside table, and then proceeded to the hearth to throw a couple of logs onto the burning embers. The growing flicker of firelight cast shadows against the tapestries and fir wood panels on the walls, invading the hovering ambiance of Broderick's presence. Davina touched her hand to her cheek where she could swear her skin still dewed moist from his hot breath. The incense and unique scent all his own still lingered.

It couldn't have been a dream! And yet, her chamber seemed as if he had never been there. Not a single trace of him remained, save for his lasting essence she began to believe her mind gave birth to. Here she sat, in her bed, when before she had been across the room in his arms.

"My, Davina, the day looks to have weighed heavily upon you." Rosselyn sat beside her on the bed and took her hand. "Oh, 'tis chilled to the bone you are." She rubbed Davina's fingers between her warm palms and then put the warm cup of tea in her hands. "Drink this down. I shall put another log on the fire." Rosselyn kissed Davina's cheek, and went to the hearth to do as she promised. Her friend rattled on about the evening, telling Davina about her own exciting encounters in the Gypsy camp as she sat on the bed's edge, ensuring Davina drank her tea. Davina tried to listen to her handmaid talk about a handsome young Gypsy she'd met, and how obvious he was about fancying her, too, but Davina's mind blurred into numbness. Was she losing her mind? How could she be insane enough to still fantasize about him after his audacious behavior this night on that longed-for encounter? He spoiled everything.

Davina nodded absently at Rosselyn's storytelling as she sipped her tea.

Broderick crunched the fallen leaves as he strode through the forest on his way back to the Gypsy camp, deep in thought. Davina's handmaid didn't seem like she would be leaving anytime soon, so he gave up for the night. He had been poised, fangs distended and the Hunger raging, when someone headed down the hall to Davina's chamber. In an effort to avoid being caught, he deposited Davina back in bed and pressed his palm against her brow, willing her to forget his exit; leaving her to think she dreamt the encounter—he hoped. He hadn't time for anything else.

Grunting, he cupped his manhood and adjusted himself under his sporran. The dream he had, their encounter in the tent, and now seeing her in that night dress put Broderick in a constant and unfulfilled state of arousal. Her fear caught him ill-prepared, suggesting she was more the victim than a willing participant. This game he played with Angus may be putting someone innocent in the middle.

He had nothing more to go on than when he'd first come to her tonight…and he clenched his fists at being in another position where Angus used a woman to try to get at him.

The music drifted toward Broderick as he neared the gathered crowd in the middle of the Gypsy camp, the chanting and clapping growing stronger. In the center of the cheering spectators, Amice's granddaughter, Veronique, swayed her hips to the beat, arched her back and thrust her well-developed breasts forward, tossing her head about, losing herself to the melody and encouragement. Broderick stood at the edge of the circle, his arms crossed and scolding eyes upon her. When the music slowed, she sashayed toward him, her arms beckoning, a smile on her lips and mischief in her brown eyes. Broderick's mouth twisted with annoyance and he focused on his boots to feign interest in some mark or flaw in the leather, and then back to her again.

Veronique laid her hands upon his chest and stood up on her toes. "Dance with me, Rick," she taunted and pushed away from him to turn her body in the dance. Her crimson skirt spread out and exposed her bare legs to the chilling night air.

Broderick remained where he stood, his eyes warning her to behave. The crowd encouraged him; the Gypsy men slapping his back in earnest and urging him to enter the circle. Glaring at the men around him, Broderick protested, and Veronique approached him once more. She unfolded his arms and slipped her hands into his, tugging on him, knowing he wouldn't refuse and humiliate her.

Resisting her, he dragged his feet into the circle and the tempo climbed once more. He half-heartedly clapped and tapped his foot as Veronique twirled about him, touching her hands to his back, then his chest, then his hips. She pressed her back to his, molding her body against him, then pushed away and danced around to face him. Broderick clenched his jaw, his face growing flush. Though Veronique had an enticing body full of youth and energy, she had been the image of a little sister too long for him to feel any attraction toward her. Having his passion still ignited from Davina, though, Veronique's intimate contact didn't do much to cool his fevered and unresolved desire.

The music's exotic beat climbed faster and faster, her body trembling to match the cadence, her eyes locked to Broderick's; then the music stopped, throwing Veronique to her knees before him, her body arched back as if in offering to him. The crowd exploded into applause and cheers. Broderick helped Veronique to her feet. He turned and stalked away, heading for their caravan.

Seconds later, her hot hand slipped into his, her chest heaving from the exertion of her dance. Broderick could also sense her embarrassment from being abandoned in the circle; but her intense determination dominated such embarrassment. Patting the back of her hand before releasing her, he scowled and said, "Behave, little sister."

She stopped and punched her fists into her hips. "*Petite soeur?*" she hissed.

Broderick whirled around and faced her. Before he could utter a scolding word, she leapt into his arms and planted a firm and possessive kiss on his lips. With ease, Broderick pushed her back and gripped her shoulders. "Veronique, Amice will blister your bum. Now behave."

Veronique giggled and licked her lips with a seductive sweep of her tongue.

Broderick spun her around and swatted her derriere hard enough to make her yelp. "Je *vais te donner une fessée!*" he said, threatening the same punishment.

Before Broderick disappeared into the caravan to escape from Veronique, Amice emerged from the tent. Though he wished he couldn't, Broderick heard the exchange in French between Amice and her granddaughter.

"Come here!" Amice ordered. "You are fortunate I did not march into that circle and pull you away, kicking and screaming in front of all those people!"

"Grandmother—!"

"Hush! Broderick is not for you! You are too young for him. You chase after him like a bitch in heat and make a fool of yourself! I will not have any more of this!"

"You know very well he can hear you!" Veronique hissed.

"He can hear you now, so stop your whispering. Go to bed! We have much to do on the morrow and you need your rest."

Broderick shook his head. Veronique made her attraction toward him very obvious, proving she was more than willing to bed him. He just wished Amice had scolded her at another time. She embarrassed the lass in front of Broderick to teach her a lesson. Broderick didn't know if such tactics would work with Veronique, and hoped this open reprimand did not encourage her to pursue him even harder just out of rebellion.

Veronique pushed past Broderick as he stepped out of the caravan, and slammed the door behind her. Broderick faced Amice and crossed his arms. *That was unnecessary,* he told her through a silent communication, implanting his thoughts within her mind so she could hear him.

Amice glared at him. *She needs to know where she stands. You do not tell her that. Your gentle rejections only make her more determined.*

But embarrassing her is not going to stop her from pursuing me, either. Broderick sighed. *She has a childish infatuation for me. Nothing more. She'll meet another man one day, more her age. She'll forget about me.*

136

Amice shook her head. *No, my son. There you are wrong. She has too much of her mother in her. I have seen this passionate determination before.*

Broderick turned away, knowing very well how that situation turned out. The heartbreak of Amice's daughter was something he did not want to be a part of. *You may be wrong about her. Give her time.*

A heavy sigh weighted upon the old woman and she said aloud, "Think what you wish, my son, but I know different."

Heading toward the woods, Broderick stomped away from the camp, not wanting to be around the tension in the air—from both the caravan where Veronique slammed and punched cabinets, as well as Amice, cleaning up the tent for the morrow's preparations.

In the isolation of the forest, he stood in the darkness—eyes closed, head back, arms out—and inhaled a deep breath of frosty evening air. The cold of winter drew near, and Broderick embraced these longer nights approaching. The summers left him little time to experience the world around him. Winter gave him the opportunity to revel in his immortality. Opening his eyes and dropping his arms, he stared up at the sliver of a moon in the blackened sky. Would she look the same in a hundred years? Would she be faithful and follow him through the coming centuries? The corner of his mouth turned up.

You may be the only one, my Goddess, who would be true. Always loving. Always there. Always watching over me.

Shaking his head, he sighed and observed the camp. Though Veronique may accept everything about Broderick, she gave in too easily to her emotions. Upset her too much, and she could be a handful. He released a soft, reflective laugh. He didn't think he could handle a few years of that, let alone a span of centuries. They were not compatible. This was all just a childhood infatuation for her, in spite of what Amice told him. He refused to believe she would follow the path her mother did. Given time, Veronique would lose interest in him if he remained consistent with his rejections. She would eventually see reason.

"Whatever you're doing, Rosselyn," Seamus said as he trailed behind her determined pace, "be quick about your deeds. I have too many things to buy at the market this day to waste time at a Gypsy camp." He snorted. "And extra honey to purchase to satisfy a sweet tooth."

Rosselyn snickered over Seamus's grumbling as they made their way into the camp, the sun rising in the late morning over the forest tree tops. Seamus shook a scolding finger at Rosselyn and continued his complaining. "She has a jar of her own honey and enough to keep any normal person happy for at least a month! But not Mistress Davina! She finishes the entire jar in half the time!"

Rosselyn rolled her eyes. "You know why she does it, Seamus. Can you not be somewhat sympathetic to her plight?" Seamus had the decency to look ashamed, and nodded. Stopping at the edge of the camp, she scanned the area. "Over there," she said, pointing.

As they passed a merchant arranging his jewelry upon a gray, wool blanket on the ground, he leapt to his feet and intercepted them. "Ah! You come to buy my jewelry!" He took Rosselyn's hand, leading her to the bulk of his treasures. "I have a beautiful necklace of peridot to match your golden eyes!"

"Nay, thank you." She pulled away from him and glanced at Seamus's impatient glare. "We seek the fortune teller. He's a large man with red hair and—"

"What would you want with him?"

Rosselyn turned to a dark-haired Gypsy, who stepped from behind a blue-painted caravan and appraised her with his black eyes. Her heart skipped at the sight of his handsome features and olive skin. "Nicabar," she breathed and stepped toward him.

His graceful, trim form stepped forward and he bowed a greeting. With a seductive sparkle in his eyes, he sauntered toward her, stopping just close enough for her to want to reach out and touch, yet too far away from her body to do so. "Rosselyn," he whispered in return. His eyes roamed over her figure, bringing heat to her skin everywhere his gaze touched. His delicious Spanish accent sent flutters through her belly. "The giant *dukker* is a strange man of dark secrets, not someone you should seek." With a raised eyebrow, the corner of his mouth turned up in a devilish smile. "But my warnings may not deter a woman such as you, with fire in her eyes and passion in her heart." He closed the distance. "Pursuing a mysterious stranger may be exactly what you seek."

Seamus made a dramatic display of clearing his throat. "Rosselyn?"

Rosselyn pursed her lips at the *dapifer* as he spoiled the mood. She returned her attention to the handsome man before her.

Nicabar chuckled at Seamus and shook his head. "His tent is there, *mi dulce*," Nicabar pointed over her shoulder. "You will not find him there, though. He never returns until nightfall."

"Nightfall? Why?"

He shrugged his broad shoulders. "Odd hours indeed, but necessary. The old woman reads during the day and he relieves her at night."

Rosselyn thanked him and departed with hesitation, staring at the dark Gypsy over her shoulder before she tore her gaze away and caught up with Seamus, who already headed for the fortune teller's tent. A small fire burned within a circle of stones and the old woman, Amice, stepped out of the tent dressed in a rainbow of colors. "Ah, you have come to have your palm read!" She reached for Seamus.

Seamus jumped away and clutched his hand to his chest. "Rosselyn, I have no time for mystic diversions."

"Everyone has time to indulge in their fantasies, *monsieur*," Amice said, taking Seamus by the hand and pulling him into the tent after her.

Rosselyn stifled her laughter behind her hands. Seamus's protests sounded from the tent, but the old Gypsy won with a noisy babble of French. Rosselyn waited with a smile, craning her neck to hear the mumbling of the fortune being told. Seamus emerged from the tent with a sheepish grin, trailing Amice behind him.

"He will wait now," Amice said with confidence. "Help yourself to some tea, *monsieur*, while I speak with this young girl." Amice stepped before Rosselyn, appraising her. "Ah!" she said with a growing smile and whispered, "Now you are ready! Come, let us discuss the matter of your freedom."

"My what?"

CHAPTER SIX

Rosselyn followed Amice into the tent. "The matter of my *freedom*?"

"*Oui*! Come sit." Amice put her index finger over her mouth, then pointed to where Seamus sat outside, and encouraged Rosselyn to sit on the stool in front of the table. Amice sat in the chair on the opposite side and held out her hands. "*Donnez-moi vos mains.*"

Rosselyn assumed she asked to see her palms and offered Amice her hands.

The old woman turned Rosselyn's hands back and forth, inspecting one palm then the other, her fingertips chasing the lines across her skin. "*Regardez*, you see this line?" she said in hushed tones.

Rosselyn nodded and leaned forward.

"Do you see how this splits? How this first section of the line is weak and this new split is deeper, stronger?"

Rosselyn nodded again.

"This confirms what I read in your tea leaves those many years ago."

Rosselyn thought back to the first time she saw the Gypsies in Stewart Glen. She and Davina made many trips down to the Gypsy camp after their first visit. "Oh, are you referring to the reading you told me about later?"

"*Oui.*" Amice grinned. "The reading I did from the cup you drank from that first night."

"Aye, I remember now. You said the shape of a bird flew from a box or a cage in the tea leaves." The memory was vague, but there.

Amice patted her hand in approval. "I remember this because I saw something else of which I did not tell you. Back then I did not think you were ready, but now you are."

Rosselyn tilted her head in anticipation.

"The bird in the cup flew toward a wagon or a cart, and the truth seeped into my old bones. You would be one of us!" Amice grinned with excitement.

The whispered words fell upon Rosselyn's ears, but they floated around the air, intangible like smoke that formed useless shapes.

"One of us," Amice repeated. "A Gypsy."

"Me?"

Amice nodded and grabbed a stack of thin, painted tablets of worn wood. As Amice shuffled them about, Rosselyn could see various pictures of colorful artwork. Amice drew a tablet from the stack and laid it down: A picture of two happy children on a horse with a blazing sun in the background. "You are a free spirit, loving life, and you are not afraid to take risks." She smiled and pulled another tablet off the top of the stack and laid it beside the first. On this tablet, a serious man, wearing long black robes like a priest, stood over two children who bowed before him. Amice frowned. "But you feel trapped by the confines of authority and rules." Shaking her head, she drew another tablet with a picture of a woman inside a wreath, surrounded by various animal heads in the corners of the tablet, which brought the old Gypsy's smile back. "Ah, and this confirms everything. This means you will finally achieve your dreams. You will break free from the bonds of rules and see the world!" She contemplated Rosselyn. "Is this not your dream?"

A lump formed in Rosselyn's throat and a moment passed before she could speak in a whisper. "Aye, that is my dream." She cleared her throat and wiped the tears blurring her vision. "How could you know this?"

"This is what I do, child." Amice laid down one more card, showing a moon in a dark night sky with wolves howling between two pillars. The old woman dropped her mouth open and put one hand upon the card and the other hand upon her heart. "I feel a great and painful secret you harbor within yourself."

Rosselyn bit her lower lip to keep it steady. *How could she know this?*

"You must settle this before you leave, I'm sensing."

The pressure in Rosselyn's chest became unbearable and her tears burst forth. "How can you see this? This has burdened me for almost a year, since the truth came to me." She wiped her cheeks with her sleeve and sobbed into her hands, releasing the built-up tension. "Telling this secret could hurt so many people. And yet keeping it inside is hurting me. I fear I'm losing my sanity. What am I to do, Amice?"

Amice gathered her tablets up and shuffled them as she closed her eyes in concentration. Hope bloomed in Rosselyn's heart as Amice might have the answers she needed. Fanning the tablets across the table, Amice indicated her head toward them. "Choose three tablets for what will happen if you do *not* tell your secret, and three tablets for what will happen if you *do* tell your secret."

Rosselyn nibbled on her thumbnail as she considered the cards. She pulled three tablets that seemed to call to her, drew them toward her, and gave them to Amice. "If I do *not* tell my secret," she whispered. Amice put the tablets aside. Glancing over the remaining tablets, she pulled three more. "If I *do* tell my secret."

Amice turned the first three over, revealing a man hanging upside-down, a tall tower being destroyed by lightning, and a skeletal figure with a scythe. "Keeping this secret, child, will result in many deaths."

Rosselyn gasped. "Surely not something as drastic as that!"

"I only tell you what the tablets reveal and how they speak to me." Amice closed her eyes and laid her hands upon the cards as if to feel their message. "There will be sacrifices made and other truths revealed, but at a great cost. There will be loss of lives, I tell you, and I do not see such things often. Death is a prediction I do not make lightly."

Rosselyn trembled.

Amice turned over the other three tablets showing a beastly creature with horns and two people imprisoned in chains to him; an imperious man with a scepter and face of stern determination; and the tablet that revealed this all—the moon with the howling wolves between two pillars. "Telling your secret will expose greed and materialism.

There is a very controlling man involved, and more mysteries will be uncovered."

"Will anyone die?" Rosselyn sat forward on her seat.

Amice placed her palms on the tablets once more. "I do not know. Nonetheless, I feel a sense of justice involved here, a kind of resolution in the end."

Rosselyn stared at the tablets as Amice's message swirled around in her head. Neither outcome sounded desirable, but revealing what she kept hidden seemed the lesser of two evils. In spite of her apprehension of what the future may hold, a wave of relief washed over her.

"I leave the choice to you, my dear Rosselyn." Amice patted her hand and gathered the tablets into a neat pile, setting them aside. She cleared her throat. "Now, to the other matter," she said, changing her tone of voice. "My son is a man of free spirit," the old Gypsy supplied.

"What? How did you know he was the reason I came here?"

"It is my job to know," she dismissed with a wave. "He has no woman in his life." She appraised Rosselyn. "Only the most unusual woman will capture his heart."

Rosselyn sat thunderstruck, still reeling at the doom-filled prediction she just received while also trying to make sense of how Amice divined her intentions.

"This is why you ask about him, *non*? To find out if Broderick has a woman in his life?"

Rosselyn gawked at Amice. "But not for me—"

"I know who you are here for." Amice nodded, sharp and determined eyes sizing her up.

Rosselyn hesitated, unsure if Amice would be honest. "I realize you may be partial, madam, but Broderick...he seems capable of—"

"If you are wondering if he would hurt your mistress—as he is a man of great size—I tell you he possesses a gentle heart." Amice tapped her chest and then grasped Rosselyn's hand. "I know only what Mistress Davina's palm has told me. Her past is filled with sorrow and loss, *non*?"

Rosselyn concurred with a slight nod of her head.

"Be watchful of her, Rosselyn." Amice searched Rosselyn's face with concern. "Her pain is not yet over, and she will still need you. The past still haunts your mistress." They stared at each other for a long moment. Rosselyn sensed Amice wanted to say more, but instead Amice patted her hands and ushered Rosselyn out of the tent. "That is all I can say, young one. Remember, mind what this Gypsy woman tells you this day." Without a backward glance, Amice disappeared back inside the tent.

"Are you quite ready?" Seamus said tapping his foot, his arms crossed.

"Aye, Seamus," she whispered, her mind still turning the incident over in her mind. "Poor Mistress Davina."

"What are you mumbling about?" Seamus snapped as he came alongside her.

"Nothing, Seamus."

"Enter!" Lilias called when Davina knocked on her chamber door.

"M'ma, have you seen Rosselyn?" Lilias lay on her bed with a cloth to her forehead. "Are you not well, M'ma?"

"My head pains, darling."

Davina sat beside her mother and rinsed the cloth in the bowl of cool water at her mother's bedside. "Rosselyn went into town with Seamus to do the marketing," Lilias rasped then sighed, a smile on her mouth when her daughter placed the cool cloth across her brow and eyes. The head pains Lilias frequently experienced lasted for hours, sometimes days. "Methinks I even heard her arguing with Seamus about going to the Gypsy camp on their way into the village."

Davina stiffened at the mention of the Gypsies. She forced herself to relax. *How intolerable.* The slightest mention of the Gypsies or Broderick affected her whole body. Damn him, she wouldn't let him have this much control over her. *You are being childish!*

"Something vexes you, darling?"

Davina looked down to see her mother peering out from under the cloth, pain and inquiry in her eyes. Davina took the cloth and rinsed it in the cool water a second time, replacing the compress on her mother's brow. "Nay, M'ma. I'm well."

"But there is such a terrible crease on your brow."

"Honestly, M'ma. Do not worry so over me." Davina kissed Lilias's cheek and left her mother to rest.

Broderick entered the chamber to find Davina lounging on her large, canopy bed. The breeze that blew past him into the room caressed her body and fluttered the thin night dress, just barely keeping his heated gaze from viewing her naked form. The dark triangle of curls at the apex of her legs and her dusty rose nipples shone through the translucent material, stoking the fires of Broderick's desire.

He grumbled as his shaft filled with need and pressed against his breeches, demanding freedom. "Och, woman! 'Tis a sight to make a blind man see, you are."

Davina's lips curled into a seductive smile, and she crooked a finger at him, beckoning him to draw near. He needed no other encouragement.

Tossing his belt and sporran aside, and lifting his shirt off his head, he enjoyed the way her eyes drank in the sight of his bare chest. The closer he came to her bed, the lower her eyes traveled down his body, until they settled on his obvious arousal.

She propped herself upon her elbow and reached out to touch him. "I want to see all of you, Broderick," she begged with her husky voice, and tugged at his breeches.

Again, no further encouragement necessary, Broderick did as she commanded and finished stripping, laying down next to her. He seized her mouth in a greedy kiss, pulling her to him, seeking to remove the barrier of her night dress. Slipping his hands under the gossamer material and finally touching her velvet soft skin, he groaned and sought to caress every inch of her flesh. So warm. So inviting. Why could he not get enough of this woman?

Davina wrapped her leg over Broderick's hip, and her hand slipped between their bodies, her slight fingers caressing his turgid shaft with feather touches.

Broderick growled. "Oh, you will be the death of me!"

"Am I not touching you proper?" Her wide and innocent eyes inquired him.

"Nay, 'tis right and proper you are, which is why you shall do me in." Broderick reached around the back of her and stroked the wet folds between her legs, causing her to gasp.

"Then if this is dying," she breathed, "Do me in, too."

Broderick chuckled. "Aye, blossom."

They stroked each other, their moans and panting escalating to a fevered pace.

"Fill me, Broderick! Take me!"

His cock, already damp with his own desire, slid effortlessly into Davina's tight wet quim, pulsing and hugging his shaft, fitting around him with perfection. He cried out, grunting her name into her silken red hair, as he angled her hips to meet him, thrust for thrust.

"Harder!" Davina clung to his back, pulling him deeper as her heels dug into his backside. "Harder, Broderick!"

This woman was a fantasy come to life, so full of passion and hunger. Broderick could do no more than everything in his power to fulfill her desires, and pumped them both to an earth-shattering climax that left them breathless in each other's arms.

Still laying on top of her, taking pleasure in her flesh pulsing around his shaft, Broderick touched his lips over her face, breasts and shoulders with languishing, adoring kisses.

"Stay with me forever, Broderick." She breathed the words, and yet it seemed to Broderick she shouted them, so shocking were they to his being.

He looked at her, his brow furrowed. "Davina, I…" He regretted the words as soon as her face melted from passion to pain. Tears welled in her eyes and she pushed away from him, donning her robe from the settee.

"I knew this would happen." She crossed her arms defensively. "I was a fool to believe you would want anything more."

"Davina, you don't understand what you ask of me." Decades of revenge surrounded his life. His immortality. The danger she would be in if he loved her.

"Nay! I understand perfectly, and I had childish dreams of a life together. 'Tis my fault. You had your tryst. Now go." She turned her back on him and sobbed. In the distance, he could hear the baying of child.

"Davina—"

"Go!"

Broderick's eyes opened and he stared at the rough rock ceiling. Aggravation knitted his brow and a frown formed upon his lips—another dream.

He sat up and rubbed his face, then groaned from his throbbing erection. Shaking his head, he breathed deep the stale air, his eyes piercing the darkness with the sensitive sight immortality gave him. Only darkness came through the parting folds of the curtain barrier Broderick placed deep inside the cave. The leaves rustled in the wind just outside.

The presence of these slumbering daytime visions perplexed him. For thirty years, nothing; and now a dream almost every day he slept. Even more unnerving than the dreams, they were all about Davina. She fascinated him, and that disturbed him to distraction.

The dreams these last few days contained visions of him visiting her chamber for romantic encounters. With minute variations as to how they engaged, the amorous meetings were similar in their structure—he came to her, she surrendered to him, and then left her crying when she asked for more than the brief coupling. All of them ended with the soft weeping of a child, lingering in the background, while Davina cried and cursed him.

Pushing the visions aside, he rose, agitated. Where was Davina now? Did she sit by the fire in her chamber doing what noblewomen do— reading, tending to needlework, reflecting on private thoughts? Or had she already left for a rendezvous with Angus, plotting the next stage in his trap?

Broderick cursed and dressed. With his silver sword fastened to his hips, he pushed the visions of Davina aside and stepped out of the cave, roaming his eyes around the darkness. Silence enveloped him, save for the distant rustling of branches stirred by the wind. Closing his eyes, he extended his senses outward in all directions. As always, he took every opportunity to extend his range by exercising his abilities. He waited. A tingling over the hairs on the back of his neck sent shivers of anticipation down his arms. "The hunt is on, old friend," Broderick growled and set off in the direction the sensation originated from.

Racing through the trees, he approached the presence of the other Vamsyrian, whom by now he knew to be Angus. He grinned in triumph when the essence still didn't retreat as Broderick drew closer. It seemed Angus couldn't sense Broderick's spirit just yet, as he had not reached the standard boundary. Broderick extended his abilities to include emotion. Though not yet close enough, he prepared to feel them when he came within range. He scanned the area, roaming over the new terrain—a different direction than when he followed the trail on his first night in Stewart Glen. Fear, mixed with frustration, hit his gut with a greater force than he anticipated. Broderick laughed out loud and drew his sword. He surprised Angus and could feel his hasty retreat! The rush of adrenaline gave Broderick new speed and he pressed harder toward his target. And then, like the flame of a candle flickering as it lost fuel, Angus's presence faded. Within seconds, Broderick lost the trail. Confusion slowed his pace as he searched the area, stretching his senses out as far as he could manage. Broderick stopped, closed his eyes and clenched his jaw, willing to reestablish the trail, but received nothing.

Broderick stood in the silence of the forest, hoping the sensations would return. After a long period of no result, his shoulders sagged in defeat. With a grunt, he shoved his sword back into its scabbard and marched in the direction he last sensed Angus heading. Just over the rise of a hill and through the trees, he found the remains of a small, stone structure. A tower, perhaps, situated at the corner of a perimeter wall. The remaining stones littering the ground around the structure indicated as much, and Broderick stepped through the open doorway at the base of the ruin. The wooden floor, not yet rotting, groaned under his weight. He glanced up to see part of the ceiling opened to the night sky.

A diligent search revealed a locked trap door in a darkened corner. Broderick kicked the boards in and tossed the broken pieces aside. As with the other lair, no physical evidence revealed who the daytime dwelling belonged to, but Broderick could smell the same spicy essence he did from the lair he found his first night in this area. The occupant had to be Angus. Making quick work of his efforts, Broderick destroyed the dwelling, busting up the boards and scattering the pieces as far as he could throw them in many directions. Though the structure could likely be repaired, Angus would still have to spend the time to do so.

Turning on his heel, he headed to the first lair he found and destroyed. Angus appeared to have repaired this one, digging out the hole once more and replacing the boulder. Broderick repeated the destruction by pushing the boulder as far from the site as possible and filling in the hole with dirt and forest debris as best he could. Neither of these methods were sure ways of destroying a lair, as was evident with Angus's rebuilding. Only sprinkling true holy water on the site would prevent any Vamsyrian from using the lair, but such a thing was very hard to come by—if it existed at all—and using such a rare item for this minor task would be a waste. Water blessed by a priest or clergy of the church would do nothing to a Vamsyrian. They were only servants of God, and bore their own faults and sins upon their heads. Water to harm a Vamsyrian must to be touched by God Himself. Broderick's teacher Rasheed said the only source known for that supply of water could be found in the deserts of Arabia, where it was rumored Moses struck a rock, bringing forth water to slack the thirst of the wandering Israelites during their exodus to the Promised Land. If Rasheed knew the exact location, he didn't share that with Broderick, nor did Broderick expect him to. Rasheed taught Broderick what he must and nothing more. Such dark secrets were shared with few.

Destroying both lairs didn't take long, and the Gypsy camp wasn't far enough away to be out of his circle of sensing, so Broderick didn't fear Angus sneaking to the camp while his tasks kept him busy. He would keep his watch on these two locations as the nights wore on. Eventually, he would catch up with Angus. With these lairs eliminated for the time being, Broderick set out to feed the Hunger.

Broderick shook his head to clear the horrid images of the thief he fed from this night. He longed for a way to feed without having to absorb such rancid experiences. However, there was at least a sense of justice from preying upon these degenerates.

He approached the curtain wall of Stewart Glen Castle. Glancing around to be sure no one was about, he crouched down for leverage and sprung up, jumping to the top of the wall. The strength immortality gave him not only made running long distances effortless, it also made jumping high almost as easy as taking a step. Hunkering down, he hid in the shadows of the turret and eyed the courtyard below, tilting his head to listen. No activity, no sounds. A frigid breeze tossed a strand of his hair across his face and he brushed it aside, sighing. Why was he here? The time of day was too early for her to be in bed. His impatience to visit her while she slept—to feed from her and gain information—badgered him and he could stand the biding no more, so he headed to her home. Now that he sat waiting in the shadows, he cursed his juvenile behavior.

Rosselyn opened the double doors to Davina's bedchamber, drawing his eyes. She emptied the water of a wash basin over the side wall from the landing, the ting of the metal bowl echoing around the courtyard as she placed it on the stone edge, and shook out a cloth. Broderick could see just past Rosselyn into Davina's chamber, and the sight made his mouth go dry. Davina stood in a shallow bathing tub, sponging off in the glowing firelight. Rosselyn hurried back into the chamber, closing the doors behind her and cutting off the enchanting view. Once again, Davina turned the tables on his efforts to catch her off guard. Dropping down to the ground, he dashed the short distance across the courtyard and leapt the height, onto the terrace. He hesitated, staring at the barred, narrow window, feeling very wrong about the strong desire to peer into her chamber. With a throbbing erection in his breeches, his desire won over and he stepped before the opening, keeping to the shadows.

Broderick's loins stirred and his mouth watered as Davina's skin glistened in the firelight, the flames reflecting on her breasts and shoulders, her taut belly and thighs...and the gnashing scars marring her perfect figure. Long slashes slanted across the backs of her thighs and buttocks when she turned around. Davina rubbed her skin and stretched. His eyes narrowed as Broderick noticed her left arm bent in an awkward way; nothing too disfiguring, but enough for him to take notice. *Broken once?* He tried to reason, at first, she may have been the victim of an unfortunate accident, but the scars on her body weren't by chance. The passionate heat pulsing through his body transformed into the flames of anger. These marks were meant to humiliate and dominate. *Angus...or someone else?*

Rosselyn closed her eyes against the scars as she washed Davina's back. Straining to perceive the maid's misty emotions, Broderick caught images of a handsome, but menacing face. *Oh, Davina!* A mixture of sadness and anger wafted from Rosselyn and swirled around Broderick. *Why did you refrain from telling me about Ian? How much you have been through, my sweet friend.*

Davina turned toward her maid and frowned. "Do not pity me, Rosselyn!" she snapped. "Pity is the last thing I want from anyone." Dropping her head and covering her breasts, she turned away from Rosselyn. "I will finish cleansing myself."

Rosselyn nodded and disappeared into the wardrobe, coming out with a whisper of lace and silk, laying the nightgown on Davina's bed. After a period of stillness, she struggled to speak. "Forgive me, Davina."

"Nay, Rosselyn. There is nothing to forgive." Davina grabbed her drying cloth and covered her body before she went to her friend. "'Tis I who should ask for your forgiveness and thank you for your concern."

Rosselyn glanced at Davina with hopeful eyes. They embraced and Rosselyn excused herself.

Standing for a moment, staring after Rosselyn's exit, Davina finally turned and stepped back in the tub to continue rubbing the scented cloth across her skin, a despondency drawing down the delicate features of her face. Kneeling down in the tub of shallow water, Davina wept, her shoulders shaking under her sobs.

This was why she winced at intimacy, why she locked her heart away and closed her thoughts so tightly. She was willing her memories away. How a man could treat a bonnie creature—or anyone— in such a way he would never understand. Those were the kind of men he ached to devour. Finding weakness in themselves, they punished those weaker to attain the power they lacked. For Broderick, those were the best to dine on. Broderick wanted to comfort Davina, but now would not be the right time. He remained outside until Davina dressed and sat close to the fire with her needlepoint.

Davina continued her endless task of poking her needle in and out of the tapestry, weaving the colorful threads back and forth into the intricate scene. Though the light was not ideal, she needed to do something for distraction. Since the mounting chores during the day gave her no time to stitch, she took this opportunity to lose her thoughts in the repetitive task of sewing. Fighting to see through her tears, she eventually left behind the emotions and memories that plagued her of Ian's cruelty, and focused on the design. At one time, keeping her mind from the past had been easier with her fantasies of Broderick, but now those caused her distress, as well. She should have dismissed the brute from her mind. Instead, she still thought about him too much, and such irrational behavior frazzled her nerves.

Davina gasped and shook her finger which throbbed from the penetrating needle. "Damn Gypsy!" She addressed the shadows as if he waited for her. "You have me so worked up, I stuck myself."

"Now, now, milady," he scolded with a gentle voice. She turned with a start. Broderick stood beside her bed, leaning against the foot post. "'Tis not my fault your mind dwells upon me."

His demeanor caught her off guard. Instead of the mocking countenance she expected on his face, his eyes held compassion, his full lips turned down in what she could only describe as concern. Recovering from her initial shock, she gained her senses and rekindled her anger. "Do I have no privacy with you!" she snapped and put her needlepoint aside. "How dare you invade my chamber again!"

"Again?" Broderick stepped away from the bed and crossed his arms over his massive chest.

Davina opened her mouth to protest, then snapped it shut and turned away from him. Had she truly dreamt his appearance? *Impossible.* Now what would she do? The arrogant bastard would think she kept fantasizing or dreaming about him so much she couldn't keep a distinction between the two. Though this wouldn't be far from the truth, she didn't want him to know. Yet if she denied his inquiry, he would think she couldn't keep the incidents straight because men invaded her chamber on a regular cycle.

"So, how many men *do* you entertain in your private chambers, milady?"

I knew it! Davina composed herself and turned to face him, her shoulders back and chin out. "Who I entertain here is none of your business. The matter at hand is your invasion of my privacy. I wish you to leave."

He flowed across the room like sweet, morning mist over a lake, very much like a specter indeed. His presence mesmerized and surrounded her when he drew near. A peace engulfed her body, and increased when his finger touched her cheek. Shouldn't she be screaming? Though his unearthly movements took her breath away, she refused to back off or show him any kind of fear, so stood before him with bold determination. That roguish grin returned and deepened her fortitude, infusing her with the urge to kick him. She pushed his hand aside.

"Nay, milady." His voice, deep and husky, seductive in every syllable he uttered. "Methinks the true matter at hand is you don't want me to leave."

She gasped and stepped back. "How absurd! I want nothing better than to see you gone and out of my life forever!"

He stepped toward her, closing the distance she just created. Davina's body trembled so with anger, she knew not what to say. Several protests and curses seemed to crowd up in her mouth at once, all fighting for escape. Yet when his head tipped forward, his mouth just a breath from hers, they all fled in a gasp. His eyes locked with hers, hooded and inviting. When his gaze slid down to her mouth, her heart thundered in her breast with anticipation. Desire coursed her body, pushing out any thoughts of protesting his presence. The corner of his mouth turned up and he stepped away from her to lounge on her bed.

She regained some of her senses. "Why you arrogant bast—"

"Ah, ah, ah! Watch that tongue of yo—"

"I care not what you think, you ox." She planted her hands onto her hips. "Get out!"

"Davina?" Lilias knocked at Davina's chamber door. "Sweet, are you all right?"

Davina shot a murderous glance at the Gypsy invader and scampered to the door. "Aye, M'ma," she called to her mother. "All is well. Go on to bed."

"But I heard voices."

Davina's voice trembled. "'Tis nothing, M'ma. I'm thinking aloud. Now please go to bed." Davina turned to Broderick and jumped when she found him directly behind her.

"Are you not going to introduce me?" he teased in a deep whisper.

Davina put her hand over his mouth to silence him, her eyes wide with the fear of discovery.

"Davina?" Lilias's voice seemed laced with suspicion.

She knew her mother heard the Gypsy's rumbling voice. This audacious man, with a devilish grin on his full lips, reached for the latch on her door. Davina gasped and slapped his hand away. When laughter rumbled from him, she clamped her hand onto his mouth again and lost her breath when he pressed the full length of his body to hers, trapping her against the rattling door. She pushed on him and choked at the sound of the door latch. Davina shoved him back and whirled around to find the door opening. In stepped Lilias, and Davina's words of explanation left her mouth unspoken.

"Davina!" Her mother rushed forward and gripped her shoulders. "What's wrong, child? You look as if you have seen a specter!"

Davina dared a glance behind her, and then stumbled with shock when her eyes beheld an empty room.

"Davina?"

"I'm well, M'ma." Davina doubted her trembling voice convinced her mother overmuch. She tried again. "Really, M'ma. I just had a nightmare. I didn't want you to worry about me." Only as an afterthought did she consider her still-made bed, and relief trickled over her at the impression the Gypsy left on her bed covers, giving evidence to Davina's lie. She hugged Lilias in haste and escorted her toward the door. "Thank you, M'ma, but methinks I should go to bed now."

Lilias stared at her daughter with narrow-eyed suspicion, then gave a gentle but hesitant kiss to her brow and closed the door behind her.

Davina sighed and fell against the door, this time securing the lock with great care. She stood for a moment, leaning against the solid wood, drawing from its strength, with her eyes closed and a few deep breaths. She started when warm breath touched her neck. Broderick stood before her, nuzzling her skin with his lips. Weak-kneed, Davina pushed him aside and toddled away from the door.

"Why did you not introduce me?" he mocked.

"Do not speak so loudly," she hissed, and made efforts to keep her own voice a ragged whisper. "You have already met my mother. Now leave."

He stood with his arms crossed, shaking his head. "I'm here to make an attempt at getting to know you better, milady. I find you fascinating."

"A gentleman's attempt at courting?" Davina laughed. "Then you should try an afternoon visit, chaperoned in the parlor if you wish to know me, sir."

"Do I need to remind you—I'm a Gypsy, not a gentleman."

"Oh, how thoughtless of me to forget." Davina pursed her lips at the ridiculous conversation being whispered back and forth.

He chuckled and began circling her. "I'm quite serious, though." His eyes fondled her form. Though he didn't continue to whisper, the low seductive tone of his voice served well to keep quiet, and sent tingles across her skin. "You are of great interest to me, milady."

"Oh, I'm quite sure," she said, raising an eyebrow, demonstrating her distrust.

He stepped closer. "'Tis the woman I wish to get to know and..." His eyes raked over her body. "...understand."

"You are doing wonders to win my heart, gallant Gypsy." Her voice dripped with sarcasm and she crossed her arms. "Now, if you don't leave my chamber, I'm not opposed to calling my mother back onto the scene to protest an intruder in my room."

"Is there nothing I can do to make you trust me?"

"Aye. Leave."

"And that's all I need do for you to trust me?"

"Never return?" she offered, with travesty in her voice.

"I regret I cannot promise you that, Davina."

The sound of her name upon his lips made her hesitate for some unknown reason. "Then I shall never trust you, shall I? What a pity." Davina marched to the door and put her hand upon the latch. "If you don't leave, I will scream for—"

"Not necessary, milady." Broderick sauntered toward her, slow, deliberate, as if trying to show her he would make no sudden moves. He stood so close to her, she could feel his breath against her cheek. Staring up into his emerald eyes, Davina pushed back against the hardwood door. The scent of incense drifted off his clothes and through her senses. His hand cupped her cheek and his warm skin held an underlying scent of lavender. She dared not disappear into the wonder of him, but kept her eyes fixed on his. Yet, she could still almost see his muscled form standing in the tent, the firelight shimmering on his bare chest, incense swirling around him. He smiled, bringing out his tempting dimple, and Davina's cheeks bloomed with heat as she knew he read her thoughts. Before she could protest his presence, he closed the small distance by encasing her in his arms. Her breath held in her chest when his lips stopped just short of hers. She gazed into the emerald depths of his eyes, expectation thundering through her heart.

"Tell me you want me to go," he whispered against her mouth.

"I...I want you to go."

The Gypsy smiled and dropped his gaze to her lips. "Nay, you do not. You cannot bide another moment for me to kiss you."

"You are arrogant and conceited." Her voice held no conviction.

"But I am right." Without delivering the kiss he promised, Broderick stepped away from her, bowed, and brought her hand to his lips. His full mouth burned a sensuous kiss upon her palm and Davina fought to keep her breath steady. "Good night, Davina." He strode through the curtains and double doors and disappeared behind the swaying fabric.

Davina stood for a stunned moment, watching the drapes stop their gentle waving until all went still. In a few hasty steps, she threw the curtains open to reveal an empty landing. "How—?" The drop was far too long for him to have jumped. She eyed the dried and shriveled vines climbing up the wall and shook her head. They couldn't have supported any weight, but she couldn't fathom any other way could he have made it down. Well, at least this time she knew she hadn't dreamt their encounter. The black, cold night encircled her and chilled her cheeks, making her all too aware of her surroundings. Drawing her robe closer around her throat, she went back into her chamber and paced herself into exhaustion.

Crouching against the tree she scaled for a better view, Veronique cursed under her breath as she watched that Davina disappear back into her chamber. She knew it! She just knew Broderick came to see her. Veronique's heart twisted, and she squeezed her eyes and fists to fight back the tears. When Broderick leapt over the curtain wall and hiked several strides from where she perched in the tree, she made special care to hold her breath and lock her thoughts away lest Broderick hear her. He disappeared into the dark forest without so much as a word. Damn him for still seeing her as his little sister! She had much more to offer than this prissy, weak-willed woman with her servants and castle. That Davina didn't know anything about what Broderick needed, or how to deal with his thirst for blood.

Veronique saw the determination in Broderick's eyes when he left. She had to be a bit more blunt in making Broderick come around to seeing her as the woman she had become. She would prove to him she was much more woman than that Davina could ever be.

Broderick didn't need fire for warmth or light. The blaze provided a simple comfort, a slight nostalgia and nothing more. The flames flickered and hissed in his cave as he sat against the crude wall, lost in reflection.

He questioned his motives for continuing into Davina's chamber after he'd seen her moment of vulnerability. She couldn't possibly be an accomplice to his enemy. So why did he continue with his intentions?

Broderick cursed under his breath, his whispers echoing in the cave. He knew why he went into her chamber—and it had nothing to do with divining thoughts or finally getting to those memories about Angus. Broderick rose from the ground and paced along the length of the cave. *You are falling for the bait*, Broderick reprimanded. *Focus on your goal, Rick.*

After some endless pacing, Broderick returned to sit before the fire. He needed to learn more about Davina and her connection with Angus. If she wasn't an accomplice, what was the brief encounter with Angus? Broderick divined just enough information to keep him curious. Angus did it deliberately to taunt him, lure him in. Davina was bait and nothing more. Angus loved the chase, the hunt, and he loved getting innocent people involved. But why did he choose her? Broderick had read the palms of several people in the town of Stewart Glen on their last visit so many years ago. Why did Angus single out Davina? This is what Broderick needed to discover, and only Davina had that answer.

I had the opportunity to feed from her, and yet I didn't take that chance. He grumbled at what this woman did to him. When he touched her, delving into her dark secrets was the furthest intent from his mind, and the dreams weren't helping curb his appetite. After learning what he did about the abuse she suffered—the abuse he foretold—he found it hard to proceed with feeding from her for information. Obviously she was Angus's victim.

Broderick had to make a conscious effort to focus on his goal, yet when he tried, she locked her mind tight against his probing. Her thoughts on this were her own, and Davina wouldn't tell him what happened, certainly, until she grew to trust him, which also meant she wouldn't give in to any intimacy with him until he gained her trust. This intimacy would lead to what he wanted. Appearing uninvited to her bedchamber could hardly be the way about this.

No more midnight visits. He'd have to try the conventional way and pay her a social call like a respectable gentleman. Again, he chuckled. He hadn't acted the Lord of Glenstrae for over three decades.

"Thinking of her?" Veronique's question held a cold bite, matching the chill in her eyes and the night air.

Broderick scowled. He was so lost in contemplation; he cursed for not hearing her approach. "I told you to never come to my resting place, Veronique. Someone could follow you. You make me vulnerable during the day." He glared at her, and yet still she stood before him, seething in defiance. He shook his head. "And just who are you referring to?"

"You know of whom I speak!"

Broderick groaned inwardly. "Veronique, don't—"

"She cannot understand what you are! She cannot give to you the way I have!" Veronique thrust her wrist at Broderick, showing him her scars, scars he knew too well, for they were made by his own mouth. They had been stranded in a place with no other people. Veronique offered her blood. Broderick was foolish enough to accept her offer and more foolish to let her keep the scars at her insistent pleas. She wore those scars proudly. The young French girl's voice dropped to a desperate whisper. "I give you my blood and my heart." Stepping closer to him, she opened her blouse, baring her breasts. "And my body."

Broderick watched her nipples pucker against the frigid air. He entertained the idea for a moment. Veronique did accept him fully. She would never reject him, but when he beheld her face, the frail child he knew so well stifled his desire. She would always remain his little sister, no matter how she matured. As much as he hated to admit it, because he did care for her, she was also too selfish for his tastes. "My interest in Davina isn't what you think. That aside, what I do and who I pursue is none of your business. Go home, little sister."

"Damn you, Broderick MacDougal!" she said, kicking and cursing at him in French. He blocked, dodged and slapped her hands and fussing away until he realized she wouldn't stop, so he threw her over his shoulder and carried her wriggling body back to the camp.

"Ouch!" Davina sucked on the tip of her punctured finger. "What did you say?"

"You heard me," Lilias said, hands upon her hips. "The Gypsy fortune teller is waiting for you in the parlor. And I don't mean Amice."

Davina put her needlepoint down with shaky hands. When she hadn't seen Broderick near on two days, she began to think he gave up his pursuit. Davina tried to shove away the growing sadness at his absence, convincing herself she didn't need him in her life. The fantasies were over, and she would continue her days free from such nonsense. So why did her hands continue to shake at the mention of his visit? With a curt, "Thank you, M'ma," she attempted to pass Lilias through the door. Her mother stepped into her path.

Lilias's exasperation melted into desperation. "Oh, Davina! Please watch yourself. He's a bonnie lad, but so was Ian."

She ignored her mother's comments and stepped into the hall.

Davina advanced the tentative steps of trepidation as she headed down the stairs. *What is that intolerable man up to?* Her steps quickened to stomps. *Was invading my privacy through my chamber not enough? Now he invades my family's life by paying a social call?* She paused and pouted. *It matters not that he accepted my challenge to do so. I've made it obvious I don't wish to see him.* Nodding at her reasoning, she stomped to the parlor door and breathed deep.

"Davina?"

She turned to see Rosselyn running down the hall. Davina couldn't keep the impatience from her voice. "What brings you here, Roz?"

"Your mother told me to accompany you. She said she didn't want you to be alone with the Gypsy."

Huffing over Lilias's lack of trust, Davina straightened her posture and jutted her chin out. "Well, he won't be here very long. I've come down to dismiss him." She swung the doors open and her breath caught in her throat. Clad in the attire of a gentleman, as regal and confident as ever, Broderick stood in the parlor. His massive arms crossed over his broad chest, fiery auburn hair blazing on his shoulders, an annoying eyebrow raised and that damned dimple next to the smirk on his full lips.

Davina stood with her mouth open at his figure clad in fine threads. How would a Gypsy come to own such rich garments? A dark-blue doublet covered his broad torso, the split sleeves contrasting with the white linen shirt beneath. The skirt of the jacket hung shorter than Davina saw in the current fashions. Albeit old fashioned, the garment complimented his trim hips and muscular thighs. The older style of the clothing betrayed him—he must have acquired them from someone else through the many towns they'd traveled. He could have traded such older but fine clothing for some of his services with ease.

Secured around his trim waist shone a leather belt holding his sporran pouch, decorated with a fur flap and metal clasp of the Scottish thistle. The pouch nestled low on his hips and—with much relief to Davina—sheltered her eyes from his groin, most likely outlined by his form-fitting tan trews. Encasing his muscular calves were a pair of soft brown leather boots, matching the color of his leather belt. Diverting her eyes back up to his face, she cursed under her breath at being caught—once again—ogling him. She would have worried about him hearing her initial gasp, but Rosselyn's gasp sounded much louder than hers.

"Nica!"

For the first time, Davina noticed the handsome, dark-haired man standing beside the Gypsy, smiling devilishly. He bowed to Rosselyn.

"Greetings, gentlewomen," Broderick said in that deep, creamy voice and bowed his introduction. "Broderick MacDougal, at your service. May I present Nicabar Mendoza, a fellow traveling companion?" Broderick stood almost two hands taller than Nicabar, his smile much more menacing. Nay, devilish didn't suit the description of Nicabar's smile. His shone with angelic luster compared to the Giant's. The Dark Lord himself.

Davina pondered his name and her brow creased. "Son of the Dark Stranger?"

"Excuse me?" Broderick asked.

"Your name—MacDougal means Son of the Dark Stranger, if I'm not mistaken." She pursed her lips and crossed her arms. "How appropriate." She sighed and stepped forward to dismiss them both. "I'm afraid I must—"

Davina stopped when Rosselyn stepped toward Nicabar, her handmaid's eyes sparkling. Davina clenched her fists. Drawing her own conclusions, she guessed Rosselyn had been down to the camp more often than the one recent visit to the market with Seamus. Rosselyn's familiarity with the dark-haired Gypsy unnerved Davina. Her handmaid acted almost as if she didn't see Broderick. But how could she miss him and his alarming transformation?

"May we have a word together?" Nicabar asked. Without hesitation, Rosselyn led him from the room by the hand. Davina was on her own. *So much for not leaving me alone with the Gypsy.*

"Chess?"

Snapping out of her stupor, she gawked at Broderick. "What?"

He sauntered toward the chess table and picked up a black marble pawn. "Do you play?"

"Very well, thank you." Davina maintained a defensive posture. "And when do Gypsies find the time to play chess?"

"I haven't always been a Gypsy, you know."

"I gathered that, considering your current attire." Davina hoped he would take the conversation further and she could learn a bit more about his past, which intrigued her. Broderick chuckled and sat at the table. She sighed with disappointment.

"Please," Broderick pressed, motioning toward the chair across from him. "Join me in a friendly game."

"Why?"

Broderick traveled his eyes down Davina's body, sending delightful, heated tingles through to her toes. "Because I enjoy your company, and wish to engage in a battle of wits." His eyes met hers, challenging.

She refused to take the bait. "Well, I do not, sir. Please leave."

"Do not wish to engage in a battle of wits, or do not enjoy my company?"

"Neither."

Broderick's head tipped back in laughter, a laughter that filled the parlor and her soul. She shook off the strange desire to join in, reminding herself he mocked her.

"I really must ask you to leave."

"I'm making a valiant effort to pay you a proper visit." Shaking his head, he crossed his ankle upon his knee. "I will not leave this room until you play me a splendid game of chess." His leveling eyes told her he meant to do just what he said. With his deep voice, he added, "If you force me to leave, I shall steal into your bedchamber in the middle of the night, and seduce myself into your dreams."

Her stomach fluttered, and Davina cursed him under her breath as she seated before him. "You are intolerable, Gypsy."

"Thank you, milady."

"'Twas not a compliment."

Broderick chuckled.

Oh, how insufferable! He was too damned comely for his own good, and he knew it all too well. He charmed her to annoyance—and he seemed to know every move she made on the chessboard! In minutes he called checkmate.

"'Tis unfair to use your seeing abilities in this game!" Davina protested.

"Madame, I did no such thing," he returned with amusement. "Your moves are entirely too predictable."

Davina rose from her chair. "Well, you have had your game. Now leave."

With a slow shake to his head, he said, "Nay, milady. I said I would leave when we had a splendid match together. 'Twas much too easy. You were not into the game at all."

Davina started away from the table. "Well, I am not playing—"

Broderick snatched her arm and Davina tumbled back into his lap.

"Damn you, Gypsy," she cursed as she continued to struggle against his impossible hold. "I will scream if you don't let me go!"

Broderick's deep chuckle rumbled from his chest through her body. "Keep moving upon my lap in such a manner, and I will have to toss your skirts up right here in the parlor."

Davina gasped so hard, she almost choked. "A pox on you, savage! Let me up or I will scream!"

"I shall enjoy the following scene, then. Your servants will come running to your rescue, no doubt your mother leading the pack, and I will have the pleasure of visiting your chamber before the sun comes up on the morrow."

Davina ceased struggling for a moment and spied the dreadful promise in his mischievous eyes. She huffed for a moment or two longer and with much reluctance, conceded. "Oh, let me up so I may take my seat!" Davina surprised herself—she had to suppress a smile.

Trying to cover her amusement, Davina made a dramatic display of plopping back into the chair and, from his seat across the table, Broderick presented a triumphant grin. With elbow on the table and chin in hand, she covered her mouth to hide her smile and helped him set up the pieces for the next game.

Broderick's rush and violent onslaught unnerved Davina. She took a particular offense to his knight's consistent pursuit of her queen.

"Must you be so brutal in your approach?" she quipped. "You give yourself no time to think about your next move. Can you at least savor the game?"

Broderick covered his mouth, making an obvious demonstration of stifling a fit of laughter.

Davina almost had as difficult a time as he did holding back her mirth, but that soon died as his pursuit became even more aggressive. She placed many obstacles in his way, sacrificing other important pieces just to save her queen, remaining defensive in her all of her moves. Protecting her queen became a single determination for her. She'd be damned if she'd let her go to that brute!

In three more moves, Davina found her piece cornered and captured. She'd lost her queen. One more move—checkmate. Her face flushed with heat, but that subsided once she remembered this game went far better than the last. Surely he would be content with this attempt. The rampant emotions running through her were confusing and uncomfortable. She couldn't decide if she enjoyed his company or couldn't stand being around him. "You have had your game. Now go!"

"The game still held no satisfaction for me, mistress. Much more challenging, I will admit. Your anger seemed to improve your game, but your efforts were not good enough."

Taking a deep breath to calm her nerves, she sat back into her chair, as casual as she could muster, and laced her hands in her lap. "I'm afraid I've given you my best, sir. Methinks I'm not as good as I thought. Or at least not as good as you are."

"Well, if your efforts were the best you could do…" Broderick shook his head with the corners of his mouth turned down in pity. "Who taught you to play?"

Now *that* hit a tender spot. Davina rose from the table and Broderick snatched her wrist. "My brother, sir! And I will have you know he was a very good chess player!"

Broderick's face softened and he released her hand. "Please accept my sincerest apologies, Davina. I didn't mean to stir grievous feelings over your late brother."

Davina rubbed her wrist, eying Broderick with suspicion as she sat back down. "How do you know of my brother?"

"When I touched you, I could feel the anguish and grief. I saw flashes of him. I could feel the depth of your affection."

Davina gazed off into the past. *Ah, my sweet Kehr. What a void I have since your death.* "Will the pain ever go away?" she whispered, forgetting for the moment she wasn't alone.

"Nay, milady." Broderick rested his elbows upon the chair's arms and steepled his fingers under his chin. "The grief may dull over the years, but it never completely fades away."

"You talk from experience."

Broderick nodded. "My family was murdered."

"Your family?"

"Aye. My two brothers, their families, and my parents."

Davina gasped. "Your entire family?" The grief of losing her brother and father was overwhelming at times, but she couldn't imagine losing everyone she held dear. Empathy swelled in her for Broderick's loss and she fought back the tears stinging her eyes. "How could you bear such a loss? How did you survive?"

Broderick shifted in his chair with apparent discomfort over the question.

"Please forgive my intrusion," she apologized with haste. "'Tis not my place to ask such an intimate question. I find I'm desperate to talk about my own losses, maybe learn to cope as well as you seem to have." A thick stillness fell and Davina stared at the chess pieces, not wanting to chance a confrontation. After a long moment, she braved a glance up, and the compassion in his eyes surprised her. "Do you ever talk about it?"

"About the pain? About what happened?"

Davina nodded.

"Nay." And he averted his gaze.

"I thought…" She trailed off, her hands fidgeting a nervous dance in the folds of her skirt.

"What, Davina," his voice coaxed.

"Well, 'tis rather…well…I actually feel relieved I'm not alone in my grief."

"Do you not grieve with your mother, the other members of your household?" Broderick leaned forward in his chair, resting his forearms upon the table.

"At first, but a short time thereafter, no one would mention their names. No one would speak about those precious times spent with them. Their deaths seem too much to bear. It has become an unspoken rule in our home, try as I might to overcome the silence."

"Names? You spoke only of your brother."

Davina cleared her throat. "Both my father and brother died at the Battle of Flodden Field."

"I suppose that senseless war left a lot of orphans and widows in its wake. I remember Kehr," Broderick whispered, staring into the past.

"You what?" How could he know her brother?

"From the first night you came into my tent. You and your brother used to steal honey from the pantry."

Soft laughter fluttered over Davina's lips. "Aye. We kept our little secret for a while. I should have taken your advice and not stolen so much at once. You—" Davina stopped, her mouth hanging open for a moment. "You remember."

The corner of Broderick's mouth turned up. "Aye. I remember."

Davina's heart slammed against her chest. He remembered her! He knew her! Then her face grew flush. "Why the charade? Why did you pretend as if you didn't know me?"

He remained seated, leaning back in his chair, at ease. "I did not."

"You most certainly—!"

"Nay, milady. I just never made you aware of my recollection."

"You conniving—!"

"I am no such thing." Broderick raised his eyebrows and studied her with amusement in his eyes. "Why, may I ask, does this vex you so, milady?" Broderick rose from his chair and swaggered toward her.

Standing and backing away from him, she stammered, "I am not...you...I..." Davina cringed over her senseless response. Damn her and her ridiculous desire for this man!

"I would say you have quite a bit of your heart invested in this. Why is it so important I remember you?"

Davina stopped and stood her ground. "Nothing could be further from the truth, sir. Methinks you displayed devious behavior."

"Devious?"

"Aye, devious! You had the upper hand and took advantage of me!"

Broderick's grin grew and he continued to advance, his voice as creamy as ever. "I wager you have been thinking about me for a very long time that I should have such an advantage over you, as you say."

"You conceited—!"

"Aye, you have."

Davina gasped as she found herself in a corner. Before she could dodge his path, he trapped her, pressing his body against hers. "Admit it, Davina," he breathed hot against her cheek. "Tell me you never stopped thinking about me."

"You are mad!" Her struggling profited nothing against him.

His lips stroked her skin, his nose pushed back her hair, revealing her ear to his mouth. "Say it," his voice caressed.

"Nay." She panted as his tongue dove inside her ear, then around it, lapping at her lobe and tapping a primitive part of her being. He nibbled his way across her jaw to her lips, where his mouth hovered for a moment, his heavy breath mingling with hers. Her own heated desire reflected in his eyes and burned her soul. Closing her eyes, she fought him no more. Broderick moaned and slanted his mouth across hers.

Lost. And for the moment, Davina wanted to be that way. Lost in the long-awaited taste of Broderick's kisses. Lost in the years she ached to have him hold her as he did now. Lost in the fantasy that his hunger proved he thought of her over the years as much as she did him. In the dream that he ached for her, trembled in her arms, swooned in her kiss just as she did his.

CHAPTER SEVEN

Broderick threaded his fingers into the thickness of Davina's tawny tresses and he pulled her harder against him, groaning into her mouth. His lips devoured her, touching her eyelids, her cheeks, her nose, claiming her lips once more and capturing the taste of her at last. Davina's yearning merged with his growing hunger to absorb her, body and soul. His mouth traveled to her throat, his tongue dancing a hot, wet trail across her skin. They seemed to cling to each other in a desperate attempt to become one in their union, leaving Broderick breathless.

Stopping for the moment, he broke from their kiss and struggled to maintain some control over his senses. The rose oil from her heated skin mixed with the scent of her blood, and his mind swirled. Opening his eyes, he searched to stave off the spell engulfing him, fighting off the dizzying effect.

Broderick's breathing, ragged and trembling, screamed a warning. He closed his eyes and fell into another ardent kiss, but more demanding, his body tense, a new and powerful yearning coursing through him. Davina's excitement, mixed with her fear, titillated his senses, making it near impossible to pull away. Her fear ignited the Hunger hiding behind his passion, and the familiar and deadly pain shot across his gums, his mouth watering, his tongue aching to sample the sweetness her blood promised. A low, guttural growl rumbled from Broderick's chest as he wrestled to keep himself from giving in, and with a sudden force, he shoved away from her.

"Broderick?" Davina's trembling voice beckoned to his instincts, a temptation too great for the immortal side of him to resist.

"I apologize for my display, Mistress Davina," he rasped, his words wooden and rough in texture. Broderick kept his back to her. Seeing her so vulnerable would be his undoing…and hers. He straightened his clothing to try and gain composure over his deadly instincts. "I enjoyed our games and hope to spend more time with you in the future. If you will excuse me." Without a backward glance, he left her alone in the parlor and rushed to the nearest exit through the kitchen. The cold night air, a welcome reprieve. No one in sight, to his relief, Broderick proceeded quickly through the courtyard and headed toward the gate. Just as he rounded the corner of the castle, the light from the parlor's oriel window caught his eye…as did the silhouette of Davina. He made an abrupt stop, seized by the vision of her staring at him. Even in the darkness, in her shaded features, he could see her lips swollen from his kisses and the sadness in her eyes. *Better the sorrow in her eyes, than her blood on my hands.*

A trick of the torches, she told herself, as his silver glowing eyes stared at her through the darkness, and yet a strangely familiar dread came over her and settled into the pit of her stomach. Davina shuddered and her heart pounded. Broderick turned on his heel and stomped out of the courtyard through the gate.

"You fancy him?" Lilias asked.

Davina turned to her mother, standing beside her. "Nonsense. He's a beast." Davina realized her hands clutched the sill of the oriel window. To avoid her mother's admonishment, Davina left and distracted herself by visiting the nursery to check on her daughter. Cailin lay sleeping like an angel nestled in the clouds. With a kiss to her plump cheek, Davina slipped out and went to her adjoining chamber.

Here, she was alone. Rosselyn had not yet come back, still with Nicabar somewhere, she supposed. With methodical routine, Davina readied for bed and slid beneath the large comforter. She lay watching the flickering firelight. Her emotions danced about like the flames, and she struggled to rein them in.

"Broderick MacDougal." She tasted his name, at last putting a full identity to the man who had given her strength and haunted her. Broderick elicited such confusing weights upon her heart. She ached for him to continue his advances because he drew out of her the overwhelming desire to surrender; and yet those very same feelings scared her to death.

Davina tossed in her bed, as if trying to make the uncomfortable feelings go away by making her body comfortable. It seemed obvious Broderick knew something about grief she did not. He seemed to have succeeded where she failed. Would time, eventually, cure the grief? Would he be open enough to share his experiences with her? And where would such confessions lead?

She shifted with unease. Davina guessed Broderick's interest in her held only primitive motivations, and she knew how those encounters ended. Were all encounters so shallow? Rosselyn often spoke of the pleasures of joining. What did Rosselyn find that Davina had not? Rosselyn talked often of tenderness and caresses. Her own mother uncharacteristically told Davina on her wedding night that lovemaking could be the most wonderful experience when one knew deep love. Yet Davina's own experience with Ian was brutal, unfeeling and painful, and especially humiliating. Her cousins even spoke of the act with disgust or as their duty. None of them mentioned love, passion or thrills.

The only men who seemed capable of such caresses and thrills were the midnight lovers. These were not the things a husband seemed capable of. So, could Broderick be a midnight lover? Davina's body tingled. He did seem capable of caresses and thrills. But, the memory of the triumphant smirk on his mouth reminded her the experience would be short-lived. She didn't think she could live with the regret of being used when the encounter ended. Broderick sought to claim her as a midnight conquest—nothing else. As foolish as her fantasy seemed, she wanted more. Yet, she didn't think she could be mistress material. She shook her head and buried deep within her covers. Nay, she couldn't be like Rosselyn. She had a daughter to think of.

Rosselyn pulled her cloak tighter against the chilling darkness as she strolled beside Nicabar through the forest. In the distance, the flickering light of the campfires and torches made the caravans and people appear as if they hovered in blackness. She smiled as Nicabar's fingers slipped between her own in a possessive grasp, her heart dancing in her breast. Something about Nicabar, something alluring and so masculine, excited her senses. His bonnie eyes and long lashes drew her in, held her captive anytime he gazed at her. The rest of the world faded away. He stopped and faced her, the distant firelight illuminating his face with a soft, orange glow. She didn't need to see his features with any clarity. His face already etched a clear vision in her mind—each thick lash, twinkling eye, roguish twist of his full mouth—all of it memorized.

"You look beautiful tonight," he whispered, as if careful not to disturb the silence of the forest. "I am flattered you dressed so deliciously for me."

To Rosselyn's surprise, her face flushed with warmth. A rare activity for her, blushing normally came during limited times of embarrassment, but never when a man complimented her. She turned away from Nicabar. "And what makes you think I dressed for you this evening?" she said in a teasing tone.

Nicabar snickered and turned her around. His arms slipped under her cloak and around her waist to her back, pulling her against him. Rosselyn stared into his striking eyes and he appeared as if he would kiss her. She hoped he would. His finger caressed her cheek. Did he pause to give her a chance to push away? Well, he wasted his time.

Being bold, oftentimes she would initiate the next move, but she melted into the helplessness of Nicabar's embrace. Then his mouth covered hers in a deep and searching kiss. She clung to him, her fingers sliding through his silky black hair, the hardness of his body against the full length of her. His teeth nibbled at her bottom lip, his delicious hands roaming over her body. Nicabar stopped and pushed her back a short distance. "I do not trust myself with you this evening," he said with mischief, his voice dripping with his lovely Spanish accent. "I will take you home."

Rosselyn sighed inwardly. In spite of her longing, though, she nodded. He hadn't disappointed her. Every man she had relations with pursued her with unrestrained desires. They went for what they wanted and didn't think twice about her feelings. Nicabar's self-control made her feel cherished, and she smiled as they loitered back toward the castle.

Croft hugged the wool blanket closer, trying to stave off the visions running rampant through his head while cradling his broken fingers against his chest. "Go away," he whispered, sweat dripping down his brow and into his eyes. The sting of sweat seemed a small comfort against the blaze of agony tormenting his mind. He shuddered and closed his eyes tight against the images, but that only seemed to make them clearer. Opening his eyes wide, his body begged for sleep, which he'd not seen in days...not since that Devil Gypsy attacked him...not since that Devil Gypsy fed from him with those vicious fangs.

The feeding had been blissful for the time they were locked in the exchange. He gave his blood and the Devil Gypsy gave him nightmares. "I promise," he prayed to God for the hundredth time. "I promise I will never touch another child. Just stop the agony, Lord. Stop the nightmares!"

"Be afraid, poor lad. They will never stop."

Croft choked back a scream as the Devil Gypsy towered over him. "Nay! You stay away from me!"

The Devil Gypsy grabbed Croft by the throat to silence him, but now that he stood nose-to-nose with him, it wasn't the Devil Gypsy, though they shared a resemblance. "I'm not the one who caused you this torment. I'm the answer to your prayers."

"Who are you?" Croft managed to rasp through the chokehold.

A slow smile spread across his lips, exposing his fangs, with the same silver glow in his eyes. "I am the Angel of Death." Turning Croft's head to the side, the Angel of Death bit into his neck, and the same euphoric sensation flowed through his body as when the Devil Gypsy fed from him. However, no demonic images invaded his mind, no scenes of hell or torment. His mind disappeared into the blissful blackness. He would finally find rest.

Broderick rose from the creaking bed, careful not to disturb the barmaid sleeping beside him. He stared down at her motionless form, a lazy smile on her lips. She was the one he saw their first night in Stewart Glen, with the generous cleavage and dazzling smile. He came to the tavern after a hasty feeding in the forest. With the Hunger raging inside him after being with Davina, he attacked a roe deer unfortunate enough to cross his path. At least with his blood lust somewhat dampened, he could control the Hunger without taking a human life, but he still needed human blood.

Soon after he arrived at the tavern, he watched the barmaid's seductive glances and obvious invitations while he gulped at the bitter ale. Not wanting to taste the salted, sweaty, stinking skin of another thief or murderer, or deal with their horrid mental images, he decided to take her offer and follow her to the room upstairs. He had no need to bed the wench—it was her blood he was after. Instead, he swept through her mind to lull her to sleep, and with a swift bite to her throat, fed from her and wiped the encounter from her memories. Though her mental images appeared less horrific, he understood what led her to live a life where she sold her body for profit. He used his blood to wipe the wounds from her skin, wishing his immortal gifts gave him the ability to change the past for people.

He sat on the windowsill, closed his eyes, and took in the last few hours of the night. His mind flooded with images of Davina's silken lips. On his own skin, he still smelled the musky rose oil she wore, and the memory of her throat lingered upon his mouth. He sighed in defeat. His face burned with regret as he remembered how the Hunger surfaced when he touched her throat. Not having fed before visiting was a foolish thing to do.

Broderick stared into the blackened sky, at the sleeping village, searching for some solace in the peace around him. But he found none. He feared losing control. A frigid breeze flurried past him and the wench stirred on the straw mattress. Broderick placed a small handful of silver *half groats* on the table beside the fireplace and left her moaning in her sleep.

Broderick stepped out onto the street, and a familiar tingling rustled the hairs on the back of his neck. *Angus!* He probed his senses outward, picked up the direction and dashed between the buildings, picking his way through the darkness. The trail led to an open door at the far edge of the village, still swinging on its hinges. In the blackness of the room, a man sat crumpled in the corner, his breathing shallow, his heartbeat weak. Broderick picked him up and the scent of blood forced his fangs to extend in anticipation. This was the man Croft he fed from a few nights before, his broken fingers cradled against his chest, his neck torn open and still pulsing a rivulet of blood.

"You said you would kill me," he whispered.

The man wouldn't survive, so Broderick took the opportunity to feed upon him and gain what information he could. In the dying man's memories and blood, Broderick saw Angus Campbell. He also saw the torment this man lived with since Broderick fed from him and poured horrific images into his mind. Aye, the man changed his ways. He had no desire to prey upon children, but he also didn't have the means to carry out his new-found transformation. The images Broderick put into his mind caused near madness for this poor creature. Dropping the man to the floor, Broderick struggled to keep the guilt from overcoming him. His intentions were to reform the man, not drive him insane. How many more had he driven to such madness?

But they deserved it! Broderick swallowed the bile rising in his throat. The death rattle coming from Croft brought him back to the moment, and Broderick forced himself to keep his wits about him. He healed Croft's wounds, not leaving any traces of the attack to avoid suspicions. The poor, mad soul would be found with no explanation for his death.

Broderick fought the grief as he rushed through the door and extended his senses into the night. Nothing. No Vamsyrian presence that he could detect. Not willing to give up just yet, he headed out of town in the direction he last sensed Angus. Why Angus pulled back and taunted from such a distance, Broderick could only guess. Perhaps he wanted to find out what Broderick's weaknesses and strengths were. Perhaps Angus just toyed with him.

Broderick roamed the area for as long as he dared, battling his conscience and the frustration at failing to find Angus. When the horizon hinted with the coming sun, he headed for his own lair. Dashing through the forest, he approached his cave and stopped several feet before the entrance. He sighed. Veronique. Her sweet, young scent wafted on the bitter air. Shaking his head and steeling for the encounter, he stomped into the cave and found her standing in the darkness—topless. He grumbled. "'Tis much too cold for you to be wandering about without covering." Continuing deep into his cave, he prepared for rest. "And you're ignoring my wishes again. Do not come here, Veronique." He pointed a finger at her. "Ever."

She stepped in front of him in the darkness, very visible with his immortal vision. Her bare breasts, round and full, youthful and proud, jutted toward him. Her blouse and shawl hung off her shoulders and at her elbows, her hands rested on her hips, still dressed in her skirt. Broderick scanned her figure and shook his head.

"I have been waiting for you," she said in a soft voice.

"Did you not give yourself time to sleep? Amice is awake at this time, needing your help. You will be no good to her tired."

"I have rested. I rose early to meet you before—"

"Veronique—"

She stepped toward him and smoothed her hands over his chest, up his neck where she tried to pull him down to meet her. She pressed her soft and eager body against him. He pushed her away and yanked her blouse and shawl over her shoulders.

"Veronique, you need to go back to the camp."

"*Pourquoi*, Broderick?" She tried to kiss him a second time, and once more he pushed her away. "*Je t'aime*, Broderick. Can you not see?"

"Veronique, you don't love me. 'Tis just a passing infatuation. You need to understand—"

"I understand you, Broderick. I embrace what you are. Will she? I am much more woman than that Davina. If she was any kind of woman, you would not have left her chamber that night."

He grabbed Veronique's wrist. "Back to the camp!" he said, dragging her behind him.

"This is true, Broderick, and you know it is!" Veronique struggled against his grip. "She will never love you like I do! She will hate you once she finds out what you are!"

"Enough!" he thundered, silencing her for a moment. Dawn threatened on the horizon. Pulling her shirt closed, he hoisted her struggling body over his shoulder. "'Tis not the time to argue, Veronique!" Broderick raced her to camp with his immortal speed, dumped her before their caravan with little care, and then raced back to his cave. He grumbled as he ducked inside the safety of his black velvet curtain, a pinkening sky on the horizon.

"You cannot take everything I have!" the woman shrieked at the man atop her horse. The surrounding farm lay in ruin, decomposing from neglect and lack of funds. "You have taken every piece of silver I have and now you're taking my horse! How do you expect me to live?"

"What makes you think this concerns me?" he asked, not interested in her answer. Such a pitiful display, with her mousy-brown hair, tangled and dirty, her clothes, rags, her calloused hands. He shuddered over the last several months he lived with her.

"After all I've done for you?" She fell to her knees in the freezing mud, clenching her hair in fists. "You used me!" She glared at him with her tear-filled eyes. "I should have let you rot! I should have never taken you in! I should have—"

He trotted over to her and kicked her face, silencing her pleas. She lay sprawled in the mud, weeping. She did what he needed, provided what any woman was bred for. She nursed him back to health from his near-fatal wounds given to him by Davina's brother Kehr; gave him a dry place to lay his head, a wench to bed, food in his belly, and now the means to leave. Snorting at her pathetic figure, he turned the horse toward the road and left the smells, decay, and tears behind. Her sobbing faded in the distance as he urged his horse down the road.

He had just enough money for his journey north, and then he would get what he needed from his father—if he was still alive. The relief of journeying to his destination and finally having his own life back blew over his body like a warm summer breeze. *This will work!* Ian gritted his teeth in apprehension of the unknown. Had he stayed away long enough for people to think him dead?

This time away from his father and his controlling nature gave Ian plenty of time to ponder his options. Ian grunted. Munro wouldn't think any differently than before. Gratitude over having the prodigal son home at last wouldn't change his demeanor. Nay, Munro would still be the one holding the purse strings.

"Not anymore," Ian growled and rubbed the beard on his face. Enough of being the puppet. The time had come to reap the rewards of his suffering and patience. "Welcome home, son," Ian said, and a self-satisfied smile spread across his lips.

"You squeal like a piglet!" Davina screamed over her daughter's uncontrollable titters. She continued to scrub her baby's ribs, causing more peals of laughter to pour from the child.

Lilias glanced from her needlework, smiling and shaking her head. "The poor child is going to suffocate if you continue to plague her so!"

Davina stopped for a moment, letting her daughter catch her breath, but Cailin wanted more. She pulled on her mother's hands to continue her tickling. And Davina did.

Lilias shook her head and resumed her needlework. "Well, at least she'll be exhausted when her nap-time arrives."

"Cailin is wearing *me* out, M'ma. I will have to nap with her!" Davina buried her face in her daughter's neck, making loud smacking noises.

"You were just as tiring as she," Lilias informed Davina. "Now you know what I had to contend with."

"You must have been a happy mother, then," Davina countered.

"Aye, m'darlin'. That I am."

Davina rose from the bed and picked up her daughter. "I believe the time has come, precious." She cradled her child and turned toward the nursery. As she suspected, Cailin began to cry. "There, there, Cailin. You'll be unbearable if I don't lay you down." Davina unlaced her bodice, and her daughter quieted as her eager little mouth latched onto her breast. She watched as Cailin's little ragged sobs softened to an easy breathing, tears glistening on the lashes of her closed eyelids, which Davina wiped away. When Cailin stopped her suckling, Davina laid her down and left her swaddled in her cradle.

Davina joined her mother back in her bedchamber, and they conversed over their needlework until Lilias excused herself to ready the kitchen for the evening meal. Davina put her work aside, and Rosselyn helped her dress for her daily ride. Over her chemise, she wore a simple woolen gown of dove gray, trimmed with maroon embroidery work Davina had sewn herself. Maroon cord laced up the front of her bodice for support. The net over her braided hair reflected the same maroon, and a low headdress of dove gray with matching maroon embroidery topped off the ensemble. Donning her heavy, rabbit lined, black cloak, she went downstairs to the stables where Fife readied her mare.

Davina studied the clouds overhead as she set down the path, into the woods bordering their property. A gray blanket of clouds hovering in the sky and set above the horizon, let the distant setting sun nestle between the two linear planes. The sun bathed everything in red, pink, and amber hues, bringing an accenting warmth to the contrasting shadows created by the clouds, which cast an equal aura of dusk and cold. The scene cast a strange essence of being caught between two worlds. The bitter breeze moving through her reminded Davina the fall months were ending much sooner this year. Winter frosted the air, which meant she wouldn't be enjoying her daily rides as often. With that in mind, she urged her horse Heather into a full gallop, as if to make up for the stagnant winter months to come.

Davina slowed when her mare began to show slight signs of fatigue. "Forgive me, Heather." She stroked her silky mane. "I was not mindful of you."

Heather nodded her massive head, as if in response to her phrase.

Davina chuckled and they continued at a lazy pace, crunching through the dried leaves carpeting the forest floor. She surveyed their surroundings and recognized the circle clearing where she had been over a year ago, when she met the dark stranger named Angus. She pulled the reins to stop her horse and a quiver rippled over her body. Angus never returned as he said he would in his parting comment. She urged Heather forward into the forest, enjoying the solitude of the trees.

A rustling of leaves in the distance snatched her attention, and she hugged her cloak tighter. Another rustling and she grabbed the knife tucked into her boot, the boot dagger with the silver inlaid design she bought for Kehr that night she first met Broderick. Holding the blade out in defense, she waited and listened. A light, frozen breeze blew past her, stinging her cheeks…but nothing else. No sounds in the distance, just the thrumming of her heart in her ears. Nothing came out of the darkness but the wind. The dagger gave her some peace of mind. She sighed and shook her head, scolding herself for being so jumpy at the slightest noise.

Davina laughed. "Peace of mind, indeed."

Heather nodded again in response to her mistress's voice.

Urging Heather forward, she kept her leisurely pace. As of late, her heart had been more troubled than ever in her life. And why? Because of some wandering Gypsy. She forever dwelled on their encounters—the feel of his lips and his hands on her body; the tremors vibrating through her from his kisses; the fire he ignited in her belly and other intimate places. All of these were new to her, something at which Ian's courting only hinted. Just as Ian's true nature had been unknown to her, she didn't know Broderick's true nature.

She corrected herself and turned her horse back toward Stewart Glen. She had a pretty good idea of the kind of nature Broderick possessed. He revealed it the first night he came back into her life—a rogue, a womanizer, a man who loved a challenge and went after what he wanted without mercy. "Nay," she said aloud. "Broderick MacDougal is not the kind of man I want in my life." Why did her words not sound convincing upon her ears? Davina harrumphed. What reason did she have to envy Rosselyn and the freedom she expressed with her body? What did such freedom buy her but a broken heart and emptiness? At least this remained the argument Davina told herself to keep hold of her convictions. Her shoulders hunched in defeat.

Heather stomped and jumped forward. Davina pulled on the reins to stop her mare and listened. A rider in the distance? The sound was strange, not quite like the hooves of a horse. Almost as if someone ran at an unnatural pace, but she shook her head at the improbability of such a notion. She turned toward the sound, but could see nothing in the shadows. The darkness startled her. How had the dusk faded into night upon her without notice? Davina gripped the knife and kicked her mount into a steady pace on toward the castle and away from the unseen person approaching. She could be running from nothing, she reminded herself, trying to calm the fear stabbing her gut. But when the pace of the pursuer quickened to match her speed, she unleashed her fear with full force. Davina leaned forward against her mare's head and slapped her crop against Heather's neck.

The nightmares of Ian came rushing back, and she whimpered. Gripping the knife in one hand for strength and the crop in the other, she glanced over her shoulder. She could see nothing, but he sounded as if he were right on top of her. Davina urged Heather faster, but the mare labored under her demands, more so now than normal if Davina hadn't run her so hard at the beginning of their ride. The curse for herself never left her lips as her pursuer yanked her from her saddle. She let out a blood-curdling scream and flailed her arms and legs about, trying to escape the solid embrace about her waist. Her captor landed squarely on the ground, still holding her. When Davina had a slight footing, she turned her knife on him, but he knocked the blade from her hand in one swipe. With ease, he wrestled her to the ground, and the air left her in one gust when he fell, full-weight, on top of her.

"Woman, you didn't even give me a chance to identify myself before you took off like a wild banshee!"

His creamy voice rumbled from his broad chest, moving over her body, leaving relief in its wake, followed by a trembling rage. At last, she had her breath back. "You inconsiderate, bumbling ox!" she screeched. She struggled to get out from under Broderick, but surrendered from the useless effort. "How could I have known you rode after me? I heard a rider coming and I dared not linger to discover who it was!" She scanned the clearing, seeing only Heather. "And where is your horse?"

Broderick chuckled.

"Besides, if I had known it was you, I might have tried harder to get away!"

Broderick rolled over, taking Davina with him, laughter pouring from his mouth. He continued laughing, her words—it seemed—more than he could bear.

A combination of the tension easing from her body, his weight lifted off of her, and the relief over being safe, caused her to drop her guard and get caught up in his merriment. Her muffled giggles soon grew to healthy guffaws, and the two of them rolled around in the leaves, their mouths hanging open with no sound coming forth from laughing so hard. When the amusement abated and they caught their breath, Broderick pulled Davina on top of him and pushed her hair off her face, some of which had come loose from the net. The darkness around them didn't afford her a clear view of him, but she could see he smiled at her. His thumbs caressed her cheeks, as his hands framed her face, then touched her parted lips and her breathing became shallow with yearning. The fierce heart beating beneath her hand in his chest seemed to pump her excitement to a fevered level, and when Broderick pulled her in for a kiss, she surrendered.

Broderick spread intoxicating kisses over her cheeks, brow, lips, and chin. His mouth fluttered lower as his hands unfastened her cloak. She gasped when his hot tongue trailed a molten path to her neckline. In seconds his fingers pulled the cord lacing her bodice and exposed her breasts to the chilling night air. With gentle hands cupping her flesh, his tongue flicked across her nipples. Davina reveled at the touch of his mouth on her bare skin, his hair between her fingers and against her lips as she kissed his brow and smelled the fragrance of lavender mixed with his own masculine essence. His mouth met hers again, their tongues performing a sensual dance, swirling, touching, teasing, and his hard shaft pressed against her belly. Broderick grabbed Davina's thighs, spreading them until she straddled him. She ground her mons against him, her breathing fast and desperate.

Davina gasped as his hands smoothed up her legs to the center of her craving. She arched into his fingers and her tongue probed the depths of his mouth, tasting every part she could explore. She nibbled at his lips, his chin, and his earlobe as he stroked the moistness between her legs. *Oh, what a divine feeling! No one talks about the wondrous sensations!*

"'Tis only the beginning," Broderick whispered devilishly, his hot breath against her ear.

Her face flushed self-consciously at how far she'd let him go, but before she could push off him, he brought her face down for another seeking kiss. Davina melted into the flavor of him. His mouth seared more exhilarating kisses across her jaw to her throat, as he rolled on top of her. Davina cried out. A sharp pain pierced her neck, and she froze in Broderick's embrace.

The sharp pain at her throat. His face buried in her neck. The euphoric feeling moving through her body. These unknown, yet familiar, memories assailed her mind.

Broderick leapt away from her, leaving her to stare at his back in a daze. Searching the ground where she laid, Davina found the dagger Broderick had knocked from her hands and realized she had rolled on top of the blade and grazed her neck. Her fingers sought the wound and came back wet and sticky. "Broderick?"

"You bleed," his voice rasped.

"I know." She rose to her feet and felt the cut again. Though a shallow nick, it bled enough for her to grab the kerchief from her sleeve. "All is well." She winced as she patted the cloth on her neck. Refastening her cloak, she reached toward him, but he retreated. How odd that such a fierce and domineering man would let something like blood bother him. "You are not afraid of a little blood, are you?" She meant the words to be a tease, but they came out much more serious in light of the strange images in her mind.

Broderick spun around, and Davina froze when his silver, glowing gaze penetrated the darkness. "The only thing that frightens me about blood," he said with a harsh rasp, "is my passion for it." The deep grating of his voice sent a shiver through Davina's flesh. Broderick seemed to tremble as his hands gripped her shoulders. "I can hear your thoughts, Davina. You know I can. What happened out here? Who was the man who attacked you?"

Her mouth fell open and she reminded herself of his mystic gifts. "I…I know not."

"What were you doing out here?" His voice grew more gruff and hoarse with each word he spoke. "Were you out riding like tonight?"

"Nay, I was—" She stopped, not comfortable enough with Broderick to tell him of the attempt at taking her own life; but then, he probably knew that now, too.

The glow in Broderick's eyes grew more luminescent and he turned away, hiding his face, his breathing ragged. Too fast for her to understand every detail of what happened, Broderick planted her on her saddle. With a sound slap to Heather's rump, the animal dashed through the trees and biting wind, Davina clutching Heather's mane in an attempt to stay mounted. Several times she tried pulling the reins to stop, but failed, the frightened animal never slowing her pace until the castle torches came into view in the distance.

With great effort, Davina pulled Heather to a stop outside the castle gate, staring back into the forest from where she came. *His passion for blood?* Did she imagine the molten silver glow in his eyes? Even in the darkness, harsh lines marred his face and he held a menacing glare. And what of his interest in Angus? How were they connected? Or were they? And what of Broderick's pursuit of her? She didn't see his horse, and yet how else could he have chased her? She urged Heather to go back and demand some answers, but her mare reared up, a whining protest shrieking out of her. Surveying the darkness and trees, Davina shivered in the lashing wind, and resigned to confront him another time. The icy breeze fondled her, and she shook from the cold penetrating her breasts. She realized in a gasp that the front of her gown still lay open, her bosom bare to the elements. Blushing and turning her horse into the shadows, she fixed her gown with trembling fingers, and then turned to trot into the courtyard.

She handed Heather's reins to Fife and hurried upstairs to her room. When she found her chamber empty, Davina concluded with relief that Rosselyn was probably at the camp with her Gypsy lover. She poured water into her basin and, examining her reflection, washed the blood from her throat and dabbed what little bled onto her gown and cloak. Her appearance disheveled, she imagined the impression she must have made on Fife and the others who witnessed her return—leaves tangled in her hair and strands which escaped the net, blood on her neckline, her mouth red and swollen from Broderick's kisses.

Lilias knocked, but entered Davina's chamber without waiting for permission. "Dear Lord, child!" she exclaimed and dashed to Davina's side. "What happened?"

"I'm well, M'ma," she said, pushing away her mother's doting hands. "Heather became startled and I fell from the saddle. 'Tis nothing serious, really."

In spite of Davina's protests, Lilias helped her dress the wound. While Davina changed into her nightgown, her mother cleaned the blood from the dress.

"Would you like me to bring up your supper?" Lilias offered.

Davina's stomach protested at the mention of food. "Nay, M'ma. Too much excitement, methinks."

Lilias nodded and planted a kiss to Davina's brow before leaving. Davina climbed into bed. Alone in her room, her fear and dread tumbled down upon her, sending shuddering waves through her body. His passion for blood and the silver glow in his eyes—was he a madman? The silver glow had to be some trick of the moonlight. Davina shook her head. She saw such a silver glow in the parlor, too, and no moon shone indoors. She closed her mind tightly against the strange memories trying to surface, of another pair of eyes that glowed with the same silver light. Davina succumbed to waves of tears until exhaustion claimed her and she slipped into a deep sleep.

Broderick tossed the wolf carcass into the fire he built, his blood lust abated for a time until he could acquire human blood to stave the final demands of the Hunger. He paced the forest clearing, furious for not feeding before engaging with Davina. He had just awakened, lying there in the dark, thinking of her. His body already tingled with arousal from the erotic dreams that continued to leave him unfulfilled and aching for this woman, so when she rode by, he threw his senses to the winds. Chasing after her on foot was another foolish move, but with everything else that happened, he believed he distracted her enough not to question it overmuch.

Broderick moaned from the bulge nestled between his legs. Davina let loose an uninhibited and blazing fire he glimpsed in their other exchanges. He finally had a thrilling dose—and he hadn't needed to charm her at all. Her feelings were genuine, which meant she was beginning to trust him. His loins stirred even more at the remembered encounter, and he closed his eyes a moment to relive her in his mind. Broderick wanted very much to be the one to show Davina what passion meant, how glorious indeed their lovemaking could be, and how to unleash the animal inside.

"Stay on target, man!" Broderick corrected himself. *This is what Angus wants!*

When Broderick tried to push away the memories of how Angus entrapped him the last time, he shook his head. *Nay! Feel that pain, he encouraged. Remember how it feels to lose everything you have ever loved. Let the pain remind you of what will transpire if you let such foolishness happen again.*

217

When he asked her about Angus, she seemed very willing to open up about the experience. He had been so close to getting the information he sought, but he didn't know how much longer he could control himself, and if he didn't get Davina away from him, he knew it would be the death of her. He had no choice but to send her away.

Broderick took another step forward and stepped on something hard underfoot. Davina's dagger—still with a drying smear of her blood on the blade. The Hunger roused enough for him to lose his senses and he couldn't help but savor this one, small bit of her. His tongue touched the blade and took her blood into his mouth. Though not enough to learn everything about Davina, he closed his eyes and tried to absorb as much as he could in this minute taste. A fury of flashes assaulted him, images of a man wielding a strap, his face twisted with rage, and a stab of fear pricked his heart. Broderick grumbled at the visions locked in his mind, at the fear he sensed as Davina's. This man, who matched the images he'd seen from her before, who caused her such torture and blocked what Broderick wanted, generated a hatred from the black depths of his soul. He longed to erase the sorrow she experienced at the hands of this brutal man, or do his best to replace the nightmares with new, thrilling, loving encounters. Broderick moaned and closed his eyes against his yearnings.

Getting married and having a family were his main goals in life. Revenge through immortality had its price, but his desires for a family never went away. Until he curbed those desires, this would be the weakness Angus would use to his advantage.

Broderick turned the small blade in his hand, and the Hunger stirred as he remembered the taste of her blood. He noted the silver Celtic designs inlaid down the length of the blade on each side. Narrowing his eyes, he wondered if this would be enough to kill a Vamsyrian. Studying the amount of silver, he honestly couldn't be sure.

He faced the direction of Davina's castle. Enough time passed. She wouldn't return. Tucking the knife into his sporran, he hiked toward the village to release his anger and frustration on someone who deserved it. He set off to feed.

Stewart Glen was, by no means, a bustling town of merchantry or growth; but it had most definitely grown over the years to have enough separation of poverty from the more well-to-do portions of the society. Wandering through that poorer section of town, such living conditions still amazed Broderick, no matter how many times he saw them. The stench of death and disease permeated his senses, and each step slopped through the mud-ridden walkways, the air stagnant and spoiled. The people here had little to offer society and begged their survival, living off scraps or left over charity. Soiled, crippled men hid in dark corners here and there, holding their empty hands out for food or offerings. Women tucked back into the shambling huts to guard their sleeping children. Broderick pressed a coin into any outstretched hand on his stroll.

The corners of his mouth turned up at the stalking footsteps trailing behind him like a ghost, and the Hunger stirred. Broderick pressed another *billon* penny into the hand of a lad and carried on. The footsteps closed in, and Broderick sauntered down a darkened street that ended at a stone wall.

A knife held out in front of him, the stalker entered the passageway, but stopped at seeing Broderick waiting for him. The man sized up his victim. Broderick could hear his thoughts like a whisper on the wind, the chap scolding himself for making a mistake in underestimating the size of his target in the dark. The man reeked of sweat and urine.

Broderick smiled. "Looking for something, lad?"

The man's mouth settled into a hard line. "Give me that coin, or you will never see the light of day again!"

Broderick shook his head, laughing at the threat, and stepped toward him.

Fear and desperation motivating him, the man lunged forward and pushed his knife into

Broderick's gut. Broderick grunted as the blade went deep to the hilt, then shook his head, extracting and tossing the blade aside. The wound closed. In a flash, he gripped the man's throat in his hand, turning his head to the side. Broderick settled his gaze onto the artery drumming against his thumb, and saliva gathered around his tongue. The man gasped. Broderick's incisors pushed against his upper lip as the familiar pain shot across his gums to his cheekbones.

Opening his mouth, he showed his fangs to the intended victim. As the man struggled against Broderick's grip, the Hunger burned in his belly, begging to be satisfied. Maintaining control, he bit down into the man's flesh and drank deep his blood. As he fed, though, guilt assailed his heart. As was his habit, he would fill his victim's minds with horrific images in the hopes it would change their ways. Now he hesitated. Though these dregs of society fed from the weak like parasites, Broderick never believed he had the right to take life away from them. Everyone deserved a chance to live, but not at the expense of others. And wasn't he a parasite, as well?

After the Hunger subsided enough, he pulled away from the encounter and let the man fall to the dirty street. Broderick stood over the man's limp and moaning form, closing his eyes tight, struggling to regain control. He breathed heavy, pressing his fists against the cold stone as the Hunger fought to finish the man off, but Broderick reined it in. This was always a struggle of wills as Broderick forced the Hunger to retreat for another night. Eventually, it would give in, Broderick once more in control of his senses.

He straightened, drew a deep, calming breath, then propped the man against the wall. Broderick pierced the pad of his thumb and smeared his immortal blood on the wounds to heal them. He grabbed the man's face and forced him to see eye-to-eye. "You have been spared," Broderick hissed, and the man's eyes grew wide with understanding. "You now know the fear to be preyed upon as you prey upon others." Broderick pressed his palm to the man's forehead, willing away this encounter and leaving only the fear of the consequences. He left the man dazed and confused, slipping into the shadows and vanishing from sight with hopes this new tactic would be a better approach.

Broderick entered the camp later than usual. Veronique scrunched her eyebrows and tilted her head. Where had he been?

"*Bon soir*, Veronique," he mumbled. He added more wood to the fire pit and prepared himself for his night of fortune telling. Broderick avoided her. This did not sit well with Veronique.

Activity across the camp caught her attention. Nicabar rode into the site with a young woman mounted behind him, her face glowing and eyes alight. She was Davina's handmaid, and Veronique grumbled. Nicabar dismounted, and then helped the woman down. Veronique snorted. *Ugly Scottish women! What did Broderick and Nicabar see in them?* Envy twisted Veronique's heart when they embraced and kissed before Nicabar led the woman into his caravan.

Veronique stomped into her own wagon and pouted on the tiny bed. Jealousy burned her face and curled her fingers into fists. *Damn that Davina!* Broderick's attraction to her left Veronique pounding her fists against her pillow in frustration. Davina's eyes were wide and took up too much of her face, like an owl, and her nose looked like a pig's! She was much prettier than that Scottish woman, and had much more to offer Broderick. She'd been with Broderick longer, knew all about him and his past, the losses he experienced and endured. She knew everything about him, and lay waiting—a ripe young woman filled with need for him. This Davina did nothing but fight Broderick. Why would he want someone who didn't want him?

Veronique's mind spun from the torrent of jealousy ripping through her. She had to find a way to make Broderick realize this Davina was not right for him. She could learn something about Davina to make Broderick not want her anymore. Veronique sat up with a new energy surging through her. She could learn something from Nicabar. She had seen his mistress trailing after Davina the night they first entered the camp. She would be very close to Davina. She must speak with Nicabar early on the morrow and try to learn what she could from him. Veronique settled into her bed with hope in her heart.

Rosselyn snuggled against Nicabar in the lamp light of his caravan. "Does the fortune teller—the large man, not Amice—does he have many love interests in the towns you travel to?"

Nicabar furrowed his brow and pushed away. He sat at the edge of the bed, his back to her. "Why?"

Confused by his behavior, she stared at his rigid form, and a wide grin spread across her face. "Are you jealous?"

He turned toward her, a frown on his mouth. "Why do you ask about the *dukker* while you are in my bed?"

Rosselyn didn't want to excite his anger anymore, though his jealousy made her giddy. "I don't ask about him for myself. 'Tis my mistress for whom I ask."

Shifting away from her again, he refused to twist around, in spite of Rosselyn pulling upon his arm to face her. "Nicabar, who am I here with this night?"

"Me, which is why—"

"Aye! And who has just made wonderful love to me, made my soul sing with ecstasy?"

He fidgeted and then turned his profile toward her. The corner of his mouth turned up at her compliment.

Rosselyn sat up and put her hand upon his cheek, making him face her directly. "I apologize for the timing of my question. Please forgive me?"

He nodded, but still maintained some of his guard.

"Think upon this: How can you possibly think I would be interested in anyone else when I have the perfect man before me?"

Nicabar's defensiveness melted, replaced by embarrassment.

Rosselyn pulled him down next to her and planted a sound kiss upon his lips, joyous that he returned her kiss with as much enthusiasm. "I ask about him because methinks he and Davina are a smart match."

"Are they, now?" Nicabar kissed the beauty mark on her right shoulder.

"Aye, but she's having trouble seeing this match." Rosselyn sighed. "Mistress Davina had a husband who beat her terribly and she doesn't trust any man, especially one as large and intimidating as Broderick." She sat up. "He would never hurt her would he? Does he give in to violent fits? I asked Amice, but I fear she may be biased."

Nicabar laughed. "Broderick? Oh, not him. He's a jovial spirit and takes nothing to heart." He cradled Rosselyn's arm and kissed the mole on the inside of her elbow.

Rosselyn smiled. "Good. Mistress Davina needs someone like him."

"Playing match maker?" His lips trailed to the mark at her wrist. Obviously, he was in one of his moods to kiss each one of the little raisin spots decorating her skin. They never meant much to her…until she met Nicabar.

"Well, I want to see her happy."

"You seek to make a match of her and Broderick because…?"

Rosselyn had been in turmoil about the predictions and insight Amice shared with her ever since that day she came to town with Seamus. Certainly, once she shared the secret she harbored since Parlan's death, Davina would never speak to her again. Turning the possibilities and situation over and over in her mind, she concluded this must be the reason she was destined to be with the Gypsies. Davina would never want to see her, and her only recourse would be to disappear. All the same, leaving Davina would be easier knowing she had someone to care for her other than family.

"Rosselyn? What troubles you?"

Snapping out of her niggling thoughts, she breathed deep and lay beside Nicabar again. "I fear Davina is feeling more and more uncomfortable about the time you and I spend together."

"I see." He kissed the mole nestled between her breasts.

"If she had someone special, methinks she wouldn't be reminded of her loneliness." She sighed. "I should return to the castle even now."

His lips claimed hers with hunger and his arousal pressed against her thigh. "We must make love one more time," he breathed against her mouth. "Then I will take you back."

Never had she been with a man who had as much desire for her as Nica. He rolled on top of her to make love for the third time that day, with as much energy as their first coupling. Tearing themselves away from their private time together, they dressed and Rosselyn mounted behind Nicabar, bareback on his horse.

At the castle just outside the gate, Rosselyn pressed her hand to his arm to get his attention. "Truly, Mistress Davina and I must spend more time together until I can convince her she and Broderick are a perfect pair, but methinks you and I won't have to sacrifice time with each other, after all. Pray steer your horse to the rear of the castle." Nicabar obeyed, and as they rounded to the back side of the curtain wall, Rosselyn pointed to the thick bushes. "There!" They dismounted and she led Nicabar over, glancing around to be sure no one was about. Rosselyn pulled him behind her and toddled around the bushes to a small space between the thick shrubs and the wall. Pressing against the stone, it rumbled beneath her fingers. As she pushed, she grunted to shove the stone aside. "Follow me," she whispered and entered through a secret door, closing the opening behind them. They stood on the other side of the wall, behind a stone and wood building. "We can meet here after everyone has bedded down for the evening. Be sure not to let anyone see you. Tell no one of this entrance." Pointing to the building, she said, "These are the stables."

Rosselyn clutched his hand and led him around to the side. She gestured to be silent with an index finger over her lips, and peered around the wall to scan the grooming area. The horses stood in their stables, and the harnesses and tack hung neatly along the wall. Fife was nowhere about, so she pulled Nicabar in after her. "There is fresh hay up there," she said indicating the loft.

Nicabar smiled in the dim lighting of the stables and took Rosselyn by the hand. "Just how fresh *is* the hay?" he asked and persuaded her up the ladder before him. When they reached the top, his mouth covered hers, muffling her laughter, and they fell into the loft, fumbling around their clothes in haste. Dizzy with desire and a sense of freedom, Rosselyn tumbled and frolicked with Nicabar.

"Jealous?" Nicabar teased.

Veronique squared her shoulders. "*Non*! I am not jealous. I just want to know who she is."

"'Tis no business of yours." He turned and continued chopping wood. Veronique's relentless pursuit amused Nicabar. He knew she struggled with the rampant emotions of a young woman just awakening to the sensations of her body—nothing more. Aye, he'd been there before with such emotions. He knew she was convinced it was true love, but one day she would reflect with understanding, and laugh just as he did.

"That Davina was with her the first night they were here," she resumed. "Is she her maid?"

"Why do you want to know?" he asked, not missing a swing.

She hesitated. "I just do."

"Then I still say it is none of your business."

Nicabar kept swinging. He split logs, continuing his persistent pounding, occasionally glancing up at her, hiding his curiosity. On occasion, he glimpsed at her, but refused to speak. Veronique stomped her foot and cursed in French. "This Davina woman is coming between me and Broderick, and I want to know more about her. If your mistress is her maid, then she knows everything about this Davina."

Nicabar chopped wood for several minutes before he answered. "Aye, she is her maid." He chopped. "Do you think to become her friend and learn something of Davina?"

"*Non*, I hoped you would tell me something about her."

"What makes you think I will tell you anything?" Nicabar stopped and met her gaze, his chest heaving from his efforts. "There is a price for my services, Veronique."

She shifted and dared to venture, "What kind of price?"

He smiled, then sauntered up to her and touched her chin with a curled finger. His hot breath streamed out of his mouth and against her cheek, like bursts of smoke on the cold air, his shiny chest heaving under his labored breaths. "Let me be your first."

Veronique stepped back. "I am saving myself for Broderick!" she protested. Nicabar shrugged and chopped wood. After a moment longer, Veronique stomped off, mumbling. Nicabar chuckled and kept chopping, shaking his head.

"A visitor?" Davina asked Myrna, distracted from playing with Cailin. She turned her gaze to the midday light through the window. How unusual for him to pay a visit. Broderick could be trying to be the gentleman, calling in the afternoon instead of an evening visit like their night of chess. Unsure of how to feel, she steadied her breath and turned back to Myrna. "Please give me just a few moments and I will be down." Myrna nodded and bowed out of the nursery.

After laying Cailin down for a nap—which proved much easier than Davina expected—Davina primped in the mirror before she proceeded downstairs to the parlor. The polite smile Davina donned faded when she entered the room, and she adopted a defensive posture. Scolding, Davina remembered she never had any direct exchange with the golden-haired Gypsy girl standing in the center of the parlor. Though, in their brief and distant encounters, Veronique may have held an obvious contempt for her, Davina would rise above the girl's childish behavior. Veronique hadn't yet turned around or acknowledged Davina stood in the room, so she changed her demeanor and cleared her throat to announce her presence. With a pleasant smile and lilt in her voice, she greeted, "What a pleasant surprise, Veronique!" and forged ahead with her hands extended.

The Gypsy girl shrank from Davina, not taking her offered hands. Davina clasped her hands before her and held her smile. "What can I do for you, Veronique? Would you like some refreshments?"

She refused hospitality with a shake of her head and showed an open disdain toward Davina, so Davina became suspicious of the girl's intentions. Veronique stood with defiance; her arms crossed and chin out. "Broderick MacDougal is not what he seems," the girl said.

Davina steeled herself. "How do you mean?"

Veronique stepped forward, her hands on her hips. "Have you noticed anything unusual about him?"

Davina crossed her arms. "Such as?"

"Such as a silver glow in his eyes."

CHAPTER EIGHT

With luck, Davina held the intake of breath threatening to give away her surprise. She cleared her throat. "Nay," she lied.

Veronique narrowed her eyes. "*Buveur de sang,*" she said. "That is what Broderick is—drinker of blood."

Davina flitted her eyes over Veronique's frame. "What are you saying?"

Veronique thrust her wrist toward Davina. "*Regardez,* see my wrist? See the scars?"

Davina leaned closer and inspected the scars—two white marks, diagonal along the length of her wrist. She nodded.

"It is true. Broderick has fed from me. He needs blood to survive. Because of what he is, he cannot face the heat of the sun. He must slumber during the day and comes out only at night, just after sunset."

Davina wanted all this to sound as preposterous as it should—and it would have had she not seen the very signs Veronique spoke of. Her heart pounded in her ears. "I've never heard of such a creature," she continued, trying to talk herself back into a state of sanity.

Veronique shrugged and stepped back, crossing her arms again. "You can find out for yourself...if you have the stomach. Cut your skin when you see Broderick next and pay close attention to his reaction. He may move away from you. He may stare at you with a deep hunger. It is then you will see the silver core of his eyes. It is a sign of the Hunger—his lust for blood."

Davina's face grew hot, and sweat sprang out upon her upper lip. Her fingertips touched the healing cut on her neck, absently fingering the scab that formed. Broderick's reaction the night she cut her neck on her dagger and his words all made sense. Davina turned away from Veronique, numb and speechless.

"You believe me, *non*?"

Gaining her composure, she turned back to Veronique with her hands folded before her. "I'm afraid this is a little foolish for me to believe, Veronique. Such a claim almost sounds comical." Davina forced her mouth into a smirk as her body trembled.

Veronique jumped in Davina's face. "You are a fool, Scot! I do not lie!" She mumbled on in frustrated French and marched toward the door. Before leaving, she turned to Davina. "That will be just fine! Your ignorance will get you killed!" The slam of the door echoed across the walls, leaving Davina's nerves frazzled in the furious wake of Veronique.

Davina sat down on the nearest piece of furniture, trying to steady her trembling legs. Though the reality of Broderick didn't match her fantasies, this new reality unfolding before her was turning into a nightmare.

"Davina?"

She flinched. Rosselyn entered the parlor so quietly, Davina hadn't heard the door open. Or, more likely, Davina's thoughts so preoccupied her mind, she blocked out any noises. "Aye, Rosselyn?"

"Pardon me for saying so, but you don't look well." Rosselyn came to her side and grasped Davina's hand. "Your hands are chilled. Come, let us get you warmed."

With mindless abandon, Davina followed her handmaid out of the parlor and up to her bedchamber, where they sat beside the fire. Rosselyn rambled about several things in their limited conversation, but Davina heard nothing.

"Methinks you should rest, Davina." Rosselyn didn't wait for her mistress's response, but carried on about herself and Nicabar while she helped Davina change into a more comfortable house dress.

"Thank you for your tending, Roz." She squeezed her handmaid's shoulders affectionately. "The rest of the night is yours."

Rosselyn stood before Davina, her hands twisting nervously as her eyes reflected an inner turmoil.

"What worries you?" Davina pulled her friend to the settee at the foot of her bed, grateful for this distraction.

Opening her mouth to say something, Rosselyn searched Davina's face, and yet no words came forth. She tried again, closing her eyes and swallowing to get past some unknown fear Davina could only guess at.

"Goodness, Roz, what has you so anxious?" Her friend's behavior began to trouble her, now.

Taking a deep breath, Rosselyn finally spoke. "It has been very difficult for me since Lord Parlan's death."

Davina's heart leapt. "Aye, Rosselyn! I hoped we would be able to share this together. You have no idea what a burden it has been to grieve alone. Or perhaps you do, seeing you're willing to share."

Tears welling in her eyes, Rosselyn swallowed and seemed to struggle to speak over her grief.

Davina hugged Rosselyn and cried with her friend. "Thank you for opening your heart, Roz. I cannot tell you how much it means to me!"

Pulling back from Davina, Rosselyn nodded, smiled, and then excused herself from the room. Davina sat staring after her friend's retreat, not sure what just transpired. Rosselyn appeared as if she would continue, but instead left. Perhaps this was all her friend could handle for the moment. Davina's spirits lifted at this new beginning.

She checked in on Cailin, who still napped, emitting gentle snores. Davina laid down upon the lounging couch and settled into the warmth for some security, while the daylight faded from the overcast sky and the recollection of Veronique's visit shifted over her like a dark cloud. She stared into the fireplace, her eyes wide and distant, shaking her head. She wanted to believe Veronique lied. Broderick had never—and she believed he would never—hurt her. Yet his words and the silver glow in his eyes gave her doubts. She always went back to those facts.

She buried her face into a decorative pillow to surround herself in the false security it offered. When she started drifting into sleep, she rose and retired to the bed.

With fresh blood flowing through his veins, Broderick combed the area for Angus and signs of other lairs, but he found nothing. He kept his search limited, though, to the immediate area, afraid to venture out too far for him to sense Angus approaching the Gypsy camp. With no progress, he made a direct path for the castle of Stewart Glen. In no time, he dashed through the forest with his immortal speed and arrived at the curtain wall on the western side.

An easy leap over the wall and a dash across the courtyard, he stood beside the stone structure, just below the landing of Davina's chamber. He crouched to make his jump to the landing and stopped.

Why am I here? He searched the courtyard, as if he would find the answer there. Regarding the landing a second time, his reasons were becoming as obscured as the moon, which hid behind the clouds. Blackness covered the sky and masked him in shadow. The day was late enough for Davina to be sleeping. Nagging thoughts about this being an excuse to get information he already knew gnawed his conscience. He rejected them.

In an instant, he jumped the height and stood upon the landing. Broderick peered into the narrow, barred window. A mound of covers lay heaped upon her bed, rising and falling with her soft breathing. Stepping to the double doors, he inched one door open without incident. He peered through the velvet curtains and into the room, lit with a glowing red light from the embers burning in the hearth. A need growing inside his belly drew him to her bedside and he closed the distance.

Davina lay on her back, her coppery curls fanned upon her pillows, a slight part to her full lips. So peaceful. She seemed without any troubles...at least until her eyebrows creased together. Davina stirred and moaned in protest. Slipping off his boots, Broderick pulled the covers back, laid his body by her side and, almost as a reflex, she turned into him. His fingers pushed the cinnamon locks from her damp forehead still creased in confusion or frustration. Placing his palm upon her brow, he closed his eyes and entered her dreams.

The dream world always held strange, symbolic, abstract images, but he managed to make some sense of her internal realm. A beast ravaged the servants of her household—a hunched over creature, snarling and drooling, blood dripping off of its canine teeth. Red hair, tangled and matted from the blood of its victims, cascaded down its shoulders and blended with the red hair on its body. Davina huddled in a corner, pleading for the beast to leave everyone alone. Broderick inserted himself into the scene and approached Davina.

"Oh, I knew they were lies!" she exclaimed and ran into his arms. "I knew it couldn't be you!"

Broderick held Davina as she wept. What lies? Who couldn't he be? Veronique stood in the far corner of the room, shouting to Davina. "He is a drinker of blood! He is not what he seems!"

Broderick turned to Davina. "'Tis over, Davina. 'Tis safe you are." She continued to cling to him, crying tears of gratitude.

Easing her back from him, Broderick said, "Davina, there is indeed a monster." Her eyes grew wide, but he shushed her. "Nay, not here at this moment, but you have met him."

She stared, confused, but that gave way to a dawning realization.

"Aye, you know of whom I speak. This man who attacked you…"

A crease formed over her brow. "He didn't attack me. He saved me." She bit her bottom lip in frustration. "He saved me from myself as I tried to take my own life."

"Davina, I need you to take me to the night he attacked you."

"I told you, he didn't attack me. Why do you keep insisting he has?" She pushed away. "His divine message told me you would be back for me, but 'tis obvious to me you don't hold the same wishes I do." She showed him her back.

Broderick could feel her mind resisting him, which meant she would be waking, and he didn't want her catching him in her bed. Trying one more time, he stepped forward and placed comforting hands upon her shoulders. "Please forgive me, I misspoke."

Turning to face him, she seemed to settle back into her dream world as her mind released her resistance.

"Can you take me to that night…" He forced himself to say the words she wanted to hear. "To the night he saved you?"

"What is your interest in him, Broderick? You asked me about him in the forest clearing." Her eyes grew wide and she stepped back. "The night your eyes glowed with silver. The night you spoke of your…" She swallowed. "Your passion for blood," she said in a whisper.

The beast returned, snarling in the corner and baring teeth dripping with blood, a silver glow pulsing in its eyes. Broderick enfolded Davina in his arms in spite of her resistance and hushed her, stroking her hair and feeling her relax. When he conveyed a peaceful influence over her, Broderick sensed her mind's resistance and Davina pressed against his chest. Her natural ability to block her thoughts was an obstacle he dare not traverse. Pushing her any further at this point would also bring her out of sleep, so he retreated.

Broderick eased out of her dreams, leaving images of soft, ardent kisses and soothing strokes on her bare skin. He did what he needed to do to keep her from thinking he was the monster in her dream, for he couldn't bear the thought of it…and yet this was the truth. He would eventually have to tell Davina what he was. Strangely enough, this all confirmed the dream he had during the day, with Davina yelling at Veronique while the young

French girl tried to convince Davina of what he was. *I'm going to blister Veronique's arse!* He sighed, though, glad to see the crease above Davina's brow gone. Kissing her lips, he had every intention of leaving her to a peaceful rest, but Davina responded with a breathy moan, catching Broderick short. Cupping her face in his hand, he probed more with his mouth, pressing his lips against hers, groaning as they opened to him and her tongue touched him with sweet, seeking caresses. The slow, lethargic ministrations of Davina's mouth in her dreamy demeanor coaxed Broderick into arousal, sending tremors through his limbs, reminding him of the built-up desire he'd been harboring for her since his first night back into this town. His hands smoothed over her back and pulled her body against his.

Davina's body trembled at Broderick's touch. They were lying on a cloud, thankfully away from the horrid images of the beast, pressed against each other in their heated exchange. The cool night air flowed around them, but nothing could cool the fire igniting her skin every place Broderick touched her. His mouth so hot against hers. His fingers like burning embers, his body, like a roaring flame against her own, and Davina wanted to be consumed by him. "Davina…" The sound of his voice saying her name sent her stomach fluttering.

"Broderick," she breathed back, and the sound of her voice caused the light, airy sensation of the clouds to dissipate. She faded back into the solid presence of her bedchamber. But Broderick still held her in his arms, kissing her, holding her, pressing his arousal against her leg, and a shudder of pleasure gushed through her. Davina's hands explored Broderick's body, feathering over his hard abdomen, the expanse of his chest, the strength of his shoulders, the silkiness of his hair.

"Blossom…"

The deep, husky sound caused her to peep her eyes open. "Broderick…" She realized he lay next to her in her bed, his magnificent form pressed against her, her body hot and eager for him. "You have seduced your way into my dreams," she whispered and grinned.

A gentle laugh rumbled from his chest, and he dove in for another taste of her, his mouth scorching a path over her chin, down her throat to the laced opening of her nightgown. She should question why he lay there, how he could have come out of her dreams, but he nibbled at her nipples through the thin material, and she arched her back in response to the delightful sensation. Clutching his head, she panted and moaned as his mouth found her bare skin and lapped over the erect buds, administering to one and then the other. He licked up the center of her breasts, pushing the mounds together. Davina winced, her milk-heavy flesh tender.

Broderick pulled back, worry creasing his brow. "Forgive me, blossom. I find it hard to control myself around you."

"Softer," she breathed.

He brushed his warm lips over hers, then turned caring attention back to her bosom, alternating between feather kisses, nibbling, and lapping, driving Davina to the point of madness. His large, muscular thigh nudged between her legs, and she welcomed the possession, opening to him. The sensation of his arousal against her hip made her feminine center pulse with anticipation and grow hot, and she pressed her mons against his warm leg…aching for him. As if he heard her body cry out for him, he swept his hand under her nightgown, caressed and massaged his way up her thigh and pulled her leg over his hip, wrapping her around him. His hand continued its molten path up to grip her bottom and pull her harder against his arousal.

Broderick groaned into the crook of her neck, and his seduction slowed. Pulling back from her, he cupped her face in his hand and pleaded with his eyes. "Dear God, Davina, with everything in my soul, I don't want to stop." He kissed her mouth, exploring for a moment. Then whispered, "But I need you here with me. I need you to be aware you're not dreaming. I am here—real and aching to make love to you—but only if you're willing, only if you're present."

Breathless, Davina searched his face, her body pulsing beneath him, a distinct wetness between her legs, and the very presence of Broderick an ardent need. At this moment, she didn't care about reputation, she didn't care if Broderick made love to her and then left her alone—she only knew she needed him. She darted her eyes across the room for a moment. A single glance at that door, and who lay sound asleep behind it, created a sobering moment.

The torment on Broderick's face seemed to mirror the thrashing of her insides. She wanted him as much as he wanted her, and she knew Broderick could read every thought running through her mind. For a long span of time, they stared at each other, until finally Davina surrendered, ready to compromise. *One night. What if we only spent one night—?*

"Nay, Davina. One night would never be enough for me." Broderick pulled her against him, driving all his yearning into the kiss he lavished on her, and with obvious reluctance, he pulled away. Covering Davina with her bedclothes, he sat beside her and pressed his lips to her palm. "I want all of you, Davina, for more than one night, and I won't stop until you beg me." After he put his boots back on, he lounged back upon his elbow, drawing close to her. A chuckle whispered out of him. He peeked under the covers at her thinly clad figure, and then grunted. "Even if you beg me, I may not stop."

Davina smiled and pulled the covers close to her. Kissing her brow and rising, he cleared his throat and bent forward for a deep and ceremonious bow, like a true gentleman. Sitting up, Davina covered her giggles with her pillow, for he was anything but a gentleman. With his roguish smile and maddening dimple, he winked and let himself out by the double doors.

Broderick took a very long hike in the cold night air, trying hard to ease his erection back down and bank the desire racing through his body. How close he'd been to tasting Davina, but he didn't want to take any chance she would feel guilty on the morrow, and blame him for seducing her while she slept. He couldn't win her trust by seducing her unawares, and he could see tonight she held no animosity toward him. That proved to him she had just been caught up in the dream. If she had her senses about her, he knew she would have resisted.

That failure came rushing back to him and dampened his arousal. Again, he came so close to getting the information. He dove into her mind, had her right where he needed her, and she resisted what he pressed for. Broderick chose the wrong words, but it was difficult for him to see Angus as any kind of savior. He gritted his teeth. His pride ruined his chance at getting the truth. He could have instead fed from her, but the more he grew to know her, the more that thought seemed abhorrent.

After what must have been several hours of brisk walking, Broderick managed to douse the fires burning within and marched back to the Gypsy camp. People stirred and began their daily preparations, and dawn approached in haste. He checked in with Amice to be sure all was well.

"Veronique is not in her bed," Amice informed him with a scowl.

He sighed. "I will send her to you if she's in my cave." Shaking his head, he headed to his lair. As he neared, Broderick slowed his pace and cursed under his breath. He could smell her. Resigned to the encounter, he braced for the state of undress she might be in. What better time to confront her? As he entered the cave, he lit an oil lamp for her benefit. He wanted to make sure she witnessed the full display of his disapproval and anger.

Veronique was not in the front of the cave, but the soft hush of her sleeping breath drifted on the air from the back. Shaking his head, he strode deep inside, parted the first set of heavy black curtains, and then the next. Pity filled his heart. Veronique lay like a child, curled up in the furs of his bedding, breathing the steady cadence of deep sleep. He studied her for a moment. He liked her like this— the innocent little sister he witnessed growing up, no deception or deviousness in her eyes. No ulterior motives or plans swirling around in her little head. A deep sigh escaped his lips. Veronique did more than scheme to get Davina to turn against him. She opened Broderick up to incredible risks— both by revealing what he was, as well as where he slept, coming to his cave over and over. Broderick took care to ensure no one followed him, and he came and went using his immortal speed and gifts to hide his tracks. Veronique left a blatant trail right up to the front door—a trail he had to conceal too many times.

Her clothes lay in a pile, beside her on the ground, and he cursed. Picking them up, he nudged her with his foot. *"Réveillez-tu, petite soeur."* He used his pet name for her with purpose this time, knowing it would hit home. "And don't start your protests. I'm getting very tired of them."

Veronique rubbed her eyes and sat up, the furs dropping from her body and revealing her nakedness. Broderick threw her clothes at her face. "Get dressed!"

Wide-eyed, she searched her surroundings and clutched the clothes to her chest. Settling her eyes upon Broderick, she came to realize her whereabouts. Broderick glared at her, his arms crossed, waiting for her to dress. Self-consciously she donned her clothing, her cheeks blotchy with color, and stumbled out to the front of the cave. Veronique turned to face Broderick, tapped her foot and clenched her jaw—but the tears welling in her eyes softened his heart, and he scolded himself for being such a bastard. Nevertheless, Amice was right. He needed to be more stern with her.

Broderick turned away, not wanting to see her tears. "I'm very aware of who and what you have become. I know you care a great deal for me." He addressed her then. "I care for you, too, Veronique."

Veronique's face brightened and she stepped toward him, but stopped when he held up a scolding finger.

"Listen to me and listen well, young lady. We will not…ever…be together the way you want."

"Because of that Davina," she squeaked.

"Speaking of Davina, you had no business telling her about me."

"She deserves to know the truth."

"Aye, she does, but not from you. 'Tis my truth to tell. And what I do with Davina is no business of yours. You are putting me at risk, Veronique! You exposed me when you told her what I was, and you expose me every time you come to my dwelling. Do you not see how you put me in danger during the daylight hours when I cannot defend myself?" Veronique stared at him with doe eyes. Broderick shook his head and rubbed his hands over his face. "You have never cared much about the women I have in my life. Why does this one bother you so much?"

Veronique remained silent, staring at some crack on the cave floor.

"Listen to me, Veronique. Quit wasting your time on me. We cannot have a relationship together for several reasons, and methinks you know what they are. I don't need to go into them. Your grandmother says them enough. She's right, so mind her well." Broderick, not wanting to start a debate, picked up her cloak and gave her the garment, then blew out the lamp. "I'm taking you back to the camp, little sister."

She huffed her disapproval and rattled in French obscenities as he threw her over his shoulder and raced toward the camp, using his immortal speed to avoid leaving footprints.

Veronique pounded her fist against Nicabar's caravan door, squinting at the late afternoon sun. She paused only a moment before she continued pounding.

"It's a good thing I am not in there having an afternoon nap," he said from behind her.

Veronique jumped so high, she almost fell off the makeshift wooden stairs. "Well, I am glad to see you are alone…for once!"

Nicabar shook his head and ambled toward his caravan. "No one in your kingdom has anything else to do but come to your beckoning call, eh?" He shoved past her and stepped into his dwelling. "Now if you will—"

Veronique followed him into the small wagon, slammed the door, and sat upon his bed, her fingers fumbling to unlace her bodice.

"Veronique—"

"Tell me, Nicabar!" she snapped. "Tell me everything I want to know about Davina! You will get what you asked for!"

Rosselyn stood with her mouth open as Veronique hefted up into Nicabar's caravan, eagerly following him inside. The door slammed and the wagon jostled a bit. Rosselyn's tongue felt thick in her mouth. Her stomach churned and she lost her breath. She tried to reason with herself about the several weeks she shared with Nicabar. He made no declarations of love. Their intimate moments together, as precious as they were to her and seemed to be to him, did not result in discussions of marriage or children or even future nights to come. Then why did her heart constrict so tight in her chest she feared it would crack?

A burning heat radiated from her cheeks against the cold. As a man of free will, Nicabar could bed whomever he wanted…but she would no longer be an option for him to choose. Marching over to his wagon, she took at deep breath before reaching for the door and yanking it open.

Too stunned for words, Veronique and Nicabar stood before his bed in the crouched space. Veronique's shoulders were bare and her breasts half covered. Nicabar's hands were upon Veronique's arms, just above her elbows. Both stood staring at Rosselyn with wide eyes and gaping mouths. Veronique's face changed from surprise to gloating satisfaction, and she grabbed Nicabar by the neck and brought him down for an open-mouthed kiss.

Before anyone had a moment more to respond, Rosselyn stepped into the wagon, seized Veronique by the hair, and tossed her out of the caravan onto the dirt. Slamming the door to the French whore's babbling protests, Rosselyn faced Nicabar. He had the nerve to smirk, which she promptly slapped from his face. "I may have held lofty ideas about spending my life with someone like you, but I'm not going to have such ideas about settling to be someone's whore! You want her, you can have her!"

"Rosselyn, I—"

"I don't need a man to help me accomplish my dreams." Rosselyn fought the tears stinging her eyes. "I have skills I can offer the Gypsies, and there are plenty of honest people among this camp who will take me with them, Amice being one of them." Before she made any more a fool of herself, she turned to leave the wagon.

"Rosselyn!" Nicabar spun her around to face him. When she twisted her head away, not wanting to see his bonnie dark eyes, he held her face in his hands, forcing her to face him. "You don't understand! I want nothing to do with her!"

"Then what was she doing half naked in your arms!" Rosselyn hated that tears coursed down her cheeks as she screamed at him.

"Veronique is a selfish child who will stop at nothing to get what she wants." Rosselyn struggled from his grip, but he wouldn't release her. "I may have made a mistake in trying to prove a point, but she asked for information from me about you and Davina, just so she could keep Davina away from Broderick. I told her if she wanted information…" He hesitated, obviously not comfortable about his next words. "…I told her I had to be her first." As Rosselyn wrestled with him, he protested louder, "I know that was wrong, but I was trying to show her how stupid she was, chasing after Broderick. When you saw her come in here, she was offering her virginity, tearing off her clothes. You came in as I stopped her and tried to point out how ridiculous she was being."

Rosselyn stared at him, no longer struggling, her heart breaking. "That is the most horrid excuse I have *ever* heard!" She stomped out of the caravan.

Nicabar came outside behind her and turned her to face him once more. "Rosselyn, please!" Eyes pleading, he wouldn't let her escape. "When you came in there and threw Veronique out, I smiled because I was proud of you, not because I was laughing at you."

Rosselyn clenched her jaw, fighting to stay angry with him, to not believe the words that sounded so sincere.

"And when you stood by what you believed, when you told me being with the Gypsies was your dream, my chest filled with more pride." He brushed the backs of his fingers against her cheek, wiping away her tears. "Though you were not born in a wagon or on the side of a road, you are a true Gypsy in your fiery heart, and I want no other woman by my side but you." Nicabar dropped to one knee before her and reverently kissed her hands. "I realize this is quick and we've had such little time together, but I know this deep in my heart as sure as I've known anything in my life. I want you to be my wife. Say you will be my wife and I will show you the world, *mi amor*."

Rosselyn stood before this man who stole her heart with such haste, her lips quivering with her tears.

"Answer the man!" a voice shouted.

A crowd had gathered, enclosing them within a ring of eager faces. Laughter bubbled up as joy overflowed from her heart. Gazing down at Nicabar's hopeful and handsome face, she nodded. "Aye, I will marry you."

As the crowd cheered, Nicabar leapt to his feet and swept her into his arms, twirling her around before planting her back on the ground and searing her with a kiss.

Ian Russell stared at the grave marker bearing his name. Beside it, another grave marker bore the name of his father, Munro. A mixture of fear and grief troubled his heart for a moment before he made room for relief. He was free. Ian straightened to reflect the independent man standing in his shoes.

"Can I help you?"

Ian faced a vaguely familiar man around his own age. Where had he seen him before? A name tickled his memory as a younger face, resembling the man before him, came to mind. Brian? Aye, a cousin he'd not seen since childhood.

"Is there something I can help you with?" Brian asked with a more firm voice.

"Aye, forgive me for not responding." Ian put on his best performance of grief. "I had come here expecting to find friends, and instead I find graves." He stared at the headstones again to make his point.

Brian seemed to drop his guard and approached Ian with compassion in his eyes. "'Tis sorry I am you had to find out like this. Poor souls. The Battle of Flodden."

"Aye, I guessed as much. Just coming back from that horrible experience myself." Ian lifted his shirt to display the ragged and blotchy scars along the right side of his ribs and belly.

Brian winced sympathetically. "A lucky one you are, my friend. Not many can say they walked away as we can."

Ian nodded and pulled his shirt back down.

"You look vaguely familiar. You knew Ian and Munro well? "

Ian offered a weak smile and nodded, scratching his beard. "That I did. You also look familiar to me."

The man stretched his hand out in greeting. "Brian Russell."

"Ian." He stayed his tongue before he said the rest of his name out of habit. "Ian Grant."

"Oh, the same name?"

"Aye, 'tis a common curse." Ian laughed and Brian laughed with him. "So, with the last name Russell, how are you related to Ian and Munro?"

"I be a distant cousin. When they passed on, the lands were sold to us."

"Sold to you?" Ian put on a mask of concern. "Pray, do not tell me Ian's wife—"

"Oh, nay, sir!" Brian reassured him with haste. "She's alive and well, thank our Lord. Nay, though we didn't get to see her, as her Uncle… What was his name? Oh, Tammus. Tammus Keith. He handled the exchange. He said Ian's wife be too grief stricken to stay at the holdings. We understood and are glad the property is back into Russell hands. We insisted on paying her a generous price to be sure she was taken care of. What with her inheritance and the funds from the holdings, she should fare well enough if she takes care of her spending."

Ian fought to keep his voice steady. "Aye, that was kind of you. It does my heart good to know she'll want for nothing."

"Would you like to come in, join us for supper?" Brian offered.

Clenching his fists behind his back, he dug his nails into his palms. "Thank you so very kindly, my friend, but I really must be going. I have my own family to go home to. No doubt they still think I'm long in the grave, considering the length of time I've been away."

"Are you sure?"

"Most assuredly." Ian shook Brian's hand and turned to get onto his horse, tied just inside the front gate. His knuckles turned white as he gripped the reins. "Thank you again, and I appreciate the information."

"God speed!" Brian called after Ian, who raised a trembling hand to wave farewell.

As Ian rounded the bend in the road, and certain he could neither be seen nor heard, he released a screech that made his voice hoarse. "That bitch!" He repeated the phrase, pounding the pommel of his saddle until his throat and hands hurt before he calmed and wiped his face. If he rode without stopping at an inn or tavern, Ian could make the journey to Stewart Glen with the small amount of money left, camping—he groaned—along the way. He had not anticipated everything would be gone, so his funds fell short. This woman ruined his life in more ways than one. "No pain will be too great for you, Davina. You will finally get everything you deserve, while giving me everything I deserve." Buying back this property was not his intention. He would reclaim his inheritance from Davina and finally be free to live where and how he wanted. Urging his horse forward, but mindful to keep the pace easy enough to last the ride, Ian grumbled curses for his soon-to-be-dead wife.

Veronique lagged far enough behind Nicabar to see his shape in the settling darkness. The sound of her feet crunching on the leaves echoed in her ears, setting her heart thumping in her chest, and she frequently ducked behind trees or bushes to remain hidden from his sight and his annoying habit of glancing behind him.

That Davina's ugly castle appeared around the craggy hill at the edge of the forest, Nicabar heading straight toward the structure. He followed along the western side of the wall. Veronique reached a rocky hill, which enabled her to pick up her pace and edge closer to him for a better view. Why did he not go through the front gate? Was Nicabar not welcome after he made his embarrassing proposal to the ugly Scot? Stopping at a thick growth of shrubbery, Nicabar surveyed the area, and Veronique ducked to avoid his gaze. Had he seen her? She listened for any signs, and then carefully peered over the rock. Nicabar disappeared! The sound of stone sliding against stone drifted on the crisp night air, and the bushes trembled. She waited. After a few moments of silence, she stepped forward with caution. A twig snapped and she jolted, her hand flew to her chest as she whirled around. Nothing stirred in the twilight, but then she caught movement out of the corner of her eye. She released her breath and near collapsed when a small deer scampered into the trees. Cursing for being so skittish, she turned back to her target. As she neared the bushes, faint amber light peeked through the thin branches and leaves, beyond which lay a passage in the wall. Veronique inched forward.

The young Gypsy made her way around the bush and flattened against the wall, alert to the muffled voices coming through the passage. Peering into the dark entrance, she saw what appeared to be the back of a building and some rain barrels. A devious grin spread across her lips, and she slipped inside. She brushed some webs away as she snuck through the passage. Seeing no one around, she hid beside the rain barrels and dared a cautious peek through the closed shutters of the window. Bits of hay littered the ground inside the building, one side opened to reveal stalls, hanging leather harnesses and mouth bits. The stables.

"Nica!"

Veronique squatted in fright.

"What? You love it when I do that," his voice teased.

Veronique narrowed her eyes and cursed under her breath. Nicabar and his ugly Scottish woman were in the hayloft, rolling around like animals. After listening to their grunts of passion, she was grateful she hadn't given up her virginity to him, but she still needed to resolve this problem with Davina. Veronique scampered around the stable to the side of the structure. Setting against the wall, she inclined her ear toward their voices above. Two minutes of their panting, moaning, and laughing was about all she could stand. She wanted information! Not a heated coupling!

Pouting, she made her way toward the other side of the stables. Ahead, across the courtyard, lay a door into the castle. A woman carrying two buckets came out of the door, a kerchief on her head. She waddled to the edge of the courtyard and dumped the water into a hole surrounded by stones and covered with a metal grate, then turned to go back inside. Not two moments later, the door opened, and a man came stomping out of the castle. He left the door open, and another woman stood in the doorway with her hands on her hips and a furrowed brow. "Oh, quit yer gripin', Seamus!"

The man stopped and took two steps back toward the woman in the doorway. "This is the third trip I'm making this month! Third trip! How much honey can one person eat?"

The woman stepped out, the lines on her brow vanishing, her voice softer. "You know her honey is the only thing Mistress Davina has left to keep the memory of her brother alive."

Seamus sighed and nodded. "Aye. I will make a short trip of it."

Veronique ran behind the stable to the water barrels, to hide and get closer to the passage. The loft became quiet and not too long afterwards, Seamus rode off on horseback through the front gate. As Veronique snuck back to the stone passage, Nicabar and Rosselyn burst into laughter and continued their frolicking. Veronique shook her head, exited through the passage, and headed back to the Gypsy camp. The grin on her face grew wider with each step. She bunched her hands into fists with excitement. She knew exactly what to do about that Davina!

CHAPTER NINE

Davina, Rosselyn, and Lilias sat in the parlor by the wide oriel window with their needlework projects. They took advantage of the mid-afternoon sunlight. Davina worked at her specialty of stitching delicate vines along the cuffs of one of her mother's chemises; Lilias sat before a tapestry stretched across a frame of a half-finished design, portraying the Stewart crest of her husband and the Keith crest of her own clan, a large piece that would go in the Great Hall once finished; and Rosselyn stitched floral designs on table linens. These quiet times were a welcome respite after their weekly chore of brushing clean all the woolen clothing in their wardrobes.

"Uncle Tammus said he would be back in a fortnight, did he not, M'ma?" Davina looked up from her embroidery when she didn't get an answer and saw her mother rubbing her temples. "M'ma?"

"Nay, Davina. In just a few days," Lilias whispered, squinting at her.

"Another spell of head pains," Davina said.

Lilias nodded. "I will go lie down and rest for awhile."

"Oh, we can go to the Gypsy camp, Mistress Davina!" Rosselyn offered. "Amice has wonderful herbal remedies for any ailment one might have!"

"What a wonderful idea, Roz. I'm amazed I never thought of that myself. I will tell Fife to accompany you while I tend to M'ma." Davina put her project aside to help her mother to bed, placing her embroidery threads in the basket beside her chair.

"Oh, but I hoped you would go with me."

Davina stopped in the middle of tucking Lilias's embroidery threads in her basket and glanced at her mother. Lilias remained seated, squeezing her eyes closed and massaging her temples. Grateful her mother seemed distracted by her head pains, Davina glared at Rosselyn.

"Don't fret, Davina. Broderick won't be there. He doesn't come to the camp during the daytime."

Davina blanched. Another confirmation of what the Gypsy girl told her.

Lilias strained to peek at the two of them. "Why are you so concerned whether or not he's there?

He hasn't hurt you, has he?" Panic laced Lilias's voice.

"Nay, M'ma." Davina made efforts to keep her voice calm. "He hasn't hurt me. There is nothing to be concerned about." Davina helped Lilias to her feet and glared at Rosselyn over her mother's head. "Tell Fife I will be down to join you after I have Myrna put M'ma to bed." She frowned at the gleeful expression on her maid's face. Just as Davina suspected, Rosselyn was playing match maker and did everything but come outright and say Davina and Broderick should be together. Well, Davina would just have to set her maid straight on the matter. Davina helped Lilias up the stairs to her chamber and fetched Myrna.

With Lilias tucked into bed, Davina joined Rosselyn and Fife and trotted out to the Gypsy camp.

They rode in silence for a while—Davina and Rosselyn side by side with Fife traveling ahead of them—before Rosselyn spoke. "Did I say something wrong, Davina?"

"When?"

"While we were in the parlor."

"Oh. Well, you know how my mother worries. She's also aware the Gypsy has an interest in me and doesn't fancy the idea of me being with a wanderer like him. I don't want to give her any reason to believe something will come of the match."

"Do you fancy the Gypsy?"

Davina pursed her lips at Rosselyn. "If I thought he was to be at the camp, I wouldn't have come with you." Rosselyn may have told Davina he wouldn't be there just to get her to come along. A part of her hoped she had, proving Veronique wrong. "He isn't going to be there, correct?"

"Aye. 'Tis just as I said; he doesn't come to the camp during the day."

She shivered, but Rosselyn might have learned another reason. "Why?"

"Nicabar tells me Amice does the fortune telling during the day and doesn't have the strength to continue into the night, so Broderick takes over the duty. I guess he's used to the unusual schedule."

The arrangement seemed logical enough. Veronique may have said such things to keep Davina away, though her reasons were unclear.

"But I didn't ask you if you wanted to see the *dukker*, Davina. I asked if you fancied him."

"The what?"

"The *dukker*. 'Tis the Gypsy word for fortune teller." Rosselyn remained silent, and Davina hoped she wouldn't repeat the question, but she did.

"I would want to see him if I had an interest in him, nay?" *There, that should satisfy her curiosity.*

Rosselyn smiled a secret smile, one which made Davina uneasy. Aye, she'd satisfied her, all right. Broderick interested Davina, and she grated her teeth at being so transparent.

They rode in silence for a few moments before Rosselyn turned to Davina, opening her mouth as if to say something, but closed her mouth when their eyes met. Rosselyn's cheeks bloomed with color and she diverted her gaze.

"Rosselyn, are you well?" Davina leaned over in her saddle and touched her friend's hand in a show of support.

Rosselyn opened her mouth, her bottom lip quivering, and then nodded. "Aye, Davina. All is well." Patting Davina's hand, Rosselyn comforted her mistress and then urged her horse forward toward the Gypsy camp.

As Rosselyn headed for Nicabar's caravan, an unexpected ache rose in Davina's chest. Rosselyn and Nicabar spent more and more time together. Was she losing her maid and best friend? Perhaps that was what Rosselyn tried to tell her on the ride over. Rosselyn deserved to be happy, and Davina never saw her friend glow like she did with Nicabar. Her brow furrowed and her protective nature bubbled up. He had better not be playing with her friend's emotions. She narrowed her eyes and encouraged her horse to Broderick's caravan, making a mental note to keep an eye on this relationship.

Fife waited with the horses at the edge of the camp, talking and laughing with a few of the Gypsy men. The afternoon chill stinging her cheeks didn't seem any different from the frostiness of the early morn. The days were definitely getting colder. "And we are in for a storm," she mumbled at the darkening horizon, watching the fading sunlight.

Amice rambled in French at her granddaughter, something about keeping to herself and not chasing after something that would never come to be. As Davina approached their site, the young woman scowled at Davina, and Amice grabbed her arm, whispering in her ear. Gasps of protest hissed from the girl who stomped into the caravan, leaving Davina alone with aged Gypsy.

"Please, join me, *chérie*," Amice invited, and Davina sat on the wooden stool opposite the old woman. From a pot sitting on the fire, Amice ladled steaming pottage into bowls and handed one to Davina, along with a chunk of grain bread. "I do not like to eat alone."

Davina couldn't refuse such a tantalizing aroma and blew on the thick brew before tearing off a piece of bread and dipping it into the bowl. Pottage never tasted so flavorful. Picking through the stew, Davina could see Amice had skills with herbs in more than medicinal ways. "Thank you, Amice, this is delicious."

"*Merci beaucoup*, Davina." Amice's grin was overshadowed by her wrinkled brow.

"What troubles you, Amice?"

Amice bit off the end of her bread. "Nothing to concern yourself with, *chérie*." She nibbled her stew before continuing. "And how is your mother?"

"Actually, she's the reason I came here today. She's plagued with terrible head pains. I know not what to do. I hope you have some herbal remedies."

"*Oui.*" Amice put her food down upon her stool and opened the caravan door. Veronique sat inside, glaring at Davina. Davina expected the impertinent girl would stick her tongue out as she'd done when she was a child. She tried not to scowl back and pondered what the girl had against her. From a cabinet under the bed, Amice pulled a large woven basket filled with herbs and oils, then closed the door, sat on her stool, and produced a jar with a large cork stopper, which she removed.

"This is a mixture of several herbs," she explained as she scooped out the seeds and dried bits, and poured them onto a piece of cloth, carefully wrapping and tying them into a little bundle. "Chamomile, hawthorn, hops, and peppermint, among others, but trust me…they will help." She corked the jar and handed the wrapped herbs to Davina. Amice cupped her hand and drew circles in the center of her palm with her index finger, saying, "Measure a small amount into your palm and make an infusion for her to drink when her head hurts. To prevent the pains from returning, tell her to eat a fresh leaf of feverfew daily between two slices of bread." Amice put her basket aside and wrinkled her nose. "The feverfew is bitter, which is why she must eat the leaf with bread."

"Thank you so very much, Amice." The two women went back to eating the pottage and bread. Davina admired the painted tent siding of the woman with flowing blonde hair and cards on a table before her. "This painting resembles your granddaughter," Davina observed, "but I saw it many years ago when she was little. Surely 'tis not a portrait of her."

Amice glanced at the painting and blushed. "*Non*, that is not of Veronique." She leaned forward and whispered with mischief in her voice. "*C'est moi!*" Amice giggled like a little girl.

Davina chuckled. "You?"

"*Oui!* Broderick is a very talented artist, *non*? He painted a picture of me in my youth."

Davina stopped chewing, surprised by the admission and the shocking aspect of Broderick's talent. She swallowed the bite of bread she'd taken. "Broderick painted that?"

Amice nodded proudly and turned her attention to her bowl, stirring the stew with her bread. "He also painted those wooden tablets I have shown you."

Davina gasped, remembering the detailed images on the fortune telling tool Amice had used during their last visit. "How amazing! You must be so proud of your son."

Amice's eyes went wide. "My son?" She laughed. "Oh, *non, chérie*. Broderick is not my son." Amice scooted forward and scooped some more pottage into her bowl, offering Davina more of the stew. After giving Davina a second helping, she settled back, licking her lips. "I will tell you the story. We made camp along the coast on the south of England, outside a large city called Portsmouth. We did not camp within or closer to the city as Gypsies are not welcome there."

"Truly?" Davina protested. "I cannot imagine you not being welcome, with all the variety of wares and entertainment you bring with you."

Amice nodded and rolled her eyes. "Oh, there are many places we are not welcome." She jabbed a thumb over her shoulder. "The large town of Strathbogie being one of them. Especially after that horrible Black Death. So much distrust. That is why we come to your little village. We make our parade through Strathbogie to announce our arrival, and those who do favor us come here. We are fortunate you are close enough for them to venture, yet far enough away for them not to bother us."

"I see." Davina knew some of the people from Strathbogie through the various marketing trips she and her family made to the larger establishment. The people from Strathbogie also came to Stewart Glen to enjoy what the Gypsies had to offer, which brought additional business to their village.

Amice waved her bread as she continued. "Veronique was only four years old at that time and wandered off. I only turned around for a moment and the child was gone! I searched the tents and wagons in the darkness of night. I asked the other people if they saw her, and then I heard her yelp— a quick, little cry, but I heard it well, and the sound froze my heart as I realized it had come from the water's edge. Running as fast as my legs could carry me to the water, I screamed for help. Many of the people in our camp ran with me." Amice leaned forward and laid a hand on Davina's forearm, whispering in amazement. "Before we reached the shore, this giant man rose from the water, carrying my little Veronique in his arms as she cried. Broderick was an angel rescuing her from a watery grave, and he has been with us since that day. He has most definitely become like a son to me through the years, though. That is why I call him my son."

"What a wonderful story!" Though the story did delight her and presented insight into the heart of Broderick MacDougal, Davina now understood why Veronique held such contempt for her. The young girl was not a niece of Broderick's as Davina presumed, but must fancy herself in love with him. No doubt the Gypsy girl knew of Broderick's pursuit of Davina, and probably saw her as the enemy. Well, the girl fretted over nothing. She wouldn't get in Veronique's way.

When they finished eating, Davina helped Amice wash the bowls and the old woman led her to the front side of the wagon. "Help me with these, *s'il vous plaît*," she ordered, and Davina struggled with Amice to pull out and uncover four life-size portraits from a long and apparently deep side cabinet. Names delicately carved on flat wood pieces labeled the bottom of each portrait.

The resemblance was striking. "Broderick's family," she whispered.

"*Oui*. All murdered by his rival clan, the Campbells."

Davina's heart ached over Amice's words. "Aye, he did share the loss of his family with me, but briefly. He said he doesn't talk about it overmuch." Knowing a feuding clan was responsible put the mass destruction into perspective. However, such brutal clan wars were not so common these days, at least not in this part of the country, and especially since such battles were outlawed since the Crown took over the dispensing of justice.

"His mother," Amice said, pointing to the appropriate portraits. "His father, and these were his younger brothers."

Standing with pride in the first painting, Moira MacDougal stared back at Davina with intense eyes so much like Broderick's, yet golden brown instead of Broderick's emerald green. Her ebony hair cascaded over her right shoulder, and she wore a red, green, and light blue plaid, which Davina assumed were Broderick's clan colors. This portrait showed a woman of a fiery nature. Courageous and forceful, Davina guessed, judging by the male garments she wore and stood in with such pride. How unusual and, Davina suspected, even frowned upon. Scotsmen loved such courage and independence in a woman, but not in open display or in such a masculine way. They also loved and reveled in a woman's femininity, as she assumed most men of any nationality would. Didn't a woman's feminine nature make a man feel all the more masculine? This woman intrigued Davina and created more of a mystique around Broderick MacDougal.

Broderick's fiery, russet hair blazed upon the head of his father, Hamish MacDougal, and most of Broderick's striking, handsome features and green eyes came from this man, as well as his demanding appearance. Hamish stood regally in the painting; as if confident he would get what he wanted when he wanted it. She snorted—like father, like son.

Davina stepped to the next painting, labeled "Maxwell MacDougal." Maxwell's black hair shimmered to his broad shoulders, his features handsome and linear. His painted brown eyes gazed back with a touch of humor and even vanity, one might say, one raven brow raised a touch higher than the other—so much like Broderick's gesture Davina had come to know. With his hands resting upon the hilt of his sword, Maxwell stood with his legs shoulder-width apart, the tip of the blade between his feet.

Donnell MacDougal's features were softer, more like Moira's, and his hair, cut in a rather old-fashioned, cropped style, fell golden red just past his ears. His sea-green eyes peered from the canvas with solemnity, his pink lips serious. He stood tall with his hands behind his back and sword sheathed at his hip. Davina pondered their old-fashioned garments, some twenty or thirty years out of date— maybe more. She narrowed her eyes in curiosity as she gazed at their clothing and then back at their faces.

"Broderick painted these," Amice said with pride.

Davina stood in awe, staring at the details and emotions brought to life in the figures before her. She almost expected them to step off the canvas and greet her. "Remarkable!"

"Broderick has lost everyone important in his life, *chérie*. Because he opened his heart, he is afraid to love again, afraid to trust."

Davina knew all too well how love and opening one's heart could cause a vulnerability others could take advantage of. She and Broderick had more in common than she realized, which comforted her. They both shared the same grief, and this commonality created a link between them, deepening at the sight of his family. She now had faces and names to accompany the facts.

"From the first moment I met him," Davina began, "I've been unable to get him out of my mind." She stepped forward and traced Hamish's eyes with her finger and noticed how Broderick's eyes were much greener. She turned to Maxwell and touched his handsome smirk, so like Broderick's roguish grin. Davina touched her own lips and smiled. "You know, I used to dream about marrying Broderick after I met him. Such girlish fantasies." She turned to Amice. "Silly, is it not? I met him so briefly as a rail of a girl, and he has plagued my dreams ever since."

Amice took Davina's hand and turned her palm up to study the lines on her skin.

"Broderick told me of my troubled future," she informed Amice, referring to the first time she'd met Broderick. "He was right. My husband turned out to be a very cruel man, and I'm not sad he's dead."

Amice gazed at her with a furrowed brow and she touched Davina's cheek. "Oh, *chérie*, you even lost a little one, *oui*?"

Davina's eyes stung and she nodded, unable to speak over the lump in her throat. Her miscarriage. "Aye," she managed after a moment. "You can see such things in my palm?"

Amice nodded.

"What else do you see, Amice? I know you haven't told me everything." She referred to the tea leaf reading she overheard Amice telling Broderick about when she was young. *Am I wasting my heart on a fantasy?*

Amice narrowed her eyes in concentration at Davina, as if she'd heard her silent question, and then studied the lines on her palm once more. She turned Davina's hand this way and that, pinching the skin to reveal the lines. *Is it fate we are to be together? Even Angus told me Broderick would return.*

Amice turned wide eyes upon Davina.

"You can hear my thoughts, too?" Davina whispered, unsure if she wanted to hear the answer.

"*Oui, chérie.* Some of them. I mostly see images."

"I never told you, but I heard what you said that night to Broderick, about the tea leaf reading. That I would steal his heart. Even a stranger made such a prediction." Davina couldn't seem to ask the question aloud.

"I would not trust what this stranger told you, Davina." Fear filled Amice's eyes.

"Do you know who he is? I've never seen him again"

Amice nodded. *"Oui, chérie.* He is not to be trusted. You must stay away from this man." For a moment, it seemed Amice would say something more, but instead, worry lines creased her brow and she cast her eyes down at Davina's palms. Closing Davina's hands into each other, Amice patted them and turned away, busying herself with covering the paintings. Davina remained rooted, unable to utter a word. Not trusting this man said what Amice seemed unwilling to say—it was not fate they were to be together. Though this confirmed what she knew to be right, she couldn't prevent the sinking in her chest. Not knowing what else to do, she helped Amice put the paintings back into the caravan.

Amice shuffled to her stool and sat down. "How do you feel about Broderick?"

Davina sat on her stool, uncertain and exposed.

"Do not think," Amice ordered. "Just tell me how you feel."

She plunged forward into this awkward moment. "I don't know, Amice. Confusion, mostly. Broderick affects me in a way no one else has. And yet…" After this confirmation, Davina didn't want to explore her fantasies any longer. They didn't have any kind of future together. "Methinks I should not come down here anymore. At least not while Broderick is here. You won't be staying much longer, will you?"

Amice regarded the darkening horizon the same instant Davina did. "That coming storm will keep us here another week or more, *chérie.*"

"I beg your pardon?" Her voice trembled with panic.

"We cannot travel in the deep snow, and the time is too late for us to pack and go. We will not make the next establishment before the storm. We will have to stay here in Stewart Glen. There is no telling how long we will be here."

This news didn't make Davina feel any better about this situation. With apprehension rising in her breast, she stood and fiddled with her cloak. Making sure she secured the bundle of herbs, she kissed Amice on her cheek, expressed her gratitude and scampered away.

Veronique approached her grandmother when Davina left the camp. "What did the Scot want?" she asked, trying not to sound too interested.

Amice pursed her lips at her granddaughter, so Veronique took to doing chores—stacking wood and cleaning their site. Swinging Veronique around, Amice pointed a scolding finger in her face. "You know very well why she was here. You sat listening during her visit. You mind your own business! I know what you are up to and you need to stop this nonsense. Broderick is not for you." Amice's implored her granddaughter, "I love Broderick, Veronique, but you have no future with him. He cannot give you children. He would not make you happy."

Veronique yanked away from her grandmother's grasp. "You do not know what I need or want. How do you know I would want children?"

Amice's hands flew to her cheeks, and then she threw her arms around Veronique. "Oh, no, no, Veronique! Do not say such things! You will put a curse upon yourself!"

Veronique pushed away and stormed from their site. Her grandmother was wrong. She didn't know her. Veronique had no aspirations to bear children. What other man could be more perfect for her than Broderick? This damned Davina would ruin any kind of future Veronique had with him, and she was running out of ideas. Veronique jerked at the crack of thunder, reminding her of what her grandmother said: *There is no telling how long we will be here.* Veronique closed her eyes and made the final commitment in her mind. She would do it tonight. Thunder rumbled again. She cringed. Maybe.

Angus closed his eyes, reaching into the darkness with his mind, searching for the usual pattern of madness, sporadic thoughts, or demonic visions. He had a difficult time concentrating, though. How to resolve his inability to approach Broderick dominated his mind with increasing frustration. Not only did he figure out Broderick rose for the evening earlier than he did, but also, Broderick sensed his presence sooner than he could sense Broderick's. Every time he tried to close in and catch him by surprise, Broderick already had a head start on pursuing him.

Shaking his head to clear his thoughts, he returned his attention to listen for the signs of prey. Still, he didn't hear the rapid heartbeat of insanity as he expected. Did Broderick perhaps feed elsewhere? Stepping through the muddy streets, he strode stealthily among the darkness, and then stopped. He raised an eyebrow. What if Broderick changed his tactics? Closing his eyes, he concentrated on being more open to the various experiences around him instead of narrowing his senses to a specific pattern. Gliding through the streets, a wave of guilt shrouded his being, and he smiled. In the darkened corner sat one of Broderick's victims.

The victim sat mumbling, worry etching his brow. "What have I done? What have I done?"

"You did what you had to." Angus stepped forward and approached the victim, who jumped in fright. Picking the victim up by the lapels, he held his stinking body in front of him. "What a filthy job, cleaning up after you," Angus said, more to Broderick than the man before him.

Not expecting a response, he turned the victim's head to the side and fed from him, draining away his miserable life and sparing him the insanity Broderick left behind. Angus enjoyed hearing the heartbeat slow, the man's body growing cold. Interrupting this euphoria, however, a presence he knew all too well now pressed in upon him. Restraining the Hunger and using his anger toward Broderick to give him strength, he broke from the feeding and dropped the victim to the ground, escaping Broderick's pursuit. He didn't want to face Rick just yet. He still needed to find out who was close to Rick, whose death would hurt him the most. Then he would strike his enemy where he had been struck—in the heart.

Angus masked his presence—a skill he could maintain for no more than a minute or so—giving him enough time to slip away from what Angus figured was Broderick's unusual range. As Angus hoped, the presence of Broderick MacDougal waned as he continued running. Broderick would finish off the poor soul he left behind just to glean whatever information he could about Angus. These last two encounters proved to be a nice way to distract Broderick. It bought Angus the time he needed…and gave him an idea.

Veronique's hands shook as she held the incense and oil. She clenched her jaw as she stood before the tent entrance, not understanding her nervousness. *What if Broderick does not like the perfume I bought?* She inhaled a trembling breath. *What if he does not notice me at all?* Shaking her head, she pushed her fear aside and put faith in what the town market vendor promised. The rich, exotic scent of the potion would excite any man who came close to her. When she sampled the vial, she agreed the fragrance was appealing, and figured if she enjoyed the aroma, why wouldn't a man enjoy it all the more? She took another steadying breath and entered the tent to perform her evening duties.

The tent was empty. Had Broderick not returned from feeding yet? Her shoulders sagged. She would exit and light the lamps for the evening later, when he would be there to watch her. Sighing, she turned to leave only to be near trampled by Broderick barging into the tent, a murderous glare on his face. She only just stepped aside in time to prevent a hard collision and save the oil from being spilled.

"Veronique!" he barked. "Must you always be underfoot?" He nudged past her, stopped, and heaved a great sigh. Turning to her, his face softened somewhat, but his eyebrows still scrunched in disapproval. "Forgive me, Veronique. I've had a frustrating start to my evening. You should not have to bear the brunt of my mood."

Relieved he didn't direct his anger toward her, she smiled and nodded. Broderick sat at the trestle table and closed his eyes, seeming to concentrate on calming his demeanor. She steadied her trembling hands and tiptoed around the tent, refilling the small oil lamps on the various iron holders. Broderick still sat with his eyes closed and his arms crossed. She grumbled and continued with her task. Bending forward in front of him to add more incense to the brazier, she provided him a generous view of her cleavage. She cleared her throat. He glanced at her, raised an eyebrow, and closed his eyes once more.

Persevering, she padded behind him to fill one lamp and, crossing over to fill the last lamp, she brushed her breasts across his back in passing. He cleared his throat this time, and she turned to face him after she finished with the oil. Broderick still sat with his eyes closed. Putting the incense and oil down on the table, she clenched her jaw to maintain control of her jealousy, thinking that Davina occupied his thoughts, and sat on his lap. *There!* He couldn't ignore her now.

His hands rested on her hips and he scowled at her. She kissed the tip of his nose. "Do you notice anything different about me this night?" she asked, hopeful. Her fingers toyed with the fiery curl of hair on his shoulder.

Broderick glanced away for a moment, and then returned his disapproving eyes to hers. "You are trying my patience more than usual?"

Veronique frowned, yet still leaned in for a kiss, ignoring his statement. But her hopes plummeted when his hands grabbed her shoulders and stopped her.

"A customer could walk in any moment, Veronique," he said in a voice laced with warning. "'Tis bad for business and I'm not in the mood."

Davina hugged her cloak tighter against the cold night. Rosselyn chatted with a small group of Gypsy women, sharing various bits of information about embroidery or household chores or whatnot. Davina really wasn't paying attention. What could she be thinking by letting Rosselyn talk her into returning to the Gypsy camp after her conversation with Amice this afternoon? She glanced at the fortune teller's tent. Trepidation filled her heart at confronting Broderick. What was his interest in Angus? Even a more frightening subject was Broderick's behavior, and these mysterious signs of something foreign, even mystical. Now that she stood brooding across the camp, near enough to see shadows against the canvas of the tent, Davina wasn't sure she wanted to know what Broderick had to say about either matter. She should discuss something on more common ground...like the death of their families. Davina rolled her eyes. *Aye, 'tis a much lighter subject to breach.* She shook her head.

Amice sat before the fire by the tent, rubbing her hands over the flames, inviting the occasional passerby to have their fortune told, but they strode by shaking their heads. Davina noticed the bustling about the Gypsy camp died down since they first arrived—a considerable drop even more so over the last couple of days with the coming cold weather. The townspeople had their fill of the Gypsies, she surmised. Time and decreased activities encouraged the Gypsies to move on.

She glanced at the black sky above. Though the darkness hid any clouds, she couldn't see the stars, which did not bode well. Just before sunset, the imposing clouds settled on the afternoon horizon. Foreboding hovered over Davina's shoulders as a faint rumble of thunder echoed across the sky.

"Go on, milady," Rosselyn encouraged. "That has to be the tenth time I've seen you look over at the *dukker's* tent."

"You certainly have come accustomed to using some of their words," Davina said, trying to steer Rosselyn to another subject. She glanced back at the tent.

Rosselyn smiled at her. "Aye, there is a very good reason for that." She cleared her throat.

"Do you know any more?" Davina threw another glance at the fortune teller's tent.

When she returned her gaze to Rosselyn, her friend shook her head and waved a dismissive hand. "Just go in and have your palm read."

"He has already read my palm. Why would I want to have it read again?"

"Davina, when you don't want to do something, you won't do it, so my talking you into coming down here with me has nothing to do with you being here. Take care of what you must." With those final words, Rosselyn left Davina alone to make her decision. Davina stood with her mouth open and watched Rosselyn march to Nicabar's caravan, rap on the door, and disappear inside.

"Hrmph."

So, why am I here? Though not willing to breach the forbidden subjects of mystical signs and Angus, she did want someone to talk to who shared the same losses she had. Davina envied Broderick's ability to deal with the past hurts. Maybe on that common ground they could delve into deeper subjects. *Aye, that would be a more proper approach.*

Feeling somewhat justified and more courageous about speaking to him, she proceeded to the tent and was surprised to find Amice gone. A noise from the wagon told her the old Gypsy must be inside, rumbling around for something. Or that could have been her granddaughter. Davina peeked into the tent, thinking Amice may be in there.

No voices came from the inside. As she leaned to peer in, taking care to be silent lest Broderick had a customer, the thick aroma of incense greeted her nostrils, a smell she had become quite fond of. Davina touched her hand to her hot cheeks at the arousal the scent stirred, but the warmth on her face paled in comparison to the sudden heat rising up from her belly, which spread through the length of her body. Amice was not in the tent, but Broderick sat behind his table, as pleasant as you please, and a rather comely woman sitting on his lap. They seemed absorbed in some kind of conversation for their ears alone—their faces so close and intimate to each other, Broderick's hands gripping the woman's arms just above her elbows.

She cleared her throat and stepped into the tent.

Davina almost gasped, but maintained enough control over her astonishment to keep her exasperation private. Amice's granddaughter sat on

Broderick's lap. Veronique smiled triumphantly at Davina, and gave Broderick a hard kiss on his lips before slipping from his lap and sauntering out of the tent.

Davina bunched her fists and her body became rigid. How dare he pursue her with such determination when he had a willing subject right under his nose! Just one woman couldn't satisfy him? Or did he have an entire string of women everywhere he went? How many other Gypsy women did he bed?

"Dost thou speak?" he asked in a mocking tone.

"Not to you!" Davina turned to leave and gasped when Broderick caught her up short by a steel grip on her arm.

"Now bide a moment, fair lady." He stole his arms around her in a tight embrace. Twisting and arching her body, she sought freedom, but he kept her pinned to his massive frame.

Davina's arms were trapped between them, so she couldn't flail her fists on him to work out her frustrations. "You ox!"

"What *has* you so riled?" His face held nothing but amusement, encouraging her wrath.

"You are a rogue!" she cursed. "Nothing but a rake! A cad! A beast! A cur!" She stuttered, continuing to struggle.

"Run out of insults, milady?"

"Give me a moment!"

He threw his head back and laughed, the rich sound vibrating through her body. After his bout of laughter, he repeated his question. "Something must vex you so, Davina."

"Nothing you should know." Her body began to tire from her constant wrestling.

"Ah, but I would very much like to know." His mouth descended upon hers, but she at least had enough freedom to dodge him.

She stopped fighting, her breath ragged. "Release me."

"I sense a bit of jealousy, Davina."

Heat crept into Davina's cheeks. "Certainly not!" she denied, even though she knew very well he could divine the truth.

"There is nothing between the lass and myself," he supplied. "In spite of what you saw."

Davina remained silent, willing away the torrent of jealousy and humiliation eating through her insides. She avoided his gaze by taking an interest in the oil lamp hanging on an iron frame.

"But why you should even care is beyond me," he breathed against her ear.

Though very entrancing, she resisted his spell. "I care not." More heat stole into her face, for even though she knew he could read her thoughts, she remained stoical as her final act of defiance.

Broderick released her, the humor gone from his eyes, and bowed with apparent respect. "Then I'm mistaken, milady, and you're free to go." Turning as if he lost interest in the subject, he sat back down at his table and crossed his arms.

Davina stood dumbfounded, not ready for this response. She expected him to continue fighting with her, pursuing her, handling her.

Broderick raised an eyebrow. "Tell me, Davina. Why are you here?"

She stood perplexed at the simple question she had barely been able to answer herself.

"To have your palm read?"

"Nay, I…" Her voice trailed off, all of the energy and reasons leaving her in a rush.

"I don't make it a habit to read someone's palm more than once." His iron gaze belied the casual conversation he attempted.

"Then I shall bother you no more," she whispered and turned to leave.

"Pray, say something to me, Davina." A great deal of emotion laced his voice, as if he struggled to maintain control over something lying just beneath the surface.

She faced him. "How do you do it?" Her voice constricted and, to her surprise, she blinked back prickling tears. Clearing her throat, she pushed through her apprehension. "How do you go on after such a great loss?"

"Honestly, I've not explored it myself." He motioned for her to sit across from him.

Davina hesitated, but not wanting to seem disrespectful, now that Broderick made efforts to open up to her with his invitation, she pushed through her fears and sat down.

Broderick sighed. "I know not how much I can help you, Davina. 'Tis much grief and underlying hate you hold inside. I've sensed them; heard fleeting thoughts about them, but you close your mind up like a steel trap." He leaned forward and held out his hand. "If you let them go, if you allow yourself to feel this pain so I may also feel it, I might be able to give you some answers."

Broderick offered his hand.

CHAPTER TEN

He could hear some of her internal struggle, but at this moment, panic dominated the battle raging inside her, and almost drowned out any other thoughts. He could sense she feared opening up to him, but he also sensed a fear *of* him and some confusion over what Broderick was—flashes of the silver glow in his eyes peeking through the cacophony of emotions. He cringed and tried to maintain an inviting and encouraging presence.

"Let me help you, Davina," he whispered.

Davina implored him with her eyes. She darted her attention from his hand to his face and back again. Finally, she stretched out her trembling hand, and Broderick released his breath at last.

He closed his eyes. Flashes of the night Broderick pursued her on horseback rushed through his mind as soon as he touched her skin. Images of his dark figure chasing her through the forest assaulted him, and a gripping terror coursed through his arms, followed by his own remorse. "I'm sorry to have frightened you so that night," he offered, his voice raspier than he expected. Visions of a menacing man invaded his mind. He recognized this man as the one he envisioned when he tasted Davina's blood from her dagger. "Who is this man? Is this who you thought of when I pursued you?"

When she tried to answer, he understood she had trouble speaking over her emotions.

Just answer me by thinking, Davina, he communicated, implanting his thoughts into her mind.

Her brows raised in surprise. After a moment, the tension eased from her body. *Thank you.* She inhaled deeply. *Aye, he's the man I thought of when you chased me, but the thought was irrational.*

Why is that?

Because he's dead.

Broderick tried to soothe Davina by rubbing her palm, massaging her flesh with the warm oil on the table, confident relaxing her would be the key to getting the information about Angus. However, that proved to illicit provocative images. Davina's thoughts went to their romantic struggle after he'd pulled her from her horse. Just as Broderick opened his mouth to warn her of straying to an erotic subject, a tremor vibrated through his body as Davina relived the sensation of his fingers touching the wet folds between her legs.

A tortured moan escaped him and Broderick swept around the table, pulling Davina into his arms. She stood breathless before him, clinging to him, with pleading eyes and full lips quivering and tempting. He came close to claiming her lips, but hesitated, trying to gain control of his urges. "Davina," he breathed against her mouth. "If you share such thoughts with me, I cannot be responsible for my actions."

Her cheeks colored and she stammered as he gazed into her eyes. He swooned from the intoxicating effect of her swirling emotions on his senses—desire, excitement, fear.

She opened her mouth to speak, but no words came forth. *I am so very sorry. I—*

Sitting down, his own legs almost too weak to stand, he set her upon his lap. He composed himself enough to ask with amusement in his voice, "Are you going to behave?"

Davina cleared her throat and tried to stand, but he wouldn't let her. This lighter subject at least allowed her to find her voice. "How can I behave, sir, if you won't let me up from such a provocative position?"

Her loitering in the jesting mood encouraged him to carry on their intimate game, and he still refused to release her.

"Broderick, must our encounters always turn amorous?" she teased.

He chuckled. "I must confess, dear lady, I can think of naught else when I hold you." What was it about this woman's voice that undulated through his body and had his cock leaping to attention? Even now, as she strained to get up, her bottom rubbed against the sensitive head. "Need I remind you—you started this with those explicit images."

She tried to rise for a second time, but couldn't yield against his strength, and giggled. "Please, I promise to behave."

Just as he was about to let her up, a deep grumble filled the tent as someone cleared their throat with a great, loud effort. Davina gasped and pushed away from Broderick, wanting to leap out of his embrace. But, Broderick made that a difficult task with his arms around her, holding her tight against his lap.

Broderick smiled at their visitor. "'Tis good to see you again, sir, but as you can see, I have another client."

Davina gasped. "Mr. Samuels! What a…" She seemed to flounder for the right words in this awkward situation. "Pleasant surprise." Davina put her hands to her flushed face at seeing one of the townsfolk from Strathbogie.

An uncomfortable Mr. Samuels wrung his hat with his hairy-knuckled hands. "Mistress Davina."

He also seemed at a loss for words. "'Tis good to see you, milady. I'm begging your pardon, Broderick. I heard nothin' inside and I saw no one outside of the tent, so I ventured in."

Without appearing to struggle, Broderick felt Davina continue to push against his arms, but he still held her tight. "This session will conclude in just a moment, sir," Broderick said calmly, and as if nothing unusual were happening. "Would you like to bide by the fire until I call for you?" *Please take my suggestion and leave!* His distress grew as Davina continued to struggle in his lap, rubbing her delightful bottom against his arousal.

"Nay, sir! I won't trouble you. I just wanted to tell you everything you said last week is comin' true, and I came to thank you." Mr. Samuels tried very hard to avoid eye contact with Davina. Embarrassment colored his cheeks, matching his thoughts about the awkwardness of catching them in this intimate encounter.

"You found the woman you're to marry? So soon, Mr. Samuels?"

"Oh, Clyde, please. And aye, the perfect woman, sir! We met eight years ago and then lost touch for a couple of seasons. She just came back into my life. 'Tis amazing how the perfect woman was right under me nose, a friend and someone dear to me family. I was blind not to see it until now. We wish to be wed in the spring and plan on havin' a few wee bairn!" Caught up in the news of his new family, he seemed to relinquish the awkward situation.

"Glad to hear it, Clyde! Congratulations!" Broderick did not stand to shake his hand.

"Thank you, sir!" He stepped forward, but stopped as if seeing Davina for the first time. The nervous energy returned and he inched forward as if hedging toward a wild animal, ready to bite if he stepped any closer. He extended his hand with hesitation and gave Broderick a small sack. Broderick tried to refuse, but Clyde insisted. "'Tis showing you me gratitude."

Broderick reluctantly stretched his hand to receive the donation, still trying to keep Davina in his lap to conceal his erection, the bag jingling as if filled with coins. Clyde bowed his way out of the tent and left them to their intimate moment.

Davina struggled to get up, and this time he let her go without a fight. "What in blazes were you thinking to keep me locked to your lap like some tavern wench!" she hissed.

Broderick smiled, tossed the sack of coins onto the table, and stood with his hands on his hips. "Well, dear lady, I very well couldn't stand in my current condition." Broderick glanced at his loins and winked.

Her eyes traveled down and locked onto the very obvious arousal pushing against his trews. Her

ARIAL BURNZ

hand went to her cheek and her eyes flew back up to Broderick's face.

"I would have been very glad to let you up once my...well...*member* went down, but you kept wiggling your sweet little bottom against it. You left me no choice." He crossed his arms and grinned with satisfaction.

Davina stood speechless. Broderick heard the rambling of her thoughts. She didn't know if her cheeks were on fire from the embarrassment of being caught on his lap by an upstanding citizen of their community, or from the fire burning between her legs at the sight of Broderick's obvious arousal, or a combination of both. She stood there, stunned.

Davina flitted her gaze to various points of interest around the tent, fighting to keep her eyes from straying down to view his enlarged groin. That didn't do anything to help him ease the tension in his breeches, so Broderick put the barrier of the table between them.

This act brought her back to her senses, but not her jovial mood. Davina stepped back and crossed her arms protectively over her breasts. "I...I..." She sighed, exasperated. Too flustered to continue, Davina dashed out of the tent.

Broderick hung his head in defeat. He had been so close to convincing her to open up! Why couldn't he control his urges around her? Never had a woman affected him the way Davina did. Broderick rose from his chair and paced the tiny space. He was an adolescent around her, his groin rearing its head every time she came near. Even now he cursed his still-present arousal.

Raking his rigid fingers through his hair, he inhaled deeply and steadied his nerves, trying to recover something from the evening. New information had come to light. The man she was afraid of, she said, was dead. This Ian, he assumed, putting all of the pieces together. But who was he? Her father? A lover? He knew it wasn't her brother. His name was Kehr.

Nothing more came to mind for Broderick. He needed answers, but every time he came close to Davina, he lost his senses. This task proved most impossible!

"Come, Davina," Rosselyn said, coaxing Davina out of sleep. "'Tis time to break our fast." She placed the tray of food onto the trestle table by the double doors, nursing a giddy excitement in her breast of the day to come. Winter made a grand entrance overnight, and she itched to share it with Davina. This turn of the weather would give her and Davina much needed time together before she set off on her new life with Nicabar. She feared, though, these days would go faster than she wanted, and Rosselyn grabbed tight to any moment she could before the Gypsies were off to the next settlement in their route. As much as she dreaded to think upon the weighing responsibility, she also needed this time to tell Davina her secret.

With the winter nights getting longer, the sun had not yet risen this early in the morning, so Rosselyn set about the chamber lighting candles and starting a fire in the hearth. The amber glow of the room warmed the atmosphere. "If we dress right for our meal," Rosselyn offered cheerfully, "and put a blanket over our laps, we can arrange to sit on the terrace. 'Tis a bonnie sight this morn."

Davina considered the oriel window. "Oh, why is that?"

Rosselyn drew back the heavy curtains and opened the double doors, breathing in deep the crisp morning air. Torches lit the courtyard so the morning chores could be seen to. The yellow flames created a sparkling vision on the knee-deep snow, blanketing the landscape surrounding the castle. Davina gasped.

"Looks as if the Gypsies—"

"Aye, Roz, I know." Davina diverted away from the doors with a frown and hunkered at the table. "'Tis too cold to have the doors open. Please close them."

Rosselyn's spirits plummeted at the foul mood the weather put Davina in. She sighed and did as her mistress wished. Pulling up the other chair, she spoke with concern in her voice. "We haven't spoken much with each other as of late." Rosselyn's heart pounded.

Davina turned a puzzled mien upon her. "We speak every day, Roz. What—?"

Rosselyn placed a hand upon Davina's shoulder. "Private talk, between friends. You once told me often of your dreams of marrying Broderick."

Davina switched her attention to her trencher of bread and cheese as Rosselyn continued pressing the matter.

"Now that he's here, 'tis in your own world you are."

When Rosselyn paused, Davina cast her a sideways glance.

"Does he not fancy you?"

Davina rolled her eyes and went back to her food. "Oh, 'tis very obvious he is about how he fancies me."

"Then why—?"

"Once that man beds me, Roz, I will never see him again."

"Has he not displayed any signs of affection?" Rosselyn gripped Davina's shoulder. "He hasn't hurt you, has he?"

"Nay, he hasn't. That's not a great concern for me." Davina fell silent, seemingly mulling thoughts about inside her head.

"What has he done that has you believe he wouldn't want more than a bedding?"

Davina seemed more ardent about this topic. "The first night he returned, he handled me like a tavern wench!" Her cheeks flushed. Whether out of embarrassment or anger, Rosselyn couldn't tell.

"How did you imagine your first encounter would be?" Rosselyn had an idea of why Davina was so disappointed, but wanted her to voice it.

She opened her mouth, but no words came forth, and then she closed her lips. Davina sighed. "They were childish fantasies to be sure, but…" She picked at her cheese, uncharacteristically apprehensive. Rosselyn knew, however, between the two of them, a more timid and childlike Davina often emerged. Though she only had two years on Davina, she knew her friend relied on her as an older, wiser confidant.

"I remember how you envisioned the reunion when you were younger—"

"In spite of that, Roz," Davina interrupted, "he still should not have handled me in such a way." Davina implored Rosselyn with her eyes. "He pretended he didn't recognized me, and I found out later he did. His behavior is so very confusing.

He kisses me like a man starving, and then pushes away from me as if he made a dreadful mistake."

Relief eased the tension from Rosselyn's body. At least they kissed. That was a good sign! Yet, Davina seemed self-absorbed in these matters. "Are you not behaving just as contrarily? Have you told him how much he has meant to you over the years? Have you shared your heart with him?"

Davina gasped. "I cannot do such a thing! He would surely stomp on it as soon as I exposed my true feelings!"

"Why are you so certain?"

She opened her mouth once more and closed it, her bottom lip trembling. Tears glistened in her eyes under the warm glow of the hearth.

"Out of concern for you," Rosselyn ventured, "because of what you have been through and the size Broderick is, I've inquired about his nature. I've asked many of my new friends at the Gypsy camp—people who have spent almost fourteen years living with him—about Broderick's demeanor, asking if I should have any valid concerns for your safety in his hands. All of them—and I stress all of them—have laughed at the notion of Broderick ever doing harm to you. I've heard many reports about his jovial nature, his light-heartedness, and his ease at taking everything with a sense of humor."

"Rosselyn." Davina's voice sounded most serious. "There are things about Broderick you don't know, things you don't understand."

Rosselyn crossed her arms. "I've also heard a few people mention a darker side of Broderick, but that has always been in the context of his being fiercely protective of those he loves. Methinks that's what you're seeing. Possibly, he too is afraid you will stomp on his heart if he shares it with you."

"Rosselyn, you just—"

"You are making excuses, Davina." She placed her palm alongside Davina's face. "I know you want to love again. I know you want to love Broderick. After all the years you have invested your heart in this man, now that you have him, you're finding excuses not to rush in. I understand you're cautious, but you cannot guard your heart the way you do." Davina's lips trembled, and tears dropped from her eyes as she closed them, making it difficult for Rosselyn to keep the emotion from her voice. "My sweet friend, falling in love is allowing yourself to be vulnerable enough to open your heart. Love is taking risks. If you want the love you have been dreaming of for so long, you must be willing to get hurt. I know the way you love him, and I've seen the way he looks at you. Do not let this chance pass by. You will regret it forever."

Optimism sparkled in Davina's eyes. Rosselyn hoped her words found their way into Davina's heart. The two women hugged each other, and unexpected tears poured from Davina as she clung to Rosselyn, who rocked her in her embrace until the tears were spent. She couldn't risk hurting Davina more at this moment. Rosselyn couldn't share her secret now.

Broderick called to Davina, but every time he tried to get near her, she put distance and obstacles between them. In the Gypsy camp, she regarded him with frightened eyes as she scampered between tents and wagons. In the forest, she ran to put trees and bushes between them. In her chamber, she stayed to the other side of the room, hiding behind furniture casting worried eyes at the double doors. Broderick went to the terrace, and a stretch of white sparkling snow covered the grounds. When he turned to face Davina, she shook her head, crying, begging Broderick to go away, and yet reaching out to him with trembling hands.

Broderick awakened upon the setting of the sun and stretched his body to work out the effects of his deathlike slumber. The furs on his bedding smoothed over his naked skin and he frowned, thinking of Davina. These dreams disturbed Broderick. He didn't understand them. At least this time he didn't awake with an erection. Dressing, he stepped out of his cave and stood in awe at the glistening sight before him. "Well, what a surprise," he said. A few snowflakes fell from the sky to join the rest over the forest floor. "Appears as if we will be in Stewart Glen a little longer than we planned." His emotions teetered between elation and dread, so Broderick pushed this uncertainty from his mind and set out to hunt Angus, and then to feed.

Broderick stood at the tent entrance, Amice sat by the fire pit, and Veronique was sequestered inside the caravan. Staring out into the Gypsy camp, so devoid of activity, an unease settled over Broderick. The cold weather kept the townspeople inside, and the Gypsies overstayed their welcome. Though a concern, because Broderick had come to view these people as his family, the more pressing concern for him lay outside this pocket of civilization…Angus Campbell.

Amice studied Broderick with her eyes, stoking the fire and wrapping her heavier shawl around her shoulders for warmth. "What troubles you, *mon fils?*"

Broderick avoided her gaze. He knew he should have warned her earlier, but he hadn't anticipated how difficult it would be to gain control of this situation. Or perhaps he fooled himself into thinking he had any control. Sighing, he turned his eyes toward her. "He's here, Amice."

After a moment of silence, she turned her eyes to the fire. She continued in French. "You think Angus has finally returned?"

"Nay, I know. I've spent every night since our arrival tracking him, but he's always just out of my reach."

"And Davina is directly in his path."

His mouth dropped open. "What makes you think that?"

"Forgive me for not making the time to tell you. Davina came to visit yesterday afternoon, asking for herbal remedies for her mother. Broderick, Angus has approached her."

"She told you what happened in the exchange?"

Amice nodded. "Not all of it, but he told her he had a divine message that you would return and rescue her."

Broderick tightened his jaw. "The first night we arrived, Angus's face was in Davina's memories. I didn't say anything because I didn't want to worry you. This is why I've pursued her, to find out how she plays a part in his scheme."

Amice placed a fresh kettle of water on the fire and sat back on her stool, waiting until Broderick joined her. "You cannot think she is a willing player in his plans."

"At first, I didn't know, Amice, and having felt the bite of betrayal in the past…"

"I understand, my son."

"Though in a dream of hers in which I entered last night, Davina told me she sees him as a kind of savior."

"Aye, I had the same impression, and I warned her not to trust this man." Amice's eye grew wide. "Only last night did you get this information? Why has it taken you so long?"

Broderick shifted uncomfortably. "She has the uncanny ability to block her thoughts, even stronger than you do, but this gift is uncontrolled."

"Why should that matter? The thoughts are nothing against the knowledge you gain when you feed from someone. Surely you considered this, to use this tool you know so well?"

He clenched his jaw again.

"You care for her too much to cross that boundary." Amice sighed. "Though respecting that boundary has put her life in danger, I am neither ashamed nor frightened to say I am glad of your fondness toward her."

The blood drained from his face. "If you think I have feelings for her, then I cannot doubt that Angus also sees what you do. I have indeed fallen for Angus's trap, just as he planned." Broderick rose from the stool and paced. The hairs on the back of his neck tingled at the approaching presence of Angus Campbell. "He's coming," he hissed. "Stay in the caravan and block your thoughts." Skirting into the darkness behind the tent, Broderick hid from wandering eyes before dashing off into the night to chase after Angus, and prevent him from entering the camp.

Broderick arrived at Davina's castle and found few, if any, windows illuminated. He needed to get to the bottom of this. He failed to find Angus. Where Broderick concentrated on improving his skills in sensing others of his kind, Angus, it seemed, had focused on improving his speed, and perhaps something more Broderick didn't realize they could do. Angus's presence would be there one moment and then the next, gone. How was that possible? Another lesson his mentor and teacher conveniently left out? Rasheed would definitely get an earful the next time they met…if they ever did.

Broderick skirted through the shadows of the courtyard to stand below the landing by Davina's chamber. The amber glow of firelight came from her narrow window, and when he leapt up to the small stone wall of the terrace, he peered into her chamber. Candles burned and a warm fire blazed in the hearth. Her restless figure paced the floor. He sighed and advanced to the double doors. Her temper would not fare well. He feared Davina rumbled around in her head with dizzying thoughts and rationalizations as she had done so many times before. The woman needed to stop trying to solve every facet of her life and learn to live it. Through his immortal gifts, he reached out to sense the details of her disposition—fear, confusion, frustration.

Though Broderick fancied his stealth entrances as a game between them, a playful mood did not seem appropriate. He entered the room without permission, moving through the curtains and standing before her shocked demeanor. "I didn't think you'd have granted me entrance had I knocked."

She crossed her arms. "You are correct, sir."

"My apologies, but we have a serious matter to discuss," he said, keeping his distance.

"Aye."

He could hear the questions bubbling up in Davina's mind about what he was, and the mysteries about him that frightened her so— questions Broderick didn't want to answer at this time. "I need you to tell me what happened the night Angus—" Broderick stopped to prevent her from defending her savior. "The night Angus and you met."

"I don't understand your connection to this man. Do you know him?"

"Aye, all too well." Broderick's voice trembled and he cleared his throat. "He's the man who slaughtered my family.

"Merciful Father," Davina gasped and sat on the settee at the foot of her bed. "Broderick, I had no idea— I cannot understand—" She shook her head. "Why did he say the things he said to me?"

"I only know you met him in that clearing. The images I've seen from your mind have been fleeting and conflicting." He crossed his arms. "I don't think you realize your gift. You're very good at blocking your thoughts, mistress."

"I am?"

"Aye, you are." Broderick sat beside her and took her hand in his. "Davina, please tell me what happened so I can gauge whether or not you're in danger."

Davina stared at him with fear-filled eyes. "Danger, but why?"

"I believe Angus is using you to get to me, though I'm not exactly sure why. We hardly know each other, and yet there are signs in the images I've seen from your thoughts that lead me to believe he thinks otherwise."

Davina nodded. "I went to the clearing upset, at a very bleak time in my life." Dropping her gaze into her lap, she took her hand from his and fiddled with the cloth of her robes. "I took the coward's escape and planned to end my own life." Tears dropped onto the backs of Davina's hands.

Broderick wiped the tears from her skin and put a comforting hand over hers. "'Tis understandable, Davina. Do not blame yourself for having such notions. Thankfully, you didn't go through with it."

She nodded and cleared her throat. "Angus is the reason I didn't succeed. I'm unsure of what happened. I only remember waking with a large bump on my head, and Angus sitting beside me, relieved he saved me from myself." She squeezed Broderick's hand. "I, too, am relieved he stopped me from such a terrible deed, which is why I don't understand how he could have slaughtered your family. He seemed so caring."

Broderick bit back his snide remarks. "What else did he say? Amice mentioned he had a divine message for you?"

"Aye, he said God led him to the forest that night with a special message of which he couldn't make sense of. He said, 'You must tell her that he will return, that he will rescue her. You must tell her not to give up hope and hold to that image of strength.' Those were the words you said to me when we first met. You said to hold to an image of strength, and that would get me through the troubled times you foretold."

Broderick rose and advanced thoughtfully to the hearth, rubbing his jaw. "Davina, I need to ask you something, and I need you to be truthful with me." He faced her. "What was that image of strength you held to?" Broderick knew the answer, but he had to hear it from her to be sure.

Davina dropped her gaze to her lap to watch her fiddling fingers. "They were childish fantasies, Broderick, foolish."

"Davina, please tell me."

"You," she whispered.

He turned his eyes back to the hearth, seeking the flames for refuge. "I feared as much." Angus gleaned those thoughts from Davina in her time of despair, and then used her as bait to get to Broderick. Angus must have learned the wide circuit of the Gypsies. It was only a matter of time before they repeated visiting the towns. Angus may have even fed from Davina, and learned much about her heartfelt feelings for Broderick that mere thoughts could only touch upon. Because Davina thought of Broderick for so long, using him to get through the hard times, Angus knew once Broderick returned to Stewart Glen, she would pursue him or at least seek him out...and those images Angus left of himself in her mind would cause Broderick to pursue Davina to learn what he could. Angus had been lying in wait. But for how long?

"Davina, when—?" When Broderick turned back to face Davina, he saw her body trembling with sobs. Rushing to her side, he touched her shoulder with concern, but she shoved him away. "Davina, pray tell me what troubles you so much?"

"Leave me!"

"Davina, please—"

Her tearful eyes glared at him as she shoved him away and stomped to the fire, putting her back to him. "You can read my thoughts, can you not? Divine what you must, but leave me alone!"

True enough, she opened her mind, and he could sense her rejection and broken heart. Broderick's last statement of "I feared as much" caused this turmoil. She had misunderstood, and he had been so lost in solving this personal mystery of his, he had not noticed her sorrow.

"Nay, you misunderstood me." Broderick stood at a precipice. He no longer had a quest to find information from her. He knew those answers now. He could just walk away and let her think what she wanted. He should. It would be easier for her to let him go if she hated him. Then why did her heartbreak touch him to the core of his being?

"How could I misunderstand? You have made it very clear you don't hold anything in your heart for me other than lust."

Broderick stepped behind Davina, aching to pull her into his arms. The fire blazed in the highlights of her auburn curls and the aroma of her blood and rose oil filled his senses. Placing gentle hands upon her shoulders, he turned Davina to face him. She shrugged and tried to step out of his reach, but he wrapped her in his arms, holding her against him in spite of her resistance. "Davina, listen to me," he breathed against her temple. "I meant that I feared Angus knew you cared for me, which is the reason he chose you to lure me into his trap." Broderick pulled back enough to gaze at her tear-stained face. "What I fear more than anything is that he has succeeded, and his success has put you in danger."

She tried to turn away, but he held her chin steady, pressing her to face at him. Her eyes squeezed shut and she pleaded, "Do not look at me as if you care! I know better. I'm not the fool you think I am."

"Look at me, Davina," he whispered.

She stopped struggling, her eyes still closed. *I cannot bear the heartache!* she screamed in her head.

"Davina…" He breathed her name.

Her eyes, filled with anguish, gazed up at him with a glimmer of hope. His thumbs brushed away the tears from her cheeks, his chest aching. How could he blame her for having such suspicions? "My intentions began with discovering your part in Angus's plan, but heaven strike me down, Davina, I cannot help myself when I'm near you." Broderick brushed the back of his fingers against Davina's throat, and his heart quickened at the warmth of her skin. His words came out in a whisper. "The sight of you, the touch of you, the very scent of you makes my soul drunk with pleasure, and I find I cannot get enough of you, blossom."

His eyes took in every inch of her delicate features and settled upon the bow of her mouth. She sighed when his thumb caressed her bottom lip, and Broderick leaned forward to taste her sigh. His mouth covered hers, tentative caresses at first, but when Davina moaned, he plunged deeper. Broderick reveled in the warmth of her arms wrapped around him. His arm swept down her body, cradling her legs around his side, and he carried her toward the bed. Their kiss broken, Davina lay back against the pillows, her eyes hooded and inviting. Broderick sat on the bed beside her, studying her. Her chest rose and fell in deep breaths. He hesitated in this moment to drink in her beauty, but also to give her an opportunity to stop him. He waited for her protests, hoping they would never come, gazing at this woman he ached for. This image would be burned into his dreams— the firelight playing upon her skin, the flames dancing in her eyes, her full mouth parted in anticipation. Davina touched her hand to his cheek, a gentle smile playing upon her lips. She then smoothed her fingers to the nape of his neck and pulled him toward her. "Davina," he breathed as their mouths joined, open and hungry for each other.

Misty images of Davina's limbs wrapped around Broderick's bare back, fluttered through his mind. Broderick groaned, his groin hardening even more, as Davina's thoughts explored the possibilities of their lovemaking. With haste, Broderick yanked off his boots, tossed his belt and sporran aside, and tugged his shirt over his head. Davina shed her house robe, her translucent night dress teasing his desire. Broderick stretched his body beside her under the warmth of the covers, providing her a cocoon of protection. Drawing her into his embrace once again, his hand slid down her back to cup her bottom and bring her against the length of his body.

Davina's breath quivered at the sensation of Broderick's erection against her belly, at the smoothing of his hand over her bottom, encouraging her to press against him. The warm, moist heat of his breath against her neck sent ripples of pleasure over her skin, and she ached to feel his mouth upon her breasts. Pushing away from him, she pulled the neck of her nightdress down over her shoulder, and his eyes reflected the desire flowing through her limbs, her soul pleading for him to do what she wanted. His full lips parted in anticipation, and he opened her gown, exposing her breast to him. Sweet, tender kisses teased her flesh as he gently cupped her breast in his hand, worshiping her body with his mouth, darting his tongue out to leave tingling trails of wetness. Her expectation released as his mouth closed around her nipple, tight with need, and she arched her back with a husky moan, reveling in his soft hair in her hands.

Putting her hand between their bodies, Davina reached for his breeches, to do away with the barrier keeping him from her. Broderick helped her push the material away and guided her hand to take possession of him. His hardness made her sex clench, tightening with hunger, pulsing with heat. She moaned, squeezing him as he breathed her name.

Pushing her nightdress to her waist, Broderick's fingers caressed their way over her hip, down her bottom, and nestled between her legs, stroking the wet folds of her hot center. He breathed against her ear, sending shuddering waves through her body. "I have ached for you, dreamed of you. I cannot get my fill of you." The sincerity in his voice dripped like honey over her heart, bringing warm tears to her eyes.

Broderick seized her mouth in a rapacious kiss and positioned his body between her legs. The tip of his shaft touched the sensitive junction between her thighs. He stroked the head of his cock along her valley of moisture, sending more twitches tingling through her body, and slid inside her, both of them moaning with the release of this anticipated moment of joining. Grunting her name, Broderick drove the length of his erection in and out with slow, coaxing thrusts, each plunge deep and fulfilling, driving Davina faint with pleasure.

A shattering cry erupted from behind the door of the nursery, jarring them both. *Cailin!* The guilt of her surrender tumbled down upon her like a load of stones. Davina glanced at Broderick's wide eyes and escaped from under him, righting her nightgown. Cailin's wailing tore at her conscience, and she fought back tears of shame. "This was wrong," she whispered, unable to face Broderick, still in her bed. She never should have listened to Rosselyn and given into her impulses. She had a child to think of. She scampered to the door, her face hot with humiliation. Before she disappeared behind the door of the nursery, she saw his bewildered expression and her heart twisted with regret. "Please…go."

CHAPTER ELEVEN

What in Hades was that! Broderick lay where Davina left him, confounded. *A baby?* He heard the name *Cailin* from Davina's mind. She cooed and soothed the child, the sounds drifting through the small crack of the open door, leaving Broderick no other conclusion except that she was the mother. Davina had a child? This explained a lot—including her sensitive breasts—but left a lot of unanswered questions. Ian, this dead man she feared so much, must have been her husband and the child's father. Why had he not gleaned this from her thoughts? Why did she not tell him? Pacing the length of the hearth, Broderick raked his fingers through his hair, questions tumbling around in his head. Scolding himself, he couldn't believe he never picked up on it. Well, he could believe his short-sightedness. He had one thing on his mind—getting information from her. *Well, two things on your mind, you rogue.*

So, the next question—why hide she was a widow? What kind of battle raged inside this woman's head?

Broderick, too impatient to wait, wanted answers now. He fixed his breeches, threw on his shirt and boots, and marched over to the adjoining room, ready to demand those answers, but the words died on his breath. Broderick stood immobilized in the open doorway.

Embers from the hearth cast a crimson glow upon Davina, seated in a chair close to the dying fire's warmth. She sat unaware of him, so intent on humming to her child, caressing the infant's cheek. Tears shone on Davina's face. In her arms lay a babe who seemed less than a year old—*Cailin*. With cinnamon curls so much like her mother's, her pink mouth suckled at Davina's nipple, her tiny hand resting on the fullness of her breast. His mouth watered at the sight. At the same time, this image of purity, motherhood, and innocence kindled a protective nature that flamed in his soul. Broderick clenched his fists. Immortality would never allow him to experience the joy of having his own children—fatherhood sacrificed for revenge. For the first time, the impact of his foolish decision pierced his heart like a blade. Who was this idiot who wasted the woman and child Broderick now ached to cherish and shelter? Surely, he deserved to die.

Davina raised her head and their eyes met. Her sweet humming stopped, as did the caresses she gave her child. Her eyes turned cold as she glared at him, wrapping protective arms around her baby. Shame swallowed him whole as he became an intruder in this delicate scene. He stared at her a moment longer before he retreated to the bedchamber.

In awkward silence, Broderick waited for Davina to finish, righting his clothing to keep his hands and mind occupied. After a few endless moments, she emerged from the room, closed the door behind her with care and marched to the armoire beside the double doors. Without offering him a single glance, she put on pair of slippers, donned her cloak and stepped out of the chamber, between the heavy curtains onto the terrace. Broderick followed her into the biting night air.

She stood rigid with her back to him. He could feel the heat in his face, flushed from embarrassment. "Davina, I—"

"How dare you!" she snapped and turned on him. "Can I have no privacy with you? Not even when it concerns my own daughter?"

"I am sorry." Broderick bowed his head in shame. Davina's silence drew his attention. She stood gawking. Did she not expect an apology from him? What kind of man was this husband of hers that any form of kindness or humbling took her by surprise? His many questions came back to him. "Why did you not tell me you were widowed?"

""Tis none of your business. None of my life is any business of yours."

Broderick ignored her scolding. "But how——? Whose——?"

"My husband was killed in the Battle of Flodden Field."

"Why did you not mention him when you told me of your brother and father?"

"As I said, 'tis no business of yours." Davina turned her back to him and bowed her head.

"He's the one from which you wanted me to rescue you." Broderick didn't ask. He made a simple statement.

He could feel embarrassment emanating from her. Davina remained motionless for a long period of silence, her back still to him, and then she nodded.

He clenched his jaw and fists, but reasoned he wasted his energy. With her husband dead, he would be unable to continue his abuse. "I cannot say I'm sorry you lost your husband."

"Nor can I."

Broderick placed a comforting hand upon her shoulder, and she shrugged him off.

"I told you to leave," she said with sorrow in her voice. "You have what you came for. You made it into my bed, now please go."

"Is that what you think this was about?" Broderick put his hands upon her shoulders, turning Davina to face him. Flashes of her husband and an overwhelming sense of betrayal assailed Broderick's mind and crawled over his body like a death shroud. The many times Ian lied to Davina, lured her in with sweet words, tender caresses and empty promises; all of them ending in violence and violation of her body and heart. Broderick almost staggered back from the mental and emotional assault.

"I cannot trust your intentions, Broderick. I cannot trust what you may say. You have pursued me in such a lustful way, I cannot believe I mean more to you than just a bedding."

Broderick fought the tears stinging his eyes. The slashing scars on her body *showed* him the abuse she endured. The rush of her memories made him *experience* the depth of the abuse from her perspective. Remembering how Davina snapped at Rosselyn for showing pity made Broderick keep his tears at bay. "Everything that just happened has meant more to me than I want to admit because of the depth of my…my love for you, Davina." He wiped the tear that ran down her cheek and stepped into her heat. "A love that may end up getting you killed. And now I've put your daughter in danger." Broderick sighed, taking Davina's hands and putting her knuckles to his mouth in a desperate kiss. "I'm torn, Davina. Tonight, I wanted to walk away from you when I thought you hated me, thinking it would have been best. But I fear I've fallen too deeply to turn away, because my enemy must already know you mean something to me. And now that I know you have a daughter, there is nothing that could keep me away from you, no matter what the threat may be. All I ever desired was to have a family, and you are all that to me."

Davina's eyes welled with more tears and she bit her trembling bottom lip. "There is a darker side to you that frightens me, Broderick. A silver glow I see in your eyes. You speak of a passion for blood. Veronique tried to tell me what you are, and though her words make sense with what I've seen with my own eyes, my heart begs for it to be lies. What are you?"

Broderick knew this moment would come. Until now, he never regretted his decision to become a Vamsyrian, and yet he hated what he was because of the fear in her eyes. One thing was certain: He wanted this woman in his life. He didn't care if this was what Angus intended from the beginning, or what set him on this path to losing his heart to her. His heart was already lost, and he would do anything to protect her, whether she wanted him or not. He would, however, rather have her love in return and telling her the truth at this time would crush that chance.

"I want to answer your questions," he began. "I want to tell you everything, to tell you the truth. I've never wanted to share this with anyone as much as I do with you, but I cannot answer your questions at this time."

A hope flickered in Davina's eyes, but the fear and uncertainty that emanated from her made her bottom lip quiver and her tears flow anew. "Why? What—"

"Please, Davina," he begged and kissed her brow. "I'm asking you to give me some time, 'tis all. I promise I *will* tell you everything, but there are certain…tasks I must see to before I can." Facing Angus and eliminating him, being the most important and pressing matter.

Davina collapsed into Broderick's arms, her body wracking with sobs as he held her tight. Her heartfelt cries drifted out over the snow-covered courtyard and disappeared into the cold night.

Angus leaned back against the wall as he sat on the ground. His grumbling was muffled inside the cellar of the small tower structure he built almost a year ago. It was the one lair Broderick had not yet found. This little dwelling was quiet, tucked away in the woods far to the northwest, too far out of the area Broderick dared to venture from the Gypsy camp. Angus didn't need anything fancy, nothing elaborate or even functional, in a mortal sense. He purposefully built the structure to appear abandoned and useless. It provided shelter and housed the hidden cellar he crafted, where he slept during the daylight hours. Angus needed nothing else as he sat waiting for the moment to spring his trap, which had, at last, arrived.

Broderick's failed attempts at finding him over the last several nights were amusing, but starting to bore him, and he grumbled once more. Two things Broderick had learned to do caught Angus off guard. First was the ability to stop feeding to spare lives. Doing such a thing went against the very nature and purpose of a Vamsyrian. Death was indeed the goal, as their Creator designed. How else was one to rack up so many sins against the soul, making it impossible to turn back toward God? Just the free-will choice to become a Vamsyrian was the axe of the executioner for their souls. Did Broderick think to spare these lives in order to avoid final judgment? Angus snarled at Broderick's meaningless quest. Did he hope to make up for the sins against his soul before he became a Vamsyrian? Broderick pretended to be a hero, a man of honor and integrity, but Angus knew the true soul that lurked inside his black heart.

These weak attempts at salvation in sparing these lives were a waste. Then again, Angus saw the benefits of such a skill. Angus wouldn't have been able to spare the sweet Davina had he not learned such a thing from Broderick years ago, by feeding from the people Broderick spared. The first time Angus tried to stop in the middle of a feeding, he failed. Not wanting to be bested by his enemy, it had taken him several attempts before he finally mastered the talent. The monumental strength of will it took to wrestle the Hunger into obedience turned out to be greater than he imagined, and the little respect he had for Broderick increased.

Davina was a means to an end, a hope that Broderick would dally with the lass as a distraction, giving Angus time to find out who Broderick really cared about. Broderick couldn't spend almost a decade-and-a-half with these Gypsies and not form some lasting relationships. Feeding from Davina helped him learn about Amice. He saw the old woman and her connection to Broderick through Davina's memories, but he couldn't count on the old woman still being around by the time Broderick arrived in Stewart Glen. And the victims Angus killed in cleaning up after Broderick gave him no pertinent clues about such things. Revenge would be to torment Broderick through the ones he loved, just as Broderick had tormented him. He had to learn about whom Broderick cared; yet, that proved to be most difficult.

Angus kicked the dirt wall in his cellar, grunting his frustration. That was the second thing Broderick learned that caught Angus off guard—his ability to sense Angus before Angus could sense him. Every time he started toward the Gypsy settlement or Stewart Glen, Broderick's presence loomed like a hawk swooping down from the sky unannounced. He didn't know if Amice still lived or who had replaced her. He couldn't even get close enough to observe from a distance.

The age-old hatred erupted, and Angus clenched his fists. Broderick knew who Angus was, and yet Broderick purposely made himself the enemy, seeking to end Angus's life. Broderick had been given everything denied to Angus, yet he still wanted Angus's blood. Angus pounded his fists against the ground upon which he sat. "None of it was enough for you!" Broderick's entire life had been a mockery of what Angus hoped to achieve. No matter how hard Angus tried to prove himself, Broderick shoved his nose in Angus's position amongst his brothers, like a dog in its own excrement. Rick even stole Angus's idea of using immortality for revenge, no thanks to Cordelia. What a fiasco that turned out to be.

Angus stood and dressed, then pushed his way out through the cellar door in a hidden corner of the high-ceilinged room. Listening to the sounds of the area to make sure he was alone, Angus heard the distant rumble of thunder from the north. Another storm. He smiled at the appropriate setting the icy weather would create. He set off down the hill, through the dense forest several miles northwest of Stewart Glen. As he glided silently over the snow, dashing between the trees, he chuckled over the new development in his plan. He needed a distraction, and the poor lovesick man with the hairy knuckles he observed in Strathbogie last night would be just the one.

Veronique's hand trembled as she pushed at the stone wall behind the bushes. With her grandmother asleep and Broderick still out for the evening, she had grabbed what she needed and slipped away from the camp with no one's notice. The darkness of the deep night made finding Nicabar's path difficult, and the newly fallen snow didn't help. Even though the white landscape provided a backdrop to at least see the shadow of trees, she hadn't the proper shoes to protect her feet. Nor did she have anything for her hands to guard against the cold.

Why didn't the wall open the way it had for Nicabar? She cursed under her breath and tried again. Nothing. Veronique's fingers crept along the cold stone in the darkness, searching and shivering from the freezing temperature. She held her shawl closer around her shoulders, not giving up. *There!* She pushed the nub protruding from the stone and the wall submitted. Breathing a sigh of relief, she pushed the wall section with all her might and stepped into the dark passage. A deafening silence oppressed her, the shadowed courtyard empty and ominous. A heavy, throttling sigh from one of the horses shattered the stillness and she gasped. Gritting her teeth, she crept along the stables, cringing at the crunching of her steps. She waited at the corner of the stables, hunting for movement. Confident she was alone, she stepped across the courtyard—thankful her footprints mingled with the multitude of others—and over to the castle wall. Listening for any sound, she tried the door she had seen the man named Seamus use, thankful the latch hadn't been locked.

The kitchen lay dark and empty. Veronique waited until her eyes became accustomed to the blackness. Tiptoeing through the hall, keeping close to the wall, she peered into the first door. The dark shapes seemed familiar. She stepped into the doorway and recognized the parlor where she told Davina about Broderick's true nature. She snorted as she thought of the stupid Scot. Now that she had her bearings, she backtracked into the kitchen.

The illumination from the open, outside door helped her make out the shape of a large table at the center of the room. She padded along the walls, trailing her hand along the wooden panel, and almost screeched at the clanging of the implements she'd touched. Stilling them, she darted her eyes around the room, waiting for someone to come running in to investigate the commotion. She could just make out two doors along the back wall. Scampering to close the outside door, she tiptoed her way blindly to where she saw the first door, and ducked inside. She waited in silence.

The thick scent of ale and foodstuff surrounded her. She listened, but nothing save the hammering of her heart pounded in her ears. The pitch-blackness of the room seemed suffocating, so she eased the door open to let in some of the dim lighting afforded by windows near the ceiling. Still no one appeared in the kitchen. She sighed and turned to contemplate the room. With her eyes now more accustomed to the dark, she saw shelves of provisions lined the walls, and several huge barrels sat in the corner. This was what she wanted! She searched franticly for the honey pot. *There!* Lifting the lid, she stepped before the pot and looked inside, hesitating.

Veronique clutched the stolen vial in her smock pocket. Autumn crocus, an herbal liquid Amice used to cure gout. Veronique remembered tasting the bitter brew when she was younger, sneaking through her grandmother's potions, intent on sampling the many exotic-scented concoctions, not knowing at all what she did. Lucky for her, Amice caught her only after trying the first vial—the autumn crocus. Even after Amice made her vomit, she remained sick for two days. The painful experience from her childhood formed a bitter tang in her mouth, reminiscent of the poison.

This honey may be eaten by anyone in the household, she surmised. *What if someone else gets sick instead of Davina?* She replaced the lid and bit her lip. What if she missed the mark entirely? Davina would still be able to accept visitors while someone else suffered and lay sick in bed, not solving her problem. She searched the contents of the cupboard for answers, as if the vegetables and dried meats could tell her what to do. Veronique stopped short and gasped with excitement. A small jar next to the larger honey pot bore the name "Mistress Davina" in the pottery surface. She opened the lid and sniffed. *Honey!* She shook her head and giggled. *The spoiled brat has her own supply!*

Putting the lid down on the shelf beside the pot, she held the vial and again hesitated. How much? Veronique tested only a little of the potion as a girl, but she drank the concoction directly not diluted, and she was much younger. What she held in this vile was enough to kill Davina. Veronique shook her head, certain she wouldn't eat the whole jar. But what if she ate too much? Did she want to put Davina through such torture? Part of her said nay, she didn't want to be responsible if things went wrong. But the other part of her quickly pushed away any of the warnings threatening her mission. This part of her wanted to see Davina suffer. She closed her eyes and imagined Broderick, seeing him pursue Davina with a passion she dreamed he would pursue her with; a passion she had not seen him pursue anyone else with, but that Davina. What made her so special? The most frustrating part was how Davina opposed Broderick at every turn. She despised him. Why did he want her so much? Why, when Veronique came to him willing and able and so much in love with him already? She swallowed the lump in her throat and gripped the potion tighter.

Veronique poured the entire contents of the tiny vial into the honey and used the wand to stir the potion about. *Davina will not eat it all*, she reasoned. Veronique grinned, very satisfied with the completed task. Putting the vial back into her smock, she replaced the small honey crock and turned toward the door. A shadow and bright light crossed the wall. Veronique froze. Shuffling steps sounded in the kitchen, and she shrank back into the pantry, trying to disappear into the darkness. Veronique's heart pounded in her ears as the door opened and she ducked behind a barrel.

The silhouette of a female entered the pantry, a candle sitting on the kitchen table providing the bright light. Though the shadows hid the person's face well, Veronique could just make out the features. She put her hand over her mouth to keep her fright in check. *Davina!* Several prayers rattled around inside the young Gypsy's head. Davina grabbed her crock of honey and left Veronique undiscovered in the darkness. She breathed a quiet sigh of relief and almost collapsed on the floor. She waited a moment before peeking through the doorway. Davina sat at the table in the center of the kitchen and Veronique sat back in her hiding spot behind the barrel, biting her curved index finger to keep from screaming her frustrations. She would have to wait until Davina finished and went back to bed.

Sitting at the long prep table in the kitchen, Davina placed the crock before her and swirled the honey around with the wand, her chin in her hand as she watched the golden liquid glistening in the candlelight. "Oh, Kehr," she sighed and closed her eyes.

She could almost see her brother sitting at the table beside her, his large frame leaning against her—shoulder to shoulder—resting on his elbows as he dipped his finger into the honey and pulled out a dripping mouthful. She chuckled. "You were always a glutton about eating our honey."

"I am not!" he retorted.

Davina pursed her lips at her brother. "Aye, you are indeed!" She dipped a delicate finger into the crock and coated the tip with the sticky treat. "You don't have to load your finger up with all the honey it can take. Just a taste, Kehr."

Davina brought her finger to her mouth and touched her tongue before she closed her lips around her finger and let the honey melt into her mouth. She opened her eyes. This new batch of honey Seamus picked up yesterday tasted bitter. She would have to speak with him and find out from whom he'd purchased it. Had he changed beekeepers? She tried another sample, shrugged and continued eating. Aye, she would indeed need to speak with Seamus. She closed her eyes once more.

"See?" she continued her imagined conversation with her brother. Davina swirled the honey around, enjoying the smoothness on her tongue and the roof of her mouth. "Savor every drop of this nectar from the Gods."

Kehr held his laughter back for as long as he could, and then burst into a mild fit. "'Nectar of the Gods,'" he mocked. "Savor all you want. I'm gorging." They giggled together in the darkness.

Davina opened her eyes to find herself alone again, the candle flame twirling its silent dance upon the wick, morphing the shadows around her, drawing her into its lazy movements. The flame glistened like a star through her tears, a half-hearted grin tugged at the corners of her mouth as she continued eating the honey, choking back her grief.

"Sorry, lass," Broderick said to the young woman sitting before him in the tent. He released her hand and smiled. "I cannot give you details. The lines do not reveal anything more than generalities." She cast him a dreamy smile. This was the third trip the lass made into their tent to see Broderick, and though he didn't normally read a palm more than once, twice at the maximum, they needed the funds. Nevertheless, she was there for more than mere fortune telling, and he didn't feel right about making her part with her coin. When a long silence passed and she failed to get up from the table, Broderick leaned forward. "I cannot give you what you seek, lass. Run along now." Her hand flew to her blushing cheek, her smile vanished from her face, and she dashed from the tent without depositing any donation. Broderick shook his head, feeling sorry for the girl.

Sighing, he sat back in his chair and crossed his arms, alone to ponder his fruitless search the night before. There were times when Broderick could sense Angus, certain he would pop out of the darkness from behind a building or tree or rock. Then the presence disappeared. No more tingling sensations in his midsection, no more hairs rising on the back of his neck. Nothing. He wanted to comb the land for his enemy, not sit here reading fortunes. Conversely, he didn't want to leave the people he loved alone and vulnerable, so he stayed to protect them.

Mulling over the failure would do him no good. He turned his attention to other matters: His dreams. They were becoming more disturbing as the nights wore on. Frowning, he recalled the frantic images of Davina wasting away—her face gaunt and her gut cramping. No matter what he did, he couldn't get near enough to help her; her cries for his assistance went unanswered. He wanted very much to check on Davina, but needed to focus his attention on Angus, and she was too delightful a distraction.

Making his way to the tent opening, he noticed Amice and Veronique sitting at the fireside. Flames performed a flitting dance in the pit as the women huddled near its warmth. The snow on the ground lay thick. The cold silence broke when hurried footsteps sounded in the camp.

Rosselyn stumbled up to them. "Amice, we need your help! Davina is ill." Her bottom lip quivered. "We fear she may die!"

Broderick's heart battered in his chest, and Amice stood. "What are her signs?" she asked.

"She has complained her stomach and throat hurt. She has been very thirsty, but taking anything has been difficult for her to swallow. And she has terrible diarrhea."

"How long has she been like this?"

"All day," Rosselyn supplied.

"Veronique, fetch my basket," Amice ordered. Veronique ran to the caravan and emerged with the basket in hand and concern in her eyes. Amice took the basket, squeezed her granddaughter's hand in thanks and turned to Broderick. Amice stopped. Her brows raised and suspicion in her eyes, she grabbed Veronique's hand again. This time, Veronique made a desperate attempt to loose herself from her grandmother's probing grasp.

"What have you done, child?" she demanded in French.

Veronique stared at Amice in shock, her hand upon her breast. "Me?"

"Do not lie to me, child!" she reprimanded. Amice squeezed her granddaughter's wrist, causing her to wince. "You know I can sense what you have done!"

"Then you can divine what I gave her!" Veronique snapped back.

Amice slapped her face. "Tell me! And I want to know why!"

Veronique gasped, but would say nothing. Amice considered Broderick.

He nodded and stepped forward. Veronique wrestled to get away, but she was no match for his speed or strength. He held her by the shoulders and hugged her to his chest. She stopped struggling. "She put a vial of autumn crocus in Davina's honey jar," Broderick supplied, speaking in French so Rosselyn wouldn't understand.

Amice gasped. "The entire vial?"

Broderick nodded and Amice wailed. Veronique jutted her chin out, pushing away from Broderick. "She will be well! She will be bedridden until we leave, but she will fare well enough!"

"You foolish child! You may have killed her!"

Veronique crossed her arms in defiance and glanced at Broderick. He turned away, too afraid he would do something regretful. Broderick went to the back of the wagon, grabbed one of the horses and swung onto its back. "Rosselyn, get Nicabar to escort you back to the castle."

She nodded, but eyed Veronique with venom in her eyes.

"Go," Broderick encouraged, waving his hand. "I will deal with Veronique later."

Rosselyn reluctantly withdrew and went to Nicabar's wagon.

Securing her basket of herbal remedies, Amice mounted in front of Broderick with his help. In minutes, they stormed through the front gates of the castle. A small team of servants led them to Davina's chamber. Davina's pitiful figure lay pale, almost shriveled amongst the bedclothes. When Amice appraised Davina, she whirled toward the people in the room. "*Sortez!* Out of the room, everyone! And I want hot water at once!"

"But I want to be with her!" Lilias protested.

"If you want your daughter to live, you must leave!"

"Tammus?" Lilias pleaded.

The tall man put a comforting arm around Lilias and urged her along. Reluctantly, she nodded and did as Amice ordered, ushering Myrna out before her. When the doors closed, Amice faced Broderick, already standing at Davina's side and holding her hand. He gasped when he touched the weakness of her pulse.

Amice placed her hand upon his shoulder. "Come, help me with my herbs."

Broderick nodded and left Davina's side to stand by Amice, awaiting her instruction.

She will not live without your help, my son, she said mentally. *We must act now.*

A knock came at the door, and Amice took the offered kettle of hot water to the table by the double doors. Broderick closed the door against the protests, giving them their privacy.

Turning her back to Davina, Amice pulled out chamomile blossoms and other sleeping agents, produced a small cup from her basket, sprinkled the herbs into the cup, and poured hot water over the medicine. She held the cup for Broderick. He brought forth Davina's knife from his sporran and cut open his wrist, letting a small measure of his healing blood pour into the cup. Uncharacteristically, the cut burned and Broderick hissed at the pain. Though the cut healed from the blade, it healed slower than usual and left a thin scar. Only one thing could scar him. Amice stared at him with question and worry in her eyes. He regarded the inlaid designs on the blade. "Silver," he whispered.

Amice's brow creased with concern, but she handed the cup to Broderick while she shuffled toward the heavy curtains and pushed through the double doors to the terrace. Her hands filled with a small amount of clean snow, she put some into the cup to cool the scalding water. Tossing the rest of the unused snow out the door, Amice grabbed the cup from Broderick and went to Davina's bedside.

"Come, child," she said, encouraging Davina to sit up. Davina's eyes opened to slits and she tried to smile at Amice. "Drink this, *chérie*." Amice held the warm cup to her lips and helped Davina sip the brew. "Drink it all, Davina."

Broderick watched and expelled a deep sigh of relief. She would be all right.

After Davina finished the tea, Amice went about making her more—this time, without Broderick's blood.

Broderick could see Davina's color already returning, and she opened her sapphire eyes. He sat at her side, holding her hand, and noticed a stronger pulse.

"How amazing. I already feel better," she whispered and squeezed his hand. Amice appeared at the opposite side of her. "What is that wonderful tea you made?" Davina asked. "I can feel the brew working its magic inside me this very moment."

Amice glanced at Broderick. With a slight shake of his head, he silently asked Amice not to reveal the healing source. Amice nodded. "A cup of chamomile tea and a special, secret ingredient, *chérie*." She gave Davina the second cup of tea and shuffled to the door. "I will let them know you are well, and we will have some food brought up to you. You will need your strength back," she said, bowing out and leaving them alone.

"I no longer feel pain in my stomach or throat," she said, her voice very much improved.

"Then Amice has done her job well. I'm glad." Broderick kissed her hand and she smiled.

When a soft knock sounded at the door, Broderick stood and commanded the party to enter, Amice in tow. Lilias rushed to Davina's side. "Thank our Lord, you look better already!" She held her daughter in a tight embrace, and Broderick could feel the relief emanating off Lilias. "Amice is a miracle worker!" She turned to Broderick. "Thank you so much, Master Gypsy. Thank you, Amice. You have both been sent from heaven!"

To Broderick's shock, he blushed and rolled his eyes. *If she only knew.* He risked a secret smile in Amice's direction, and she winked at him.

Lilias called through the door, "Myrna, you may bring Cailin in. Davina is well!"

A large woman with a faint resemblance to Rosselyn waddled through the door, holding a tawny-haired infant with sapphire eyes that locked on to Broderick. The air stilled a moment and Broderick could hear nothing else in the room. Cailin's cherub face sparkled with wonder as she stared at him. A twitter of giggles poured from her like bells, and Broderick swallowed the lump forming in his throat.

"Well, Master Gypsy," Myrna said, grinning. "She seems to fancy you!"

The scene refocused, and he witnessed the many faces cast in his direction. Broderick took two steps toward Cailin, and she fairly launched into his arms, much to the surprise of everyone in the room, especially his.

"I've never seen the like!" Lilias exclaimed. She and Davina exchanges astonished glances.

"Nor have I," she whispered, and a smile formed on Davina's lips.

Broderick struggled to keep the tears at bay with Cailin in his arms, her little hands touching his face and pulling at his lips, to everyone's amusement. How much time had passed since he held a babe in his arms? His nieces and nephews were the last, over three decades ago. Broderick never allowed himself to get this close to something he couldn't have. A warmth wept over his heart and spread across his chest, threatening to envelop his soul. He breathed in Cailin's scent, and fought another lump forming in his throat at the sheer joy of holding her and sharing her essence.

He winked at Davina while Cailin tugged his bottom lip down to his chin, causing Davina to cover her mouth and stifle a laugh. He chuckled, turned to Cailin, and blew a puff of air at her, which caused her to hide her face in his chest, laughing. Broderick savored the warmth of her affections.

After a period of everyone fussing over Davina, who showed improvement every moment, Amice insisted they should leave Davina to rest. They all filed toward the door to exit, and Myrna came forward to take Cailin. Broderick kissed the top of her head, and all, save Broderick, left the room. Lilias lingered at the door, frowning at Broderick, and then Davina.

"'Tis all right, M'ma," Davina assured her.

Eying them both with caution, Lilias exited the room, closing the door behind her, but not before giving Broderick a warning glance, as if to say, "Behave yourself, Gypsy." He hid his smile until she left.

Davina turned her eyes to him. Aye, she did fare much better in just the short amount of time since she drank the tea. One more sigh of relief escaped Broderick's mouth.

"She has always worried so over me," she said, the raspy grate gone from her voice. Davina seemed to notice, too. Her hand went to her throat and she visibly swallowed. "Amazing."

"Aye, Amice is quite the miracle worker." This time stretching his body beside her, he held her hand in his as he propped onto his elbow.

"I've never seen Cailin behave in such a way," she said and smiled. "It seems you have that effect on women."

"Nay, just bonnie redheads," he said and pulled her in to taste her lips. Though he longed for more, he withdrew. "You need your rest, and the food should be coming soon." He stood and leaned against one of the canopy columns. They stared at each other for quite some time, Broderick studying her features. *How can she be more beautiful than the previous day?* His gut twisted at what Davina did to him…to his heart…and how deadly that would be for her. He had to ensure her safety. "I will leave you to rest now."

Davina smiled and nodded.

"Goodnight, Mistress Davina." Bowing, he exited the room by the chamber door and almost ran into Lilias, waiting in the hallway. He was glad he didn't leave by way of the terrace. Lilias would have questioned Davina about his exit, raising suspicion about other ways into her chamber. He raised his eyebrow and crossed his arms. "Greetings, Mistress Lilias. I hope I didn't keep you waiting overmuch."

She matched his stance, crossing her arms. "Too long for my taste, Master Gypsy." They stared at each other for a lengthy stretch of uncomfortable moments. "I hope you have good intentions for my daughter, Gypsy. She has had enough grief and loss in her life. Do not burden her heart with more."

Broderick cringed inside and nodded. "Point well taken, milady." With a curt bow, he left through the front door.

Scanning the area to be sure the way was clear, Broderick kept to the shadows and worked his way to the back of the castle. He listened at the kitchen doorway. No sounds, so he slipped inside. Distant voices lingered through the halls, indicating something else occupied the staff for the moment. He nosed around the room, using the memories he gleaned from Veronique to find his way to the pantry. There on the shelf sat Davina's labeled honey jar. Broderick lifted the lid and sniffed. The bitter aroma mixed in with the honey sweetness made him crinkle his sensitive nose.

Alert to any noise through the halls, he waited for any movement or sounds signifying people milling about. Silence. He stalked over to one of the side tables. Broderick cleansed and rinsed the jar in what appeared to be remnants of the dish water from this evening's meal. With the jar bathed and dried, he replaced it on the pantry shelf. Now to catch up with Amice.

Broderick led the wagon horse and started his way back down the path to the Gypsy camp at a steady pace. Davina's mortality hit him harder than he wanted to admit. Seeing her pale and ashen from being poisoned, his heart constricted with an ache that left him uneasy, but that settled once the tea mended her. A smiled tugged at the corner of his mouth. It was love at first sight with Cailin. In an instant, he lost his heart to her, too.

Ahead of him, Amice trod along the road, slow and weary. Dismay rolled off her like a heavy fog as he drew near. His heart went out to her. He knew this grief for her daughter, Veronique's mother, and also the familiar heaviness of regret and guilt. "You must stop blaming yourself for her death, Amice."

Her head still bowed, she nodded. "Aye, my son. I understand what you tell me. My heart will not listen, though."

Broderick ambled alongside his old friend. Placing a comforting hand upon her shoulder, he drew her close as they continued down the road. "Though I didn't witness her death first-hand, remember, I know everything. Your whole life is within me, just as if I experienced it, when I fed from you those many years ago. Veronique..." Broderick wanted to tell her Veronique wouldn't follow the same fatal path of obsession as her mother, but reflecting over Amice's memories of her daughter, he had to admit he shared the same fears.

"Even you cannot tell me Veronique is unlike her mother. She has gone as far as poisoning Davina to make you her own. What will she do next? Unless you surrender to her need, she will not stop…or she will…" Amice choked back the words and stood before Broderick with pleading eyes. She grabbed his shirt in desperation. "I cannot stop her, Broderick. I cannot make her realize love is not one-sided, or as much as her heart hurts, she must let go of someone who does not love her the same way. I do not understand this obsession. She tells herself again and again she is following the right path. I feel it every day from her, Broderick, and I'm helpless to stop it."

Broderick held Amice in his arms, her delicate, old body wracked with sobs, her heart breaking. Was this a demonic possession? Was this a generational curse for Veronique? Why could she not see reason or the truth? What compelled her to use everyone around her in the name of what she called love? Frustration surfaced. "I can perform simple mind tricks on my victims, or wipe away horrific memories from helpless children. Why can I not change Veronique's mind on this, though I have indeed tried?"

"Nay, my son. Altering memories is one thing. Changing someone's free will is an entirely different matter."

He nodded. "Let me try one more time to speak with her," Broderick endeavored. "There must be some way to reach her. We have a slight advantage in the legacy of her mother's death. Methinks she'll see the mistake Monique made and be the wiser for it."

"Oh, Broderick, I have tried for so long! I have seen the signs since she began growing into womanhood and you were so prominent in her life. You became her hero as her protector and that is my fault. I should have never asked you to take on that role."

Broderick pushed Amice back and held her by the shoulders, boring into her eyes. "Pray never regret meeting me or my joining you and Veronique. I love you as my own mother, and she as my sister. You have both been my light in the darkness. You have filled a void created so many years ago." He sighed. "Whether I or any other man came into her life, Veronique would have made the same choices." He hugged her once more, and then they continued down the path. "Come. We will go back to the camp and talk with Veronique. This conversation is well overdue."

When Broderick and Amice approached the camp, he sensed the panic rise in her. "Where is she?" Amice checked inside the wagon and around the campsite. "Veronique?"

"She is here, Amice." Nicabar peered out of his caravan, and then ducked back inside. Struggling against both Nicabar and Rosselyn, Veronique made a desperate effort to get away from her captors. "We were headed back to the castle when she tried to leave the camp." Nicabar and Rosselyn each held Veronique by the arms, dragging her to Broderick and Amice. In one final attempt to escape, Veronique bit Rosselyn's hand, who yelped and slapped Veronique across the face.

"Why, you little vixen!" Rosselyn grabbed Veronique's hair and the two began fighting. Nicabar tried to grab Rosselyn, but the women flailed around too much for him to do anything.

Shaking his head, Broderick marched up to the two women, grabbed them by the back of their bodices and yanked them apart. "Enough." He threw Rosselyn toward Nicabar, who caught her and held tight. Veronique kicked and scratched at Broderick, but he threw her to the ground. "I said, enough!"

Amice went to her side, but Veronique pushed her grandmother away. She stood her ground, eyes wide as she glared at Broderick. "How dare you—!"

Broderick stood towering over her and with one step, silenced her. "How dare I? I should slap you across that audacious mouth of yours. You almost killed a woman, yet you have the gall to condemn *me* for putting you in your place?"

Veronique sat in silence, her chest heaving and fire in her eyes.

"Have you no remorse? Do you not understand that you almost killed Davina over your selfish ideas of love?"

"Veronique," Amice said. "You must understand the seriousness—"

"Do not plead with her, Amice!" Broderick growled and turned back to Veronique. "How can your selfishness rise to the point of disregarding someone's life?"

"I did not intend to kill her." Veronique wiped her eyes and stood, stepping back from Broderick and Amice, and dusted the dirt from her hands and skirt.

"But you would have! You almost did! Had it not been for what Amice did for her, she would be dead!"

Veronique reached trembling fingers toward his cheek. "Do you not see how I love you, Broderick? Can you not see she is wrong for you?"

He stood aghast, his mouth open, and slapped her hand away. Anger tumbled down upon him like a landslide, blurring his vision, and though he tried to stop, this was too much for him to understand. "She almost died," he thundered, and Veronique quailed, her eyes wide. "You think *you* are more suited? Your selfishness knows no bounds. Why would I want to spend any time, let alone an eternity, with a self-centered, conniving bitch like you?"

Amice gasped and stood between Broderick and her granddaughter. "Broderick!"

"Nay, Amice. This should have been said long ago. This is an obsession, Veronique. An obsession that has nothing to do with me. Your idea of love has nothing to do with anyone but yourself and the fantasies you created in your twisted little mind." He closed the distance, Amice still standing between them, but he ignored the old woman and spoke over her head. "Understand, Veronique, that you're not the center of everyone's attention, or you'll end up dead like your mother."

"That is enough," Amice cried out and turned to hug her granddaughter, but Veronique pushed the old woman aside once more. A guttural screech poured out of Veronique's mouth, and she disappeared inside the wagon.

Broderick could feel the heartache of both Amice and Veronique, but he didn't care. Turning his back on them, he stomped into the forest, waiting until he was out of sight to run through the trees, almost blinded by his anger. The Hunger flooded his body, fueling his speed, bent on taking advantage of the first opportunity to unleash its fury.

Clyde Samuels raised a hairy knuckle to the side of Rhona's face and caressed her cheek, wiping away her tear. "Aw, I speak sweet words to you and you cry?"

"Oh, tears of joy, my love, tears of joy." Rhona smiled and kissed his nose.

She shifted her position on the rock, perhaps getting more comfortable, and she snuggled in closer to him. On the stroll back to their home, the night was cold, but she wanted to admire the moon and stars peeking through the clouds, so he humored her. While she gazed at the sky, he gazed at her lovely face and knew he was the luckiest man in all of Scotland.

"Clyde, you're everything I hoped for in finding a husband, and I think of what a fool I was not to see it earlier. You have always been a good friend. Why did I not see? All the time we wasted—"

"Now, none of that talk," he said, placing his fingertip on her lips. "We cannot change the past. We can only take what we have and move forward."

Her smile returned and she nodded. "Wise words. I will say nothing more on the matter."

Kissing her mouth with reverence, he took her hands and pulled her to her feet. "'Tis cold out here. What say we go home and do this before a warm fire?" Hooking her arm in his, Clyde led her back to their original path where they stepped together down the road, their footsteps crunching in the snow.

"Did the Gypsy truly tell you we would wed?" she asked with wonder.

"Aye!" Clyde squeezed her hand in his excitement. "Well, he didn't say you by name, but he said I wouldn't have to bide long before me land would bring forth new wealth, or before I married and had children. Not a fortnight later, I needed to see your brother, and there you were, visiting him at the same time. You took me breath away and came back into me life. I say it was meant to be, and therefore what the Gypsy foretold." A rustle from the brush off the road drew his attention, and he peered into the darkness.

"Did you hear something?"

Clyde nodded, his eyes searching for any movement. "A noise in the bushes," he answered. "Aye, probably just a rabbit."

They continued walking and a low, menacing chuckle came from the same direction of the rustling. Rhona squeezed his hand. "Come, Clyde," she whispered. "Let us quicken our pace home."

He nodded and wrapped a protective arm around her as they pressed into a faster gait. Rounding the bend in the road, the way became darker as the path went under the heavy limbs of the trees and the moon ducked behind the clouds. "Just a bit more, Rhona," Clyde encouraged.

Rhona gasped as Clyde stopped short and crushed her to his side. A tall figure stood on the road before them, blocking the path, most of his face hidden in shadow. The wide shoulders and the red hair caused Clyde to relax. He breathed a sigh of relief.

"Broderick," he said. "I didn't expect to see you all the way up here near Strathbogie. You gave us a start. We were just talking about you."

As the man stepped closer, Rhona shrank from him. Clyde noted his intimidating size and deliberate movements, which seemed unnatural, and understood her reaction. Nevertheless, Broderick's lack of return greeting gave even him pause. How odd that this man wore a thin linen shirt on such a cold night and yet seemed unaffected by the harsh temperature. Before Clyde could open his mouth to say anything, the Gypsy pounced on them, pushing Clyde down into the snow so hard, something snapped as he put his arm out to brace his fall. The sharp pain in his left forearm followed, and Clyde cried out, hugging his arm to his chest. Turning his head, he tried to see Rhona through the tears in his eyes. Clyde blinked to clear his vision, and still he didn't believe what he saw. The Gypsy fortune teller stood bent forward, holding Rhona's limp body in his arms, his mouth latched onto her throat and blood staining the back of her dress. Her heavy shawl lay tossed to the snowy ground.

"Rhona!" Clyde struggled to get to his feet, but stopped when the attacker glared at him. Even in the shadows, he could see the blood flowing down Broderick's chin, and his eyes glowing silver like a cat peering from the darkness. The Gypsy smiled and dropped Rhona like a sack of grain before dashing into the forest like an apparition.

Tears dripping from his face, Clyde crawled toward Rhona, whispering her name and grunting from his broken arm. His knees and hand stung from the wrist-deep snow. His progress slow and painful, he inched toward her for an eternity before he reached her side. Her pale form lay with her limbs at odd angles. "Nay, Rhona," he whimpered. "Please be well. Please, dove." Her skin was cold, unresponsive, missing that element of life and he cried harder. He threw his right arm around her and nuzzled his face against her cool cheek, rocking in his sorrow. "Why?" he groaned. Shouting into the forest, he demanded of the absent Gypsy, "Why would you do this to her? Why would you foretell our marriage and then take her away from me?"

"Because he's a heartless monster," a voice said from behind him.

Clyde turned with a grunt to see a man standing in the road. He stood tall in the pale moonlight, his auburn hair tied back, a heavy coat over his broad shoulders. "Let me help you, friend."

"Did you see him? Did you see what he did?" Clyde clung to Rhona, moving aside so the stranger could see what the Gypsy did to the woman of his heart.

"Your cries led me here," he said, stepping forward and kneeling. "I'm sorry I was too late. I've been hunting him for many years, and I know his pattern too well."

"He has done this before?" Clyde shuddered.

"Aye, that he has, but you can help me stop him."

Clyde stared in disbelief. "Injured as I am and you have been hunting him for years? How can I help you?"

"Do you want to help me catch him?" The man grabbed his shoulder for emphasis.

"With my last dying breath, if I can, but how?"

"We must first get you mended." The man rolled his sleeves up and took a knife from his belt. Examining Clyde, he reached for his broken arm. "We have to set the break first, so this is going to hurt, but not for long. Can you bear it?"

"Do as you must." Clyde gritted his teeth, bracing himself.

With a nod, the stranger grabbed his arm, pulling and twisting while Clyde let out a guttural cry. Quickly, the stranger cut Clyde's arm open near the break and then cut his own arm, letting his blood fall into Clyde's open wound. Before Clyde could back away from this ghastly procedure, the pain vanished from his arm, the wound healed, and he could almost feel the bones mending under his flesh. The stranger's cut healed even faster.

Clyde sat with his mouth open. "What are you? Who are you?"

"Angus Campbell," he said standing. "And you're welcome."

"Oh." Clyde stood. "I apologize and I'm very grateful. Thank you. I'm Clyde Samuels. But—"

Angus nodded and then stared at Rhona. "I'm truly sorry for your loss, but we must move quickly. Let us take her to your home to keep her body safe. I will explain everything—who I am, what I am, and how you can get your revenge against the Gypsy, Broderick MacDougal."

Broderick cursed and tossed another log onto the campfire. Sparks burst and floated into the air in a dazzling display. The Gypsy camp lay quiet, all asleep in their caravans and wagons. Broderick paced in the small space before the fortune-telling tent. He had enough sense to calm the Hunger with the blood of animals, before he actually found a thief in Stewart Glen on which to satisfy the

Hunger enough to hold back its demands. After that, he'd spent the night combing the area, searching for any signs of Angus, and came up with nothing. Still, he dared not venture too far from Stewart Glen or the Gypsy camp to put those he loved in danger. Images of Davina and Cailin falling into Angus's hands flashed through his mind and he shut his eyes, helpless as he sat and waited for Angus to make his next move.

The hairs on the back of his neck bristled, and Broderick clenched his jaw as he turned his head in the direction he sensed Angus. Ensuring he had his silver sword strapped firmly to his side, he took off toward his enemy, pumping his legs as fast as his immortal strength could muster. The cold air whisked past his face and ears in a rush as he dodged trees and brush, through the forest and across the pathways, gliding over the snow while leaving no tracks. Angus's presence grew closer and faster, as if he was running toward Broderick, which caused him to smile, certain that Angus still didn't sense Broderick's presence. Angus would be in for a surprise. Pushing even harder, he pressed on toward a hopeful encounter and finally the opportunity to confront Angus. This would be over tonight.

There! Broderick knew the standard boundary had been reached, and he could feel Angus retreating. Drawing his sword, he turned as Angus's presence changed direction and headed north. Broderick reached his limit on speed, unable to go any faster, but refused to give up the chase. This time he would catch up with Angus, and confidence rushed through him. Tracks appeared in the snow and Broderick followed them. He closed in on Angus, but something nagged at him. Something didn't seem right. Angus never left tracks before. Another tingling at the back of his neck caused him to slow his pace—a different tingling. Angus's presence faded, replaced by another Vamsyrian presence, pushing in toward Broderick. He slowed to a stop and scanned the forest with his eyes. Angus's essence lingered just slightly before it completely dropped off. This new Vamsyrian spirit dominated his senses, heading straight for Broderick. He stood his ground, waiting for the arrival of this stranger. Crunching through the snow, a silver glow in his eyes, a familiar figure ran toward Broderick. He stood flabbergasted as Clyde Samuels—a Vamsyrian with rage in his eyes—charged forward, screaming at Broderick with his hands outstretched. Broderick quickly sheathed his sword and dodged the crazed man to avoid hurting him.

"I will see you dead this night, Gypsy!" Clyde took another leap at Broderick.

CHAPTER TWELVE

Amice rose with a start and glanced around the tiny caravan, her eyes falling on nothing but the faint light of fire coming through the cracks in the door. She shivered at the vision of the man in her sleep. She had to get out of here to keep him away from Veronique, if she could. Dressing in haste, she grabbed her heavy shawl and eased out of the wagon with as little noise as possible, so as not to wake her granddaughter, who lay under a mound of covers in her bed, a lock of golden hair shining in the firelight. Latching the door behind her, Amice tended the fire and put some fresh snow in the pot to boil.

Moving into the tent, she lit two of the four lamps and sat at the table, shuffling her tablets. Placing three down, she gazed through the dim light at the painted images. The Magician, the Hanged Man, and the Moon. She sighed and put her hands upon the tablets, closing her eyes. This master manipulator will sacrifice others to gain hidden knowledge. "But sacrifice whom?" she whispered in her native tongue.

Amice left the tent and went to the fire to see the water steaming. Taking her herb basket, she sprinkled some tea leaves into a cup and poured the water warm enough for her task, but cool enough for her to drink. She closed her eyes, concentrating, drank the tea and shuffled back into the shelter of the tent to read the cup. Her heart quickened. *I should not have read the leaves!* Putting the cup down, she closed her eyes and concentrated all her efforts on clearing her thoughts and blocking her mind. With much effort, her hands ceased trembling. Her breathing slowed.

"At last."

The deep voice caused her to flinch. She opened her eyes and beheld, in the flesh, the man she saw in her vision, the man Broderick showed her in his mind. "Angus Campbell."

"What a pleasure to finally meet you, Amice."

"Do what you came to do and be done with it," she snapped, and refocused her concentration on blocking her mind and clearing her thoughts.

Angus stepped forward, a smirk on his face, his eyes searching hers, one eyebrow raised in curiosity. "Why is it I cannot hear your thoughts, old woman?"

Amice sat motionless and silent, maintaining her concentration.

"Interesting." Angus stepped around the table and beside Amice, who continued to keep her eyes forward on the tent flap. He grabbed her by the shoulders and made her stand before him. "You know I only need to feed to know everything about you—and, in turn, about Broderick."

A tear slipped down her cheek.

Broderick pushed Clyde's arm up behind his back as he forced his chest into the ground, sitting atop the man to keep him still. Eventually, Clyde stopped wrestling and surrendered.

"You cannot win against me, Clyde. I've been a Vamsyrian much longer than you. Now let us talk. Who did this to you?"

"You did, you bastard!" Clyde sobbed into the snow. "I've nothing left to live for now that you have killed her. Why would you do that?"

"Killed who?" Broderick rose, letting Clyde go. Snowflakes floated down from the sky, a peaceful act in contrast to the agitated atmosphere between the two immortals.

Rising to his feet, he turned his rage on Broderick. "Rhona! Me wife-to-be! The one you foretold I would marry."

"What makes you think I killed her?"

"I saw you! I saw you take her right before me eyes this very night!"

"Clyde, I don't know what you saw or what has happened, but I didn't—"

"Nay! He said you would deny it all! He said you would try to trick me!"

"Angus Campbell, is that correct?" Broderick clenched his jaw to maintain his control.

"I know you two have been bitter enemies for decades. He told me everything, how he sought immortality to get his revenge against you and you sought it so you could continue to fight him! And now I'm going to help him end your brutality and ruthlessness. How could you do that to her?"

"Angus has lied to you, Clyde! Did he tell you that he was the one who transformed me?"

Clyde contorted his face with confusion, but held to his rage. "He didn't say who transformed you, but it matters not!"

"Lad, what would I have to gain from killing Rhona? And why would I not just kill you now and end this charade?" Broderick stopped and digested Clyde's words. "You said you saw me do it this very night? That means you were transformed just this evening?"

"Aye, but why—"

"Clyde! You never faced the Vamsyrian Council for your transformation?"

"What council?" His features softened in light of their conversation.

Broderick paled. "Angus has sentenced you to a torturous death, my friend."

"I expected to die, Broderick MacDougal, in my efforts to kill you. What does that matter?" Clyde dropped to his knees and sobbed, "She's dead. At least as an immortal, I had a fighting chance, and gave Angus the time he needed—"

Broderick turned and hastened back toward Stewart Glen and the Gypsy camp. He would have to deal with Clyde Samuels later, if the Vamsyrian Council didn't catch up with him first. No one could be transformed into a Vamsyrian without the approval of the Council. Anyone who had been transformed without approval was called Rogue and was brutally tortured as an example. Additionally, the maker of the Rogue would also be hunted down and destroyed. Somehow, the Council knew whenever a Rogue was made and the hunt was on, or at least that's what Rasheed told him. How they found out, Broderick didn't know, and perhaps it was just a scare tactic. Angus had taken a great chance to create a Rogue as a distraction. Regardless, it worked.

Angus coasted over the ground, using his immortal speed to travel without making any footprints in the snow. Heavy snowflakes pattered his face, caught in his eyelashes only to melt and fly from his view. The newly fallen snow covered much of the evidence of traffic, so he maintained his course along the side of the road. His immortal senses let him hear anyone approach at a great distance, allowing him ample time to hide. He dashed into the cover of the bordering trees or bushes and disappeared from sight.

Angus waited patiently, downy flakes and icy gusts trying to make a frigid impression on his skin, but to no avail. Eventually, she came stomping up the road, snow crunching under her feet, grumbling. A shawl wrapped over her head against the weather, but Angus could still see the golden tendrils framing her face. "And just where are you going, Veronique?" Angus whispered from his hiding place. She mumbled something in French as she plodded along, hefting a bag higher onto her shoulder. Having fed from a few people who spoke French, Angus knew the language well.

"You can have her," she managed over a quivering voice, thick with animosity. She stopped and glared down the empty road. "I do not need you!" she screamed at no one in particular.

Angus smiled and shook his head at her rash display. The lass would get killed, stomping through the night and yelling like a fool, drawing unwanted attention from anyone in the area. And dangerous people were in the area, waiting for victims like her to be stupid enough to venture out alone. *Such as I, sweet Veronique.*

"I hope she rejects you until the day she dies." She threw a clump of snow to make her point and whirled back around to continue her determined pace toward Strathbogie. Angus swaggered forward and met her out on the road. Veronique stopped and hugged her shawl close to her throat.

Angus bowed. *"Bon soir, mademoiselle."* He glanced around at the pressing dawn only his immortal eyes could see. "Or should I say good morning?" He took cautious steps toward her as she inched backwards. "'Tis a stormy night for you to be traversing the road…alone." She stared at him with wide eyes, but said nothing. He stopped a few feet from her. "Where are you going, Veronique?"

Her eyes grew wider and she turned to run, but Angus snatched her up before she took a step, her bag dropping at their feet. Angus stifled her scream, her body wriggling against him as he held her, tickling the Hunger and his desire to the surface. The sharp pain of his fangs extending traveled over his gums. As soon as he drove his fangs into her warm neck, she stopped struggling and nearly collapsed in his arms, moaning. He already fed, so it wasn't difficult to stop feeding from her once he gleaned the information he needed. He dropped her limp body to the ground, where she panted and moaned.

He glanced down at the girl, who slowly gained her faculties. "Come, Veronique. We must bide our time until the eve on the morrow." Adjusting his growing erection, he grinned. "Perhaps we can do something about your virginity." He hefted the girl over his shoulder and dashed over the snow, gliding at immortal speed to avoid marking the snow toward his faithful structure.

Broderick finally came bounding into the camp to find Amice by the campfire, sobbing, with Nicabar and few other Gypsies comforting her.

"Amice!" Rushing to her side, he discerned the bite marks on her neck.

"She is gone, Broderick!" Amice clung to his shirt. "Veronique is gone!"

"Angus has her?"

"*Non*, at least not for the moment, I hope." She considered the small crowd and switched to French. "He fed from me, so he knows everything, Broderick. Everything. He went to the wagon to take Veronique, but she was already gone. I do not know when she left, and I fear she ran away before

I even lay down myself. Her bed only had pillows under her covers. She even cut a lock of her hair to look as if she lay in her bed. Confident he would find her, Angus left me here. He knew I would rather die than let him use me against you. We must find her, Broderick." Amice collapsed in his arms with weak sobs. Carrying her to the caravan, he encouraged her to lie down and rest. Too weak to fight, she nodded, and he closed the door of the wagon.

"Nicabar, organize a search party, but do not have them leave until day breaks."

Nicabar nodded and turned to his task.

Broderick turned his attention to the snowy horizon. The slightest beginnings of dawn approached. He didn't have enough time to do any searching on his own, and they could use the daylight to their advantage. When Nicabar issued the orders and they prepared to leave, Broderick pulled Nicabar aside. "If you find Veronique, her captor, Angus Campbell, will be sleeping. You won't be able to wake him, nor do you need to. He may even appear dead." He drew a breath to ready for what he had to tell his friend. "If you find him…whether dead or alive, you must behead him and bury his head."

Nicabar's mouth dropped open, but he recovered and cleared his throat. "*Sí*, Broderick. I will do as you say."

"Remember, do not leave until day breaks." Broderick shook Nicabar's hand and turned to head in the direction of his cave. Biding didn't fare well with him, but bide he must. He couldn't do anything until the next evening. This was one time he was grateful for the lethargy of his daytime slumber. Otherwise it would be a sleepless time for him. As Broderick slipped into sleep, an unearthly cry echoed across the forest. Broderick uttered a silent prayer for Clyde Samuels. Better the fire of the sun to take him than to die at the hands of the Vamsyrian Council.

Amice groaned from the cold in her aged joints, jolting as their horse trudged through the ever-rising snow. Nicabar rode with her, holding her in front of him. She clutched Veronique's shawl in her hand, prayers of protection fluttering over her lips for her granddaughter.

"It is not much farther," Nicabar informed her. He had gone off with a searching party as Broderick instructed, and they found tracks, almost covered in snow, leading away from the camp and heading toward the main road out of the village. Following those tracks led to evidence of a struggle, with Veronique's shawl and belongings partially buried in the snow. He brought those back with him when he came to get Amice. Amice had to see for herself. She had a gift for touching things and seeing images, among other talents. The stronger the emotions, the stronger the images. She saw nothing from Veronique's belongings. They must have separated from her before Angus made off with her, if that's what happened.

"Here, Amice!" Nicabar urged the horse forward over to the spot.

The snow covered a lot of the tracks, taking away the sharp edges of the footprints, but they were deep enough to tell the story. Indeed, there seemed a struggle, and yet no footprints seemed to leave the spot. "Help me down, Nicabar," she rasped. When he set her upon the ground, Amice squatted in the snow, placing her palm in the center of the struggle. She closed her eyes and quieted, ignoring the cold and wind. As if out of the smoky mist, a vision of Veronique, wide-eyed and open-mouthed, stared back at Amice. Blood, fangs, and the menacing smile of Angus Campbell.

A whimper of distress seeped out of Amice's mouth. *"Mon dieu!* He has her! You must find her, Nicabar. Do as Broderick has asked. Find his lair and slay him as he sleeps." Hope died upon her words, though. They may have the advantage of the daylight hours, but Angus was no fool, and her tea leaves were rarely ever wrong. He could be anywhere in the surrounding land, miles from their location. Nicabar helped Amice back upon the horse and turned in the direction they came from. "Back to the camp," she whispered and cold tears slipped down her cheeks.

Cailin jumped up and down on Davina's lap, and she grunted and groaned at her daughter's weight, still a little weak after the sickness. "Oh, 'tis enough, Cailin." She laid her daughter down on the bed. Davina covered her eyes with Cailin's feet, feeling her little toes against her forehead, pulled Cailin's feet away and blew a quick gust of air on her baby's face. Cailin blinked and laughter tittered out of her mouth. She repeated the game, her child laughing harder at each round.

Cailin's playful nature stimulated the memories of seeing her daughter respond so openly to Broderick. A spark of hope flickered in Davina's heart that the dreams she harbored for nine years would become the reality Amice predicted.

You still have many questions that remain unanswered, the voice of reason reminded her.

Davina puffed another breath of air at Cailin's face, pushing down the rising doubt. *He said he would tell me everything once he finished his task,* she argued and clung to the images of those heated moments in his arms, aching for more of their lovemaking, wanting desperately to believe he did indeed care for her as much as he said he did. She clung to the sweet assurance in his eyes and the love he confessed. *He is not Ian, who was filled with broken promises and lies…and always brought pain.*

But what of the silver glow in Broderick's eyes? 'Tis unnatural.

A single tear ran down her cheek and soaked into the folds of her skirt.

The chamber door opened and Rosselyn inched her way into the room, her eyes wide and a deep furrow on her brow. "Rosselyn?" Davina rose from the bed. "What is it?"

Her friend closed the door behind her and faced Davina, worrying her bottom lip with her teeth, tears forming in her eyes. Her mouth opened once, then twice, as if to say something.

Davina stepped forward and took Rosselyn by the hands. "Come, sit and speak with me. You have been wanting to tell me something for too long." She led Rosselyn to the settee at the foot of her bed, glancing at Cailin, who lay on the comforter playing with her toes. Brushing a lock of Rosselyn's chestnut hair aside, Davina smiled encouragingly. "All is well, my friend. I've ears to hear you."

Rosselyn closed her eyes, tears spilling down her cheeks, and swallowed, nodding. "I've kept silent for too long on this, Davina." Opening her eyes, the words poured out of her mouth in a rush. "I only found out shortly after Lord Parlan died. I was told not to say anything, and it has been eating me alive inside since then. We thought we would be thrown out of the household if the truth was known. My mother believed all these years she would be thrown out, and now she has shared this burden with me, but if I do not say anything—"

"Rosselyn, whatever you have to say, you will not be thrown out of our household. You are family. We love you. Why would you think that would happen? Say what is on your heart."

Rosselyn's eyes searched Davina's, and she eventually nodded. "Davina…we are sisters."

"Of course, Rosselyn, that's how I've always felt about you. Go on."

"Nay, Davina, we truly are sisters." She breathed deep. "We share the same father."

Davina sat numb for a moment, unable to qualify Rosselyn's words. A warm flush came to her cheeks when she realized what Rosselyn implied. "How do you mean we share the same father? How—"

"Lord Parlan…" Rosselyn swallowed. "Parlan lay with my mother, Davina, and she became with child. No one knew but Parlan and my mother."

Davina rose and turned her back on Rosselyn, her face hot and her eyes stinging with tears.

"When my mother told her betrothed what happened, he abandoned her and left the village.

Your mother has always thought I was the daughter of the man who left, and my mother let her believe that out of fear."

Davina clenched her fists and faced Rosselyn. "Why would you say such a thing! My father would never have done that! What is this about? Why are you telling me this?"

"Amice told me I was holding a secret, and she said it would be worse if I did not come forth and tell you the truth. She said lives would be lost if I kept quiet! I do not know how that could happen, but I believe in Amice's gifts, and if lives would be lost for keeping silent, then I would gladly risk my security in my home to save those lives. Davina, this is true, I swear to you. I've always been honest with you, and keeping this to myself was torturing me!"

The chamber door opened and Myrna stepped into the room, fear in her eyes. "What are you saying, child!" She dashed to Rosselyn's side, covering her mouth. "What lies are you telling Mistress Davina!"

"Mother, stop! We can keep this from Davina no more."

Davina stood and watched Myrna scolding her daughter with such fear and panic, her actions spoke more than her words. "'Tis true. You deny this, but I can see the truth in your eyes." Davina fought back her tears. "How could you do this to my family?"

Myrna turned pleading eyes toward Davina. "Nay, Davina. I—" Myrna wept into her hands. "Rosselyn, why did you tell her?"

Davina's mind swirled with all the information, at the guilt on Rosselyn's face, at the sorrow Myrna poured out. Rosselyn tried to reach out to Davina, but she backed away. "Nay, I cannot…" The love she held for these two women—women she knew and shared her home with since her birth—clashed with her anger. Davina and Rosselyn were sisters, and she wanted to be joyful over that revelation, but at what price? The betrayal of Myrna, of her father, both of them toward her mother? They lived a lie all these years. Before Davina said anything she might regret, she scooped Cailin from the bed, wrapped a blanket around her daughter and grabbed her cloak. "I need some time," she mumbled and left Myrna and Rosselyn behind, heading for the back entrance through the empty kitchen. Tears coursing down her face, Davina held Cailin close under her cloak as they stepped into the cold. Davina knew it would be best to bring Cailin with her, not wanting to arouse suspicion in her mother, as she didn't feel comfortable leaving her baby with Rosselyn and Myrna. Not right now. She just needed a few moments in the fresh air to clear her mind. She would normally jump on her horse to escape, but not with Cailin. *Just a short walk along the property.* She wouldn't go far.

Davina ducked behind the stables and snuck inside the hidden passage through the back wall. Somehow this exit gave her a separation from the castle and its members within, as well as not attracting any attention going out the front gate. Closing the wall behind her, she stepped out and faced the bordering forest. Tall and strong, the trees offered refuge from the anger, the betrayal, the confusion, and gave her some measure of strength. She stepped forward and ambled amongst the trees, seeing the flakes of falling snow from the sky and the branches above. A forceful breeze kicked up and caused her to duck into the warmth of her cloak with Cailin until the pressing wind passed. Clods of snow fell from above, dropping around them.

She sighed and gazed back at the castle. From here she could make a better effort at being more objective. The pain of Myrna's betrayal stabbed her gut. Still, the reality that her father had been a willing participant nagged at her conscience. She didn't give Myrna time to explain, yet at that moment she didn't want explanations. Anger and betrayal ruled her mind. Davina hated the idea, but it might also be possible that Myrna was *not* a willing participant, which cast her father in a very undesirable light. She shook her head. Her own experiences with her father, doing what he wanted for his own benefit in spite of the sacrifices others made, also tugged at her resolve. Forcing Davina to marry Ian to better the family situation—in spite of the pain he caused her even after her father knew the truth—did override his ability to dissolve the marriage when they had the chance. It crushed Davina to think he would take his position this far and have his way with Myrna.

Leaning against one of the trees, she closed her eyes and absorbed the sturdy energy emanating from the towering pine, her cheeks wet and cold from crying. Cailin's hand touched her cheek and she opened her eyes to view her daughter. With an uncanny intelligence, her baby girl searched Davina's face, almost as if offering her support, as if to ask what she could do. Davina kissed her daughter's cheek and buried her face in her neck, holding her close and keeping her warm.

Davina gasped as a hand clutched her hair and forced her head up. Cailin wailed as Davina stared into the murderous glare of a man she thought she would never see again, his knifepoint pressed against her cheek.

"Surprised to see me, Davina?" Ian gritted over Cailin's cries.

Davina's mouth hung open as she struggled to maintain a grip on her daughter.

"You saved me a lot of trouble," Ian said with that familiar menacing grin. "I'm very glad you decided to come out of your own accord, or I would have had to kill a few people to get to you."

Davina couldn't utter a word, so filled with terror at seeing Ian risen from the grave, her and her daughter's lives in his hands. Cailin's continuing cries echoed through the forest.

CHAPTER THIRTEEN

"Ian!" Rosselyn stood several feet away from them. "My God, what are you—?"

"Shut up!" Ian turned to face Rosselyn, using Davina and Cailin as a shield. Davina could feel the cold blade against her throat. Thankfully, she was able to get a better grip on Cailin, and did what she could to calm her by rubbing her back.

"Ian, please let them go!" Rosselyn stepped forward, her hands outreached.

He hugged Davina and Cailin closer, pressing the blade harder against Davina's flesh, causing her to wince as the tip broke her skin. In a calm steel voice, Ian said, "You go back inside and tell Tammus to come out here, and we will discuss what I'm doing here and what I want. Do so quickly, or their blood will be on your hands."

Rosselyn nodded and turned around without hesitation, sprinting back toward the castle and the front gate of the perimeter wall.

Ian pushed Davina toward the ground, and she made every effort to keep from dropping her daughter as she tripped forward into the snow. His eyes fell to Cailin, still crying, and a frown turned down the corners of his mouth. "I should have beaten her out of you, too," Ian sneered, steam rising from his mouth in the cold air.

"Bastard!" Davina turned Cailin away from Ian and rubbed her child's back. "Why can you not leave me alone! What—!"

"I would like nothing better than to have you out of my life!"

"Then why are you here?"

"Because you have what belongs to me! You, my father, your father...you have all kept me from what has rightfully been mine since birth!" He stood over her, almost nose-to-nose. "You have my inheritance, and I mean to have it!"

"Money?" Davina stood in shock as she watched him pace in frustration. "Is that all this has ever been about? Money?"

He turned incredulous eyes toward her, his mouth open. "You think I'm here for you?" He laughed, a most maniacal sound that sent shivers through her. "You think I ever wanted to be shackled with you and a child? I did everything I could to get out of our marriage."

"You had your chance to get out of this marriage!" Davina countered over the wailing of her daughter. "When my father said he would dissolve the marriage if you kept abusing me, you should have just continued to beat me! I do not—"

"That may have dissolved the marriage, but my father would have still withheld from me!" Ian shook his head. "Women are so stupid, and you're the worst of them all. In order for me to get anything, I had to be the model husband. Proving you were stupid and crazy was my way to save face, you stupid bitch! I was so close to getting that, too, and then you became with child, locking us into the marriage!" He pointed to Cailin and stalked to tower over Davina. "You just needed to swallow your pride and—"

An arrow grazed Ian's shoulder and he growled, clutching his arm. Standing on a garret on the perimeter wall, one of the patrols had an empty crossbow and an ashen white face realizing he'd missed his target. Leaping forward, Ian grabbed Davina and Cailin again, stood behind her and put the point of his blade to her throat. Tammus ran forward and cautiously stepped as he approached them, his hands out in front of him and a scowl on his face. "Ian, you let Davina—"

"Shut your mouth!" Ian demanded over Cailin's screams. "I want my inheritance! Four thousand gold *unicorns*!"

Tammus blanched. "Four thous—! Ian, we do not have that kind of—"

"I know you sold my holdings, and I know the money and my inheritance upon my father's death went to Davina! Pray you didn't spend it all by now, because if you did, I will take it out of her."

Tammus inhaled a deep calming breath, but his voice still trembled. "Ian, this will take time to obtain."

"I understand that, Tammus," Ian said in his icy-calm tone that always belied the foul expression on his face. "Until you gather my money, I will have Davina and her child with me. I want the keys to the Stewart Glen New Lodge, provisions, a new horse, blankets and anything else you can think of to make Davina comfortable."

Davina knew any comforts her family provided would be for Ian.

"It may take days to get that kind of money together, Ian. Or longer."

Ian pressed the blade into Davina's chin, and the tip pierced her skin. The face of her uncle paled. "The longer I have Davina, the more she'll suffer. I suggest you get the money as quickly as you can."

Tammus grunted and turned to the man on the perimeter wall. "Do not let them out of your sight!" he called to the man, who nodded. Tammus turned to Ian. "You understand, of course."

"Of course," Ian said, cold humor in his voice.

Tammus stopped with horror in his eyes. Davina had the exact same reaction to Ian's evil calm the first time she witnessed it.

Ian remained standing behind Davina, holding her against him. She realized he wasn't going to let her go since they had a crossbow trained on them. Cailin began quieting down in the lack of activity.

"It has been a long time, Davina." He nuzzled her neck, and she shuddered. "Do you not miss me in your bed?" He chuckled at her silence. "'Tis much time to be made up for, *wife*."

Davina held Cailin tighter. *Please God. Let night fall swiftly.*

"Nica!"

Dusk settled on the horizon as Amice watched Rosselyn stumble toward Nicabar, who just came back from a day of searching for Veronique. Other than the place where he took Amice, he and their party found no signs of Veronique, or any lair to speak of. Her heart ached with the realization she may never see her granddaughter again. Amice stressed that they return before nightfall. They did so empty handed. Rosselyn's hands clutched at her skirts as she stumbled into the snow. Nicabar rushed toward her and she rose only to fall into his arms. Amice shuffled toward the frantic woman.

Rosselyn panted and clung to Nicabar. "Oh, God, Nica! You...have to help...her! He has...taken her away!"

Nicabar helped her to a stool and rushed to get a blanket.

Amice came over as he pulled the blanket under Rosselyn's chin and bruised cheek.

"What happened?" he demanded. "Who did this to you!"

Amice patted his shoulder. "Let her rest, Nica. She cannot answer you if she collapses."

"I'm well enough," she said, catching her breath. She implored Nicabar, "He has taken her and the baby! Please, we have to—"

He knelt before her and held her hands in his. "Slowly, Rosselyn," he told her. "Who are you talking about? Who has taken—?"

"Ian has taken Davina and the baby."

"Who is Ian?"

"Ian is Davina's husband." She darted her eyes at Amice, Nicabar and some of the others who gathered around. "We thought he was dead, but he has come back!" Her words hitched through her sobs. "We must go after them!"

Nicabar held Rosselyn and caressed her cheek as he spoke. "Easy now, *mi amor*. Which way did they travel?"

"West, into the forest." She breathed deep and addressed Amice. "Broderick can find them. He'll go after them, will he not?"

Amice studied the dark, overhanging clouds that crawled in from the North throughout the day. Though they couldn't see the setting sun, evening traveled fast upon them. Broderick would rise very soon. "*Oui*, I am sure he will."

"Where is he now? Should we not find him?" Rosselyn asked.

Amice patted Rosselyn's hand in assurance. "He will know where we are. Let us go to the castle and organize supplies for him." Amice walked in a fog, her senses numb. The loss of her granddaughter weighed heavily upon her, yet other lives were now at stake. Her old heart would not take much more of the chaos. Drawing a deep breath, she succumbed to the numbness, knowing it would help her through the next several hours.

Grabbing her basket of herbs, she allowed Nicabar to help her over to one of the camp horses, a younger Gypsy pulling Amice into the saddle in front of him. Nicabar mounted his horse and Rosselyn joined him. With haste, Nicabar led everyone through the snow and toward the castle.

Davina's hands had grown numb. The ropes, bound tight about her wrists, cut into her skin and grew tacky with blood, which trickled down her arms and stained the sleeves of her dress. Dots of her blood littered the front of her gown, and her cloak hung around her neck, down her back, choking her as she trekked through the knee-deep snow. Ahead of her, through flakes as soft as thistle down, she stared at the rigid form of Ian's back. The rope—long enough to keep her away from the horse's hooves but not from the up-flung snow—remained a constant reminder of this man's savagery.

Cailin sat before Ian in the saddle, bawling, her howls causing Davina anguish too great to ignore. Hours passed since Cailin had eaten. The bodice of Davina's gown stiffened, sticky with her milk, and her breasts ached from the need to release them.

"Ian!"

Under Cailin's sobs, she could hear Ian humming some nameless tune. She watched him gorge on a chicken leg her family packed, eating in front of Cailin and purposefully pulling away from her any time her tiny hands reached for the food.

"Ian! Cailin needs to eat!"

"Be quiet," he said, and continued humming.

"Damn you, Ian! She's hungry!"

Ian kicked his heels into the side of the horse, and Davina yelped, struggling to keep up. Her skirts tripped her and she fell, dragging behind the horse, the snow scraping her face as she fought for air. Her hands, deadened from the cold, would surely tear from her body. Somewhere along the way her cloak ripped from her shoulders. At last, Ian stopped the horse. Turning onto her back, she drew deep, icy breaths and gritted her teeth.

"Had enough?"

She struggled to open her eyes.

Ian smiled from his position in the saddle, mocking her. "It wouldn't do Cailin any good to have her mother killed. Who would protect and feed her?" He laughed, turned the horse, and continued his lazy pace. Before he could drag her again, Davina staggered to her feet. A deep hate—like nothing she'd ever known—burned inside her.

"Broderick!" Davina's hands reached out from the darkness, an unseen force pulling her back. Cailin wailed in the distance and his heart reached for both Davina and her child. "Broderick! Where are you?"

"I'm here, Davina!" Broderick ran into the black forest, dodging trees and stumbling in the snow. Blood spots littered the front of him. Stopping, he searched to find the source of

the wounds. Blood trickled down his arms from his bound wrists.

Davina called for him again, but she sounded miles away. "Davina!" Running toward her fading voice, he turned the corner of a ridge and stopped with fright—Ian's menacing face nose-to-nose with him.

Broderick's eyes opened and he stared at the craggy ceiling, motionless. These dreams were becoming too coincidental over the last several nights—they reflected the waking world around him as he slept, all of it connected to Davina. He clenched his jaw, rose and worked out the stiffness in his body. Broderick tensed from the rustling inside his cave. With lightning speed and sword drawn, he burst out from behind his curtains in a fighting stance, waiting to confront whoever came into the cave.

Amice gasped and stood wide-eyed before him. When her eyes went down his body and her cheeks bloomed with color, he dared to follow her eyes. He was naked. Broderick's own face burned with embarrassment and he disappeared behind his curtains to sheath his sword and dress in haste. Trying to keep his voice even and calm, he cleared his throat. "I hope you have good news for me." The silence gave Broderick pause, and a heavy cloak of dismay disturbed his heart.

"Angus has Veronique. They could not find his lair."

Broderick clenched his fists.

"And Ian has Davina and her baby Cailin."

The dream. Half-dressed, he emerged from behind his curtains and Amice's sorrowful eyes revealed her turmoil. They stood staring at each other, the unsaid situation hovering between them like an evil entity. Angus pulled his heart in one direction and Ian pulled his heart in another. Amice would not make him choose, yet he was the only one who could rescue both of these women who meant so much to him.

Stepping back behind his curtains, he slipped into his shirt, grabbed his sword and threw the baldric over his shoulder, nestling his blade at his hip. As he stepped out onto the snow, he fastened his belt and sporran. Amice came up behind him and put her hand upon his arm.

Through her sobs, she said, "You cannot be in two places at once. No one but you can face Angus, and yet..." She faltered in her words. "I do not know how much hope is left for Veronique, my son. Oh, that you could save them both, but I have come to the truth today that my Veronique may already be dead. My tea leaves have said as much."

Broderick knelt before his old friend. Wrapping her in his arms, he let her cry.

Amice gained her voice again and framed Broderick's face with her wrinkled hands. "Davina has a better chance at surviving her situation, but I greatly fear for her baby." She swallowed and fought a new flow of tears. "It is her you must go after, my son."

He kissed Amice's brow, and sweeping her into his arms, he set off toward the castle of Stewart Glen, amidst the snow flurries, using his immortal speed to glide over the snow.

As they approached the castle, he slowed to a more acceptable pace lest anyone see them, and headed straight to the front entrance. Rosselyn stood waiting to show them the way. Dashing down the hall, Broderick turned into the parlor. A rush of people surrounded him, all speaking at once. Myrna, Nicabar, Lilias, and a few other people he didn't recognize.

A man with chestnut-brown hair stepped forward, who Broderick recognized from the day Davina took ill from the poison, silencing the rise of voices. "Thank you for coming, Broderick. I'm Tammus Keith, Davina's uncle."

Broderick nodded. "Amice briefed me about most of what happened on the way here. How long ago did they leave?"

"Almost three hours. Ian took them to a small summer lodge the family has just west of here, and should probably be there by now, if the weather hasn't been too unforgiving and they maintained a steady pace." Tammus frowned, worry in his eyes. "He demanded four thousand gold *unicorns* and I haven't been able to gather the ransom just yet."

"You won't need the money," Broderick growled. "Which—"

"But he said if we didn't bring him the ransom—"

Broderick stepped forward, piercing Tammus with his eyes. "Dead men don't need money, my friend."

Tammus opened his mouth to protest. Broderick heard the man thinking of the safety of his nieces, but Tammus's thoughts and mask of concern melted with understanding.

"I will let nothing happen to Davina and Cailin," he vowed. Broderick easily slipped into his old role of the Lord of Glenstrae, and motioned for Amice to come forward. "Please stay here for your safety." Amice understood he had concerns over Angus getting to them. Though the castle wasn't complete assurance of their safety, it fared better than a wide-open Gypsy camp. He turned to Tammus. "After I'm gone, I want those gates locked. Do not let anyone in unless you know them personally, and even then, I would raise caution. No one should be coming here at night."

"Agreed. 'Tis already ordered." The corner of Tammus's mouth turned up in approval, and Broderick nodded.

"I'm assuming Ian took provisions with him?"

Several people nodded.

"I hope the same will be packed on my horse, including extra blankets."

"Already been done," Tammus assured him.

He turned to Lilias. "Did you pack an extra change of clothing for Davina?"

"Nay, I didn't think to." She dabbed her eyes, wiping the tears falling since Broderick arrived. Lilias nodded. "Myrna, would you please—?"

"Aye, milady," the heavyset woman whispered with a nod and waddled out of the room.

Fife poked his head into the parlor. "Master Broderick, a horse is ready for your journey."

Broderick nodded, and a team of people followed him into the kitchen. "Will someone please ensure I have a cake of soap, a small wash basin, drying cloths and washing cloths?" Rosselyn volunteered to fill his request, and Broderick turned to exit through the door to head to the stables. The snow, falling steadily since he rose, grew heavier as they headed through the courtyard, the wind growing fiercer. There, a horse stood ready for him as promised. "Who has taken the journey to this lodge and is most familiar with the route?"

Lilias stepped forward. "I know the route well, Master Gypsy."

Broderick stepped before her and cupped her tearful face in his hands. "You must do something for me, Mistress Lilias," he said with kind encouragement.

She nodded.

"Close your eyes and think of your journey. See yourself going to this place, the familiar and noticeable landmarks along the way."

Lilias nodded and closed her eyes, and so did Broderick.

He absorbed the images flashing through her mind. "See the front of this building as you approach. See the inside of the lodge and its rooms." Broderick held Lilias's trembling shoulders as he committed to memory as much as he could. Kissing the crown of her head, he whispered his thanks.

She opened her eyes and met his gaze.

"I will find them…and bring them back."

Lilias stared at him with watery, sorrow-filled eyes. *Will they be alive or…?* She stepped into his embrace.

After a brief moment, Broderick impressed her to Amice's side, mounted his horse and habitually checked to see his sword cleared his scabbard, ready to draw if needed.

Rosselyn came running down to the stables, waving her hand and yelling for Broderick to wait. Rushing to his side, panting and handing him a hefty bundle, she said, "The soap, cloths, and the extra change of clothes!"

He thanked her and secured the bundle in the fully-packed saddlebags, squeezing it in where he could. Kicking his steed into a full gallop, Broderick bolted out the gates and reined the beast west and to Davina. Though he could reach Davina faster on foot, carrying all the provisions would have made the journey difficult.

Broderick glanced heavenward. "I know you have a deaf ear to my kind, Lord, but hear me for her sake. Let her strength be enough to survive this."

"So Broderick is going to play hero," Angus said, pondering this new development, the lifeless body of the perimeter patrol at his feet in the snow. He approached the Gypsy camp with the intention of confronting Broderick with Veronique's life. However, Broderick's presence was absent from the area. Broderick hadn't come out to meet him as he expected. Listening to the thoughts of those around the camp led him to the castle at Stewart Glen, and this poor soul at his feet gave him the last bit of information he needed. Whoever this person was, this thought-to-be-dead husband of Davina's may have thwarted his plans for the night, but he didn't necessarily ruin everything. The fact that Broderick went after Davina instead of Veronique made it obvious who meant more to him. Broderick was immortal and would most definitely win against this mortal…if he made it to her on time. If he did, all would go as planned. If not, Davina's death would make Broderick weak enough to take the fight out of him, while Angus used Amice and Veronique to deal the final blow.

CHAPTER FOURTEEN

Broderick continued through a blinding curtain of egg-sized flurries. The tracks he followed disappeared under the new cover of snow. Curses flowed from his mouth in hot breaths as he pushed forward. Though Lilias's memories showed the way to the lodge through a valley of connecting glens, all he had were images of summer journeys. Snow, which kept building, covered the route and made the landscape indefinable. He tried to keep his fear at bay with the faith he proceeded in the right direction. Though immortality granted him supernatural night vision, he couldn't see through snow. The poor visibility made it more and more difficult to see the landscape, and he had to right his horse through the rising ground to get back into the center of the guiding glens.

Breathing deep through his nostrils, the scent of blood caught his attention and the Hunger stirred.

He inhaled another breath. Nothing. Another. There…the unmistakable scent of blood. He slowed his mount and jumped from the horse, smelling the cold gusts of air. More blood. His gut tightened both from the Hunger and over whose blood it might be, but he quelled his rising uncertainties. The scent of blood didn't seem strong, indicating there wasn't a lot of it.

Broderick had not fed prior to departing—and for once, that worked in his favor. The Hunger, not yet satisfied tonight, made his senses all the more acute for what it needed most. Taking another step forward, his foot landed on something in the snow. He pulled on the large cloth under his foot. Davina's cloak. The smell of her rose oil and essence sent a wave of comfort through his body, but he tensed at the smell of her blood. Swinging back up into the saddle, he pushed the horse forward, allowing the Hunger to reach out for any more signs of blood. Coming forward through the falling snow, a familiar rock formation appeared on the right. Excitement drummed his heart as he recognized this landmark as being the last large marker just before the lodge. He was close!

As quietly as possible, Davina worked at the ropes tying her hands behind her back. A blazing fire radiated from the hearth across the room, and from her corner she took advantage of the warmth.

What Ian built for his own comfort, also helped cease her shivering. Numb and lethargic, her hands made the effort difficult. Her breasts, hard and aching with milk, added to her discomfort. She rested for a moment, the left cheek of her bottom throbbing, and then tried to straighten her legs from their curled position under her body. She winced. They were stiff and one leg tingled. The rest of her body ached from the hard miles. Tears stained her cheeks and stung the open scrapes. Still, all the soreness in her body paled next to the wrenching in her heart.

Cailin had stopped crying when they reached the lodge. Davina hoped her daughter was asleep. But as she stumbled to Ian's horse, he swung the limp child down only by her arm, and Davina cried out when Cailin's arm snapped. Ian hefted Cailin into Davina's bound arms with little care, and Davina used all her strength to keep from dropping her baby. She fell to her knees, crying, and stretched her legs out to put Cailin onto her lap, covering the babe with her skirts. Only after Ian strolled through the lodge and found the accommodations suitable, did he come back outside and cut Davina's bonds. He left her to battle her weakness, lifting Cailin and staggering to her feet. When she struggled inside, he prodded her through the front area and into the dining hall where she collapsed on the nearest bench and hurried to unbind her breasts. She just put her hands to her neckline when Ian grabbed her by the shoulders and dragged them both, Davina clutching Cailin to her breast, over to the corner and pushed them to the floor.

"Have a seat, Davina," he mumbled. Then he snatched Cailin from her grip. Davina reached for her daughter, frantically tugging and pulling at Ian's arms, but he batted her attempts away. Grunting, he slammed his fist into her face. When she came to, she was seated in the corner, wrists tied behind her back, ankles bound even tighter, her head spinning from the blow she received.

From her position in the corner, Davina surveyed the area while she struggled to regain her bearings and assess her situation. Ian gorged on more food at the table to her right. Davina's stomach rumbled in response. Beside Ian's trencher lay his dagger. She turned her attention back to his face for fear of him catching her covetous eyes upon his knife—the only weapon she could find in the room. Davina tried to gauge any suspicious reactions, any signs he might see that she tried to break free. She concentrated to ensure her movements were as minute as possible.

Cailin lay on the table next to Ian, her face pale, her tiny chest rising and falling in rapid, shallow breaths... *At least she still breathes.* Cailin's broken arm was deformed and blotched with purple skin. Davina gritted her teeth and fought the helplessness welling inside her. Until she freed herself, she could do little for her daughter, and time ran short. Davina twisted her hands and pulled at her bonds, pain climbing up her arms like fire burning her flesh. Though getting free was the first goal, more importantly she needed Ian out of the way. Only then would she be able to help her daughter. That insurmountable task weighed down her spirit. Her limbs trembled from exhaustion. Weakness lorded over her body. Where would she find the strength to come against Ian? More tears slipped down her cheeks. She eyed the dagger in vain.

"So, tell me, Davina," Ian spoke casually over his food, a piece of grouse flying onto the floor. "Did you ask your brother to kill me, or did he just decide to do that on his own to protect his little sister?"

Davina remembered Kehr's last words to her before they went off to war. "I swear to you, Davina," he whispered against her ear. "You will never have to see him again."

Ian finished eating and wiped his hands on a cloth that held some of the food. "Oh, he tried to strike me down." Strolling around the table, Ian picked up Cailin and laid her gingerly on the floor, just out of Davina's reach. "A very good attempt, I must say." Ian lifted his shirt and exposed ugly, blotchy scars all along his right side. Dropping his shirt, he smiled. "But I remained conscious long enough to see him die. How glorious, Davina! To see a great English spearhead emerge from his chest like the birth of a foal, dripping with blood and flesh! What an exquisite sight!"

He bore his crazed eyes into hers, and she turned away.

"Upsetting?" he asked with sincerity. "Does it rip your heart apart to hear the details of your brother's death?"

She glared at him, and he grabbed her shoulders, his fingers biting into her flesh.

Ian pulled her to her feet and shoved her onto the bench, straddling her lap and pushing her hard against the table. She gritted her teeth to keep from crying out. At least she sat in a better position to fiddle with her bonds. A devious smile spread across his face and he put his mouth against her ear, laughing. "You know I love it when you fight, Davina!"

Let him think what he wanted; fine by her.

"Aye, it has been a long time, wife." Ian's hands groped her milk-hardened breasts, and she gasped from the soreness, his lascivious eyes upon her. Davina wanted to vomit. Oh, how she despised this man! Nothing made her want to retch more than what came next. She closed her eyes and concentrated on her hands. *Please, dear Lord, give me strength!*

"Did your Gypsy dream lover ever come back for you?" he teased against her ear as he continued to molest her. His whiskers scraped against her raw skin. "I thought I saw the Gypsy caravans by the village." He laughed.

Free! My hands are free! Davina turned her head, took his ear between her teeth and bit as hard as she could, wincing as his screeching wail pierced her ear. He jumped off her lap and put his hand to the side of his head. Davina spit the piece of flesh onto the floor, stifling the urge to vomit, fighting the gagging convulsions.

Ian bent forward, grunting, blood dripping through his hand.

Before he recovered, she grabbed the dagger off the table, her arms heavy like they dragged through mud, but then she lost her bearing. She toppled to the floor in front of the chapel door, dizzy. Shaking her head to clear the confusion, she realized Ian had recovered and knocked her aside. Struggling to crawl away, she stumbled onto her face. Her feet were still bound. Ian grabbed her ankles and pulled her toward him. Disorientation conquered her senses. The room flopped back and forth as Ian dragged Davina around. Nausea threatened to claim her and she covered her mouth, closing her eyes.

Severing the bonds at her ankles, he cut through her kirtle. The sound of tearing cloth grated her nerves. The coolness of the room hit her skin through her thin chemise, and Ian straddled Davina, pinning her arms at her side with his knees. Forced to view him in his dominant position, she saw his snarling face, the room still spinning. He raised his arm high, clenching his fist. Davina wiggled beneath him and he punched her face. She lay still for a moment, stunned from the blow, then resumed struggling. Another blow and a warm trickle oozed from the side of her mouth. Fighting once more, she managed to free one of her arms and snake her hand up between his legs, squeezing and twisting his sack as hard as she could. Ian yowled. Davina bucked her hips, and he fell forward, enough for her to scoot out from under him. Davina struggled to her knees before Ian pounced, still nursing his groin. Two more crushing blows to her face rendered her helpless. She had no more strength to fight. She searched for her daughter in hopes Cailin still lay unconscious, unable to witness what she knew came next.

At breakneck speed, Broderick arrived at the lodge nestled in the small valley. The wooden door was shut against the cold and no lights flickered in the windows. His body tensed. What if Ian didn't bring them here? Where would he look next? Could they already be dead? Digging his heels in, he galloped down the slope and leapt off his horse at the gate, bolting to the front door and shouldering it open. Empty. But the thick scent of blood hung in the air. His fear dominated the Hunger, keeping it under control. Broderick barreled through the front hall into the next room.

Davina lay almost unconscious, moaning and thrashing her head from side to side. Her breasts were exposed, and straddled on top of her knelt Ian—the man he saw in the image from the taste of Davina's blood; the face staring back at him in the dream tonight. Rage gushed through Broderick's body, and he clenched his fists.

The scent of blood assailed his senses and the Hunger demanded an audience. Snarling, Broderick pulled back his control, allowing the Hunger to come forth. The familiar pain shot through Broderick's gums as his incisors extended. He hunched forward, his breath gusting hot from his lungs, and a snarl boomed out of his mouth, causing Ian to cease in cutting Davina's chemise. Ian, wide-eyed and open-mouthed, dropped the dagger to the floor.

Ian grunted and Davina gasped in relief when his weight lifted. She couldn't see, her eyes swollen to slits and head still spinning from his blows. A loud crash of furniture made her flinch with fright. She lay for a moment, trying to gain her senses.

Move! She ordered her body to obey. *Get to Cailin!* With groggy motions, she rolled onto her side and crawled away from the commotion. What happened? Was Ian pleading? Did he beg for his life? Or did she have deluded fantasies, lying on the floor underneath him as he violated her? Davina's fingers touched something soft and warm. *Cailin!* She squinted through the darkness of delirium and found her daughter's limp form on the floor. Gathering the babe into her arms, she scrambled to the edge of the room and cried as she held the soft bundle against her breasts.

Ian's blood-curdling scream pierced her ears, and Davina ducked into a ball to protect Cailin. She slapped a hand over her own mouth when a sickening gurgle echoed along the stone walls, followed by the gruesome crackle of ripping cartilage, like a chicken carcass being dismembered. Davina searched the dining hall with squinted eyes, and her breath left her in a gust of disbelief.

Broderick stood facing her, the fire behind him silhouetting his figure, Ian's limp body in his arms. Blood—streaming black in the dimness—flowed from Ian's neck and down his arm, outstretched toward the floor, lifeless. Ian's body hit the floor with a thud. Davina swallowed hard when the firelight exposed his throat, gaping and shredded. Her heart thundered in her ears. She gazed up at Broderick. That molten silver glow shone in his eyes through the dimness. His chin glistened, and black liquid stained the front of his white shirt. What was that black liquid? Davina's eyes widened with horror. Could that be blood coming from his mouth? Did blood stain his chin and shirt? She glanced down at Ian and then back to Broderick, who turned his back to her in haste. His arm made a sweeping movement, as if he wiped his face clean. In a smooth motion, he tore his shirt off and tossed it aside. Her chest heaved as she panted, panic overwhelming her.

"Davina." What she heard of Broderick's voice over the thudding in her ears sounded hoarse, and harsh. Just like the night she cut her neck on her dagger. The night he said, "The only thing that frightens me about blood is my passion for it."

Davina searched the room for a weapon and saw Ian's dagger. She put Cailin down on the floor and with a glance at Broderick's expansive back, lunged forward and grabbed the knife. Standing like a lioness over her child, she held the dagger in front of her, shielding Cailin on the floor behind her. Broderick turned around and stepped forward, his hand outstretched. "Davina, please…"

Please what? She bit her knuckle to stave off a scream. Her other hand trembled with the sharp knife poised at Broderick.

"I know what you have just seen is more than you can bear at this moment, but put the knife

410

down and let me help you. I can help you." Broderick pleaded with his eyes, the silver glow gone. Yet his chin still held signs of Ian's blood, his bare chest still gleamed black in the firelight.

Davina bent forward and retched onto the floor. She fell to her knees, struggling to keep the knife before her. Scrambling back against the wall, searching for Cailin, the knife slipped from her grasp and she moaned as the strength left her body. All went black.

Broderick rushed to Davina's side and cradled her. He almost didn't recognize her, so deformed and discolored was her face. Cailin's condition was far worse. The infant inched so close to death, Broderick didn't have much time.

Laying Davina back on the floor with care, he swept the baby into his arms and, using Lilias's memories of the lodge, rushed to the bedchambers off the front hall. "Stay with me, little one," he cooed, brushing her red curls off of her tiny brow. Dust clothes covered the furniture in the bedchamber. With a quick yank, he exposed the lounging couch before the hearth and lay the baby down. Broderick drew a calming breath and began his ministrations. He pulled and turned her arm, setting her bone. From his sporran, he produced Davina's dagger.

With the blade, he made a small cut in the crook of Cailin's arm where it splotched of purple and deep red. Her blood pulsed out slow, indicating the weakness of her heartbeat. Cutting his own wrist, he winced from the laceration, remembering the silver blade a little too late, and let his blood drip onto her fresh wound. Without a scar, the incision on her arm healed. The bruises faded away. Cutting Cailin's wrist, and then his own, he joined them, letting a very small portion of his blood flow into her veins…just enough to heal her without any repercussions. The cuts closed and color crept back into the child's face. Within moments, all of her bruises faded and her breaths became deep, healthy, and strong. Cailin would live. He sighed with relief and kissed her brow. Some of his blood flowed through her veins now, and would for a short time before her body absorbed it. But without the damaging effects of a Blood Slave infection, because he had not consumed any of Cailin's blood. This bonding of blood was the closest he would ever be to having a child of his own. He stared at the face of this precious bairn, her small features reflecting the beauty of her mother, and Broderick's throat closed with emotion. With one last kiss to her brow, he uncovered the massive canopy bed in the room. No mattress. Grabbing all the dust clothes, he shook them out, folded them up and placed them on the hardwood base of the bed, creating as much of a mattress as possible.

Back in the dining hall, Broderick picked Davina up from the floor and placed her in the chamber on the mattress. With a kiss to her scraped brow, he went about doing what he could to make them both comfortable by starting a fire in the bedchamber hearth. He grabbed a pot from the kitchen house to melt snow and provide hot water, and brought in their provisions and packs.

Laying her on some blankets by the fire, Broderick examined the extent of Davina's injuries. He stripped Davina of her torn clothing and washed the blood from her wounds. She stirred every now and then under his ministrations, but never woke. Broderick tended to her in the same way he tended Cailin, his healing, immortal blood working its miracles on her wounds and injuries. Though the blood he did force into her cuts and abrasions would go deep enough to heal some of the soreness and any internal damage, she would still ache on the morrow, considering the beating she received.

Checking to ensure he healed everything he could, he covered her with a blanket and stood with his hands on his hips, finally calming his nerves over the intense moments that just passed. Davina was safe. Cailin was safe. He almost lost them both. With overwhelming relief bubbling up in his chest, he bowed his head and his eyes fell to the dried blood upon his chest...Ian's blood. Thankful for the distraction, Broderick refilled the basin at the wash table and paused at the monster staring back at him from the looking glass. His mouth set into a hard line. Even though he wiped the blood from his face, plenty remained for Davina to have seen. It coated his chest in crimson and now the blood had dried and cracked on his skin. What a gruesome sight she must have witnessed. Regret washed over him.

After cleaning up, he tossed the bloody water outside, rinsed the basin again and replaced it on the wash table, then turned his attention to the packs. Among the baby clothes and Davina's chemises and dress, a large, moss-green man's shirt and a pair of dark brown breeches were stuffed in the sack. Broderick smiled at Myrna's forward thinking. Although getting into the garments didn't prove too difficult, the breeches fit tighter and hung shorter than he liked. They would have to do, though. He tucked the pants cuffs into his boots. The moss-green linen shirt fit much more to his liking, and had the draped freedom of garments he preferred. He buckled his belt, tucked Davina's dagger into his sporran, and left the front of his shirt partially unbuttoned. Broderick burned their soiled clothes in the hearth. Thankfully, the Stewarts packed plenty of extra blankets and he laid a couple of the thicker ones over the makeshift mattress.

Broderick observed Davina lying before the hearth, her skin rosy from the warmth of the fire. The swelling of her eyes and mouth had all but disappeared, restoring the bonnie face he had grown to love. He sat on the floor beside her, stroking her hair and letting the tension of the events melt from his body. Clenching his jaw, he steeled against the dread threatening to rise up and consume him. He almost lost her. How could loving Davina wrench his heart, and at the same time fill the chasm left from the emptiness of losing his family? This deep affection for her flowed through him, bringing peace in its wake. Broderick thought he would never love again after Evangeline's betrayal; and yet his ardor for Davina surpassed anything he felt for Evangeline. Had he *ever* loved her? Cogitating on the night Angus massacred his brothers and their families—the night Broderick anchored a large portion of his hatred—could he honestly say Evangeline's betrayal had driven him mad? He squeezed his eyes shut and bowed his head, recalling that night to find the source of his vengeance.

Admittedly, Broderick held a measure of responsibility for neglecting his wife. He devoted himself almost full time to getting his family's estates in order. They built three keeps, one for him and each of his brothers, Maxwell and Donnell. As a result, Broderick hardly came home, let alone paid any attention to his new bride. When he apologized for slighting her, she admitted to being unfaithful. The passing weeks were tenuous between them, but Broderick accepted culpability for his part in the affair, in spite of how much her infidelity hurt. But on reflection, could he say what hurt worse—his heart, or his pride? Broderick and Evangeline agreed they would get through this setback and start working on their family. Nothing was more important than continuing the bloodline and producing heirs. However, this was not the true betrayal that drove him to choose immortality.

Two months after their reconciliation, on the eve of the May Day celebrations, his brother Maxwell told him Angus Campbell asked for an audience. Their enemy awaited Broderick outside the castle keep at Glenstrae, declaring he came in peace.

"Peace is not an option," Broderick said more to himself than Maxwell, who trailed after him holding a lantern to light their way. They stomped up the narrow staircase in the gate house, heading toward the top garret. "He's not here for the ale."

"Agreed," Maxwell mumbled, and they marched the length of the allure—the walkway along the top of the curtain wall—to stand at the front of the keep, straining to see Angus in the orange glow of the torches. Night had just fallen.

Angus sat atop his horse a goodly distance from the gate, relaxed and at ease. He waved, exuding the friendly neighbor and peacemaker. Broderick didn't like it. "State your business!"

"Why, I am here to wish the lord and lady of the castle a joyous May Day celebration," Angus hailed merrily. "Ah! And here is the fine lady of Glenstrae! Good evening to you, milady!" Angus bowed in his saddle. Broderick could just make out Angus's smile in the dimness.

"Do not let him out of your sight," Broderick growled at his brother. "Get back inside, Evangeline." Turning to face his wife and usher her back down into the keep, Broderick paused. She shook her head and put her hand over her pale lips, staring wide-eyed at their unwanted visitor.

Angus called from below, "I also came to tell you I enjoyed bedding your wife! I had a rowdy time teaching her all manner of…"

"*Him?* You were rutting with *him?*"

"I didn't know," she whimpered. "He said his name was—"

Broderick grabbed Evangeline and dragged her down the stone steps. He never heard anything she or Angus said, his mind numb to any noise around him, his eyes only seeing red. The cacophony of his brothers' shouts and the pulling at his limbs went unheeded, but they at least impeded his murderous intent upon Evangeline. With a degree of control, he struggled away from his interfering brothers and dragged her to the gate, opened the latch, and threw her outside, banishing her and withdrawing his protection.

That was all the moment Angus needed. He issued his battle cry and charged the keep.

In retrospect, Broderick and his brothers should have been able to shut the gate against Angus before the reinforcements were upon them. Yet, miraculously, Angus jumped from his horse, leapt the impossible distance and blocked the opening with his body. Not so miraculous now that Broderick knew he was immortal and possessed the strength of at least twenty men.

Dread and guilt blossomed in his chest. His love for Davina illuminated the truth of Broderick's anger. Evangeline was the means to an heir and fair to look upon. A broken heart didn't drive him to throw her out of the keep—pride did. Rage filled him because he was made the fool, not because she betrayed his love—so, in truth, he could no longer blame Evangeline.

Broderick opened his eyes and rubbed the self-pity from his face. The same set of circumstances loomed before him once again: Angus exploited Broderick's weakness, by hurting the ones Broderick loved. At this point, his heart was in too deep. He couldn't walk away. Broderick brushed her coppery curls away from her brow, the beauty of her face and spirit causing his heart to ache. Aye, this love made him vulnerable enough for Angus to strike, but Broderick swore he would never let Angus harm Davina or Cailin, no matter what he had to do to ensure their protection. Even if their safety meant sacrificing revenge.

With a brief kiss to her brow, he picked up Davina and carefully set her on the bed. Grabbing Cailin and returning the lounging couch to its place before the hearth, he nestled Cailin by Davina's body and secured the blankets around them. Davina snuggled inside their warmth, instinctively pulling her child into the protection of her arms. Broderick touched his mouth to Davina's mended face, caressing her cheeks, her lips, her eyelids. One last lingering kiss to her mouth, and Broderick stood and sighed. At ease that both she and Cailin were well, warm, and out of danger and pain, he turned his attention to the next task—cleaning up the mess.

Broderick stomped through the lodge at a determined pace and through the front door, secured the horses, and headed toward the kitchen house just across the back courtyard from the stables, their provisions in hand. He searched the root cellar and pantry and found a half-filled cask of vinegar. That would do well to clean up the blood. Broderick grabbed the jug and headed back into the house through the back door, setting the vinegar just inside the dining hall on the floor.

Using one of the smaller dust cloths from the other bedchamber, he covered and picked up Ian, hefting the dead weight in his arms, and carried the body to the dense forest behind the stables. Trekking through the snow a good distance from the lodge, he found a rocky area containing large stones. Rock formations jutted up from the forest floor. Placing Ian's body along one of these outcroppings, he used the loose stones around the area to bury the remains, the ground too frozen for digging.

With that done, he raced back to the lodge, performed the grisly task of cleaning up the blood, and returned to the kitchen house.

Broderick stood at the prep table, organizing the supplies, and a wave of exhaustion hit him. He leaned back against the brick oven to steady himself. Fear seized his body, and he spun to see the horizon through the open door. Dawn! He lost track of the time! Broderick needed a place to hide before the fatal powers of the sun scorched him, and just as it was for burying Ian, the ground was too frozen for digging in the forest. Very young in immortal years, no clouds could hide him. The recent cries of Clyde Samuels—still echoing in his mind—reminded him of that death. The sky lightened to charcoal gray, and Broderick's face grew warm as he stood in the entranceway. Slamming the door, he turned to the cellar entrance in the floor, and his eyes drooped as the next wave of exhaustion hit him. His limbs went numb and his body abandoned him. Fighting to close the door behind him, he struggled into the dark chamber, and collapsed to the floor. Broderick had just enough time to roll onto his back before a deathlike slumber settled upon him, and he disappeared into the blackness.

Davina opened her eyes and stared at an unfamiliar bare canopy above her. Her brow creased with confusion, and then her eyes grew large as the previous night came rushing back in a wave. She moved to sit, but nestled at her side, her sweet daughter laid breathing and twitching from her dreams, a subtle smile upon her bow-like mouth. Relief washed over Davina at the sight of her daughter, warm and alive. She sobbed. *Thank God Cailin lives!*

She eased up onto her elbow and groaned from the tenderness in her joints. Davina urged Cailin to wake. Her child opened her eyes enough to see her mother's nipple and her eager little mouth latched on with obvious hunger, settling into a feeding nap.

Davina winced, but then sighed from the liberation of the release. Poor little darling hadn't eaten since the afternoon the previous day. Remembering when Ian so carelessly and cruelly snapped Cailin's arm, she opened Cailin's blanket and examined her delicate limbs. Davina's mouth hung open when she found no signs of any trauma.

Her mind twirled with confusion. She recognized the room where they lay—her parents' chamber at the New Lodge. Touching her face, she prepared for the worst. With tentative fingertips Davina explored her skin, and to her surprise, she found nothing unusual—no soreness, no swelling, no abrasions. Her breath left her in astonishment. Had it all been a nightmare? They were at the lodge, and her muscles were tender, indicating the horror did happen, yet on the surface, all seemed well.

Cailin looked for the other breast and Davina pulled her attention back to her baby. Once Cailin finished nursing, she settled back into a deep sleep. Davina showered grateful kisses across her baby's face. *What would life have been like without her?* Tears wracked Davina's body for a short time, but she steadied her breath. Cailin lay safe and alive—but how? After what Ian did to her little girl, Cailin's condition before Davina lost consciousness, the child should not have survived.

Broderick! It *had* to be Broderick.

The last thing Davina recalled, she stood over Cailin while a blood-soaked Broderick pleaded with her to let him help. Then she fell unconscious—vulnerable to him and the monster he was. Broderick must have tended to her and Cailin. Did he have more of Amice's miracle cure? Or had he used something more supernatural to aid him in his ministrations? She shuddered.

Sitting up in the bed and pushing the dread aside, she threw the covers back to reveal her naked form. Broderick must have undressed her, as well. She covered herself and recoiled into the safety of the blankets, but then remembered the way Ian had shredded her clothes. For certain, Broderick didn't have much choice except to remove her spoiled clothing. Shame prickled her conscience. She grabbed one of the blankets and wrapped it around herself.

Kissing Cailin's cheeks, Davina left her baby on the bed, and sat on the lounging couch to ponder. If not for the soreness and being in the lodge, she would have thought this all a horrible delusion. Flashes of the night before played in her mind. Images of Ian pinning her to the floor, his hand raised and the many blows he dealt, brought stinging tears to her eyes and she covered her face, sobbing. She allowed this time to grieve over the experience.

Her tears spent, she explored the room and found the bags on the floor, the supplies scattered about, amongst which she discovered some of her clothes and her cloak. She picked what she needed out of the pile and returned to the hearth, where burned the last red, dying embers.

Someone packed a thick linen chemise and a warm woolen dress, which she thankfully donned to cover her chilled skin. Lacing up the bodice, she searched for something to plait her hair, but found nothing. Her boots were still in good order and she found some hose amongst the spare clothes. Donning her cloak, she inhaled deeply and stood before the entrance of the chamber, her trembling hand upon the latch. She pulled open the heavy door and shivered in the cold air.

The wide front hall lay bare. The front entrance, centered on the south wall to the left, lay open. Walking to the door, she pushed it shut and noticed the splintered wood of the frame. She fought the smile of pride and gratitude tugging at the corners of her mouth, imagining Broderick bursting through the door when he arrived. A flash of Ian's throat, mangled and torn, assaulted her mind, stealing a measure of the warmth from Broderick's deeds. She closed the door as best she could against the cold, turned around, and eyed the door to the dining hall, where the events of the previous night took place. Swallowing hard, she rubbed the cold from her arms and marched across the room. She braced and opened the door.

Davina scrunched her eyebrows in confusion as she eyed the empty room. Only minor remnants of the night before remained—the sprawled furniture spoke of the struggle Ian gave at Broderick's hands, the heavy scent of vinegar accounted for the lack of blood on the floor, and the ash in the hearth held remnants of a blood-soaked shirt.

Stepping into the room, she went to the spot where Broderick killed Ian. What did Broderick do with Ian's body? She saw the faded ring outline of Ian's blood. The blood. Down Broderick's chin. On his chest. The sickening sounds of Broderick ripping Ian's throat apart. Davina collapsed to the floor on her knees, squeezing her eyes shut against the images pounding her mind. Shaking her aching head, she pushed the memories away and rose from the floor. "I cannot think upon this now," she said, using her voice to silence the internal turmoil.

Davina went back into her parents' bedchamber to make a further assessment of the supplies available. "Stay occupied, Davina," she grumbled. She scurried to the hearth, filled with ashes, and started a fire to chase away the coldness swarming the room and her soul. With that done, she turned to the supplies on the floor, knelt and gathered them into the bags, setting them aside.

Cailin's whimper brought her out of her activities. Davina rose to gaze over the large foot board and found her daughter sitting up in bed, looking a little lost and afraid. Cailin's hand in her mouth, soft trails of a tear or two down each cheek, she half-giggled-half-whimpered and Davina's heart constricted. Cailin seemed to reflect the emotions tearing through her own soul and mind, not knowing whether to laugh or cry at the sight of each other. Davina rounded the bed post toward Cailin's outstretched hands and lifted her daughter into her arms, holding her close and crying into the crook of her downy soft neck.

"'Tis over, precious. M'ma is here." Davina pulled back from the embrace and gazed into Cailin's crystal blue, smiling eyes. As she wiped the tears from her baby's cheeks, Davina's stomach growled in protest. Cailin started at the noise and her mouth formed into a little 'O'. She glanced down at her mother's stomach and back up at Davina, then burst into giggles, dragging her mother into the merriment. "We should get something to eat, aye?" Davina asked through her laughter, grateful to turn her attention to simpler tasks.

She kissed Cailin's nose and dressed her in the clothes provided among the supplies, before wrapping her in the soft baby blanket. Davina made her way through the lodge to outside, the cool, crisp air hitting her face and causing her to tremble. She wrapped the cloak about her daughter, and they stood on the back step in the silence, her heart dropping into her belly. She squinted in the sun, reflecting off the vast blanket of white snow spread out before them. The snow lay so deep, she almost couldn't discern the landscape.

"Dear God," she whispered. "How will we get through this?" Davina drew her quivering bottom lip between her teeth to still her nerves and hugged her daughter closer.

Stepping out into the courtyard, Davina surveyed the area. The stable lay off to the right, and she breathed a sigh of relief—the large structure housed the horse Ian had taken, and served to block off some of the snow which covered the grounds overnight. Broderick's horse also stood tethered in the stable. The presence of the horse meant either he was still here, or at least he would be coming back. The animals grazed in peace from the trough. Sculpted peaks of white ridges hugged and bordered the stone structures around the courtyard, as if frozen in some kind of arching dance, and glistened like diamond dust in the sun. Davina caught her breath at the sight—something she had not seen since her youth, and then only at their castle, since she mainly visited the lodge on occasional summers. Though snow frequented Scotland these many winters past, such a heavy snowfall didn't happen as a regular occurrence.

Eventually, Davina picked through the peaks of snow and settled with gratitude inside the already cozy kitchen house. Setting Cailin aside on her blanket, Davina surveyed the small building. Broderick had been here as well. Wood lay stacked in piles next to the brick oven, where dying embers crackled in the pit under the main chamber. The door to the pantry stood open a crack. Herbs and salts were scattered beside the food stuff, laid out on the preparation table next to the saddlebags, as if Broderick were readying the food for them. Her brow creased. *What stopped him in the middle of his tasks?* Cailin remained content in playing with the edge of her blanket.

Davina gazed down at the root cellar and Veronique's voice echoed inside her head. *Because of what he is, he cannot face the heat of the sun. He must slumber during the day and comes out only at night, just after sunset.*

She swallowed and urged her feet to move, but they remained rooted to the floor. After a moment, she realized she held her breath. Inhaling deep, she clenched her fists and shuffled to the door. She heaved it open. Darkness greeted her eyes, so she lit an oil lamp and headed down the stairs. She hitched her breath and covered her mouth, her eyes wide. Broderick lay on the cellar floor by the back wall, his body still and motionless—including any rise or fall of his chest in slumber's breath. A lump formed in her throat and she ran down the stone steps to Broderick's body. Her hand still pressed over her mouth in a struggle against the rising grief, she studied him.

Broderick lay on his back, hands at his sides, his chin close to his left shoulder, his face angled toward her. The probability that Broderick may be dead sent a cold shiver through her body. She crouched beside him and searched his face for any signs of life. His skin seemed normal, not pale or translucent. No deadly signs were evident in Broderick. She reached out a trembling hand and touched his cheek, half anticipating a hardness to his flesh. An unexpected wave of relief surged through her when her fingertips came in contact with his pliable and warm skin. Though Broderick didn't burn with the heat she normally experienced from him, he was not ice cold either. His skin felt almost cool to the touch, but still very much alive. So why did he not breathe?

This was more proof of his state of being, the creature Veronique warned her about. This deathlike slumber—half-dead, half-alive position of serenity—gave Davina great pause, and her eyes lingered over his facial features. Her fingers touched his full, masculine lips and a tear slipped down her face. She touched his chiseled cheek with her thumb, brushed her fingertips over his brow, and then pulled back when a soft, deep moan came from Broderick, holding her hand to her throat. He *was* alive! His brow creased for a moment and then smoothed. Davina searched his face for any more stirring. Eyeing Broderick's large chest, his shirt open, exposing the fiery hair sprinkled across his skin, glistening in the lamplight, she waited. No movement. She prayed—nay begged—for his chest to rise and fall with breath, wanting this all to be an illusion. Leaning forward, Davina laid a tentative ear to his chest.

"Please," she breathed. Silence. No heart beat. No sound of breath. Only that of her own heart pounding in her ears. Though Broderick's flesh didn't feel as if he were dead, and though he moaned and voiced his existence, he held no signs of belonging to the living.

Davina's body shook as she sobbed. She sat back upon her heels, her hands covering her face as she cried. She begged for the reality to be a nightmare. Broderick was exactly what Veronique warned—a drinker of blood. The molten silver glow in his eyes, the blood flowing from his mouth and his proclaimed passion for it—they all connected. But no evidence of the monster she saw last night made sense against the man with whom she fell in love. Davina scooted into the corner, curling into a ball, and wept. And God help her, she ached to have Broderick cradle her in his protective embrace.

Cailin let out a soft giggle in the kitchen above, bringing Davina back to the problem at hand. She glanced at Broderick and her lip quivered, tears stinging her eyes anew. Davina reflected on that moonlit night in the forest clearing, her knife poised over her heart. She would do anything to protect her daughter from violence. This dark side of Broderick's being. The danger of Angus. Were these threats any different? Nay, they were even worse. Davina couldn't put her heart above the safety of her child.

She crawled to Broderick's side and touched his cool cheek, the visage of his bonnie face distorted through her tears. Pressing her lips to his, she framed his face with the shroud of her cinnamon hair, and savored one last taste of his lips. "You will always be my image of strength," she breathed upon his mouth. "My Gypsy rogue."

CHAPTER FIFTEEN

Kneeling in the white snowy center of a clearing, Davina reached toward Broderick, tears coursing down her anguished face. Dark trees surrounded her like sentinels. Snow fell in soft tufts from a gray sky, drifting and swirling around her sobbing form. Her wailing cries—white mist on the cold air—tore Broderick's heart in two. Cailin's laughter echoed through the trees.

"Davina!" Broderick strained to run to her, his limbs sluggish as if weighted. "Davina!" Every labored step he made pushed Davina farther from him.

Her anguish melted into sorrowful resignation and she turned a steel gaze to his. "'Tis for the best, Broderick. Cailin must be safe."

Angus emerged from the black forest behind her, a wicked grin on his face. He stalked toward Davina and Broderick wrestled to run faster. Chuckling, Angus continued his lazy stroll toward the weeping desire of Broderick's heart.

"Do not come for me, Broderick." Davina rose and dropped her gaze to her hands. Turning her palms up, she showed Broderick. They were stained with blood. Red splattered the snow on the ground. "Stay away to keep us safe." She turned and walked into Angus's waiting arms, and the forest swallowed them in darkness.

"Davina!" Broderick bolted upright, shaking off the delirium of his daytime slumber. The darkness of the cellar and the scent of lamp oil surrounded him, mingled with the unmistakable scent of what he had grown to love as Davina.

Rising to his feet, he staggered to the stairs as the slowness in his body lingered. Working toward the cellar door, he pushed. It wouldn't open. Cursing, he stepped back down into the cellar and walked off the lasting effects of the lethargy. With a growl, he bolted up the stairs and smashed his shoulder into the door. It flapped open and slammed to the floor. Inhaling a calming breath, he stood in the center of the kitchen house—a clean kitchen house. Nothing remained of what he set out to prepare for Davina and Cailin, except the ashes in the hearth, now cold and gray. Dread settled over his soul as he stepped outside into the winter. His night vision revealed footprints to the stable where Ian's horse stood tethered. He could not, however, see the horse he brought, and the ground around the stables lay trampled with signs of several horses, and footsteps from more than Davina's tiny feet.

Broderick stomped through the snow to the back door and rushed inside, past the dining hall and into the bedchambers—both of them empty. His heart sank. This confirmed what he guessed about the dreams. Somehow he and Davina shared a mystic link. The thoughts Davina had about Broderick during the day seeped into his mind while he slept. They combined with his own thoughts, and created dream-like images. If he guessed correctly, the dream today not only showed Davina as she sat here, anguishing over the truths she knew about him; she also felt leaving him would keep her and Cailin safe…which put both of them in danger, without his protection.

Davina had straightened up any sign of them being there, replacing all the dust cloths over the furniture. The silence pressed upon his ears and heightened his fear. A folded note lay on the dust-covered lounging couch. He snatched the paper and opened it with frantic fingers:

Broderick MacDougal,

After the horrific events of last night, I have no doubt you will understand why my daughter and I could not stay at the lodge. Not only because I could not face the memory of my dead husband—at last dead—but to remain here, so uncertain of what our next encounter would bring. My Uncle Tammus has arrived to take us home, so know that we are safe and taken care of. Do not pursue us.

I write this letter to appeal to the man I know is still inside your heart, in spite of what I saw last night. I beg you to lead Angus away from me and my family. Please keep us safe.

With sincerest and gravest intent,

Davina Stewart-Russell

Crumpling the paper in his fist, he tossed it into the gray ashes in the hearth and raked his fingers through his hair, a sickness settling in his stomach. Davina walked right into Angus's hands. Grabbing his sword, still waiting in the corner behind the door, he dashed out the front door and down the pathway already created by Davina and Tammus. Securing his sword to his hip and ensuring it was clear of his scabbard, he hoped he wasn't too late.

Sitting before the hearth in her own bedchamber, Davina shook her head. "Nay, I do not want to see him again," she lied to her Uncle Tammus for the third time.

Tammus sat beside Davina on the lounging couch, and took her hand in his. "Davina, can you at least tell me what happened out there?"

Avoiding her uncle's gaze, she fixed her eyes on the dancing fire. "I've already told you, Uncle."

"But where is Broderick?" Tammus had urged her for answers for almost an hour, his voice soft and encouraging. "If he saved your life by killing Ian, the man who would have killed you and Cailin with or without the ransom, then why is he not here with you? What has he done to make you shun him? By all accounts, he's a hero, and yet you want nothing to do with him."

What could she tell him? She had only said that Broderick rescued her from Ian, killing him before she lost consciousness, and she assumed Broderick buried Ian's body somewhere in the woods. When she awoke, Broderick was gone. How could she tell him what Broderick actually did? How could she explain the extent of their injuries; that Cailin had been on the verge of death and somehow Broderick made them well? How could she explain the way he laid in the cellar under the shroud of death, and yet living?

"I do not want to see him again." She whispered the lie once more, biting her bottom lip to stay her tears.

A long silence stretched between them before Tammus sympathetically patted her hand. "I do not understand, Davina. And there is nothing more I can do. But be assured that you have but to ask and I will listen." He kissed the crown of her head and walked from the room, closing the door behind him. Davina sat numb, staring into the flames, hugging the decorative pillow to her chest.

A shuffling on the landing drew her attention. Through the window, Davina saw the darkened sky, and her heart thundered. She failed to notice the descent of night. Did her heart beat so rapidly out of fear or anticipation? Would Broderick lead Angus away? Could he? Padding to the double doors, she parted the curtains and stepped onto the empty landing. The harsh cold greeted her face. The snow on the landing had been disturbed, and her breath hitched in her throat. Several large footprints milled around the narrow space, as if someone stood outside, waiting. Peering over the side of the stone wall into the courtyard, a set of footprints both came toward and led away from the wall. Heart thrumming wildly in her breast, Davina warred between excitement and fear. Had Broderick just been here in spite of her wishes? Had he overheard her conversation with her uncle? The words from her own mouth that she didn't want to see him again, and then decided to respect her wishes after all? Davina stared into the night, searching the darkened forest beyond the curtain wall, and she blinked away her tears.

Broderick followed the tracks Davina and Tammus made earlier in the day. There had obviously been no snowfall since last night, their tracks still fresh and remained uncovered. With the air clear, Broderick could see the castle of Stewart Glen far off in the distance. "Almost there," he breathed and turned his eyes back to the trail ahead of him. In a few strides, he pulled up short. "Oh, Veronique…"

Broderick ran to the side of the road. Stretched between two trees, Veronique's pale, cold, body hung displayed like a limp puppet. Rope bound her wrists and her head hung to the side, her beautiful blond hair lifeless and tangled. Broderick pushed her hair aside and the blood drained from his face. Two fang slashes marred the white skin upon her neck, dripping with fresh blood. "Angus," he hissed. He bolted toward Stewart Glen. "Nay!" Broderick left Veronique behind, gliding over the snow as tears flew from his eyes.

Rosselyn, Myrna, Amice, and Lilias, holding Cailin in her arms, all filed into Davina's bedchamber. Their faces each a mask of fear, and they huddled around Davina. Angus Campbell stepped into the room and closed the door behind him, latching the lock. "Nay, ladies," Angus said, pointing to the nursery door. "In there, please." They all looked to Davina, worry etched on their faces. Once they disappeared into the adjoining nursery and Angus closed the door behind them, he ambled to Davina's armoire. Davina blanched as

Angus shoved the massive piece of furniture—surely twice her height—across the room with a loud grating racket, but with no apparent effort. He settled the cabinet before the nursery door and smiled with satisfaction. The women now barricaded inside the nursery, shouted and pounded on the door. "Silence!" Angus boomed, and they obeyed.

Angus turned to her and grinned. "I told you we would see each other again. 'Tis my pleasure."

"Forgive me, but I do not share your sentiments." Davina stood rigidly by the settee, hands clasped to keep them from trembling. "What do you want?"

He bowed graciously. Straightening, he removed his cloak and laid it upon the lounging couch, revealing broad shoulders and a sword at his hip.

Dawning realization flowed over her like a wave of cold water, and she sat down. "You planned this back when you saved me from killing myself." Feeling foolish, she wondered, now, how much saving he had really done.

He nodded and raised an eyebrow. "As for what I want...well, 'tis a rather long story, and I don't think I have much time." Angus rushed in on Davina too quickly for her to react. He trapped her in his arms, forcing her head to the side, exposing her throat as he clutched her hair. A deep chuckle rumbled from his chest as he cupped her bottom and pulled her hard against his groin.

Davina gasped as his mouth pierced her flesh and he drank deep of her blood. She moaned, her mind swirling as all resistance fled.

Breaking the crimson kiss, he jerked his head to the side, and inclined his ear toward the double doors. A smirk formed upon his lips, glistening with her blood. "Ah! Our hero arrives." Angus pulled a dagger from his boot and in an instant, spun her around so he stood behind her. He held the blade over his own wrist, keeping Davina trapped within the circle of his arms.

Angus faced the landing where Broderick entered, sword drawn and eyes menacing.

Broderick stood ready to do battle, and Angus tightened his gripped on Davina, pressing his knife against his wrist. Angus licked blood off his lips, and Broderick noted the marks on Davina's throat. "Step any closer and she'll be my Blood Slave, Rick."

"Let her go, Angus. Your fight is with me."

"Have I given you enough time to determine the limits and powers of what you have become?" Angus leaned forward and narrowed his eyes. "Are you a worthy opponent yet?"

"Let us find out. Are you game for a little swordplay to start?"

"And lose my advantage by releasing the desire of your heart?" Angus said, nuzzling his captive. "I think not."

Broderick locked eyes with Davina. A glimmer of joy sparkled on her face, but he clenched his jaw, struggling to maintain a stoic mask.

"Aye, Rick. 'Tis indeed wise not to argue that point. I've already fed from her." Angus nudged Davina's ear with his nose. She tried to turn away, but Angus held her by the hair.

Broderick fought the helplessness needling his gut, and gritted his teeth.

Whispering, Angus toyed with Davina's life, taunting Broderick. "You wouldn't have forsaken poor Veronique to save Davina if it were not true." He inhaled and sighed. "Nor would you be here if the lass meant nothing to you."

Broderick stepped toward them, but stopped when Davina cried out as the tip of Angus's blade pierced her delicate skin. She bit her trembling lip, and a tear slipped down her cheek as a trickle of blood leaked from her throat and soaked into her neckline. Angus lapped at her neck.

Broderick growled. "Do not make this about her! Let us finish this senseless clan feud that our fathers left as their legacy!"

"Our *fathers*?" Angus grimaced and a maniacal laugh fluttered out of his mouth. "You hate the thought of us being brothers to the point of denying who *sired* me?"

Broderick's throat clenched and he froze, unable to speak. The two immortals stared at each other in disbelief, neither seeming to understand the other. Broderick swallowed and forced the words out of his mouth. "What are you implying?"

Angus growled and Davina cried out as he tightened his grip on her. "Do not stand there feigning ignorance over my parentage! 'Tis the reason your family has plagued mine these decades! Why *you* have been bent on destroying me!"

"I've sought your blood for the slaughter of my *own* family! What madness do you speak of?"

"Do *not* insult my intelligence by feigning you do not know we are brothers!"

Broderick almost stumbled forward in disbelief. "*What?*"

Angus's convictions seemed to falter for a moment and his grip on Davina went slack. When she tried to step away, he grabbed her anew, and rage contorted his face. "I'm no fool, Broderick MacDougal! I know this is why—"

"What lies have you been fed? You are mad!"

"Hamish is our father, and you have never been able to stand that betrayal!"

Broderick's breath pumped in his lungs as he tried to make sense of Angus's words. The feud between their families began in his youth, and

Broderick searched his memories for anything that would give evidence to this insane claim. He never understood Angus's obsession with the endless conflicts, his seemingly insatiable thirst for MacDougal blood. Angus's taunts through the years finally made sense, though—an open contempt for Broderick's position as the eldest son, an obvious jealousy Broderick never understood. Angus was the eldest son of Fraser Campbell and so would inherit his lands…unless he was indeed the bastard son of Hamish MacDougal. If that was so, then Angus slaughtered his own brothers on that bloody May Day massacre. Broderick tightened his grip on his sword and gritted his teeth. "You knew we were brothers and yet you still killed Maxwell and Donnell and—?"

"No more than what all of you have done!" Angus gripped Davina's hair and her whimpers emphasized his words. "You lived a privileged life, boasting your inheritance and estates, while you pursued my blood with vengeance! Yet you question *my* motives? I have no fault in this but my birth!" Angus titled his head back, an unearthly cry pouring from his mouth, slit his wrist open and forced his blood into Davina's mouth. Tossing her choking form aside, Angus leapt at Broderick.

In chaotic flashes, the two immortals clashed swords and slashed at each other, each unleashing decades of fury. Broderick hacked with his sword and met with Angus's blade. Sparks flew as Angus relentlessly pounded against Broderick, using his own grief and loss to fuel his defenses. Metal clashed against metal.

In the blink of an eye, Angus dashed across the room toward Davina, but Broderick anticipated his move and headed him off, blocking his path with his sword, coming close to clopping Angus's nose clean off his face. A small nick at the tip of his nose made Angus hiss from the wound. The slow-healing gash caused him to pause, wiping away the blood.

Broderick smirked. "Never thought to have a blade fashioned of silver?"

Angus's mouth twisted as he growled and leapt for Broderick, wielding his dagger and swirling both blades in unusual maneuvers Broderick had not encountered in swordplay.

Broderick pulled Davina's dagger from his sporran and matched Angus blow for blow as they danced around the room, thrusting and blocking, sparks exploding around them. Their limbs blurred through the air with immortal speed as they dodged and parried in a frenzy of motion.

Davina crouched into the corner by the head of her bed, out of the way, refusing Angus the opportunity to take her up as a hostage again. The grin on Angus's mouth gave Broderick a creeping dread that tickled his senses. With actions almost too quick for Broderick to perceive, Angus poured a battering of thrusts, slashes, and swings that Broderick struggled to meet, dodge, or parry. His relentless pounding drove Broderick into the corner by the wardrobe, limiting his movements, and Broderick lost his sword in the mind-spinning assault. Ducking while rotating and slashing with Davina's dagger, Broderick side-stepped a killing slash from Angus...and to his advantage, the gesture exposed Angus's chest. Seizing the opportunity, Broderick thrust Davina's dagger into Angus's heart.

Slack-jawed and stunned, Angus stumbled back, dropping his dagger to grab at the handle of the knife embedded in his body. Turning to Davina, Angus dove for her, but Broderick tackled him, pounded his fist into Angus's face and dragged him through the double doors. Shoving Angus over the side of the landing wall, Broderick tumbled with him over the edge and both crashed to the ground below with a grunt.

"Broderick!" Davina screeched.

Shaking his head to recover, Broderick shoved away from Angus, lifeless beneath him, the dagger protruding from his chest and blood staining his cream-colored shirt. Broderick let out a sigh of resignation, but dwelled only a moment on the death of his enemy. Davina was in trouble.

Leaping to the landing, Broderick nearly toppled into Davina. He grabbed her shoulders, ushering her back into the chamber, and searched for any noticeable changes in her demeanor. "How do you feel?"

Davina threw her arms around Broderick and planted a hard and possessive kiss on his mouth. He melted and lifted her sweet body against him, their mouths hungry upon each other. Setting her feet upon the floor, he pulled back enough to gaze into the sapphire depths of her eyes.

She framed his face with trembling hands. "I'm grateful you did not heed my letter. I love you, Broderick. I cannot help but love you!"

Her confession brought Broderick to his knees, and he laid his cheek against her belly, embracing her warmth, reveling in the caress of her fingers through his hair. "I love you, Davina, and will never let you from my sight again."

Concern for her safety flooded his heart, bringing him back to his senses. Broderick stood and gripped her shoulders. He searched her face, her eyes, her throat. "Oh, Davina…" Broderick brushed the hair from her shoulder and examined her neck…where the fang marks from Angus should have been. Only blood marred her skin.

She glanced down at the blood stains on her dress and nodded. "I'm well."

Broderick shook his head. He grasped Davina's hands and guided her to the foot of her bed. "Davina, you're not well, and we don't have much time. I must explain what has happened to you."

She flitted her fear-filled eyes over his face, nodded and gave him her attention.

"Angus fed from you, did he not?"

Broderick touched her throat and she nodded.

"Did you drink the blood he forced into your mouth?"

Tears welled in her eyes and she nodded again.

His gut tightened into a knot. "Davina, Angus has done something to you in this exchange that—"

Davina gasped and huddled close to Broderick, her eyes darting as if she searched for something swirling around her.

"What is it?" He grabbed her shoulders, forcing her to face him.

"I feel him! He's here!"

Broderick dashed from her side and went to the landing. An impression in the blood-stained snow, along with Davina's dagger, were all that remained on the ground. Broderick leapt over the side of the landing and knelt, grabbing the dagger. Though there may have been enough silver to create some kind of damage, obviously the blade was not enough to kill Angus. Studying the tracks leading from the spot where he laid, no doubt Angus

447

stumbled away from this too weak or wounded to come back up and finish the fight. This also confirmed that Davina had become Angus's Blood Slave, since she had sensed his presence.

Broderick jumped to the landing and came back into the room. "You are correct. He's here…or was. He lives to fight another day, but the more pressing issue is what has happened to you." Putting the knife on the table at the side of the double doors, he guided her to the settee where they sat. "You have become what is known as a Blood Slave. What Angus did to you is difficult to explain, and I can go into more detail later on, our journey, but—"

"Journey? I am not leaving to go anywhere!" Davina stood and put some distance between them.

"Davina, you're going to die if I don't get you to the only people I know who can help you."

Davina staggered back a step, fear numbing her body, unable to speak. The women pounding at the nursery door drew her attention, interrupting the shocking effects of the words Broderick just uttered.

"We must make preparations to leave immediately," Broderick said, moving closer and keeping his voice low. "The journey is at least two nights ride from here and we must travel at night, as you do not know the way. We have the advantage of the long evenings in winter, so we might make good time. The sooner the better, as your condition will worsen as time progresses."

The women pounding at the door increased, and Davina stepped before the armoire. "Mother, please stay calm. I'm well. Do not worry. We will get you out of there as soon as we are able." The commotion ceased. Davina turned back to Broderick. She didn't want her mother to hear the conversation, so she guided Broderick to the opposite side of the room, which now lay in disarray after the fight. Everything happened so quickly and she tried to make sense of the confusion.

"How is Cailin?" Broderick seemed to sense her mood.

Davina nodded, grateful for a change of subject. "Aye," she rasped. "She's well, but I do not know how. Her arm was broken. She was on the verge of death. You…?"

"Aye, it was me. The blood running through my veins has healing powers. As gruesome as it sounds, that's what I used to heal you and Cailin."

"Your blood? How?"

"By using it like a liniment." Bowing his head in what appeared to be shame, he then glanced back up at her. "Or like a potion in some tea…" His voice trailed off, leaving her to interpret the tea Amice administered when she was ill.

"I consumed some of your blood?" Davina felt the warmth drain from her face and she sat on her bed to steady her weakening legs. "But how is it that I consumed your blood and I was not in danger, but with Angus's blood I am?"

"Angus fed from you first, and then he fed you his blood, which was mixed with yours. As I said, it is difficult to explain, but this infusion causes your body to try to turn into what we are."

Now that she had the chance to ask her multitude of questions, Davina didn't know if she wanted to hear the answers. She swallowed her apprehension. "And what is that? What are you?"

Broderick inhaled a deep breath. "We are known as Vamsyrians. We are a race of immortals—once mortal, who have gone through a transformation through a blood infusion. The process of transformation normally drains the mortal of blood to the point near death, and then they drink from the Vamsyrian who drained them. This mixture of blood takes over the body to complete the transformation. However, in your case, you didn't have enough blood drained from your body to make the transformation complete." Broderick sat beside her and grasped her hands. "Davina, your body will die trying to fight the transformation if we do not get help." Deep sorrow filled his eyes. "I'm sorry I didn't have the chance to tell you all this. This is what I wanted to explain to you, but I wanted to get you out of danger first, because I knew Angus was using you to get to me."

"And I played right into his hands." Davina shook her head. "I thought I was—"

He placed a finger on her lips. "None of that matters now. Blossom, if I do not get you to the Vamsyrian Council as soon as we are able…" He stopped and his brow furrowed. "Come, let us free your family from the room and make haste."

Davina nodded, her head swirling with fear and confusion…as a dark heaviness crept over her soul.

CHAPTER SIXTEEN

Davina fell to her hands and knees on the stone floor, screaming at the pain slicing through her body once more. Drops of sweat soaked into the sandstone as she trembled, struggling through the effects caused by her condition. Though the pain was intense, they made the journey before her condition was too far along. Broderick told her of his experience, standing right where she did, facing the same choices. If his condition was further along by the time he reached this point, Davina paled at the agony he must have endured. When the wave passed, she heaved heavy breaths as Broderick helped her to her feet.

The Elder named Rasheed stared at Broderick, as did the other two Elders at the table flanking him. "You say that Angus Campbell is your brother?"

Broderick still struggled with that information; the tick in his jaw gave evidence to his clenched teeth. "Aye, my brother he is."

Davina noticed on their journey—which took two nights to traverse—that her senses seemed more acute. She heard the slightest sounds, noticed the slightest movements in facial expressions, giving away subtle hints as to what others may be feeling...just as Elder Rasheed did now. Broderick's answer seemed to increase the alarm in Rasheed's eyes, and yet he did everything to maintain an even façade so as not to reveal his emotions. Surely Broderick noticed these subtle changes as well, with his magnified senses, but he gave no indication.

"Did you know this when he transformed you?" Elder Mikhail asked.

"Nay, I did not. I discovered this two nights ago."

The three Elders exchanged fear-filled glances, almost seeming to wait for one another to make the next move. Even Broderick looked uneasy at their silence. Rasheed inhaled a deep breath and nodded. "Davina Stewart-Russell, you have a choice before you. You can either become a Vamsyrian and join our race, or you can choose to become a member of the Army of Light."

"I've explained the choices, Elder Rasheed, and what each of them entails."

Rasheed nodded. "Then take her into the room where she will face a member of the Army of Light."

Broderick helped Davina cross the room to a large wooden door, which two hulking men opened and ushered them through. Sitting her on the chair in the center of this room, Broderick stood at her side. One of the Vamsyrian guards tried to lead Broderick out, but he shrugged off the efforts. "I'm staying with her."

The two men glanced at each other, shrugged and closed the door, retreating into the back corners of the room, settling into the dimness. The lighted brazier to one side did little to give the room light and Davina shivered. Before too long, a bolt thrown back on the other side of the door caused her to jump and the door creaked open. A cloaked figure entered the room, frail and small. The door closed and the bolt clanged again, locking them in together. This figured turned and faced them, revealing strands of silver hair spilling out from the hood of her cloak. She fell to her knees in a gasp. "Father, why do you curse me so!" she said, clasping her hands together before her.

Broderick stepped forward and pulled her hood back to show the anguished face of a woman who appeared in her fifties. "Evangeline?"

Evangeline trembled at the sight of Broderick and the agelessness of his choice so many years ago. *Why, Lord!* She anguished internally. *Why have you brought me back to this?*

"Evangeline?" the woman in the chair whispered. "Your wife?"

"The marriage was annulled," Evangeline responded and looked pointedly at Broderick, who nodded.

The beautiful woman doubled over in pain, and Broderick rushed to her side, comforting her through the wave of what Evangeline recognized as the Blood Slave condition. Through the soft whispers of Broderick's soothing words, she learned her name was Davina. Evangeline had a curse on her soul, carried through the years of not being able to save Broderick from this damned life of becoming a Vamsyrian. Now she would be the agent of sending another innocent soul to hell—or of taking her away from Broderick if this woman chose to go with the Army of Light. *Have I not devoted my life to you to make up for my sins, Father? Was that not enough?*

Davina recovered from the pain and turned her eyes to Evangeline. "I understand you're to explain to me the other side of my choice. Please do so."

Evangeline nodded and swallowed. "You have become a Blood Slave. If you choose to come with the Army of Light, God will heal you. But if you choose to come with me, you will…" She hesitated, knowing the impact this may cause on Davina and Broderick. "You will never see Broderick again."

Davina gazed back at Broderick, who stood by her side like a sentinel, anguish in his eyes. "And if I choose to become a Vamsyrian? What will this mean other than the immortality and this life at night I've seen for Broderick?"

With all the gravity and truth she could muster, in hopes of saving this woman's soul, Evangeline said, "You will be turning your back on God, child. Vamsyrians rarely elaborate on the details of this choice, but they're creations of Satan because—"

"What?" Broderick took a faltering step forward. "Vamsyrians are no such thing!"

"Broderick!" Evangeline was aghast. "How can you lie to this woman? I see you care a great deal for her, but are you bringing her here to give her immortality for your own selfish reasons? I thought at least you would have told her the truth!"

"You never said this on that night I was faced with this choice! You only said I would be turning my back on God."

"What did you think that meant, Broderick?" Evangeline's mind went back to that night she faced him. Broderick had been filled with so much rage, grief, and betrayal at seeing her—redeemed from her sins and with the chosen few of God—and he suffered from his condition and loss of his family. "What I tell you is true, Broderick, and I'm amazed they never explained this to you after all these years. Even if I had finished my explanations, you wouldn't have listened to me. You had made up your mind."

Broderick glared at her, searching her face, and the anger and accusation in his eyes faded to resignation. He nodded. "Aye, you're right, Evangeline. Continue."

"Davina, Vamsyrians are Satan's revenge against God. In his eternal hatred of man—God's special creation with free will—Satan struck a bargain that would trap man's soul for eternity. Satan's new creations developed a thirst for blood so they would slay innocent lives for their immortality, thus adding a never-ending list of sins against their trapped souls." Evangeline hesitated at the horror on Davina's face, but she pushed on. "They are a mockery of Christ's salvation, my child. They gain immortality for the shedding of innocent blood. Humanity gained eternal life for the shedding of Jesus' innocent blood. What the *Tzava Ha'or*—the Army of Light—offers is a chance at a new life, and protection from the Vamsyrians. They're not permitted to harm us or anyone we take with us or they'll incur God's wrath. Choose to come with me and you can also be healed. This is what I set before you." She sat back on her heels, waiting for Davina's decision with hope in her heart.

Davina looked to Broderick and back to Evangeline, who could see the struggle of this young woman's heart deep in her tear-filled eyes. Fighting another wave of pain, Davina clutched the chair as Broderick kissed her sweaty brow, encouraging her to make her choice. Davina nodded and gained her breath. "I choose to become a Vamsyrian."

"Davina, nay!" Broderick grabbed her by the shoulders as he knelt before her. "Nay, you must choose to go with Evangeline!"

"This is the choice you wanted me to make all along?" Davina's bottom lip trembled with a new flow of tears. "Why did you not tell me this is what you wanted?"

Broderick bowed his head into her lap. "Because I feared you wouldn't come with me. I didn't want you to transform, but I couldn't bear to see you suffer the death before you." He lifted his head. "This is the only way. You won't be turning your back on God and you can still be with your daughter."

"But if I choose to become a Vamsyrian, I can have both you and Cailin in my life. Why are you doing this to me? How can you expect me to give up the one true love I have with you?" Davina clutched Broderick to her, and Evangeline's heart ached for them.

What has Broderick done to be cursed like this, Lord? Why have you asked me to be the one to deliver your judgment? Evangeline wiped the tears spilling down her face.

The first sign will be the sacrifice of a troubled heart. This sacrifice will spawn the forgiveness needed to release this heart trapped by guilt and heal.

The words floated through her mind, causing a peace to settle upon her soul. "The prophecy," she whispered. Only now did she understand what it meant. Evangeline burst forth with tears of joy. *Thank you for making me your instrument of peace!*

"Broderick…Davina…there is another way."

They both turned hopeful eyes to her. "Come to me, child." Evangeline rose and encouraged Davina to stand before her. She embraced Davina, who doubled over from another wave of pain. Easing Davina down onto the floor, cradling her in her lap, Evangeline searched the high ceiling for the next instructions from God. Davina trembled with her knees bent, curled into a ball. Evangeline bunched part of her cloak as a cushion for Davina's head and arranged Davina's skirts to be sure they covered her legs…and noticed the dagger sheathed in Davina's boot.

The first sign will be the sacrifice of a troubled heart.

Evangeline nodded, peaceful with this path chosen for her. Slipping the knife out of its sheath, Evangeline plunged the blade into her own

MIDNIGHT CONQUEST

troubled heart before Broderick could do anything to stop her. Evangeline's hand—holding tight to Davina—burned and Davina arched her back, screaming. A surge of healing energy flowed through Evangeline from the crown of her head through her limbs and into Davina. The pain Evangeline expected in her heart never came. She pulled the knife from her chest. The blade gleamed with no blood. She sat confused, uncertain why she didn't die. Did she misunderstand?

Broderick rushed to their side, examining them, frantic eyes searching Evangeline's face. "Why would you do that? What have you done?"

"Broderick?" Davina sat up, perplexed. "'Tis gone. The pain in my body from the blood is gone."

Evangeline touched Davina's face. The burning of the fever was gone as well. "But the prophecy said my sacrifice would…" She realized at that moment God spared her from death. She had made the sacrifice in her heart, forgiving herself for how she had betrayed Broderick, freeing her heart from the prison of guilt she created over these three decades. God never wanted her to kill herself. All she had to do was let go of the guilt…*sacrifice her troubled heart*…and He would do the healing through her hands. Spying the dagger when she heard the words of the prophecy were a coincidence. *Thank you, Lord, for sparing my life in my*

460

rash decision! Evangeline's grin nearly split her face and she laughed. "He is a *loving* God, thank the Lord!" Evangeline gave Davina back her dagger.

Broderick helped both women to their feet and crushed Evangeline in his embrace. "Fool woman."

She laughed in his chest and pushed away from him. "Aye! And I thank the Lord He took pity on me. I thought I was about to meet him."

"What in Hades made you do such a thing?"

She marveled that her healthy heart beat rapidly at her narrow escape. "There is a prophecy, Broderick, that speaks of redemption for your kind. I do not know but one line of text from the ancient scripts. It speaks of signs, and I recalled this particular line: 'The first sign will be the sacrifice of a troubled heart. This sacrifice will spawn the forgiveness needed to release this heart trapped by guilt and heal.' This one line became revealed to me only a year after you had been transformed. I didn't know what it meant until this moment."

"Yours was the troubled heart you thought to sacrifice?"

Evangeline nodded at Broderick's question.

"How did you know it would cure Davina's condition?"

"Because the words came to my mind when I asked God why this was happening, why I was here again to face you. These assignments are few and far between, and I've had only two such assignments. Both times, Broderick, have been with you and me in this room."

The two Vamsyrians standing at the back of the room exited with haste, leaving the three of them to ponder this new development.

"They are not going to let us leave this place alive," Broderick grumbled.

"That's yet to be seen, Broderick MacDougal," Evangeline said with the conviction of her faith. "God wouldn't save this woman to have her killed, and I'm certain you're meant for a greater purpose than either of us know." Evangeline turned and knocked on the door behind her. The bolt slammed and the door opened. "Come with me. They cannot come through this way."

Ushering them through the door, Evangeline met her mentor standing in the stone corridor, eyes wide and mouth open.

"Hurry!" Evangeline urged. "Lock the door! We must make haste!"

The woman did as instructed and led them down the hallway toward their only entrance into the Vamsyrian Fortress. "Praise be to God, sister!" she exclaimed over her shoulder. No one has made the choice to join the Army of Light in over a century! You saved—" She stopped and stared at Broderick, and then Davina. "There are two of them? How can there be two? I thought they only—"

"Walk, Sister Elspeth!" Evangeline encouraged her mentor forward. "Though we have the protection of the scriptural incantations, and the Vamsyrians dare not do us any harm for fear of God's wrath, I do not wish to invite risk. 'Tis best we all get as far from this place as we can manage."

They stepped into the cold night and scrambled for the waiting horses, but Evangeline blanched as she remembered they only had two beasts on which to travel. Turning to Broderick, she opened her mouth to voice her concerns, but he held up his hand.

"Go, now! Davina and I traveled on foot. I can take her from here."

"On foot! How are you—?"

"Evangeline!" His warning glance stopped her protests. "Do you forget what I am so quickly?"

She shook her head, feeling foolish. "God be with you, Broderick MacDougal. And you, Davina."

Broderick stepped forward and embraced Evangeline once more, but with warmth instead of admonishment. "Thank you, Evangeline." He hesitated, and then knelt before her small frame. "'Tis a long time coming, but I've forgiven you and I hope you can forgive me."

Evangeline placed a trembling hand upon his cheek. "Aye, Broderick." She kissed his brow and patted his face. She also hugged Davina. "Now go!

You are not so protected. Please make good your escape."

Broderick nodded and swept Davina into his arms. With a speed that took Evangeline's breath away, he dashed off into the night, proving the essence of his supernatural existence.

"You have a lot to tell me on the trip back, it seems," Sister Elspeth muttered and mounted her horse.

Evangeline nodded. "That I do, sister." She mounted her own horse and stared off in the distance to where Broderick and Davina had disappeared. "We have some research to attend to, my old friend. It seems the prophecy has begun."

Ammon stopped his pacing as Rasheed marched into the Grand Hall of the Vamsyrian Fortress, Mikhail storming in after him.

Mikhail grabbed Rasheed's shoulder and spun him around. "You cannot let them leave this place alive!"

"Are you mad?" Rasheed pointed to the front entrance, where they had watched Broderick and Davina make a hasty retreat. "He has already completed a small measure of the prophecy with this incident. It has already begun. We do not know enough about the prophecy. Killing him may destroy us."

Ammon stepped toward them and gritted his teeth. "Then what do you suggest we do? We cannot let him walk away to do his own bidding."

"We will watch him and keep a close account of both him and his brother." Rasheed paced, his hands clenched behind his back.

Ammon dared to mention, "Rasheed, the Creator cannot know that—"

"I know!" Rasheed closed his eyes, raking his fingers through his jet-black hair. "I was a fool not to see what that woman was up to. Cordelia has obviously learned of the prophecy and has manipulated it to begin."

"Surely, you are not saying that half-wit of a woman knew what she was doing in bringing these two brothers before us." Mikhail punched his hands into his hips.

"Have a care, Mikhail! Cordelia Harley is not the fool she pretends to be, and she has tricked us all into starting this chain of events. She is the one we must hunt down and eliminate or the Creator will take great pleasure in torturing us." Rasheed paced across the stone floor, arms crossed, eyes lost in his thoughts. After moments of silent pondering and agitation, he turned to Mikhail and Ammon. "No one else must know about this. Watch these two brothers closely. Be sure they do not do anything else to bring about our destruction. And we must delve deeper into the prophecy to find those missing pieces or their conflict will be the annihilation of our entire race!"

EPILOGUE

Broderick burst through the door, carrying Davina in his arms, and she clung to his neck, stifling her giggles over his eagerness to enter their wedding chamber.

"At last! I have you all to myself." Placing her down on the floor, his mouth covered hers in a greedy kiss, sending flutters throughout her stomach.

She licked the tip of his nose playfully when he gave her a chance to breathe. "They may come pounding on our door once they have discovered we avoided the public bedding."

"Nonsense! They have plenty of food and drink to keep them busy. Where we are will be the last thing on their minds. I won't bide another moment to make love to you."

Laughter from the hall caused both Broderick and Davina to turn and see Nicabar carrying

Rosselyn past their doorway. "The way is blocked!" Rosselyn said through her laughter as Nicabar advanced up the stairs to the next floor, where their own wedding bed had been prepared.

Davina cast a puzzled look to Broderick as he closed the door and pulled her toward the large four-poster bed.

"A rather large group of Gypsy men of my acquaintance have orders not to let anyone pass." He nuzzled her neck in a warm embrace. "Now, to the matter of bedding my wife."

Her bosom bloomed with warmth at hearing Broderick's words. "I shall never tire of hearing you call me that."

"I do hope not," he whispered, a trace of sadness on his face.

Davina touched Broderick's brow and brought his head down to meet her lips, kissing away the furrowed lines. "I will never regret," she said between kisses, "becoming your wife," another kiss to his neck, "in spite of the world you belong to." Pressing her hands to his shoulders, she urged him to sit on the edge of the bed and stood between his thighs. She floated her lips to his temple and feathered another kiss, then to his other cheek. Slowly, lovingly, she caressed Broderick's face with her mouth. *I adore you, my love. You are my protector, my champion, my husband, my sweet lover and I am eternally yours.*

Possessing her mouth with his, Broderick returned her affections, his hands and mouth worshiping her flesh. *And I adore you, blossom. I vow to protect you and all those you love with everything in my power, for all eternity.*

The love Davina had harbored for years and the fantasies of their lovemaking since she met Broderick, poured from her like a flood, and she couldn't take everything that was Broderick into her fast enough. Her hands tore at his shirt, ripping the fastenings down the front and exposing his chest. Broderick removed the leather strap about his waist and tossed the garment aside, baring his torso to the golden light of the chamber.

Fumbling with the laced kirtle of her gown, both of their fingers danced around each other to work her dress off her body. Davina could feel frustration mounting as the dress created a barrier between them. Broderick stayed her hands. That adorable dimple emerged as he grinned and raised an eyebrow, then promptly ripped the dress open in one swift movement and tossed it aside, leaving her clad only in her chemise. She didn't have a chance to smile, or even protest as Broderick's hungry mouth was upon hers. Davina reached for the fastening of his breeches, but he stopped her. Pulling away from their kisses, he cupped his hands around her face.

"Nay," he said breathlessly. "I have been yearning for this moment since you came back into my life and stepped out of my dreams. I want to savor every moment." Broderick rose from the bed and stood back, still breathing heavy. He held her hands out to her sides, as if they were wings. Eyes flowing down her body, drinking in all he gazed through her chemise, they touched every inch of her flesh like flames tickling over her skin. Her nipples grew tight, drawing his eyes, which only made them more taut. Broderick brushed the back of his hand over her left nipple. Davina sighed. Then he caressed the other. She arched her back in anticipation, pushing her breast into his hand, causing him to moan. In an instant, he slipped his arm around the back of her and pulled her into him, bending forward to pull the material back and take the erect bud into his mouth. Davina gripped his silken hair, holding his head against her and using him for support, for surely she would faint from the pleasure surging through her body at the lapping and sucking of his hot mouth.

Breathing her name against her skin, Broderick suckled, licked, and nibbled his way over to her other breast. Her legs gave from under her at the same delicious ministrations of his mouth. Broderick swooped her from the floor and laid her on the bed, his mouth still devouring her flesh. The pulsing heat that formed between her legs increased when his knee parted her legs open. "Let me see you," she breathed, and reached for his breeches again.

Broderick pulled back from kissing her and smiled, eyes searching her face. "Explore me, Davina. I am yours to command." He straightened and towered over her on his knees. Sitting up, Davina gazed with hunger at the form-fitting trews molded to his muscular legs and hips. She could see almost every curve and crevice of his erection through the material and she grew wet in response. Panting, she peeled the material back and his erection sprang forth. His member stood proud and hard before her. She glanced up at Broderick's smoldering gaze and her stomach fluttered. Looking back to his erection, her lips parted in anticipation. Tentatively at first, she reached up and grabbed his cock. Her heart pounded at the purely masculine, contrasting sensations of his velvet smooth skin encasing his rock-hard organ. Broderick moaned and his hand covered hers. "Harder," he encouraged, as he squeezed with her and began moving her hand up and down his turgid shaft, a glistening drop forming at the tip. The ridges beneath her hand, as she stroked him, sent pulsing, hot throbs into her mons.

She studied Broderick's taut belly, the ripples of muscles across his chest. Her tongue tingled to explore the contours of the v-cut in the sculpted valley trailing down to his hips. "I want to see all of you," she whispered, tugging at the breeches he still wore.

Broderick bent down to taste her mouth then stepped off the bed and stripped of any remaining clothing. Pulling her from the bed and turning her to stand in the firelight, he gingerly removed the chemise, kissing the skin he exposed as he undressed her. When his mouth licked past her hips, and the thin garment dropped to the floor, his fingers came up to the wet folds between her legs, and she threw her head back in a gasp. Gripping his shoulders as he knelt before her, Davina shuddered as he explored her hot center and fluttered his finger over her sensitive nub. Broderick eased her onto the bed, lying beside her. His mouth sought hers and their tongues and lips met in a slow, silky dance of sensuality, sweet touches of mutual tenderness and adoration. Returning his fingers to stroke the sensitive bud of her wet cleft, he coaxed her need to a frenzy. She gave into the urges to buck against his hand, panting as she clung to him.

"Aye, blossom," he pressed. "Come for me."

Her whole focus became his fingers sliding in the velvet wetness between her legs. A building sensation settled in her belly, and Davina sensed a promise of something just out of reach. With an alarming swiftness, that promise came crashing against his hand, and Davina quavered in his arms as wave after wave of bliss pulsed down her limbs. Once she caught her breath, Davina pulled back from Broderick to stare at his hooded gaze, the wonder of her experience still overwhelming. "Did I come for you?"

Deep laughter rumbled from his chest, and he held her face in his palm. "Aye, blossom, that you did! Would you like to do it again?"

Her mouth fell open and she nodded wordlessly.

With that devilish smile, his mouth made a hot, wet trail across her breasts, down to her hip and belly and settled between her legs. Pulling her bottom to the edge of the bed, Broderick's hands coaxed her limbs to fall over his shoulders as he knelt on the floor. Davina reveled at the sensation of his cheeks upon her inner thighs, while his tongue lapped her into a state of total abandon. His moans mixed with hers as she squirmed. Holding her tight against his mouth, his hands on her hips, Broderick's tongue lapped even faster at her already sensitive bud, charming her body to respond with pulsing rolls of pleasure until Davina cried out in another climax.

He lovingly kissed, licked, and caressed her center, still throbbing from orgasm. Standing before her, Broderick gripped his shaft in his fist and guided his tip over her bud where he stroked her swollen, wet folds. In one easy motion and with a loud groan, he entered, and Davina gasped as Broderick filled her. She grabbed his hands on her hips as he undulated slowly in and out of her. Bending forward, Broderick crawled up onto the bed and cradled her against him, his hand moving underneath her body to grip her bottom and angle her up to him. He buried his face in her neck and Davina clung to Broderick's back as he pulled his cock out to where the head hovered just above her center for a brief caress, and then plunged deep inside her, again and again, each kiss of his tip aiding in driving her closer to another climax. Another swelling of promise bloomed where she felt the full length of him stroking, Broderick rocking against her body until Davina clutched her husband as if she hung on a precipice. With a velocity that stole her breath, the culmination of their joining thundered through her body. Broderick cried out and shuddered, grunting her name. His hips slowed and he wisped sweet kisses across her face and shoulders and breasts.

Every ragged breath he sighed against her skin sent waves of pleasure through her soul. Broderick pulled back and his eyes met his hers, his still-rigid cock undulated into her as his hands framed her face. The love in his eyes reached into her spirit and covered her heart like warm sunshine. "I love you, Davina." He shook his head. "Such shallow words compared to depth this love reaches into my heart. My soul belongs to you, my dove," he breathed against her mouth.

Davina could hardly see Broderick through the hot tears welling in her eyes. "How I have ached to hear you say those words, dreamed for so many years to hear you say that very sentiment. They are not shallow words at all, my darling." She moaned at the slow, deliberate strokes of Broderick's shaft inside her. Placing her hands upon his face, she poured her passion and love into her kiss. "And I love you, my Gypsy."

He groaned against her cheek when she pushed her hips forward to meet his. "Ah, but my days of being a Gypsy are over. We must settle down and build our home."

She smiled and touched his full mouth with her fingertip. "Settle down and build our home we will, then. I welcome it with great pleasure! But you will always be my Gypsy rogue."

Broderick smiled with that maddening dimple that always set Davina's heart to fluttering, and they disappeared into the bliss of their eternal love, as their moans of pleasure drifted out onto the night air.

Davina bit her bottom lip, trying to stay the tears threatening to make this more difficult than she wanted. "Will I ever see you again? We've just come to know each other as sisters and now you're leaving."

Rosselyn let her tears fall freely, dragging Davina into a heart-wrenching farewell. "I honestly do not know, my dearest friend. If I ever find a way to get a letter to you or find we can travel back toward Stewart Glen, I will leap at the chance."

The two women clung to each other amidst all the Gypsy wagons, loaded with their wares and supplies, ready to set out to the next establishment. Davina's mind twirled at how much harder this parting would have been if Broderick had not come into her life. The Gypsies stayed a short while longer after the snow melted, the extra time enabling Davina's family to throw the double wedding and a hearty feast. The festivity of the Gypsies and their family in their Great Hall was an event to remember, and would be talked about for years to come.

Broderick hugged Amice, almost as if he wouldn't let her go. "Are you sure you want to leave?" he asked. "You can stay here with us. It would be safer."

"Bah!" Amice scoffed. "I am too old to change my ways now. I would not feel good about staying in one place. I was born in a wagon. I will die in a wagon." She leaned in toward Broderick. "And if the devil Angus wants to kill me, may he choke on my old blood! I think that is the way you should rid yourself of him!" She winked at Broderick and he shook his head, laughter rumbling from his chest.

Davina could see the apprehension in his eyes, though. When they had returned from the Vamsyrian Fortress, he became uneasy over the safety of everyone he loved. He took his concern as far as foolish talk of leaving Davina in order to draw Angus or the Council away, but she convinced him his ideas were rash and impulsive. Away from her or with her, Angus already knew they were in love, and the Vamsyrian Council would have already pursued them by now if they wanted them dead. Davina was safer with Broderick at her side...and she was most certainly happier!

Amice hugged Davina, and then Broderick once more. In French, she said, "Let your spirits rest in each other." She put a wrinkled hand upon each of their hearts. "Know that I will always be here." She put a hand on her own heart. "As I know both of you will always be here. Until we see each other once more, mind what this Gypsy tells you this day!" Amice winked and turned away to climb onto her wagon. A sadness crept into Broderick's eyes.

Rosselyn stepped toward him. "Nicabar and I will take good care of her, Broderick. She will never be from our sight."

He nodded, not having any other choice.

They all embraced one last time and waved tearful farewells as the wagons made their noisy path out of the village of Stewart Glen.

Davina wanted Rosselyn to be happy, truly she did, and she knew being married to Nicabar and traveling with the Gypsies would fulfill her sister's dreams of living a free-spirited life. Admiring Broderick in the light of the torches, she hugged him close, reveling in the strength of his arms and the joy that her dreams, at last, had also come true.

The End

SNEAK PEAK AT BOOK 2

MIDNIGHT CAPTIVE

PROLOGUE

Stonehenge, England—1530

Cordelia Lynn Harley stood beside one of the stone sentinels in the monolithic circle. Eyeing the ancient cragged surface, she traced her finger along a crack while she waited. She scanned the horizon for any sign of the prophetess and, again, saw none. The new moon above, like a silver claw in the black sky, lent little illumination to the landscape. Her immortal eyes beheld only far-stretching flatlands of fields and grass dotted with sheep and cattle.

"Thank you for coming on such short notice."

Cordelia started and spun to face Malloren Rune. "I still do not understand how you can sneak up on me, being mortal."

The prophetess smiled under the glow of the lantern she held, her brown eyes sparkling with mischief. "You weren't paying attention, *Vamsyrian.* I'm sure your mind was exploring the possibilities of the news I have for you."

Cordelia's heart hammered and she followed Malloren to one of the fallen stones of the monument. The prophetess sat on the sleeping giant, setting the lantern beside her. Cordelia knelt in breathless anticipation with her hands clenched on her lap. "You found the second sign?"

"That I did."

Cordelia near collapsed from the wave of relief. "'Tis just as you foretold and everything is falling into place. What *is* the second sign?"

"That cannot be revealed until certain events take place. First, you must deliver an important item for me." The prophetess patted the stone, encouraging Cordelia to sit.

Though disappointed at the delay, Cordelia became excited over the new task. "An item?"

"Indeed. One that will spark a chain of events to move the prophecy along and ensure the second sign can be fulfilled." Malloren produced a small leather pouch a hand's width across and three fingers deep.

A wire-and-wax seal secured the flap closure. Cordelia recognized the seal of the *Tzava Ha'or*— The Army of Light. "What is the item?"

The prophetess curled a finger under Cordelia's chin to draw her gaze. "Listen to me, dear one."

The grave expression on Malloren's face made Cordelia shiver.

"You must not open this pouch or you will undo all we are working toward. Do you understand?"

"Yes." She swallowed.

Malloren presented a folded piece of parchment. "You will take this pouch to the location detailed on this map."

Cordelia set the pouch on her lap and pried open the edges of the paper.

"You must be at that designated location just after nightfall three days hence. Not one day sooner or later. A man will be waiting for you. The pouch is for him to open and none other. He has further instructions inside."

Cordelia met the intense gaze of the prophetess and nodded. "Why are *you* not delivering the pouch?"

"Because I cannot wipe his memory of our encounter. Your abilities as a Vamsyrian are why you must deliver the pouch. Give him the satchel and leave no trace of your face or my instructions to meet you in his mind. He should wake up with the satchel in his hand and my instructions to guide him." She pursed her lips in disapproval. "And you must not wait for him to open the pouch. You deliver it and leave. You will meet me here again on the first full moon after the summer solstice."

"'Tis almost a year hence! Why—?"

"During that time, certain events will take place to advance the prophecy so we may perform the second sign. Besides, you will have other errands to run."

Cordelia dropped her jaw at the enormity of her mentor's previous statement. "*We* will perform the sign?"

Malloren kissed the top of Cordelia's head. "Yes, child...we will."

CHAPTER ONE

Leith, Scotland—1531

The cold steel of the blade pressed so hard against Cailin MacDougal's throat, she couldn't swallow the lump forming there—nor could she be sure her eyes watered from fear or her attacker. He smelled atrocious! His body odor and bad breath hovered around her like a fog, and she struggled to breathe. Grand appreciation filled the stranger's blood-shot eyes as they raked over her face and neckline, the corners of his mouth forming an evil grin. "Oh, ye shall be a tasty treat for ol' Jasper before I hand ye over!"

Cailin cursed over falling for the trap. She had heard of this happening—a young child asking for assistance, luring unsuspecting yet helpful strangers into alleyways, only to be jumped by someone waiting to rob them of their goods...sometimes worse. Where the young lad she followed had gone to now was hardly her concern. The chance that this Jasper might be working for Angus Campbell—which was a constant fear of her family's—pressed upon her as acutely as his knife pressed against her throat.

She tried to squirm out of Jasper's grasp—his one beefy hand holding her wrists behind her—only to be pressed harder into the barrels against the back, hidden corner of the alley. With the sharp edge against her skin, the dread over falling into the hands of her father's enemy, and the frustration of her attacker stepping on her skirts, effectively pinning her in place—Cailin's mind swirled. She fought the images of Angus feeding from her mother Davina in the dark cell he'd taken them to, his taunting eyes, Davina's blood on his smiling lips. She willed her emotions into submission. If she didn't calm down, she would never be able to concentrate on escaping and would suffer the same fate as her mother.

Jasper removed the knife from her throat to caress her cheek and she breathed easier, finally able to swallow and find her voice. "Sir, you have my purse. If you would just—"

He grabbed her throat. "Be still, ducks."

Heat rose in Cailin's cheeks when he trailed the blade to her neckline, cutting through her material. How she allowed this lout to pin her in such a confining position was beyond her, and she would never forget such a stupid mistake. This was what she deserved for underestimating him in his slovenly appearance. Admittedly, her skirts made hand-to-hand combat most difficult, so she allowed herself some forgiveness. Training in a gown would be next on her agenda, but until then, she still had this situation to manage. If she could just get her hands on her daggers, hidden within the folds of her dress! She ventured one last glance down the narrow passage. No one had yet come running up the alley, so evidently her initial cry for help went unheard. She was on her own.

There! The idiot shifted to straddle her leg, no longer pinning her, and rubbed his erection against her hip. Ignoring the blush that heated her face, she seized the long-awaited opportunity to pivot her weight, push him away and bring her knee up between his legs, gladly making contact with his offending member. Jasper collapsed to his knees, howling. Hiking her skirts, Cailin kicked the dagger from his hand, brought her foot back and swiped it across his jaw. He curled into an infantile position, groaning and clutching his groin. Cailin dusted her hands in triumph. Not wanting to make the same mistake twice, she pulled at least one of her daggers out at the ready. Shaking her head at his pitiful display, she crouched beside him and searched his vest for her pouch.

A deep, rumbling laugh echoed against the brick walls and she contemplated the raven-haired figure standing at the entrance of the alleyway, a long dark cloak concealing his rather large frame. "And just who is robbing whom?"

Pale-green eyes assessed her as he sauntered forward, crossing his arms. Something seemed vaguely familiar about this man. A delightful shiver tickled over her skin when his eyes fell upon her breasts and the smile melted from his mouth.

He swallowed hard. "If you do not close your bodice, my dear, I cannot be held responsible for my actions."

His deep voice flowed over her body like warm water from the Mediterranean Sea. Cailin glanced down at her bodice—the top of her bosoms flushed pink and rounded above her torn neckline. She narrowed her eyes at him. "Your *actions* may lead you to join this poor soul on the ground."

With the knife clutched in her left hand—giving her a little more courage than she should probably dare—she searched the robber with her other hand while keeping her eyes trained on the intruder. Jasper stirred as she retrieved her belongings and she diverted her attention just enough to deal him another blow to his jaw, causing him to slump into unconsciousness.

She tucked the purse into her dress pocket. Standing, she raised an eyebrow, the corner of her mouth lifting in a smirk, and faced the wide-eyed and slack-jawed handsome stranger.

At a quick intake of breath, he stepped before her and stole his arm around her waist in one motion. Pressing her against the full form of his hard body, he pushed her breasts even more over her torn neckline.

"Unless you wish to keep your private jewels intact," she warned, "I suggest you keep your distance, sir." With her dagger at his groin, she tilted the silver-plated blade up to make her point.

His body stiffened against her and fear flickered across his eyes. Taking one step back, he peered down at the dagger between them and fingered the cut she sliced in his breeches. He hitched his breath and offered a respectful nod, retreating. But the sneer returned to his lips. "I see the lady is handy with a blade." He studied the dagger before his eyes roamed her body and he crossed his arms again. "And how is it a gentile maid such as yourself came to be so experienced at close combat with such expertly crafted weapons? Mind you, I use the terms 'lady' and 'gentile' with much reluctance." He snickered.

Cailin narrowed her eyes. "Obviously you underestimate my skills."

"Obviously." When Cailin tried to step past him, he countered to block her exit. "You also dodged my question."

She clenched her jaw at his arrogance. "Aye, 'tis unbecoming of a *lady* to have such extensive training, but I have likely seen more tutelage in this area than you could hope to dream of, *sir.*"

Cailin resisted the urge to sigh at the rich laughter that rumbled from his chest and, at the same time, she wanted to punch him square in the jaw.

"Do I detect a challenge, my dear?" His eyes near sparkled at the prospect.

Oh, why do men always have to prove themselves? "Nay, dear sir, 'tis a simple fact I pass along to you for your own good. Now, if you will excuse me."

Another bout of laughter poured from him. "As a good citizen, I cannot let you pass without extracting some justice for this poor soul you have robbed and rendered unconscious."

It was Cailin's turn to laugh. "Good citizen? With the crime that riddles this port? Surely you jest at dispensing justice."

"Precisely why I can only assume a woman wandering such dangerous streets alone can only be up to ill intent." He grinned.

Cailin stepped left, as did he. She stepped right, only to meet his expansive presence again. Not wishing any further delays, she half-heartedly swiped her dagger at him to feign him off, which he dodged effectively. She stepped back and drew her other dagger from the specially tailored belt crafted for her weapons. With it positioned low on her waist, the leather-and-steel sheaths lay against her hips and hidden amongst the folds of her gown. Narrow crossbars made it easy to withdraw the silver-plated Wootz blades, which she twirled in her hands before facing him, poised and ready. She reveled in a certain measure of satisfaction at seeing a dumbfounded expression replace his cocky demeanor. "Please step aside, sir, so that I may pass. Do not force me to do something you may regret."

A fire blazed in his green eyes, which gleamed like opals at her challenge, and that sensuous mouth curled into a smirk. Jasper moaned and the bonnie intruder stepped forward to give the man on the ground a quick jab to the jaw, knocking him silent again. He stepped back and resumed his arrogant position.

Under different circumstances, she'd be very taken with this man. And she still couldn't help wondering where she'd seen his face.

Throwing his cloak back over his shoulders, he revealed a broad chest that rippled under the thin material of his black shirt as he reached across his hip for his sword.

Cailin blanched. Not many men carried swords on their person in the port city of Leith—daggers were the weapon of choice and easier to conceal—and those that did rarely matched the craftsmanship of this blade. This was not a cheap, decorative sword. *Out of one mess and into another.* She swallowed her fear and stood her ground.

"I suggest a wager." He winked.

"I am not a gambling woman."

Tilting his head back, he laughed and Cailin clenched her jaw, her cheeks blooming with heat again. Amusement twinkling in his eyes, he ignored her comment. "A challenge. If you win, I shall let you walk free."

"And if *you* win?"

The amusement in his eyes transformed into smoldering desire. "I shall have to take you in hand and see you submit…" His eyes raked her body. "To the proper authority." He folded his arms in front of him, the blade of his sword sweeping up and standing erect from his fist.

Cailin's breath left her in a rush and fire surged through her body—from the fluttering in her stomach to the tingling in her toes. She did not miss his twofold meaning, and drew a deep, steadying breath, biting her tongue; though keeping her tongue proved more difficult to manage. "We shall see about this, *sir.*"

With a chuckle, he advanced. Cailin had the upper hand with two blades and extensive training. Twirling her arms and bending at the waist, she parried his thrust, continued through her movement and landed a sound kick to his side, sending him sprawling into the barrels. Once the loud clatter of boxes and debris settled, he shook his head. Her opponent gazed at her with large eyes while she widened her stance and readied her blades.

His brow furrowed and he rose to his feet, adjusting his shirt and positioning his sword. "Shall we try that again?"

"I can repeat that if you are a glutton for punishment, but I think you are fool."

He laughed. With a sweep of his sword, he forced Cailin to switch her stance to block his blade. To her dismay, he also pushed her off balance and wound his arms around her, pinning her hands behind her back. She faced him, chest against chest, seething at the advantage he had taken.

"'Tis dangerous you are with those blades." He wrested the daggers from her and tossed them aside. "Now, how do you suppose we should settle this matter?"

She grumbled. "He tried to rob me. I defended myself and you interfered. What is there to settle?"

"You must understand, from my perspective, I saw quite the opposite."

Cailin wriggled, making a concerted effort to free herself, but gained no purchase against him. Huffing in defeat, she said, "I care not what you *think* you saw. He trapped me and I was forced to defend myself." She wiggled again and stopped when his arousal pressed against her belly. Heat stole into her cheeks and she gazed into his sea-green eyes, growing stormy with desire.

Before Cailin could utter another word, his mouth descended upon hers, capturing a seeking kiss. Surely her lack of will to resist was due to the ordeal she'd just experienced. But the flutter in her stomach told her she enjoyed this man's touch far too much to blame exhaustion. The daydreams of her first kiss with her promised groom—what the experience would be like, how she would respond—all vanished like smoke on the wind. She never imagined this hungry, carnal reality. When his tongue teased along the crease of her lips, she opened her mouth to him, inviting a new swirl of quivers down her spine as their tongues danced. A primal heat stole into her belly and sank to settle between her legs, which wobbled and threatened to give way.

"Cailin MacDougal!"

As if a bucket of cold water had been thrown in her face, Cailin stumbled back, sputtering and struggling to gain her composure. Jasper was gone and the handsome stranger stared at her with his mouth open and his cheeks red. With a purposeful stride, Davina MacDougal marched down the alley toward Cailin and the man who had so wonderfully assaulted her mouth. Cailin rolled her eyes.

"Child, I should slap that expression from your face!" Davina stood before them, huffing her frustration, then clasped Cailin in a tight embrace. "Why must you insist on venturing out alone? This is not a jesting situation. Your life is in danger every time you wander about unescorted."

"M'ma, Ranald and Will *were* right behind me, but there is something I— "

Davina held up her hand toward Cailin and turned to the man standing with his mouth open. "Well?"

He gawked at Cailin. "Mouse?"

Cailin swallowed and gaped at his face with understanding. "James Knightly," she whispered and the blood drained from her face. Well, at least this explained why he seemed so familiar.

NOTE TO THE READER

Thank you for taking the time to read MIDNIGHT CONQUEST. I hope you enjoyed the story! Visit my web site at http://www.ArialBurnz.com for additional information and facts, updates on my latest tales, appearances, contests, and writing tips. I love to hear from my readers, so be sure to leave a comment on my blog OR drop me an e-mail at arial@arialburnz.com.

ABOUT THE AUTHOR

Arial Burnz has been an avid reader of both paranormal and fantasy fiction for over thirty years. With bedtime stories filled with unicorns, hobbits, dragons and elves, she had no choice but to craft her own tales, penning to life the many magical creatures roaming her mind and dreams. And with a romantic husband who's taught her the meaning of true love, she's helpless to weave romance into her tales. Now she shares them with the world. Arial Burnz lives in Rancho Cucamonga, California, with her husband (a.k.a. romance novel hero, and who is also a descendent of Clan MacDougal) along with their dog and two cats.

Made in the USA
San Bernardino, CA
05 May 2020

70630104R00309